DISPOSABLE ASSET

DISPOSABLE ASSET

John Altman

This first world edition published 2015
in Great Britain and the USA by
SEVERN HOUSE PUBLISHERS LTD of
19 Cedar Road, Sutton, Surrey, England, SM2 5DA.
Trade paperback edition first published
in Great Britain and the USA 2015 by
SEVERN HOUSE PUBLISHERS LTD.

British Library Cataloguing in Publication Data

Altman, John, 1969- author.
  Disposable Asset.
  1. Moscow (Russia)–Fiction. 2. United States. Central
  Intelligence Agency–Fiction. 3. Soviet Union. Komitet
  gosudarstvennoi bezopasnosti–Fiction. 4. Mafia–Russia–
  Fiction. 5. Spy stories.
  I. Title
  813.6-dc23

ISBN-13: 978-0-7278-8509-8 (cased)
ISBN-13: 978-1-84751-612-1 (trade paper)
ISBN-13: 978-1-78010-663-2 (e-book)

All Severn House titles are printed on acid-free paper.

Severn House Publishers support the Forest Stewardship Council™ [FSC™],
the leading international forest certification organisation. All our titles that
are printed on FSC certified paper carry the FSC logo.

Typeset by Palimpsest Book Production Ltd.,
Falkirk, Stirlingshire, Scotland.
Printed and bound in Great Britain by
TJ International, Padstow, Cornwall.

For my father

ACKNOWLEDGEMENTS

Thanks to Steve Sims, Richard Curtis, Leslie Silbert, Robert and Jane Altman, Daniel and Sima Altman, Margaret Gray, Judith Rosenberger, Kate Lyall Grant, Rachel Simpson Hutchens, and Charlotte Loftus.

A prince should have a spy to observe what is necessary, and what is unnecessary, in his own as well as in his enemy's country.

Hitopadesha, twelfth century

PROLOGUE

SOUTH-EAST OF MOSCOW

She cruised in at fifty feet, the wind at her back.

A pre-dawn hush lay across the Russian countryside. Beneath a quarter moon, the backcountry roads were dark ribbons crossing featureless black landscapes. To anyone on the ground, the fiberglass and anodized aluminum tubing of the ultralight Flightstar would be just a furtive glimpse of chrome, an unremarkable twinkle in the night.

Nearing the police cordon, she killed the Rotax 530 engine. In relative silence, then, she glided over a patch of land manned by half a dozen oblivious sentries. The dacha lay before her, dark and insensate; she aimed for the silhouetted peaks of the roof. Reaching down, she set the bricks of RDX on their thirty-second timer. *Thirty* . . .

Here came the roof, monochromatic through her night-vision goggles. From her belt she selected a white phosphorous grenade and then held it tightly, waiting for her moment.

Twenty-eight . . .

Raising herself out of the pilot's seat, she clung to the glider with the strength of a single index finger. Two sentries stood atop the rapidly-approaching roof, as expected.

Twenty-six . . .

The tallest peak of the roof was passing beneath her. She triggered the phosphorus grenade and then jumped, rolling out behind the forward propeller, releasing the grenade as clouds of thick white smoke pulsed up around her.

For a few instants she was in terrifying free-fall, tumbling forward and down at forty miles per hour, stomach lurching. Then she hit the roof, tucking and rolling, spending off her momentum.

Twenty-two . . .

Gaining her feet, she took quick inventory. A rib on her left side felt bruised but not broken. The hazard suit, lined with charcoal, seemed intact. The Flightstar was passing overhead; the roof's two sentries, confused by the pulsing smoke, emptied their weapons after it.

Crouching in the shadow of a brick chimney, she drew a silenced

Remington, small enough to fit nicely in her hand, and straightened her night-vision goggles. A strand of long blonde hair had come loose; she tucked it efficiently back beneath the black-knit cap.

Eighteen . . .

On the far side of the dacha, the Flightstar hit the earth with enough force to shudder the house's foundations beneath her feet. Paying no attention, she sighted on one of the sentries, took careful aim, and fired.

Down he went. Climbing a peak, crouching in another shadow, she tried to find the remaining guard. A dog somewhere started barking hoarsely. Floodlights, mounted all around her, switched on, shining out on to the lawn.

Fourteen . . .

Locating the remaining guard, she took aim and fired. He spun away, clasping one hand to the side of his throat before crumpling off the roof.

Using the chimney to orient herself, she summoned the dacha's blueprints to mind. The master bedroom should be four meters west of her current position and two south. She began to pace it off—

—but someone was shooting; she had to duck back behind the chimney.

Ten . . .

With a mirror mounted on the Remington's stock, she tried to locate the shooter. Another guard on the roof? A sniper by the helipad? Failing to find him, she was forced to improvise.

Six . . .

From her spot behind the chimney, she hastily arranged four cutter charges in a square on the roof and then backed away, ducking and covering.

One!

Right on schedule, the bricks of RDX stashed in the Flightstar exploded, filling the night with a semblance of daylight. At the same instant the cutter charges flared thermite, slicing a square clear down to the dacha's first floor.

Donning a gas mask, she lobbed a tear-gas grenade through the hole she'd cut in the roof. Spitting and hissing, it discharged its contents. Hanging from her fingertips, she followed the grenade, dropping on to a charred lip of second-floor carpet.

The first guard she encountered was already unconscious. The second was still twitching. Sparing him only a fleeting glance, she consulted her mental blueprint again. Two doors opened off the corridor in which she found herself. Which way to the master bedroom? She fought to concentrate. Every instant she hesitated, the element of surprise slipped farther away. Outside, dogs continued barking; an alarm joined them, pealing wildly up and down.

Go!

She chose a door.

Inside the room, a tiny figure – a little girl – cowered in a bed. '*Otkuda vy?*' the girl whispered.

Cassie closed the door and went to sit beside her, stroking dark hair off a tiny forehead. '*Nichevó stráshnovo,*' she murmured through the mask. 'I'm an angel. Go back to sleep, honey.'

After a moment, she crossed to a door on the room's far side. Behind it, she should find a walk-through bathroom; beyond that, the adjoining master bedroom.

She led with another tear-gas grenade, followed by a fragmentation grenade. Spider-like, close to the floor, she pressed forward. Bedclothes were burning. Heavy tendrils of smoke and gas clogged her night-vision goggles; she tore them off. She glimpsed the target: wearing a silk bathrobe, patting desperately at flames dancing across his torso. Solidly built, tiers of muscle going to fat, receding gray hairline. He was alone in the room – but his bodyguards would not be far away.

Three steps put her beside him. She brought up the Remington 1911 R1. Despite the flames dancing across his chest he froze, eyes widening, at the sight of the semi-automatic hovering inches from his face.

A suspended instant; then she pulled the trigger, sending a parabola of blood and brains splattering across the wall.

She spent another heartbeat looking down at him. The ruined face, sheeting off the skull like snow off a mountainside beneath a hot sun. A stunningly ordinary face, she thought, for the man she had built up in her head to superhuman proportions, for the man who had—

Security thundered through the door. As they opened fire, she dove to her right. The sharp smell of Primex powder assailed her nostrils. The wall behind her sprouted smoking holes. She kept moving, rolling behind a chaise settee. Falling on to her back, she planted her feet against the settee and sent it airborne, buying an instant.

Another shot – *zwip* – and wood splintered, grazing her temple. She turned and leapt toward the window, hitting the pane high, slicing apart the hazard suit and opening a wide gash on her forehead. Twisting in mid-air, she managed to get a grip on the dacha's facade, helped by tiny adhesive hairs in her gloves, and avoided tumbling two stories to frozen earth.

Scaling quickly down, she dropped lightly on to a side patio. Parked in the adjacent driveway were an Infiniti, a Bentley, and a Porsche. Nearby was a fourth vehicle, a Polaris snowmobile: large, chunky, and insectile, painted black and gold, like a yellow jacket. Her hands shook as she found a latch to open the cowl, then removed the air box and worked free the back of the key switch. Five slots, two wires . . . The engine roared to life.

Throwing one leg over the saddle, she opened the throttle. An instant later she was whipping past sugar-coated pines and stands of white birch.

Her temple pulsed. She had lost the knit cap; long blonde hair flayed her face and cheeks. Her ears strained for a descending whistle, for the grenade that had her name on it. None came. Fixing the night-vision goggles back across her eyes, she leaned low over the handles and exhaled: a sigh mixed with a sob. After a moment she risked a look back. No pursuit – not yet – but they would be close behind.

She passed a wooded meadow and a potato field. The trees gained grandeur. Soon she would hit the road. Then she could dump the snowmobile, find the motorcycle she'd hidden, and vanish.

She had done it.

She forced out another shaky breath, made herself focus. Beyond a copse of birch stood a tall chain-link fence, topped with barbed wire; beyond the fence, the road. Skidding to a stop, she abandoned the snowmobile. From a singed pocket of the hazard suit she withdrew a pair of wire-cutters.

Slicing a gap in the fence, she discarded the cutters and slipped through. Hidden in shadows, dusted with snow, her motorcycle waited. She jumped aboard and started the engine.

She had done it.

With a tight smile beneath the mask she whipped back into motion, bending low against the wind.

PART ONE

ONE

BELIY GOROD, MOSCOW

The hazard suit had been traded for soft brown boots, crisp blue jeans, and an ordinary hooded parka; twin wounds on her temples had been cleaned with handfuls of snow. To anyone watching, she would look like an average young woman of nineteen or twenty, perhaps a bit prettier than most, out past her curfew.

Moving swiftly, she crossed a cobblestoned street. With its wrought-iron lamp posts, medieval monasteries, and picturesque eighteenth and nineteenth century cottages, the snow-hushed neighborhood evoked a Russia of a bygone era. Approaching a darkened doorway, she felt like Rodion Raskolnikov skulking through shadows after the murder of an elderly pawnbroker . . . or Anna Karenina, determining in a moment of desperation to fling herself beneath the carriage of an onrushing train.

Grasping a heavy brass door-knocker, Cassie delivered three soft raps. Then she waited, hugging her elbows and counting. One-thousand-one, one-thousand-two, one-thousand-three—

The door opened. Her contact absorbed her impassively, stepped aside, and waved her up a narrow staircase. Neither spoke until they were behind a closed door on the cottage's second story, inside a simple room sparsely decorated with religious icons, smelling vaguely of liniment.

The man was tall and slim, in his middle forties, with cool eyes and a thin, peevish mouth. After locking the door, he turned to a roll-top desk. 'There's a white Mondeo parked outside.' He tossed something, which she caught reflexively: keys. 'Go to the Mayakovka House on Tverskaya Ulitsa. Pull up outside the lobby. A man will approach the passenger side. Small white bandage on his left hand—'

Later, thinking back, she was unsure what had tipped her off. His voice might have tightened, or she might have noticed a tension in his carriage. Whatever the case: by the time he turned from the desk, gun in hand, she had already sidestepped and advanced. With her right elbow she struck his Adam's apple, hard.

On his knees, emitting small strangled cries, he grappled after the weapon. She bent, pulse thudding in her throat, to recover the silenced GSh-18 before he could reach it.

Still working on instinct, she opened the door and slipped back out into the narrow stairwell. Again the image of Dostoyevsky's haunted murderer flashed through her mind. Banishing it quickly – the man might have backup, even now closing in – she turned up, keeping to the sides of the risers, and made for the roof three steps at a time.

TICONDEROGA, NEW YORK

Inside the rambling lake house, Ravensdale hung his windbreaker on a hook and then helped the boy take off shoes and coat. 'Go and play, buddy, while I get dinner ready.'

His son pattered dutifully, with two-and-a-half-year-old gravity, off into the living room. After watching for a moment, Ravensdale carried his groceries into the kitchen. Putting on water to boil, he began transferring packages into cupboards and refrigerator.

At the sound of tires against gravel outside, a crease appeared between his eyes. Lifting a curtain, he saw a gray Ford Escort with Maryland plates pulling up beside his Volvo S40. When the Escort stopped, brake lights remained dark. Ravensdale's scowl deepened. Surveillance vehicle drivers, he thought, sometimes disabled tail lights so that wary targets would not catch the car changing speed to keep pace.

In the mud room he found the shoebox on the high shelf, withdrew the old Beretta, checked the safety, and slipped the gun into the back of his chinos. Covering the stock with his oversized black T-shirt, he returned to the kitchen, peeking again through the curtain. A figure was moving carefully up the icy walk.

Opening the front door, Ravensdale caught his visitor in the act of reaching for the bell. Beneath a tweed overcoat and crimson scarf, Andrew Fletcher looked essentially unchanged since their last encounter: high corrugated brow, sandy widow's peak, pale-blue eyes crackling with intelligence behind stylish Dolce & Gabbana frames. Upon his promotion to Moscow Station Chief, the man had gained a few pounds; now back inside the Beltway he had lost them again, making the boyish cleft in his chin stand out.

'You should have called,' said Ravensdale curtly.

'I tried. The number you gave me's no good.'

'Boom!' said Dmitri from the living room. 'And red car says, I mad! And blue car says, no, *I* mad! And red car says, no, *I* mad!'

For an uncomfortable moment, Ravensdale refused to cede the

doorway. Fletcher looked at him evenly, expectantly, breath forming frosty plumes on the cold air. At last the larger man moved grudgingly aside, gesturing his guest into the kitchen without offering to take coat or scarf.

In the kitchen, Fletcher spent a moment soaking in the surroundings: percolating water on the stove, shoddy fit of doors in frames, framed photograph on one wall – Ravensdale in happier times, with one arm around Sofiya – and mournful winter twilight beyond a wide picture window. The lake in January was a sad, gray presence. The houses speckling its banks looked small, inconsequential, impermanent. He said dubiously, 'You like it up here?'

'Suits me.'

'Ha.' Fletcher loosened his scarf, fixed a cufflink poking out from beneath one overcoat sleeve. 'I thought retirement might have mellowed you. No such luck, I guess. Well, hell. You must be exhausted. I can't even imagine chasing after a toddler at this age. These weary old bones.'

Ravensdale leaned against a counter – the Beretta poked uncomfortably into the small of his back – and said nothing.

'You've seen the news?' asked Fletcher mildly.

Ravensdale raised his eyebrows.

'Blakely's been killed. Just a few hours ago. Outside Moscow.' At the blank look on Ravensdale's face, Fletcher blinked. 'Good Christ. Benjamin Blakely . . .?'

Ravensdale shook his head.

'I don't care how deep your head's buried in the sand; there's no way you could have avoided Benjamin Blakely. One of the whiteboard jockeys back at HQ. Decided to steal every secret he could lay hands on, eighteen months ago, and then pass them over to anyone who cared to have a look. In the name of transparency, he said. Really, for the greater good of Benjamin Blakely.'

Ravensdale's eyebrows climbed higher.

'Cocksucker leaked classified information that, taken out of context, doesn't exactly make us look good. The Russians, of course, gave him sanctuary. Anything to turn the screws. But now it's caught up with him.' Fletcher couldn't keep the satisfaction from his voice. 'Karma's a bitch,' he said.

Ravensdale grunted.

'He was protected by the best private army the Kremlin could offer. Someone penetrated one hell of a security cordon to reach him. Methinks I detect the whiff of a paramilitary operation.'

'You think, or you know?'

'I had nothing to do with it.' Fletcher took a wax apple from a bowl on the countertop, eyed it suspiciously. 'Not that I mind. Son-of-a-bitch did more damage than . . . This is a good thing, Sean. Take my word.'

Ravensdale stroked his salt-and-pepper beard and held his tongue.

'For all we know, it's Russian internal politics at work. Someone wanted to embarrass the Premier-ski, take away his trophy. But there's the possibility . . .' Fletcher put down the wax apple, shrugged. 'The old guard at the agency, you know, hasn't been too happy lately. And some of us have never been too good at turning the other cheek. But, hell, look who I'm talking to.'

'What do you want, Andy?'

Andrew Fletcher spread his palms. He had an expensive manicure, Ravensdale noticed: fingernails buffed and neatly clipped.

'Bottom line: I can't say for certain that our hands are entirely clean. Which puts us in a tight corner, Sean. The Russians have identified a suspect. Currently at large – but they're pulling out all the stops. If they get her, God only knows what she might tell them. Just twenty minutes ago, they released a statement: "We harbor no suspicion for this heinous act toward our American partners," et cetera. But you know how their *Novoyaz* works. It's all between the lines. They're pointing a finger, in their own special way.'

Wind lowed outside, making loose chunks of ice clump in the half-frozen lake. Upstairs, a branch caught in the breeze scratched against a window. In the living room, Dmitri had lapsed into uncharacteristic silence.

'Sean. I know you just want to sit it out. But come on. Special circumstances require special—'

Ravensdale shook his head.

'You're looking after your boy. I appreciate that. But consider the bigger picture. Things are goddamned tense right now. It's a goddamned tinderbox . . . and this gets pinned on us, it's just the spark to set things off.'

Ravensdale said nothing.

Visibly, Fletcher controlled his temper. He opened his mouth, closed it, and then opened it again. 'I passed a coffee shop on my way down. The Sticky Bun, it's called. Said it's open until ten. I'll wait there. Because I know you want to be a good father, Sean. But think it through: that means leaving your son a world worth inheriting.'

With a final reproachful glare, he retreated from the kitchen.

Moments later an engine turned over in the driveway; then tires tickled icy gravel again.

Ravensdale looked at the stove. The water was boiling.

MOSCOW

Yaroslavsky Station had been constructed, over a century before, in the style of a fairy-tale castle, with frosted windows and imposing dark gables. A bird-shat statue of Lenin stood out front, surrounded by *bomzhi* – homeless – holding bottles in brown paper bags.

The early morning schedule was thin; no train left for half an hour. A solemn hush hung in the air. Cassie found a private corner, away from a group of derelicts, and sat cross-legged on the dirty floor, taking in her surroundings. An abundance of street people helped her blend in. The troika of Leningrad, Yaroslavsky, and Kazan, collectively called Three Stations, served as a Mecca to the city's indigent.

During the next five minutes, she did her best to identify the security presence in the station. Four pairs of blue-suited *politsiya* circulated, and at least three plainclothesmen, the latter betrayed by the slow, steady sweep of their eyes. Two soldiers, wearing camouflage and Kalashnikovs, stood near the boarding concourse. The soldiers and police held small leather-bound digital tablets, which they consulted discreetly.

Bestirring herself, giving the authorities a wide berth, Cassie visited the gift shop and spent eighty rubles on a pair of dull scissors and a black magic marker. Moving into the ladies' room, she allowed herself an instant of self-reproach. She had fled the three-story cottage in Beliy Gorod so quickly that she had not even paused to take the man's wallet. As a result, her funds were severely limited.

Inside a bathroom stall festooned with graffiti (*If you had a million years to do it*, Holden Caulfield had said in her favorite book, *you couldn't rub out even half the 'Fuck you' signs in the world*), she chopped her hair short and colored what remained black with the magic marker. The result, choppy and unevenly two-toned, could pass for punk. After a moment of deliberation, she hid the GSh-18 inside a toilet tank and then flushed the keys to the Mondeo down into Moscow's antiquated sewage system.

By the time she emerged from the bathroom, another clump of soldiers had appeared by the ticket counter – and still another, by the departure board. She walked brazenly between them, past a bench on which a mother sat with a young child, and lifted the woman's purse. Inside a faux-alligator wallet she found fifteen hundred rubles.

Dropping purse and wallet into a trash basket just two meters from a gun-toting soldier, she approached the ticket window and bought passage on the next train leaving the station. Get out of the city; that was the priority.

Over the loudspeaker, her train was called. Waiting on the platform, she lost herself in the thin crowd, avoiding to the best of her ability prying eyes and security cameras. When doors hissed open, passengers boarded in a slow, halting line.

She took a seat across the aisle from a young man reading a Japanese comic book. Two *politsiya* passed outside her window, consulting their tablets and peering owlishly into the train; she turned her face away.

After five interminable minutes, a whistle blew and the rusty old car jolted into motion. She rocked gently along with the sway of train on rails, trying not to think too much. Through the foggy windows passed first the Moscow suburbs, weed-choked and indistinct in darkness – full light would not come until almost ten a.m. – and then forests of birch, dotted with humble dachas.

After a few minutes, the young man beside Cassie closed the comic book, took out a knock-off phone, and opened *Yandex.ru*. She peered over his shoulder, straining to decipher the Cyrillic lettering without being too obvious. The headline sent a chill wandering down her spine:

ASSASSIN IDENTIFIED
by Andrei Dubov

MOSCOW – The Prosecutor General's Office has opened an official investigation into a 'person of interest' with regard to the murder of US defector Benjamin Blakely.

Represented in the police sketch below, the suspect appears to be a young woman in her late teens or early twenties, with shoulder-length blonde hair and a slight build. Last seen early Monday morning at the government dacha in Turygino where Blakely was killed, she is considered armed and dangerous.

At approximately 2:30 a.m. on Monday, January 9th, sixty kilometers south-west of Moscow Oblast, Benjamin Blakely was viciously murdered by an assailant or assailants. The former CIA officer was protected by no fewer than thirty security agents at the time of his death, three of whom perished defending their charge. (See PROFILES OF VICTIMS, page 8.)

Government representatives charged with handling the Blakely case were left speechless by the cowardly early-morning assassination. A universal round of finger-pointing quickly followed.

Benjamin Blakely left the United States eighteen months ago, carrying a digital cache containing evidence that the CIA has codified illegal policy, including entering the homes of US citizens to conduct warrantless searches. How many of Blakely's documents have thus far been released remains unclear . . .

The article was accompanied by a photograph of Benjamin Blakely – same receding gray hairline and layers of muscle going to fat, but different, pre-surgery, nose, brow and chin – caught in the act of leaving a restaurant, looking surprised, surrounded by FSB agents. Beside the picture was a rudimentary police sketch of Cassie's face. The shape of the jaw was wrong . . . because of the gas mask, of course. Otherwise, the likeness was uncomfortably near the mark.

The boy scrolled to a sidebar and clicked a link, bringing up a photograph of a gaunt, well-dressed man with a pretty little mustache and short blond hair, addressing a crowd of reporters.

INVESTIGATIVE COMMITTEE URGES VIGILANCE
by Natasha Yurganova

MOSCOW – Speaking from Investigative Committee Headquarters on Bauman Street, Senior Inspektor Piotr Vlasov urged nationwide vigilance in the wake of the early-morning assassination of Benjamin Blakely.

'A brave and noble man has been murdered in cold blood,' said the Inspektor. 'But with the help of our faithful and watchful citizenry, the cowardly criminals responsible for this heinous act will soon be flushed from the sewers like the rats that they are. And to whomever is behind this travesty, we remind you of one incontrovertible fact: retribution is inevitable . . .'

'Tickets, please.'

Cassie handed over her ticket without looking up.

The world seemed to be shutting down, fading to a colorless blur. Her fingers pinched the thick part of her thigh. The world sharpened again. She accepted the punched ticket.

For a few minutes she pretended she was back in a safe place: the old hang-out pad in the East Village, or one of the better foster homes, or, going back farther, the small university town in which she'd been raised. But the memories were fragile, dissolving almost as soon as she managed to find them. The train rocked insistently, rolling her head on her neck, bringing her back again to the here-and-now. At last the thought she wanted to avoid above all others rose stubbornly to the surface, demanding recognition:

Quinn had set her up.

Her target had not been a *mafiya* kingpin, as she had been told, but something else. Benjamin Blakely. An American defector. Probably not even—

A gray coolness clicked in; emotion guttered and died. First things first. She must put some distance between herself and Moscow. Then – once she could exhale and get her head on straight – she could begin untangling the knot of what, exactly, had happened in the Turygino dacha and the little cottage in Beliy Gorod.

Staring fixedly out the window, a light sweat drying on her collarbones beneath the parka, she concentrated for the moment on thinking of nothing at all.

TICONDEROGA

For a long time after Fletcher had gone, Ravensdale sat watching his son, listening to ice shifting in the lake outside.

Eventually, the distant bell at Saint Mary's marked the hour, making him start. Pushing out of his chair, he returned the Beretta to its shoebox and then fixed a simple dinner. As he and Dmitri ate macaroni and cheese, Dmitri described a complex and obscure drama involving Elmo, Nemo, Thomas the Tank Engine, and cars of various colors.

At seven thirty they climbed creaky stairs, brushed teeth, and sat down before bed for a story. Dmitri chose his current favorite book, *Frog and Toad Are Friends*. Ravensdale read absently, his mind far away. 'Frog ran up the path to Toad's house. He knocked on the front door. There was no answer . . .'

Bottom line: I can't say for certain that our hands are entirely clean. The Russians have identified a suspect. If they get her, God only knows what she might tell them.

But once upon a time, Fletcher had not needed to add, Ravensdale's connections had been the best in Moscow. If anyone could pull the strings required to steal the prize away from the Kremlin, it was he.

'Frog walked into the house. It was dark. All the shutters were

closed. "Toad, where are you?" called Frog. "Go away," said the voice
from the corner of the room. Toad was lying in bed. He had pulled
all the covers over his head . . .'

*I know you want to be a good father. But that means leaving your
son a world worth inheriting.*

Did that mean a world in which the killers of Benjamin Blakely
escaped justice? Ravensdale had played dumb. But of course he was
familiar with the man and his actions. Moreover, a large part of him
approved. Any empire allowed to expand unchecked – any empire
that could not look at itself and ask the hard questions – was an
empire destined for collapse. The breakdown would come first at the
expense of that empire's own citizens, whose civil liberties would
have been systemically stripped away, whose homes would have been
illegally searched without warrants, and who, if they'd dared cause
a ripple in the master plan, would have been detained indefinitely
without trial or counsel. An empire which accrued total power among
the ruling elite, history had shown, eventually used it. And there were
all too few Benjamin Blakelys standing up to challenge the status
quo. Most Americans – Ravensdale himself, if he wanted to be brutally
honest, among them – had chosen to sit back and watch things play
out on TV. *The People have abdicated our duties*, Juvenal had said;
*for the People who once upon a time handed out military command,
high civil office, legions, everything, now restrains itself and anxiously
hopes for just two things: bread and circuses.*

But there was another reality to consider. A confession to the
Kremlin from an American assassin would give Russia substantial
leverage for her own geopolitical ambitions – the last thing the world
needed right now. Mother Russia's – *Rodina*'s – dictator in charge,
her supreme leader for life, her empire-building and saber-rattling
czar, wanted more than anything to flex his muscles and reassert his
right to sit at the grown-up table. And so he would seize any opportunity
to push harder against his borders, stoking ethnic fires, engineering
armed rebellions, driving a wedge into NATO, playing a game of
brinksmanship which could lead only to more war, more death . . .
perhaps even to the ultimate war, the ultimate death. *It's a goddamned
tinderbox . . . and this gets pinned on us, it's just the spark to set
things off.*

Would Fletcher really be displeased by that? Over the years the
man had washed gallons of blood from beneath his manicured fingernails, sometimes literally. In the process, he had cultivated a steely
hatred and searing disdain for his opposition. Mortal combat with

Russia was his life's work, his divine calling. Not for Andy Fletcher the joys of *glasnost*. A ramping up of tensions meant larger budgets, less oversight . . . more power. Every move made by the enemy justified a countermove. Anything short of Armageddon actually served the man's purpose.

Fletcher, thought Ravensdale, must have another, unstated reason for wanting this nipped in the bud.

The Russians have identified a suspect. If they get her, God only knows what she might tell them.

What she told them, perhaps, would lead back to Fletcher himself.

That Ravensdale's former boss ran his own game on the side was beyond question. But anyone who might be able to shed light on the details had an uncanny way of turning up dead.

But this time, the girl was still out there.

Get her for himself and Ravensdale might redeem, with one bold stroke, a multitude of past sins: defusing the tinderbox, calming the international waters, and then dragging the assassin before the higher-ups at Langley, providing evidence at last of Fletcher's overreaching, pinning his former boss to the wall.

Sitting in his father's lap, Dmitri suddenly craned around. 'Why Toad sad?' he asked.

Ravensdale forced a smile, tousling his son's dark hair. 'He's not sad, kiddo. He just doesn't want to go outside.'

'Toad sad. But Frog make him happy. Frog nice.'

'Absolutely correct,' agreed Ravensdale gravely. 'Frog is nice, indeed.' Clearing his throat, he continued: 'Toad blinked in the bright sun. "Help!" he said. "I cannot see anything . . ."'

After switching off the light, he found his address book, ran a finger pensively down a list of potential babysitters, and reached for the phone.

Twenty minutes later he was pulling into The Sticky Bun's parking lot. An hour before close, the shop was mostly deserted. Stella Cohen, the owner, was running vinegar through the espresso machine. Norm Harding sat at the counter, toying with the flaps of a red plaid hunter's cap.

Andrew Fletcher was stationed in a corner where nobody could surprise him. As Ravensdale slid on to a chair, Fletcher almost – but not quite – managed to hide a victorious smirk. 'Here's the plot,' he said. 'We take my car to a field a mile away. Helicopter from there to Buffalo/Niagara. In eight hours, we'll be on the ground in Moscow.'

'And then?'

'Then you work your magic.'

'My bridges have burned.'

'You'll find a way. Whatever it takes. Put the blame on Carlson, maybe.'

Ravensdale said nothing. A long shot . . . but there might be something to work with there. Jack Carlson, part of the FBI's Transnational Criminal Enterprise Section, had been Ravensdale's erstwhile partner in Moscow. Neither had been eager to work with the other, but the increasingly international landscape had made cooperation – 'Force Multiplication', in the language of the day – unavoidable. While Ravensdale had ultimately left his agency in disgrace, Carlson's career had taken wing; receiving a promotion, he'd moved back stateside to run, from Washington, the Bureau's Eurasian Organized Crime unit. In absentia, he would make a handy scapegoat.

'Make the deal sweet enough,' Fletcher was saying, 'and they'll let bygones be bygones. The purse strings are wide open on this one. The overseers are looking the other way. All that matters is results.' He inspected the placid surface of his coffee. 'Nobody wants to see how bad this thing could turn. The way things have been going lately . . . I think you've reached the same conclusion. Otherwise we wouldn't be talking. So let's not dawdle.'

After a few seconds, Ravensdale nodded. Fletcher pushed back, scraping his chair across the floor. Moments later they stepped together out into the cold night, side by side like two old friends.

TWO

20,000 FEET OVER THE ATLANTIC

Beneath the Gulfstream's window, mountains gilded with moonlight had fallen away; criss-crossing skeins of electric light had followed, and ever since there had been only limitless black.

The plane pitched violently, sending the lone steward grabbing for a seat-back. Ravensdale sat up straighter, wiping at his face. Beside him, Andrew Fletcher displayed a reassuring smile, touched with contempt. Behind gleaming lenses his eyes looked bright and artificial, like the glass eyes of a toy. 'Try to rest,' he said.

Another gust of wind rocked the jet; Ravensdale's stomach gave a queasy answering roll. He took solid hold of his armrest. The turbines hummed. The rocking of the plane settled. Eventually, Ravensdale's stomach settled too.

Closing his eyes, he pictured Dmitri waking up in the morning to find himself consigned indefinitely to Tess Mackinnon's care. The boy, he told himself, would be OK. Dima had proven adaptive. He took that from his mother. Ravensdale himself was a creature of habit, preferring careful planning and known quantities to sudden unexpected detours.

Setting his jaw, he tried to rest.

Sheremetyevo-2 was crawling with soldiers.

After landing on a secondary runway, the Gulfstream taxied into a small hanger. There they sat for almost half an hour. Fletcher peered out his window, awaiting a signal. At last he caught the eye of the steward, nodded, and quickly stood.

A black Mercedes with tinted windows of bulletproof polycarbonate had pulled up beside the plane. They left the airport via a rear gate, waved through by an official who pointedly looked away. Once Sheremetyevo was receding behind them, Ravensdale dialed a number from memory. He was placed on hold. Several minutes passed. Then the voice returned and told him the request had been granted; his personal visit was expected within the hour.

They proceeded to follow a serpentine surveillance evasion route around Moscow. The familiar sights gave Ravensdale a queer sensation of doubling, as if the old him and new him sat side by side in the rear of the car. They passed Three Stations, where Kazan's seventy-meter spired tower rose into the cloudy afternoon, and the Manege, where Tolstoy had taken his first riding lessons. Krymsky Bridge spanned a backdrop of Gothic-Stalinist monoliths. Outside Gorky Park, the elaborately carved two-tiered carousel spun lazily. The Moskva River looked more polluted than ever, clogged with a swill of trash and filth.

They stopped at a liquor store: God have mercy on the visitor in Russia who showed up empty-handed. Then they headed toward Serebryany Bor – the silver forest – one of the most distinguished addresses in all of Moscow. Here, within easy range of the city's center, on a tiny island covered with towering silver pines, lived the elite: oligarchs, entrepreneurs, rock stars, top-ranking FSB operatives, *nomenklatura* who had been senior members of the Party system, and pre-eminent *mafiya* like Otari Tsoi.

Nearing the bridge that crossed on to the island, the Mercedes pulled on to a rocky shoulder. Parked just ahead was a silver Jeep Commander. Fletcher handed Ravensdale a single glittering key. 'Good luck.'

Ravensdale nodded.

'I'm at the Marriott. In the lobby every day at noon and midnight.' His voice turned low, insinuating. 'Remember: whatever it takes.'

At the guard booth by the bridge, Ravensdale was waved from behind the wheel.

His wallet was taken, flipped through, and returned. His phone was confiscated. Invasive hands explored his shoes and cigarettes, poked up beneath the collar of the oxford shirt he'd donned at Fletcher's insistence inside the Gulfstream. '*Izvinitye*,' said one guard insincerely as Ravensdale was jabbed and nudged: *Forgive me.*

Only after the guards had sampled the cognac was he allowed to keep the bottle. Back inside the Jeep, he drove a few hundred meters more before reaching a familiar gate. The grand old mansion at the end of the private driveway had twin machine-gunner nests mounted above a lopsided facade. Inside, Ravensdale followed a bodyguard down a corridor of Art Nouveau architecture, past a library, an enviable collection of original art, and a glassed-in display case featuring Uzbek daggers, Red Army bayonets, and *kinjal*, the ceremonial dagger of the Caucasus. More bodyguards – 'flat tops', as they were known, with their severe crew-cuts – lurked in corners and doorways, arms folded before broad chests.

He was shown into a lavishly appointed sitting room, and there sat Otari Tsoi himself, reclining on a leather couch with his arm around a willowy girl of perhaps seventeen. Tsoi's close-cropped hair was still black, his jaw still leaden, his olive skin still pocked with acne scars. His thick neck, visible beneath the open collar of a poplin shirt, was still intricately tattooed with colorful skeletons, serpents, knives and angels. This man was one of the *siniye*, the tattoos announced: the blues, the old guard of the *Vorovskoi Mir*, Thieves' World.

At Ravensdale's entrance, Tsoi stood – short, stocky, powerfully built – and delivered a crushing bear hug. 'Elena,' he told the girl, leaving one massive hand on Ravensdale's elbow. 'This is an honor you do not deserve. Meet James Bond. The real-life version, I admit, is not quite so dazzling as the one from the movies. But believe me, this is as close as we are ever going to get.'

The girl disarmed Ravensdale by standing, delivering a shy, girlish curtsy, and batting glitter-coated eyelids.

'You see the disappointment on her face? She expected Daniel Craig.' Tsoi's chuckle was lightly self-deprecatory, as if he considered himself the true brunt of the joke. 'Darling, go brush your hair or something. Let the men talk.'

Accepting the bottle from Ravensdale, he inspected the label with satisfaction. At a bar in the corner, he poured two glasses of the strong cognac called *tutovka*. Handing one over, he fell back into the couch and removed from a breast pocket a tin of *khat* leaves, fitting a pinch of the leathery green root between cheek and gum.

As Ravensdale found his own seat facing Tsoi's, his gaze lingered for a moment on the large window opening on to the backyard. Beyond tall silver pines, a gentle grade sloped down to a patch of scrubby snow-covered beach. He remembered that beach: the crunch of a shovel biting into rocky sand, the grunt of flat tops lifting a body, the spray from the river, the sweet hint of brandy on Tsoi's breath. In the far distance, Moscow's skyscrapers shone like dusky jewels.

'You look well,' said Tsoi, in a tone which suggested otherwise.

Ravensdale grinned and sipped his cognac, which ran down his throat with a pleasant sting. 'It's good to see you, my friend. But I think that I owe you an apology.'

'You left me with my dick hanging out, yes. But I managed to zip up fast. Only cut myself a little.'

'It was Carlson. He gave me no warning . . . Well, you must have heard the story.'

Tsoi lifted his chin inquiringly: *Enlighten me.*

'Turns out the Bureau's man in Sicily was working both sides. Carlson panicked, called everybody off the field. That included Force Multiplication. Direct violation of orders for me to stay without him, he said . . . which turned out to be true.'

With surprising delicacy, Tsoi picked a flake of *khat* root from his tongue. His scarred face gave away nothing. He examined the flake on his fingertip critically. 'You couldn't get me a message?'

'Carlson,' said Ravensdale shortly.

'I didn't realize the man had such power over you. I'd assumed you were equals.' Tsoi scanned, to make sure the insult had registered, and then smiled. 'But that page has turned. I forgive you, *tovarish*. It's good to see your ugly face again, and that's the truth.' He flicked away the *khat* root. 'To what do I owe the pleasure? Something to do, perchance, with a certain armed assault early this morning?'

'You see through me. As always.' From an onyx cigarette case on the end-table, Ravensdale helped himself to a Sobranie. 'So you know what I need.'

Tsoi snickered. 'You've got balls. I'll give you that.'

'I'll make it worth your trouble.'

'Look around. Do I need your money?'

'A pound of flesh, then.' Ravensdale struck a match. 'Or a head on a platter.'

Intrigued, Tsoi frowned. Ravensdale could guess his line of thought. The man's network of connections, *svyazi*, reached from the storied corridors of the Kremlin to the underground gambling dens of the local gangs, the *shpana*. He kept on his payroll chiefs of police, commanders of the OMON paramilitary strike force, and deputy directors of the FSB. But connections went both ways, and with so many allegiances came complications. There were always flies in the ointment, and always loyalties which made removing said flies untenable. During their long acquaintance, 'pest control' had been one of the services provided by Ravensdale. In exchange, Tsoi had handed over an equal number of smugglers of raw fissile material.

'Tempting,' allowed Tsoi after a moment. 'Anybody?'

'Anybody.'

'But you're asking for a lot. How about five anybodies?'

Ravensdale puffed his cigarette and shrugged.

Again, Tsoi chuckled. 'You're crazier than ever, my friend.'

Ravensdale only feathered smoke from his nostrils.

'Tempting,' the man repeated. 'But be careful what you promise. I'll take you at your word. There's a fellow from the German BND who's been giving me headaches. And another from the French DGSE. And another from Mossad, and an MI6 agent who robs me of my sleep.'

Ravensdale kept his face blank.

'Now, see: that makes me suspicious. A German . . . of course, you'll throw him to the wolves with pleasure. A Frenchman . . . with a show of reluctance, but ultimately, *oui*. But a Brit? An Israeli? These are your kin. Your brothers.'

'This takes priority.'

'Last time, you disappeared on me in the middle of the night. Didn't even say goodbye. Created some problems.'

'Don't you believe in second chances?'

'Tempting,' said Tsoi again. 'Tempting. Tempting.' For a final moment, he deliberated. Then a smile lit his face, turning the acne

scars upward, baring unnaturally white false teeth – the real ones had
been lost to scurvy in prison. He raised his snifter in a toast. 'To old
friendships,' he said brightly, 'given new life.'

Together, they drank off their glasses.

SERGIEV POSAD, NORTH-EAST OF MOSCOW

A sign of pearled neon advertised a bar called Russky Dvorak.

She walked in with chin held high, lifting the first purse she passed.
Inside the bathroom she went through lipstick, mascara, hairbrush,
henna, cigarettes and lighter, cell phone, credit cards, and several
thousand rubles in cash. With the henna, she could even change the
color of her hair – but it would take time. For now, she made do with
a quick spit-and-polish using the make-up and hairbrush. Pocketing
the dye, lighter, and cash, she slipped the rest back into the purse,
and the purse itself into a garbage receptacle.

Outside, the temperature was dropping. Nevertheless, the streets
remained crowded – the town of Sergiev Posad, a prime destination
in the Golden Ring surrounding Moscow, was flypaper for tourists
– and finding an unattended car proved impossible. She wandered
packed narrow avenues, past souvenir stalls, curio and coffee shops,
bars and restaurants, boutique clothing stores, museums and fast
food joints. Beyond low rooftops, a glimpse of a more ancient
Russia loomed: the Cathedral of the Assumption, larger than its
inspiration and namesake in the Moscow Kremlin, thrusting six
ornate pillars topped with onion domes into the pastel smear of
the setting sun.

When the wind gusted, she shivered. The cold was intensifying
. . . and the ranks of police were growing ever thicker. If she couldn't
get off the streets soon, she'd be sunk. But a single girl checking
alone into a hotel would be all too conspicuous, and the railroads
were crawling with *politsiya*.

A pair of soldiers holding tablets paced slowly up the opposite
side of the avenue. Cassie developed a sudden interest in a curio shop
she was passing. One hand moved to her mouth, so she could gnaw
on a fingernail. Behind sunset-honeyed glass glinted carved *dymkovo*
toys, clay hussars, wooden eggs, lacquer boxes, Crimean lamps, silver
snuffboxes, and antique specimens of *kovsh*, a drinking vessel with
a boat-shaped body and a single handle, and *korob,* the small wooden
chest used to hold a peasant girl's dowry. Her weary eyes lingered
on a *matryoshka* doll, representing a tiny girl with tapered lashes,
bee-stung lips, and a brightly-flowered scarf.

Otkuda vy? the girl inside the dacha had asked. *Where are you from?*
Nichevó stráshnovo. Never mind. *I'm an angel. Go back to sleep,*
honey.

In the glass, she watched the hazy reflection of the soldiers pass
behind her.

She moved again. Ten minutes later she found a free stool at a
tavern four blocks from Russky Dvorak. At the far end of the bar sat
a man in his middle years, blond and well-fed, handsome but dull.
His eyes had the hungry, searching quality of a soldier's whose R&R
was almost up. A pale band on his left hand testified to a recently
removed wedding ring.

Ordering a glass of Zauberman, she waited to be approached.
Looking her best, she could hardly take two steps without fighting
off some misguided Lothario. At the moment, however, she apparently
looked far from at her best. She kept waiting. When her wine arrived,
she took a dainty sip. Her stomach growled a warning. Olives sat in
a bowl; she ate two, chewing carefully. As she warmed up, she
unzipped the parka. Another sip, and she pushed the glass reluctantly
away. Had to keep sharp.

At last the man slipped off his stool. Moments later he was beside
her, smiling. 'American?' he asked in English.

She affected wariness. 'How could you tell?'

'Sixth sense, I guess.' He offered a hand. 'Owen Holt.'

Guardedly, she shook. 'Heidi.'

'Where you from, Heidi?'

'Connecticut. You?'

'Tampa. We're both a long way from home.' Sliding on to a stool
beside her, he caught the bartender's eye and pointed at her glass.
'What brings you here?'

'My thesis.' She leaned slightly away. With pro forma politeness:
'You?'

'Business. Leaving tomorrow, actually. I was supposed to stay
another week, but with this travel advisory . . . The head honcho
thinks it might be safer back stateside.'

She nodded. 'I'm a little nervous myself.'

'We'll be OK if we stick together. Where you staying?'

'Youth hostel.'

'Is that safe?'

'When I was with my friends, sure. But they went on to Penza
yesterday. I stayed behind, to visit a few more museums . . . but now,
with them gone . . . I'm wondering.'

'Like I said: we've got to stick together.' He leaned closer, peering at her temple. 'Looks like you've already got scuffed up a bit.'

'Low ceiling.' She laughed. 'Vodka. Bad combination.'

The bartender set another glass of wine on the bar. Owen Holt leaned back, gesturing for the check. 'How about after this round,' he said, 'we find something to eat? My treat. Drink up.'

Afterward, she lay looking up at slats of light on the ceiling, listening to his labored breathing.

Eventually, she left the bed, slipping into the bathroom. The hotel's modest amenities – single-serving shampoo and lotion, saran-wrapped toothbrushes, cardboard-covered drinking glasses – struck her, after just a day on the street, as outrageously decadent.

She showered leisurely – the quick rinse before hitting the sheets had taken off only the surface layer of grime – and then, beneath gentle recessed lighting, conducted a thorough examination of her poor, battered body. The left side of her ribcage was mottled with bruises. The ribs themselves stood out clearly. The abrasion on her left temple had become an angry red welt. The right temple was not so bad.

Toweling off, she climbed back into bed, naked. Owen Holt stirred sleepily. 'Hey, you.'

She smiled. 'Hey.'

'You smell good.'

He reached for her again. She did not resist.

When it was done, he was back asleep within three minutes. She lay awake, staring at the slatted light on the ceiling.

Now what?

No easy answer presented itself. Her plans had gone only as far as completing her mission and then meeting her contact, whom she'd believed would provide safe extraction.

Beside her, Owen Holt emitted a stertorous grunt, followed by a muffled fart. He rolled away, revealing a bald spot on the crown of his head.

Maybe she could glom on to this man, talk him into delaying his return to the States. A couple traveling together would be less notice-able than a young woman traveling alone. And every kilometer she gained from Moscow would increase her chances. But sooner or later she would need to cross a border or board an airplane, and when it came to navigating an international line, Owen Holt would be of no appreciable use.

Maybe she was going about this wrong. She might just hunker down, avoid borders, and lay low. But then, of course, she would never get back to Quinn.

Her heart thumped. *Quinn.* He had tricked her – dangled the lure, made her jump, and then stabbed her in the back—

She breathed. When the emotion served a purpose, she would give it free rein. Until then, it would only work against her.

With or without Owen Holt, she realized, her chances were not good.

She had no documents, no tickets, no identification. A reasonable likeness of her face was splashed across the media. Worse, they might have recovered her scent from the knit cap she had lost. There might be dogs to contend with. Trying to pass through an airport would be asking for serious trouble.

Escape by sea, then. Reach the coast and she might board a ship. But, of course, they would be watching the ports too. An ordinary-looking young woman hardly blended in among sailors and merchant marine. On the other hand, a pleasure cruise – if she could find one – might not be out of the question. But with eyes everywhere, how would it look to purchase last-minute passage with cash? And here, too, would be the problems of documents.

That left the borders. Russia sprawled over one-eighth of the earth's inhabited land mass, covering ten time-zones. That meant a lot of border to patrol, with infamously corrupt militiamen patrolling it. A relatively short jaunt to the west would bring her to Lithuania, Belarus, or Ukraine. Safer would be the long trip east, toward Kazakhstan and Mongolia . . . or north, toward Finland.

The more she thought about it, the more plausible a border crossing seemed. Realistically, they could not keep all those miles of frontier secure. Out in the remote countryside, far from the scene of the crime, she could hop an unguarded fence or seduce a crooked sentry. If necessary, she could take another life. When circumstances required, as recent events had proved, she was capable of doing terrible things.

It was a plan – at least the skeleton of one – and she immediately felt easier inside.

She forced her eyes closed. This was her chance to rest.

For many long minutes, the wheels in her head kept spinning. She rolled over, fluffed the pillow, forced out breath between clenched teeth. At length, she quieted. Gradually, her breathing turned even.

Sometime later, she dozed.

NEW YORK CITY: ONE YEAR EARLIER
'Run,' a voice breathed into her ear.

Lights danced through the darkness. When she sat up, one burned directly into her eyes.

She kicked the sleeping bag aside and flung herself off the mattress, on to bare floor. Even sleep-addled, she realized immediately that there were only two ways out of the room: the window and the door. The lights were coming from the door. She went for the window.

'Police!' a voice cried. *'Don't fucking move!'*

Fumbling at the lock, she pushed the window up. A gust of cold air ruffled her hair. Michelle was right behind her, breathing hard. 'Hurry,' Michelle said.

Someone was coming into the bedroom. By then Cassie was slipping out, on to the fire escape and into the frigid night.

The tenement was on the fifth floor. She looked down the air shaft, at the garbage cans and the rustling rats, and then up, at the roof and the night sky beyond. She began to climb, dimly aware that Michelle hadn't made it out behind her.

'Police! Freeze!'

The fire escape was slippery with ice. She went heedlessly up anyway, throwing herself at rungs before finding firm grips. A moment later she was on the roof. Between this building and the next was a gap of perhaps six feet. Her tongue came out to scrape across chapped lips.

A man was coming off the fire escape behind her.

She licked her lips again and took a running jump.

She landed hard, rolling on to one shoulder. Her wind was knocked out, and for an instant the world shrank to almost nothing: broken glass crunching beneath her, the ripe smell of her own unwashed body filling her nose. Giving her head a quick shake, she scrambled to her feet.

Rattled down another icy fire escape, grabbing the handrails and sliding the penultimate two flights. Then she was in a garbage-strewn alley, sprinting toward the mouth—

A brown Cadillac sedan came out of nowhere, jumped the curb in front of her.

Doors sprung open; three men emerged. She reversed – but now two others were descending the fire escape.

She reversed again and came to an abrupt halt. Three small, ugly guns pointed unshakingly at her face and chest.

Slowly, Cassie Bradbury raised her hands above her head.

*　　*　　*

She woke to the smooth sound of interstate unfolding beneath tires.

For a few moments, she couldn't remember where she was. Then it came back to her: squatting in the tenement, the midnight raid, the rooftop chase. Now she was in an unmarked police cruiser – driving, it seemed, between reefs of hulking dark forest.

The clock on the dashboard read 1:24 a.m. The man who was driving glanced in the rear-view mirror, saw that she was awake, and returned his eyes to the road without comment.

Trying to sit up, she discovered that her wrists were still cuffed behind her back. The circulation had been cut off; her hands felt like two numb, disembodied balloons. Surreptitious exploration convinced her that the cuffs were secure.

She leaned back into the vinyl upholstery. *Strange.* She knew from unhappy experience that Manhattan had police stations every few blocks. What was the point of bringing her out here, into the country?

Presently, they left the highway. They drove through a small town, past old-fashioned porches and darkened dormer windows. Then farmland: barns, silos, fields, frozen ponds. Eventually, they turned again, by a mailbox featuring the words 'COBBLER'S COVE', on which two carved pheasants nuzzled.

They reached a high iron gate – so tall that Cassie, from the back seat of the sedan, couldn't see the top – and then paused, idling, for what seemed like several minutes. At last the gate creaked open with a long, low, theatrical groan. They rolled forward again. The night sky was overcast, and she could pick up only ghostly impressions of the house they were approaching, surrounded by stands of pine.

The house was a red-brick colonial, two solid stories, with porches and additions giving the illusion of a slowly spreading spill. Ten windows in front, trimmed white; an ivory portico topped with an American flag, which sagged slightly in the middle. History and old money in the air, alongside pine sap and chilled rosemary.

In a circular driveway, Cassie's chauffeur parked behind a gray Ford Escort with Maryland plates. He came to the back of the car, took her rucksack in one hand and her elbow in the other, and guided her across a flagstone walk scrupulously denuded of snow.

They entered a dim foyer furnished with Yankee unfussiness. Then a living room straight from a Williams-Sonoma catalogue: dark wood, light fabric, couch and chairs and throw pillows and lamps skilfully arranged before a cold fireplace. She could feel the house sprawling and looming beyond arched doorways. The echoes were curious:

unexpectedly dampened in some ways, unexpectedly sharp in others. Later she would discover that this was because some rooms possessed strange characteristics: padding and mats in the gym, antiseptic metal sharpness in the lab.

A man stood before the fireplace. He looked as if he'd been standing for hours, just waiting. He had a sandy widow's peak, pale-blue eyes behind stylish frames, and a pronounced cleft in his chin. He wore a black crew-neck cotton sweater, blue slacks, and brown loafers. To Cassie he looked like nothing so much as a kindly uncle – the intellectual variety, who maybe taught comparative literature at a small local college, and maybe puffed a J or two on a Saturday night with his sexy, horned-rimmed-glasses-wearing wife.

For a few seconds the man considered her, in the dim light, in silence. 'Have a seat,' he said then.

The one who had been driving set down her backpack, removed the handcuffs, and went to stand inconspicuous guard by the doorway.

'Julian Quinn,' said the kindly-uncle type as he settled down beside her on the couch.

He reached for her bag and browsed blithely through her few possessions – clothes, notebook and pen, bowl and stashbox, macramé bracelets, baby wipes, candy bars, dog-eared copy of *Catcher in the Rye*. It had been her father's copy, recovered from the attic after his death, marked up in his own hand. Of all the books she'd discovered up there, this had been her favorite, the only one she'd chosen to take along once she had started traveling light.

The man set the backpack aside. Leaning away, he said, 'I'm told you led the cops on quite the merry chase.'

Cassie raised one finger, still tingling with pins and needles from the handcuffs, to part the lank curtain of blonde hair hanging over her eyes.

'What's your name?' he asked.

'What do you want it to be?' she replied acidly, and sullenly parted her hair again.

'That's the second time you've touched your hair, young lady. It's what we call a *negation behavior*. Tends to indicate discomfort or evasion. In this case, I think both. Yes?'

She blinked and forced both hands into her lap.

For another few moments, he looked at her in silence. Outside, the wind whickered and moaned. Finally, he reached again for the bag. He withdrew the stashbox, turning it over. 'You do hard drugs?'

She said nothing.

'Whatever you've done before,' he said, pocketing the box, 'is not my concern. But from here on out, you're clean. You're in training.'

Her hand tried to go to her mouth so she could chew on a cuticle; she prevented it.

'As it so happens,' he said, 'I already know your name.' From an end-table behind the couch, he lifted a buff manila folder. 'I know quite a bit about you, Cassie Bradbury. Enough to put you away, as it happens, for quite a few years . . . Have a look.'

A thick sheaf of photographs inside the folder. Some were blurry – captures from surveillance cameras, obvious long-lens shots – but all were clear enough, she guessed, to serve as evidence in court. She saw herself picking pockets, hot-wiring cars, shoplifting with Michelle, breaking into abandoned buildings . . .

'Am I going to be arraigned?' she asked dully.

'Not if I have anything to say about it.' Gravely, he took back the folder. He handed her the rucksack, and then gestured to the man standing guard. 'I've spent too much time looking for you, my dear, to let you slip away so easily. Get some sleep. Breakfast's at six.'

THREE

SEREBRYANY BOR

Senior Inspektor Piotr Vlasov had sunken cheeks, short blond hair, a neatly waxed mustache, and a soft little mouth like a child's. He wore a cream-colored Anderson & Sheppard suit that might have cost him a thousand pounds on Savile Row and held a thin brown cigarette in the English manner, between thumb and middle finger.

He was telling a story about two prostitutes who murdered their clients and then harvested organs for sale on the black market. Ravensdale, with thunderclouds of fatigue gathering inside his skull, had lost the thread. Otari Tsoi, wearing a polite smile, seemed not to have bothered picking it up in the first place. His attention was divided between the bare thigh of the girl sitting beside him and the arriving *zakuski*, the traditional first course of a Russian meal. Crystal bowls, seemingly without end, offered large-grained gray Beluga caviar, button mushrooms in marinade, beets vinaigrette, pickled cucumbers, cured anchovies, stuffed eggs, hard cheeses, and the fine ring-shaped bread called *kalach*. Dapper servants in tie and tails circulated smoothly and unobtrusively, keeping crystal glasses filled with water, wine, and vodka.

'But of course,' said Vlasov, after providing a wealth of grisly details, 'this is hardly appropriate dinner conversation.' He stabbed his cigarette into a cut-glass ashtray and reached for a deviled egg. Leaving space for someone else to seize the conversational reins, he popped the egg into his mouth, masticated, and swallowed. When nobody spoke, he went on: 'But it does bring to mind a similar case from last year. A clinic in Mirny. Patients would die, accidentally-on-purpose, and their kidneys would be removed, packed in ice, flown west. The mastermind behind it? An Israeli national.' An expressive gesture terminated in a circumspect reach for an olive. 'As soon as we got on the scent, the man vanished like smoke. The surgeon who removed the organs, too. Both Jews. Try extraditing a Jew from Israel!'

Elena, microskirt riding dangerously high on twig-thin legs, listened raptly.

'When we asked for them back, they claimed political persecution. Israel's Supreme Court upheld their citizenship and called the charges "groundless". And they wonder why the world despises them.' For the first time since their introduction he glanced at Ravensdale, inviting a comment, or perhaps a confession. 'You're not a Jew, are you?'

Very slightly, Ravensdale shook his head.

As the next course was delivered – a hot, unctuous soup of indeterminate ingredients – the Inspektor touched the corners of his mouth with a napkin. 'I'm no bigot,' he said. 'But they're the cause of so much suffering in the world. It's just a matter of time, I tell you, until someone gets organized and finishes what so many have started . . .'

After dinner, the girl went upstairs; the men retired to Tsoi's study.

The room had been furnished with every advantage except taste. Carved nymphs and pixies capered on a granite hearth. A burnished harpsichord gleamed beneath a crystal chandelier. Ormolu swans, shells, scrolls, cupids, and mermaids tumbled across wainscoting and boiseries. Finding a seat, Ravensdale squeezed his eyes briefly closed against the onslaught of ornamentation.

He listened to Tsoi pour *tutovka*. A grandfather clock in one corner chimed dully, eleven times. Presently, Ravensdale opened his eyes and tasted his cognac. Through the window, a coppery quarter moon hung behind a scrum of cloud.

After consulting his phone, Vlasov found his own seat. The three men went through various rituals with tobacco and *khat* root. Vlasov balanced his snifter carefully on the scalloped arm of his chair, arranging it with neat precision.

'So.' Tsoi smiled blandly. 'The Inspektor is a dear old friend. I trust him completely.' He faced Vlasov. 'You were able, I understand, to have the investigation reassigned?'

'It took a bit of doing. But the Chairman owed me a favor. So, yes; you are now speaking with the man in charge.'

'And once the girl is captured, she'll come here?'

'First we'll need to parade her in front of the cameras, let the Kremlin soak in some glory.' Vlasov made a final tiny adjustment to the alignment of his glass. 'But after that, she'll vanish from her cell and come directly your way. I'll make sure of it myself.'

'But before any interrogation,' cautioned Ravensdale.

'Never fear. We all understand the . . . delicacies . . . of the situation.'

'What measures have been taken?'

'A cordon was in place around Turygino. But she must have evaded it; otherwise we would have her already. That is the bad news. The good news is, a new perimeter has been established. It reaches west almost to Rzhev, south to Serpukhov, east to Orekhovo-Zuyevo, and north beyond Sergiev Posad. Mobile search-parties comb every centimeter within. In the unlikely event that she has moved outside this sphere, we've established strategic checkpoints across the country-side. Three-hundred kilometers out in every direction. The Kremlin is determined to take this very seriously. Foreign interests cannot act with impunity on Russian soil whenever the urge takes them.' His eyelids flickered ironically. 'Officially, we are certain she will be brought to justice. Unofficially, we are guardedly optimistic.'

Listening, Tsoi wore a neutral expression.

'But the more we know about her,' continued Vlasov, 'the better our chances. Where she's come from, the extent and nature of her training, who she knows in Russia . . .' He trailed off artfully.

Ravensdale took a moment. 'I don't know anything for certain.'

Vlasov waited.

'My guess – and it is only a guess.' Ravensdale covered the sour taste in his mouth with a drag from his cigarette, a gulp of cognac. He took another moment to arrange his thoughts. When he had first noticed the pattern years before – agency business in Moscow under-taken by anonymous young assets whose bodies then surfaced in the

Moskva, fingertips cut off and faces bashed in to frustrate attempts at identification – he had brought it to Fletcher. He'd been ordered to let it go. And he had. But not before meditating on the problem; not before comparing Fletcher's schedule against windows that would have fit the training periods. He had found motive, means, and opportunity . . . and then he'd become swept up in developments with Sofiya. Put out to pasture, grateful just to have avoided Title 18 prosecution. Dmitri had come along. The question of Fletcher's side-game had been set aside . . . but never, it seemed, entirely forgotten.

'She was picked up off the street, I think. From a big enough city that a disappearing girl wouldn't leave a ripple. Whether we're talking about the US or Russia, I can't say.' Another gulp of cognac. 'She was a runaway. Perhaps an addict. Someone nobody would miss. She was trained in a secluded location, by a single officer or very small group. Absolute *razdelenie*, compartmentalization.'

Vlasov's slim eyebrows had climbed to maximum altitude.

'We can assume standard paramilitary techniques and trade-craft. Once in the field, she would have had no contact with her case officer. He's . . . He would be too careful for that. A network may have been made available to her for supply purposes. But no one – including the contact charged with disposing of her after the operation – would have known details of her mission.'

Dead air. Ravensdale smoked again. 'Just guesswork,' he said.

Vlasov and Tsoi exchanged a glance.

'We are to believe,' said Tsoi slowly, 'that a runaway – a drug addict – managed to gain access to one of the most guarded men in the world?'

'I'm telling you the way I suspect it's been done in the past. Whether you believe is up to you.'

Vlasov sat watchfully, a fisherman scrutinizing a bobbing lure.

'This . . . street urchin.' Tsoi picked at a seam of his pants. 'Her motivation would be . . . patriotism? Allegiance to the good old red, white, and blue?'

'Doubtful. I think she'd have had previous run-ins with the police, impressed them with her initiative. The man who tapped her would have assembled a file. He found some soft spot on which to push, to get the result he wanted.'

Another glance passed between Tsoi and Vlasov. The latter nodded somberly. 'It's possible,' the Inspektor conceded. 'Considering how much evidence was left behind, we are faced with a remarkable surfeit of dead ends. We recovered hair and blood from a knit cap, but found no matches in any database. Because, I suppose, there is no pre-existing profile. She has effectively come from thin air.'

Ravensdale signaled assent with his cigarette, sending a wisp of smoke curling toward the ceiling.

'She used grenades,' Vlasov went on. 'Explosives. A handgun. We have fragments and spent shells. We have the remains of the aircraft with which she made her incursion. But all trails lead nowhere: to the black market, and then to brick walls. Very neat. Clean margins.'

'That's the idea.'

'So we should forget about where she's been, I imagine, and concentrate on where she's going.' The Inspektor peered into his cognac with hooded eyes. 'Which would be . . .?'

'Her last contact tried to kill her. She won't trust another. Her face is in the newspapers. She knows we're looking for her.' Ravensdale shrugged. 'Fight or flight. She's running blind.'

'We have confidence in our sketch. I dare say she will be found, in the end, with the active assistance of the citizenry. Muscovites are the most vigilant people on the planet.'

Silence descended again, grew heavy. The clouds beyond the window skimmed across the moon, giving Ravensdale the sensation that he, too, was moving. At last Tsoi shifted in his seat. 'Gentlemen,' he said. 'I cannot forget my duties as host. Mister Ravensdale has traveled a long way. And the Inspektor is no doubt required at Bauman Street. If anything develops, we'll pounce. Until then . . . we have food for thought.'

The guest room was on the mansion's second floor.

The sheets were Egyptian cotton, the bathroom stocked with artisanal soaps and lotions. There were only two possible exits: the door, and a beveled window overlooking the front drive. With the heel of one hand, Ravensdale wiped a swath of condensation from the window. Flat tops were posted at regular intervals along the driveway. From above, he could make out the bulge of firearms beneath their overcoats.

He washed his face with scalding water. Then he sat on the edge of the bed, massaging the bridge of his nose with two fingers. In America, eight hours behind, Dima would just be finishing his afternoon snack. With luck, Tess wasn't letting the boy eat too much junk food. Dima could be damned persuasive when it came to securing junk food . . .

An engine turned over outside. He moved to the window again, saw a ZIL-41047 limousine just pulling away. The Inspektor, it seemed, had dallied for a private word with Tsoi.

After a long moment, he turned slowly back toward the bed. He was reaching for the oxford's top button when a knock sounded at the door. 'Come.'

Tsoi smiled apologetically. 'The room is to your liking?'

'Perfect. Thank you.'

'I was speaking with the Inspektor.' Broodingly, Tsoi closed the door. 'An interesting fact came to light. He recognizes you, he says, from his intelligence days.'

Tiny hairs bristled on the nape of Ravensdale's neck. It was possible. During his stint in Moscow, he and Carlson – and later he and Sofiya – had been shadowed around the clock by FSB operators. For the most part the surveillance teams had remained faceless, elusive figures behind sunglasses and trench coats. Vlasov might well have been among them.

'He has seen your file. And he connected some dots for me. I knew that Sofiya Kirov had disappeared around the same time you went back to America. But somehow I hadn't put two and two together.'

They stood facing each other, motionless.

'I'm not here to wag my finger.' Tsoi's blunt pockmarked face remained unconcerned, as if they discussed the weather. 'From what I understand, you've paid a high enough price already for your choices. Drummed out of service, until this recent development necessitated your return . . . and worse, you didn't even get to keep your prize. Is this so?'

'It is.'

'What happened?'

Ravensdale looked at the swath he had wiped clean on the window, now obscured again by fog. In that shape one could see a scythe, a wheel, a carousel. 'What did the Inspektor say happened?' he asked quietly.

'A touching story. Two enemy agents, in a race to see who can develop the other first, fall in love. They tender their resignations and run back to America. For a time, it seems they'll get away with it. Then, after a suitable period of waiting, the FSB decides to make an example, and . . . how do they say? . . . the lady vanishes.'

Ravensdale nodded.

'Is she dead?'

'No doubt.'

'You saw it?'

'Vlasov didn't give you the gory details?'

'He said they took her from a playground. Left your son crying in a sandbox. You were across town, getting the tires on your car rotated.'

'Close enough,' said Ravensdale tonelessly.

Tsoi's forehead crimped sympathetically. 'You must have turned over every rock.'

'I did.'

'Except one.' Before Ravensdale could reply, he continued: 'I thought that we were friends, *tovarish*.'

'We pretend. It greases the wheels.'

'You should have come to me.'

'If I'd thought you could help, I would have. But there are too many shallow graves in the world, Otari, for even you to find them all.'

'Also, you feared I wouldn't forgive past transgressions. Yes?'

Ravensdale said nothing.

Tsoi nodded grimly. 'My friend: accept my most sincere condolences.'

'*Spasibo.*'

'But if we're to work together now, there must be trust. And that requires complete honesty.'

Ravensdale gave a gallows-humor grin. 'Next time.'

Tsoi sighed. Idly, he picked up a small decorative *kovsh* shaped like a dragon and ran a thoughtful finger along its porcelain length. He set it down again, flashed a surprisingly easy smile. 'If you need anything during the night, knock on the door.'

'I'll be fine.'

On his way out, Tsoi paused and looked slyly back. 'Not that I don't trust you,' he said. 'But I should clarify: once the girl arrives here, she will not be released until your end of the bargain has been honored.'

'Of course.'

'Pleasant dreams.' Tsoi closed the door behind himself softly, with insulting politeness.

Ravensdale sat again on the edge of the bed. After a while he undressed, crawled beneath a cashmere blanket, and switched out the light. He dreamed of dark wolves running through dense forest, past open graves and chain-wrapped corpses.

SERGIEV POSAD

She listened as Owen Holt moved around the room, as light on his feet as an elephant.

Before opening the door he paused, as if reconsidering. She could still open her eyes, catch him in the act of leaving, and convince him to take her along. But an undependable man would be a liability, not an advantage; best to look elsewhere.

The door opened and closed. She sat up slowly, looking around. Outside the window: full daylight. Holt had taken all of his personal effects . . . and not even left a note, the charmer.

Quickly, she dressed in yesterday's clothes. Inside the parka's pockets she discovered the cash, lighter, and henna she had stolen at Russky Dvorak. From the minibar she scavenged a bottle of water, two packets of peanuts, and a bag of mushroom and sour cream potato chips – only in Russia.

A maid's cart was parked just down the hallway. Cassie turned the other way, forsaking the elevator – coming up the previous night, she had noticed a convex mirror which probably concealed a security camera – in favor of the stairs.

Before stepping into the lobby she paused, gathering a sense of the room. Immediately to her right: the front desk and a series of inoffensive watercolors depicting the town's history of woodworking. A clerk was checking in a tourist couple. Coming out of the elevator to her left: a drop-dead gorgeous brunette wearing three-inch heels, a king's ransom of jewels, and a sorrowful expression. Two teenaged girls laughed loudly by the gift shop. Two soldiers stood near the revolving door. In the center of the lobby sat a bellboy on his luggage cart, looking lost. In a sunken vestibule by a grand piano, a man in an overstuffed chair turned a page in a newspaper. From the cast of his torso, Cassie gathered that his attention was focused everywhere but on the paper he held. According to Quinn, signals sent by the body wall – the carriage of head and trunk – were primal, coming directly from the movements of the first vertebrates, the jawless fishes. As such, they were harder to control than higher-functioning cues involving fingers, hands, legs, and feet. This made them more trust-worthy; or as Quinn had put it: *The most honest gestures come from the torso, not the limbs and face.*

She exited the lobby through a side door, maintaining the greatest possible distance from the soldiers and undercover detective. The day was unexpectedly sunny, almost mild. In the turnaround before the hotel, another tourist – fortyish, perspiring, small pot-belly encased in a tight powder-blue sport shirt – was arguing with a valet. His hapless family milled nearby, trying to dissociate themselves.

'But it certainly was *not* here last night.' The man spoke British-accented English; even his annoyance sounded gracious. He was indicating a white scratch on a rear flank of a red Lada Samara hatchback. 'I know that for a fact, because the rental agent and I walked around the car with a checklist.'

'Then it must have happened,' said the valet wearily, 'as you drove. Not here, sir, I can assure you. Sergei is the very best we have. He has never once damaged—'

'Let's ask Sergei ourselves, shall we?'

'I'm afraid that's not possible. His shift has ended.'

'Then I will speak with your supervisor. I must insist.'

The man's wife – broad shoulders, fair curly hair – was sucking on the inside of her cheeks, broadcasting frustration and impatience. The kids, both in their early teens, had wandered off toward the end of the turnaround, concentrating on their phones. The hatch of the Samara stood open. One heavy piece of luggage had already been loaded, but two smaller suitcases awaited attention.

In a fraction of an instant, the decision had been made. A few steps brought Cassie to the rear of the hatchback. She slipped inside, then reached out and picked up both small suitcases. Pressing herself flush against the cargo shelf, she covered herself.

Then she lay flat, breathing shallowly, heart fluttering. If anyone had seen her, the consequences would come . . . now.

She could hear the valet and the tourist still arguing, the first doggedly refusing to admit culpability for the scratch, the second refusing to accept the insistence of the first, demanding with increasing (yet still gracious) vehemence to speak with a supervisor. She could see close-up luggage tags (HARRIS; 384 WHITE STUBBS LANE, LONDON, ENGLAND) and smell the sharp pinched fragrance of a new car. Through cracks between suitcases, she could see fine blue lines crossing the rear windshield, and beyond them the pebbled ceiling of the turnaround's roof.

Ten minutes of stonewalling passed before good Mr Harris gave up. Then the suspension creaked with the weight of four additional bodies; the hatchback was slammed closed. The engine turned over, and the Samara lurched forward, on to the road.

'I've half a mind to write a letter,' muttered the husband.

To which the wife rejoined, 'Dear, it's not worth it. Why not let it go?'

To which the husband retorted, 'Why can't you ever take my side?' In the back seat, the children poked each other and giggled. Beneath shifting luggage, Cassie tried to figure out which direction they were going. They had turned right out of the hotel – north, away from Moscow.

As minutes passed, they retained the same bearing. The family settled into silence. The rollicking motion of tires across uneven roads was lulling, the sunshiny air warm. But she needed to remain alert, of course. At any moment could come a roadblock, a checkpoint, armed men, barking dogs . . .

She would not sleep. But she could half-drowse, like a cat. Conserve energy, recharge her batteries . . . and when the moment came, she would be ready.

COBBLER'S COVE: ONE YEAR EARLIER
They moved out from the porch, past an armed guard and on to a snowy path.

For a few minutes they walked without speaking, ice crunching softly beneath their feet. Beyond the woods, blue mountains rose into the dawning sky. As they walked, Cassie felt herself warming, but she kept her hands jammed into her pockets, her shoulders hunched, her body language closed.

'This land,' Quinn announced suddenly, 'goes on about eight miles that way—' he made a hatchet-blade with his hand and pointed straight ahead – 'and about sixteen miles that way—' he gestured to the left – 'and it's all raw wilderness: woods and creeks, and lakes and fields, and not a single house except for that one right there. There's not this much unspoiled land left anywhere else in the whole state.' He took out a pack of Merit Lights, lit one without offering to share, and French-inhaled the smoke.

She looked around uneasily, into the glittering ice-caves of the woods. Cameras were hidden somewhere, she thought. This was some kind of reality show, something like that, and her every reaction was being filmed.

He seemed to be waiting for acknowledgement. Warily, she nodded. 'Bum a smoke?' she ventured.

'Absolutely not. What part of *you're in training* do you not understand?' He stepped carefully over a twisting branch. 'You are very skilled,' he continued conversationally, 'at picking pockets, at stealing cars, at evading pursuit. The only major deficit in your skill set, so far as I can see, is the ability to take a life. Sound right?'

She hooked an errant strand of hair behind one ear. 'Who *are* you?'

'Make it through the day, and I'll explain everything. Until then, don't ask. Believe me: once you learn the whole story, you'll be glad I found you.'

'How long have you been watching me?'

'End of the day.' His tone brooked no argument. 'Unless, of course, you want to call my bluff. Then we can take a ride, see a man about a judge.'

She said nothing.

'So. There are a very limited number of ways to take a man's life. For our purposes, there are only seven: by vehicle, by fire, by explosive, by hand, by knife, by poison, and by gun. Each has advantages and disadvantages.'

'You really think I'll kill someone just to stay out of jail?'

'Once you learn the whole story: gladly. And when it's done, you'll thank me for giving you the opportunity. But let's not get ahead of ourselves. Now, please, pay attention. No target is going to stretch his throat out on a chopping block for your convenience. You'll need to make your own opportunities. But if you're patient, chances will present themselves. Sun Tzu: *Options multiply as they are seized.*'

Again he paused, waiting, until she gave a short, tight nod.

'Once you've considered options and consequences and decided to proceed, you will not hesitate. If you undertake the beginning of an action, you will see it through. Hesitation will ruin you. Whether you hesitate because of procedural reasons – doubting the consequences of your actions – or because of moral reasons, makes no difference. *Hesitation will ruin you.*'

The still-rising sun hung low in the sky. They picked their way over a fallen tree trunk, through a patch of tangled shrub. 'Can you drive?' he asked.

She nodded.

'I'm assuming you can't pilot a boat or an airplane.'

She shook her head.

'Let's not put "vehicle" out of the equation just yet. If you can handle a car, a boat's not hard. Planes can be a little trickier, but with some training . . .' He flicked ash from his cigarette with a thumb against the filter. 'Fire is the most economical method. It takes only a match, and a match is usually close at hand. Death results from burning, from asphyxiation by superheated air and smoke inhalation, from carbon monoxide. But fire is imprecise. Are you listening?'

She nodded.

'Explosives, under the right circumstances, may be just what the doctor ordered. You might home-brew, or you might use something prefabricated. I'll provide contacts in the field who will be able to get anything you might need. A plastique charge is easy to hide, easy to move, and so stable you can put out a cigarette in it.'

'Uh-huh.'

'*Yes* is the better answer. So. Hand, knife, and poison. All focused; all silent. You're not a big girl, and killing someone with bare hands isn't easy. But whether it's accomplished using accessories – a blunt weapon, a makeshift garrote, even a pen – or just with what God gave you, it's possible. At the most basic level, it doesn't matter how strong you are. It matters where you hit the guy. You hit first, and you hit hard. Once the target has been disabled, several holds and locks will result in death. First, however, he must be incapacitated. Certain vulnerable points on the human body will cause such incapacitation. I'm talking about eyes, nose, Adam's apple; temple, ears, back of the neck; upper lip, kidneys, and groin.'

'Am I supposed to remember all this?'

'Not yet. When attacking with a knife, realize that the first thrust doesn't need to be fatal. Disable your target by slashing a muscle and he'll be unable to defend himself. *Then* you'll find your fatal attack, your vein or your vital organ.'

'Uh-huh.'

'*Yes* is the better answer. Poisons. Any average household is full of them, and your contacts will have access to specialized pharmacies. The trick is knowing how to use them – what effects they'll create, how detectable they are, how long they'll take to work, how fatal they'll be.'

A clearing opened on the right. At the far end, several human-sized figures stood beneath black cloth. Beside the figures, soda cans were lined at neat intervals along a low, ice-caked wooden fence. Drawing to a stop, Quinn pinched out his cigarette and pocketed the butt. 'Gun is the most certain – but it's loud. Almost certain to attract attention, unless you've got a silencer. Have you ever fired a gun?'

She shook her head.

From somewhere in the back of his waistband, casually, he produced a small pistol. 'There are five basic rules to shooting. One: the gun is always loaded.'

She accepted the weapon, surprised.

'Two: never point the gun at something you are not prepared to destroy. That means point it away from me, please.'

After an infinitesimal hesitation, she did.

'Three: always be aware of what's behind your target. Bullets penetrate things. Walls are not bulletproof.'

She nodded.

'Four: keep your finger off the trigger until your sights are on the target. Got it?'

She nodded.

'Five: don't draw unless you mean to shoot. Now as it happens, this gun *is* loaded. It's a .22 pistol – originally a single-stack Springfield Armory .45 caliber, but I've replaced the top end with a Wilson Combat .22 conversion kit. You're going to use a two-handed grip. Say you're drawing, or picking up your weapon, with your right hand. The other hand should travel out and up from below to join the first. The right thumb flicks off the safety. The gun moves to eye level, and you focus on the target. Then refocus on the front sight, so it comes into sharp focus and the target goes blurry, keeping your forearms and the gun level . . .'

She raised the gun and took aim at a distant can of Mountain Dew, which looked preternaturally distinct in the clean morning air.

'Don't be afraid of the recoil. Don't close your eyes in the second before you fire.'

Cassie focused on the can. Refocused on the sight. Put her finger on the trigger.

'Go,' he said.

She fired.

The gun bucked; pain flared in her wrist. A gout of wood leapt from the fence.

'Try again.'

She fired again and missed.

'The key to shooting is coordination. If you want to hit someone with a baseball bat, go pump iron. If you want to hit a target with a bullet, jump rope. Starting tomorrow, you'll put in one hour per day.'

She raised the gun again, took aim.

'Know your weapon,' he said. 'Power matters less than accuracy. Mossad agents will often *reduce the load*, as they say, meaning reduce the amount of explosive charge in a cartridge. What they lose in range, they make up in accuracy.'

She fired.

The Mountain Dew can spun end over end into the forest.

'Good. But don't get cocky. A motionless target on a clear day, no wind, at fifty paces . . . If there were wind, you'd have needed to compensate. First you'd have calculated your wind speed. Wind under three miles per hour creates no effect. Between three and five, you can just feel it on your face. Between five and eight, you'll see foliage blowing, but the trees stay still. Eight to twelve, paper blows and dust swirls. Twelve to fifteen, you'll actually see the trees swaying . . .'

FOUR

RED SQUARE, MOSCOW

Perhaps it was his mood, but everything on which Aleksandr Marchenko's gaze fell seemed weighted with significance.

The gun slots of Arsenalnaya Tower, wide enough for heavy cannon, symbolized the endless metaphorical siege under which they found themselves. The prominent clock of Spasskaya represented the time always slipping, slipping away, never to be recaptured. Most symbolic of all, of course, was the deceptively modest structure of granite and labradorite just fifty yards from Spasskaya. Let the wags make their jokes, calling the preserved corpse inside *kopchuska* – 'smoked fish'. To most of Mother Russia's one hundred and fifty million loyal citizens, the tomb of Vladimir Ilyich Lenin served as a reminder of all Russia once had been and all it could be again. Inside, Premier Lenin – author, lawyer, revolutionary, philosopher, lover of children and cats, icon and idol and inspiration and legend – lay serenely on his back within a crystal casket, wearing a black suit and dark-blue polka-dotted tie, softly spotlit. At peace.

They crossed through the restricted zone, passing the mustard-colored ionic columns of Building Fourteen, pulling into the inner courtyard of the Senate building. An aide opened the Mercedes' rear door, escorting Marchenko to a brick portico which led directly into the president's private office.

Seated behind a wide maple desk, the President of Russia looked smaller than on TV – somehow deflated, like a failed attempt at a soufflé. His dull dark business suit seemed a clumsy fit, too snug in some places, particularly around the judo-thickened shoulders, and too generously cut in others. But of course, thought Marchenko, he was in essence a man of action. Put him shirtless on horseback or squatting with a rifle over the corpse of a tiger, and he would radiate command and easy authority.

As Marchenko accepted a firm handshake, he absorbed the four other people seated in the dim office. They were the chief of staff, the secretary of the national security council, the Director of the FSB, and the chairwoman of the upper house of Parliament. Every person in the room, including the President, was an alumnus of the *Komitet Gosudarstvennoy Bezopasnost* – the KGB.

Marchenko took the sole free chair before the desk. From the blotter, the President lifted a folder: dull-blue cover, criss-crossing black stripes. As their *Vozhd* glanced through the file, Marchenko looked around circumspectly, pulling at his silver goatee. During his long career he had never before been inside this office, and he knew that he might never be again. Sconces on the walls illuminated a creamy ceiling. The window was heavily curtained. A golden Fabergé clock ticked on a small inlaid table. A porcelain tea service on a sideboard had collected a fine layer of dust.

At last, the President closed the dossier. His eyelids flickered. 'Your recommendation?'

He was addressing Marchenko, who sat up straighter. 'The net draws ever tighter. She cannot hope to remain free for long. The complication comes, of course, in the person of this man Ravensdale and his allies within the *mafiya* and Investigative Committee Headquarters.'

'The solution,' declared the Director, 'is simple.' He was a tall, dour man with a road map of bluish veins criss-crossing his temples, who had perfected the art of lecturing a room while speaking to nobody in particular. 'Crush this corrupt Inspektor Vlasov like the scorpion fly he is, before he can get his stinger in. Then the American has nothing to work with.'

'But then we risk some other rogue element making eleventh-hour trouble.' Marchenko aimed his words toward a sconce on the wall behind the Director. 'The *vory* Tsoi—' *Vory v zakone*, literally 'Thief In Law', an elite member of the *mafiya* – 'has powerful allies within the cesspool of the Prosecutor General's Office. And they are vulnerable, over there, to the lure of deep pockets and numbered accounts. Better the enemy we know. Feed the good Inspektor enough rope; then Tsoi is not motivated to find another instrument within the PG.'

'So arrest the *vory* himself,' suggested the Director.

'And then the American finds another instrument.'

'So arrest the American.'

'And then the CIA sends another in his place. If I may – I have a better idea.'

A battle raged behind the President's cold blue eyes. The man of action, thought Marchenko, would have neutralized the corrupt Inspektor Vlasov even for entertaining the thought of *izmena*, treason. But the intelligence professional, the lifelong veteran of the Game, recognized the value of leaving a compromised asset in play when said asset could still be of use.

'There exists,' said Marchenko, 'a better option. Upon realizing who the American was, I made some inquiries. Evidently, his wife still lives. She is in a prison camp in Norilsk.' He shrugged diffidently. 'He has proven in the past his willingness to betray his own for this woman . . .' Trailing off, he sneaked a glance at the President, to see how the man was reacting.

The President looked intrigued. The ex-spy, of course, could not help but relish the elan of using an American traitor to execute the master stroke, putting a triple-spin on the treasonous Inspektor's double-cross.

The chief of staff and the secretary of the security council swapped a glance. 'If *I* may,' said the former: a lugubrious, slow-spoken septuagenarian, with thinning white hair combed sideways across a pink scalp.

An impatient gesture from behind the desk: *proceed.*

'With Blakely gone, continued analysis of his documents presents . . . challenges. If this traitor is really so eager to betray his own, we have a mountain of intelligence which might benefit from his attention.'

The President thinned his lips. And suddenly Marchenko could see his operation – the first to allow him access to this inner sanctum – being wrested from him.

'You make assumptions,' Marchenko proclaimed crisply. 'That the intelligence offers some profound value. That the fact of the assassin suggests they were determined to deny us continuing assistance in deciphering it. More likely, I submit, it was a ploy designed to create the *illusion* of value – to help us in swallowing the wrong lure. Either that or they are just petulant children, upset that their playmate has made new friends.' He shook his head emphatically. 'And you assume that Ravensdale is equipped to offer insight. We have no guarantee of that.'

'The fact remains,' said the chairwoman. She was sixty-something, wearing bifocals, a single-breasted Chanel business suit, and gray hair pinned into a bun. 'The cache offers an unprecedented opportunity.

Yes, there are no guarantees. It might all be *dezinformaciya*. But it also might offer a chance to examine the internal workings of our enemy more clearly than ever before. It might be a coup to make Hanssen and Ames look like trifles.'

'Eighteen months of analysis already,' said Marchenko with a sniff. 'And what do we have to show for it?'

'But adopt the long view. An undertaking of this magnitude requires time. And attaining clarity in this sphere is worth more than the assassin . . . whose work is, after all, already done.' She slipped off her bifocals, polished them briskly on one sleeve – unnecessarily, thought Marchenko, purely as a rhetorical flourish – and returned them to her nose. '*Za dvumya zaitsami pogonish'sya, ne odnogo ne poimaesh.*' Run after two rabbits, and you'll catch none. 'We should concentrate on what we have and not get greedy for more. Curious Varvara's nose, as we all recall, was cut off.'

The President's ice-blue eyes glittered inscrutably.

Marchenko faced the man directly. As he did he tipped his ring, a symbol of Imperial Russia, to subtly catch the light tilting upward from the sconces. More than anything, he knew, their leader coveted a return to the glorious past, a resurgence of the noble Russian Empire. That meant, in part, snapping the West across their treacherous snout. No longer content just to kidnap Russian nationals from third countries, America had now extended herself to an armed assault within the Motherland – the latest and most blatant of a long string of insults, hypocrisies, and broken promises.

'Should we sniff around the droppings of the Americans, trying to determine which might be a jewel and which might be just shit? Or should we boldly take the reins in hand? Think what we can accomplish, with this woman's confession to wave in the hypocrites' faces! God gave us balls not for beauty, but for use. We must avenge the insult to our sovereignty, capture their assassin, obtain her affirmation of guilt, and then hang her in Red Square beside Vlasov, within sight of Lenin's tomb, for all to see.'

Beneath his ill-fitting dark jacket, the President rolled his thick shoulders. 'The assassin,' he decided, 'takes priority. Once we have her in hand, we can consider trying to extract further value from the American.'

Sage nods all around. Everyone in the room knew better than to continue arguing and risk being branded a troublemaker. When there was a person, it was said inside the Kremlin, there was a problem; if there was no person, there was no problem.

Marchenko tried not to look smug. The President checked his watch. 'Keep me apprised,' he said and reached for another file on his desk. Marchenko nodded, pushed back his chair. The meeting was over.

NORTH OF TVER

The brakes caught; the Samara hitched.

Cassie woke with a start. Pretty streaks of red laced her glimpse of the sky through the rear windshield. Harris muttered something to his wife: part reassurance, part warning. The car slowed, then stopped. A window skimmed down. The sinking sun had lent the rear windshield the quality of a mirror, and Cassie could see the dim reflection of the man who wandered over to the driver's side: a policeman, thickset, weaving slightly, possibly drunk. On the sleeve of his right arm she glimpsed the triple-banded insignia of a sergeant.

'*Litsenziya,*' the man demanded.

'Er, I'm afraid I don't—'

'License,' the man said in rough English.

Harris found his wallet and passed something over.

'Tourist?' the policeman asked.

'Yes, sir.'

'UK?'

'Yes, sir.'

'Coming from where?'

'Sergiev Posad.'

'Going where?'

'Saint Petersburg. But tonight I think we'll stop at Novgorod. I've always wanted to see Lake Ilmen . . .'

'Tariff. Eighty euros.'

Crinkling bills.

'Go,' the policeman said, and the Samara jerked back into motion. As they pulled away, Cassie watched the roadblock – two green-and-white Zhiguli-8s parked in a V, surrounded by a dozen men bearing Kalashnikovs, smoking cigarettes and sipping from flasks – recede into twilight.

'That was a shakedown,' said Mrs Harris crisply after a moment.

'Very perceptive, dear.'

'You didn't even argue.'

'He had a machine gun, dear.'

'Yes, but he had no right to extort money from you.'

Cassie exhaled a measured breath. No guarantees, she thought.

But she may just have survived the greatest challenge she would face until she reached a border. She may just make it, after all.

She woke again to the rattle of the Samara leaving the paved road.

They bounced over loose gravel, pulling into a parking lot. Tires settled with a sigh. The engine died. She steeled herself. When the hatchback opened, she would lead with a kick. *You hit first, and you hit hard . . .*

'Stay here,' said Harris curtly.

A door opened and then closed. Footsteps crunched away. Cassie carefully shifted position, moving one slow centimeter at a time, to look through the rear windshield. A parking lot, a flickering street lamp, a few skinny kids sitting on a low concrete wall, sharing some kind of cigarette. Moments later, Harris was back. 'We're in luck. But it won't be the Savoy.'

Again doors opened and closed; the Samara's suspension breathed relief. Cassie heard the sound of footsteps gritting away. For the moment, they seemed to be leaving their luggage untouched.

She moved swiftly: slipping from beneath the suitcases and into the back seat, taking care to remain low in case anyone glanced toward the car. Before reaching for a latch, she peeked again through the rear windshield. The Harris family stood clustered around a ramshackle door, struggling to work a key in a lock. The kids sitting on the concrete wall watched the family's efforts with stoned indifference.

She stepped out into the night, gentling the door shut behind herself. Beside the parking lot, a cracked sidewalk paced a narrow road. The next storefront down was occupied by a dodgy-looking tavern, its own lot half-filled with an odd assortment of trucks, cars, and cycles.

Avoiding pools of light cast by street lamps, keeping away from the tavern's single large window, she found a battered red Minsk motorbike. Beneath moonlight she worked quickly and surely: locating the Minsk's three ignition wires, following them back to the engine, skinning the insulation with one ragged thumbnail, bridging the slots. The engine coughed to life.

The town consisted of one dirt road, several squat crumbling apartment buildings – five-story *Khrushchyovkas*, built under Khrushchev as a temporary solution to a housing shortage, never intended to remain standing for more than a few years – and countless taverns. Neon signs in dirty windows advertised Baltika beer and Lvivske Porter, and Heineken for the tourists.

Soon the town ceded to rolling hills, the unpaved road to a wide rutted track. She passed a broken-down tractor, a low crumbling fence, a half-dozen penned goats with ribs standing out. A coverlet of snow glimmered on a frozen lake. Railroad tracks came and went in moonlit glimpses. The wind was freezing; despite her gloves, her hands quickly turned so cold that they burned.

With one eye always on Polaris, she continued north. In Saint Petersburg she would find crowds, warm rooms, hot food, plentiful tourists with documents to pilfer. Then she could slip through to Finland, or Sweden: neutral territory, from which she could plot her next move in relative peace. And then back to America. Back to Quinn. And he would answer for his crimes. He would answer for the blood all over her hands – the blood of a defector, a good man who had tried to expose people like Quinn. The blood of others: bodyguards, rooftop sentries. (See PROFILES OF VICTIMS, page 8.) Innocents just doing their jobs. All Quinn's fault. Had there been any truth at all to what he had told her?

He would answer. Oh, would he answer. He would answer for everything.

Her hands had gone numb. Pulling over, she removed her gloves and spent a few fruitless minutes blowing on her fingers, trying to regain feeling. She remembered a Jack London story in which the protagonist froze to death and experienced his encroaching demise, paradoxically, as comforting and warm. At the moment, that didn't sound so bad.

As long as she could still steer, she guessed she would drive on.

She clumsily ate one packet of peanuts, told herself to save the other for later, and then gobbled down that one too. After chugging half the bottle of water, she donned gloves again and kicked the bike back on to the road.

Twenty minutes later, a warm glow broke the darkness ahead. Pulling over again, she killed the Minsk's headlight. The safest course of action would be to hide until the vehicle had passed. A low snowy rise to her right would do the trick nicely. Except something suggested that the light did not belong to an approaching vehicle. For one thing, it didn't seem to be getting closer. Nor did it spread out the way headlights should . . .

She kept studying it: a faint aureole of luminosity, not quite at the horizon, but close. After a few moments, she decided that she was probably looking at another roadblock.

Her mouth set in a grim line.

She trundled the bike from the road, leaving the headlight off, and embarked again across frozen rocky fields. She would head north-north-east until she had given the cordon a wide berth; then she would loop back around.

Passage across raw countryside proved slow, bumpy, and risky. She was acutely aware that a spill from the bike might crack open her helmetless skull. Somehow the cold seemed even sharper out here. She stopped again, to constrict the parka's hood as tightly around her face as the drawstring would allow. Even the weak heat generated by her own breath against the inside of the hood offered some scant relief – although within seconds the condensation froze, rubbing painfully against her lips.

She pressed on. Countryside spread around her as far as she could see, a wonderland of birch, fir, elder, hazel, linden, oak, and larch. She passed shaded glens, rolling snow-covered meadows, frozen ponds, imposing and magnificent rock formations.

After twenty minutes more, with the road left far behind, she began to doubt the wisdom of having turned into the country. Out here, there were no options. *General Winter*, the Russians said. *The one general who defeats all her enemies.* Napoleon Bonaparte and Adolf Hitler had both underestimated the fury of the Russian winter. Charles XII had lost his empire to her arctic death-grip. Now Cassie had made the same mistake. To General Winter, one lone girl on a stolen motorbike was beneath contempt.

She began looking for shelter – even for a stand of pines thick enough to act as a windbreak. Survive the night and she would continue in the morning, beneath sunshine. But the woods were sparse, the cold wind merciless. In Manhattan, she had survived freezing nights with the aid of heating grates and back alleys and, when push came to shove, the shared warmth of other huddling runaways. More than once she and Michelle had zipped up inside the same fraying coat and slept in each other's arms. But out here was nothing and no one.

Soon the lack of feeling migrated from her extremities, up her arms and legs. Ice crystals formed on her eyelashes. Her teeth chattered so violently that she feared for her tongue. The night sky, far removed from any source of artificial illumination, looked bright as daylight: milky in some spots, ashen in others, brimming everywhere with coldly impassive stars. A worm of fear wriggled inside her stomach. She could die out here, for real. After everything, she could die of exposure: cold, pure and simple.

Cold. It had worked its way into her skin, her bones. The motorbike felt weightless, suspended in mid-air, as if it floated on clouds. A white moon shone overhead – the same quarter moon under which she had glided at Turygino. How long ago had that been? Cold like this made time meaningless. She remembered the surprising mildness of the day, the way Mr Harris had perspired in his sport shirt. That had been only hours ago. Impossible.

The motorbike's gas gauge read one-quarter full. She could still turn back and risk the roadblock. Hell, she could *embrace* the roadblock. She would be arrested, probably tortured, and perhaps executed – but before that they would put her in a warm car and drive her back to Moscow, and that would make it all worthwhile.

When she came upon the dachas, they looked at first like gingerbread houses, not quite real, and she thought her frozen eyes must be playing tricks.

With effort she brought the Minsk to a stop and, after a moment of tottering, remained upright. The rows of holiday houses were laid out in a maze: inexpensive wooden sheds barely the size of outhouses, roofs of corrugated tin peeking out from beneath vanilla-frosting layers of snow. Lacking electricity and indoor plumbing, the cabins would not satisfy many Americans' conception of a vacation home. But during summers the shrubbery would be flush with wild berries; the gardens would overflow with cucumbers, tomatoes, and *oblepikha*, the so-called Siberian pineapple, and no lack of Muscovites would be grateful for the brief respite from the city heat.

She wheeled the motorbike between two cabins, sighting in the process a rough road leading away from the other side of the colony, and forced her way into the nearest shed. A cheap padlock gave without offering even token resistance. In the gloom she found one cluttered room with a claustrophobically low ceiling. Filthy windows blocked out much of the moonlight. She spent a moment exploring, picking listlessly through frosty old papers: a 'Grandpa Ilyich' primer, the Soviet equivalent of 'Dick and Jane'; brittle magazines including the sky-blue *Novy Mir*, the red-and-white historical journal *Znamya*, the notoriously anti-Semitic *Culture And Life.*

She found no mattress, but a decaying old chair. She collapsed into it, shivering violently. At least she was out of the wind. She made sure her parka was zipped to the top, the fur-lined hood drawn as tightly as possible. She pulled papers on to herself, making a blanket of sorts – any little bit helped – and jammed gloved hands into pockets. It occurred to her that she hungry. And she might conceivably build a fire. But she lacked the energy even to move, and in the next instant she was asleep.

COBBLER'S COVE: ONE YEAR EARLIER

After building a roaring fire, Quinn came to join Cassie on the couch.

Another ordinary manila folder waited on a Williams-Sonoma end-table. Opening it, he passed her a glossy 6x9 inch photograph.

As she looked at the photo, emotion flared; then a cool, gray fog descended. She knew this fog well, having found refuge in it during her most difficult times. They called it *denial*, she supposed, or possibly it was *disassociation*, or some combination of the two.

When she spoke, she perceived her own voice through the dim mist: faint and dissipated, like a faraway melody. 'Photoshopped,' she said weakly.

Reaching again for the folder, he passed over another photograph. Then another, and another.

'Photoshopped,' she managed again.

But more pictures were coming. And more. And more. 'Fake,' she insisted faintly.

'Real,' answered Quinn with conviction.

A gust of wind chased down the chimney, making the fire jump.

She must have looked distressed. Above the Dolce & Gabbana frames, his brow gathered. 'It's OK to be afraid,' he said after a few seconds. 'Courage is resistance to fear, mastery of fear. Not absence of fear.'

She said nothing.

For a moment more, he considered her closely. Then he collected the photographs, returned them to the folder. He reached out to move a strand of hair off her forehead – a gesture at once fond, paternal, and intimate. His hand smelled of tobacco and aftershave. 'Let's call it a night,' he said. 'Another long day tomorrow.'

Closing her eyes, she felt herself sinking into the soft bed.

The cool dense fog surrounded her on all sides. Silhouettes flickered behind it, but they remained comfortably at a distance, like actors moving behind a scrim.

Once, when reading a biography of John Lennon, she had come upon a passage that described the fog perfectly. The doctor who'd treated Lennon after he'd been shot had come to see Yoko Ono in the waiting room. *I'm sorry to tell you that your husband is dead*, the doctor had said. *There was no suffering at the end.* And Yoko had looked straight back at him – dry-eyed, according to the author, and seemingly in complete possession of her faculties – and asked, *You are telling me that he is asleep?*

This was that same mist. Cassie had first sensed it creeping in around the edges after her mother had died. After Daddy's death it had massed, advancing aggressively.

Mommy had died of breast cancer. Daddy had been killed when his brakes cut out and his car slammed into a street lamp, and in one instant everything Dennis Bradbury had been – a father, a widower, a consultant, a world traveler, a passionate lover of books, a fast and generous draw with a highlighter, a middling amateur chef, a lousy amateur painter, a secret reader of *People* and *Us* magazines – had vanished from the planet in a sudden fireball, leaving Cassie forever alone. The official diagnosis of *mechanical failure* was so inadequate in expressing that loss that it felt dishonest.

Lying in the soft bed, she thrust out her chin. Her brave little chin, Daddy had called it. Look at Cassie with her determined, brave little chin. He'd had the same habit. That was probably where she had gotten it.

After she'd given up on the foster homes, going to New York for good, she had started recognizing the value of the cool gray fog. As life had grown ever harder, she'd drawn it around herself protectively. Fights in shelters, nights spent in the Tombs, hook-ups for the sake of a roof over her head, friends lost to overdoses, endless hunger and cold and pain and fear and loneliness – none could penetrate the carefully cultivated state of twilight half-sleep. Denial: good for what ails you.

You are telling me that he is asleep?

She had maintained. Existed. Survived. Still carrying, then, a heaping handful of Daddy's books, losing herself in them whenever possible, paying particular attention to the passages he'd highlighted, the nearest thing she had to hearing his voice, his advice, his point of view. Soldiering stubbornly through whatever cruelties life threw her way, her brave little chin outthrust . . .

Her eyes opened.

The quality of the moonlight streaming through the bedroom window was silver, hollow, eerie – but it was real, she thought.

This was real. It was not a trick. There were no hidden cameras. Quinn's photographs had not been faked.

The moon shone through the window like a spotlight, piercing the cool dim fog at last. She had been chosen, said the moonlight.

And now, after years of half-sleep, she would finally be awake.

FIVE

THE VALDAI HILLS

The blanket of newspaper crackled as she sat up: thin sheets of frost breaking, sending tiny crystals of ice puffing into the air. Her entire body felt numb. Her teeth were still chattering, had chattered even through her sleep. A strange weight seemed to lie atop her eyelids, her lips, her heart. When she pushed out of the chair, the parka stuck stubbornly before tearing free.

A shaft of sunlight lanced through the filthy window. Maneuvering into it, she propped her back against one wall. For several minutes she just sat, soaking in the warmth. By degrees, a film of moisture appeared on her cheeks. Tears, she thought at first . . . and then realized that the moisture was melting ice.

One by one, her systems began to fire. She was thirsty and – encouragingly – starving. When she tried to reach into the parka, however, her fingers refused to bend. Skinning off the gloves with her teeth, she examined her hands in the sunlight. They were neither visibly frostbitten nor gangrenous. They just wouldn't function.

Keeping her back against the wall, she managed to stand. A wave of light-headedness washed over her. When it passed, she leaned open the door and stepped out into bright blinding sunshine.

In daylight, the snow-frosted colony of miniature dachas looked more than ever like a fairy-tale kingdom. Flecks of poplar floated in a light breeze. A deer stood shockingly close, holding so still that she almost thought it was a statue. Then an ear flicked, a tail quivered, and the statue bounded away.

She strolled between cabins, working her way outward in expanding circles, trying to get her circulation going. As she walked, she kept her eyes peeled for anything that might come in handy. Through crusty windows she spied vast jumbles of junk – books, lamps, sleds, barbecue grills – but nothing resembling food or winter clothing. Many dachas, however, had small generators attached, which for now she left untouched.

Once her blood was moving, her fingers came back to life. Then she fumbled the bag of potato chips from her pocket, tore it open awkwardly, and poured the contents into her mouth. With her belly momentarily quieted, she felt halfway human again. She tried the bottle of water, found it frozen solid. Instead she scooped up and consumed handfuls of clean snow.

In a shallow valley to the east, the snow was deeper, pulling at her boots with each footstep. She plodded stolidly ahead, thrusting out her determined little chin. Wind rose and fell, phantom-like, whipping grains of ice against her face.

Coming back around toward the Minsk, she started checking generators. The first three were bone-dry. The fourth had a centimeter of fuel still inside. With one shoulder she allowed herself access to the nearest dacha, from which she scavenged a rusted watering can and a grease hose. Dipping hose into generator, she sucked until a sour metallic taste hit her tongue, then siphoned gas into the can.

Clearing the taste from her mouth with another handful of snow, she kept moving. Twenty minutes and six generators later, she had a watering can half-filled with petrol, which she carried back to the Minsk and fed carefully into the tank.

Inside the dacha in which she'd slept, she folded ancient paper into a battered old samovar, added a few chips of frozen wood, and – after a few tries – managed to ignite it with the cold cigarette lighter. In a cracked flowerpot, she melted snow. Combining hot water with frozen dirt, she slathered mud across the motorbike's license plate until the tag was covered.

She melted more snow, which she used to dampen her hair. Then she took out the henna. Adding dye to the water, she stirred until a thick paste resulted. She applied the stuff to her skull, taking care to avoid dying the skin. Then she sat and waited, letting the color bake, near enough to the dying fire to relish its warmth.

ENERGETICHESKAYA ULITSA, MOSCOW

Nothing about the three-story building of yellow brick hinted at its unique place of dishonor in Russia's history.

From the ordinary suburban street, a visitor gathered no hint of Lefortovo prison's famed K-shape. (On the question of whether the design was purely functional, or reflected purposeful homage to Katherine the Great, historians disagreed.) No screams echoed, and no tractor engines ran in the courtyard, as they once had, to drown out the sound of firing squads. But quiet, thought Ravensdale as he entered the sally port, should not be mistaken for serenity. Although official ownership of Lefortovo was always changing – from Peter the Great, for whom it had originally been built, through Stalin's

KGB and Interior Ministry, to the FSB and most recently the Ministry of Justice – the prison's function remained the same: Lefortovo housed Russia's most important inmates in secrecy and seclusion, offering interrogators a handy array of physical and psychological weaponry, not least the reputation of the building itself.

After passing through security, Ravensdale and Vlasov visited the command and control room located at the intersection of the three spokes of the K. Uniformed guards watched video screens, listening to feeds from hidden microphones. To Ravensdale's eyes these men were *kachki*, distinguishable only by their liveries from thousands of other young hoodlums in the city. The word, describing an entire subspecies of thug, was short for *nakachivat'* –'to pump up one's muscles'.

With passes clipped to breast pockets, they struck off in lockstep down a wide corridor, the main line of the letter K, behind a guard. 'In the past forty-eight hours,' said the Inspector quietly as they walked, 'we've received six hundred calls. Of course, five hundred and ninety-nine were cranks. Anyone with a grudge against an ex-girlfriend can seize the opportunity. But every lead must be investigated. And so my people got around to interviewing this fellow only this morning. He is an American businessman: wireless infrastructure. In Sergiev Posad for the past week, taking meetings with a local company. Credit card records and security camera footage confirm his presence at the hotel. The company with which he was meeting confirms his bona fides. At eleven o'clock yesterday morning, he approached an official at Sheremetyevo-two, saying he recognized the sketch in the newspaper. He claims to have spent Monday night with her.'

The passageway was lined with black wooden cabinets, hollow pipes, darkened bulbs atop heavy cell doors. They climbed a narrow metal staircase hanging from a wall, Ravensdale bringing up the rear. On the second floor the cells were smaller, the hallway danker, smelling more powerfully of niter and quicklime.

'The camera in the hotel's elevator,' Vlasov continued, 'confirms the presence of a girl. We get a three-quarters view, relatively clear. In my estimation, she matches the police sketch. We're now tracking down everyone who checked out of the hotel yesterday morning, in case she managed to hitch a ride. Also going over our businessman's room with a fine-tooth comb and trying to recover any unwashed linens from the laundry . . .'

The guard stopped before a cell. The Inspector's expensive cream-colored suit jacket seemed to float, wraithlike, against the gloom. 'Stand behind me,' he commanded. 'Do not address the prisoner directly.'

The cell had been designed for four, but was occupied by only one. As the door creaked open, Ravensdale saw, shivering on a bunk, a man in his middle years, wearing a rumpled dress shirt and pleated slacks, good-looking in a minor key. The man struggled to a sitting position, sandy hair standing on end.

'Comrade,' said Vlasov magnanimously, in English. He moved far enough into the cell to allow Ravensdale entrance behind him, and the guard closed the door. The room featured two bunk beds, a combined sink and rimless toilet, a single naked light bulb in the ceiling. 'How are we, this fine morning?'

The man focused blearily on the Inspektor. Rubbing a crust from the corner of one eye, he turned his attention briefly to Ravensdale. When he spoke, his voice was hoarse but keen. 'Are you from the consulate?'

'My name is Senior Inspektor Vlasov, from the Investigative Committee. And I have good news, comrade. If no unforeseen problems arise, you'll be escorted back to the airport and allowed to depart this afternoon.'

'This . . . afternoon?'

'If all goes smoothly – and you continue to cooperate fully – yes.' A reassuring smile, only slightly wolfish. 'First I'd like to hear your story myself, if you'd do me the honor. To corroborate certain details and so forth. Begin by stating your name.'

The man planted a hand against his face, slowly rubbed down. 'My name,' he said, 'is Owen Holt.'

'What brings you to Russia, Mister Holt?'

'I'm representing the firm of Fowler, Weinraub, and Hicks. From Tampa. I was meeting with Anatoly Starostin. Project manager at XE Airband.'

'In Sergiev Posad?'

'Yes.'

'Which is where you met the young woman in question.'

'Yes.'

'When was that?'

Measuring out the words: 'Monday night.'

'Explain the circumstances, please.'

'Bart – Bart Fowler, my boss – told me about the travel advisory. He suggested I wrap it up early. Better safe than sorry, he said. So I switched my ticket to Tuesday morning, the next flight I could get. Then I went to grab a drink near my hotel.'

'Your hotel was . . .?'

'The Rodinki.'

'And the bar?'

'I don't remember.'

'Was it called Bierhof? Pivnoj?'

'That was it. Pivnoj.'

'Go on, please.'

'I started talking to this girl. An American girl. She said she was working on her thesis. Said she was afraid to spend the night alone. So I took pity on her.' Holt's eyes darted to Ravensdale, back to Vlasov. 'I'm a married man, I had no designs, but she was a young girl, frightened, so I took pity and told her she could share my room. So she did. And in the morning I left and went to the airport, and while I was there I saw a sketch in the newspaper, so I went to the customs agent and told him I might recognize that face, and next thing I know I'm here. Left alone all night long, no phone call, no lawyer, no food, not even any *water*, for Christ's sake. It's not right. I was trying to help! I was putting myself out there and—'

'The name she gave you?'

'Heidi.'

'Last name?'

'No. Just Heidi.'

'Hailing from?'

'Connecticut, she said.'

'Working on her thesis?'

Holt nodded.

'Her university?'

'She didn't say.'

'Her subject?'

'She mentioned museums, so I assumed it was, you know. Folk art. Something like that. Who gives a fuck?'

'Were you intimate?'

'That's . . . I'm a married man.'

'Just between us.'

'We had a few glasses of wine. Things may have gotten a little out of hand. We were both . . . But that's neither here nor there. My wife doesn't need to—'

'You had a few glasses of wine. Where?'

'At that bar. Pivnoj. And then at a restaurant down the street.'

'Named?'

A shake of the head.

'Café Greenfield? Yamskaya? Trapeza Na Makovtse?'

'The last one, I think.'

'Describe the girl.'

Holt compressed his lips. 'I told your people already—'

'Now tell me.'

'For Christ's sake. Can I at least have a glass of water?'

'First describe the girl.'

'Ordinary. Pretty. Young.'

'And the police sketch . . .'

'Close.'

'But not exact.'

'Not exact. But close.'

'Where was the sketch wrong?'

'Her hair was shorter, in real life. Streaked black. You know – punk.'

'Height?'

'Ordinary.'

'What's ordinary?'

'Five three, maybe.'

'Weight?'

'Slim.'

'Fifty kilos? Sixty?'

'One hundred pounds. One ten, tops. Slim.'

'Identifying marks? Scars, bruises, scrapes . . .?'

'No. She was . . .' Holt shook his head again. 'There was a scratch on her forehead. She said it came from a low ceiling.'

'A deep scratch?'

'Noticeable.'

'On which side of her forehead?'

'Fuck if I know.'

'She was wearing . . .?'

'Ordinary clothes.'

'What's ordinary?'

'A parka. Blue jeans. Ordinary clothes.'

'What color parka?'

'Blue. Or black. Maybe dark blue. Christ's sake. I didn't know there was going to be a quiz.'

'Hat? Gloves? Scarf?'

'Maybe in a pocket. Not that I saw.'

'Did she have a phone? A computer?'

'Not that I saw.'

'A weapon?'

'God, no.'

'Jewelry?'

Owen Holt frowned, trying to picture it, and shook his head again.

'Money?'

'Not that I saw. But I picked up the checks.'

'A handbag?'

'I don't . . . think so.'

'Didn't that strike you as odd? An American girl, alone, no purse, no friends, no phone?'

'I assumed she'd left stuff back in her room. I wasn't worrying about it.'

'What room?'

'At the youth hostel.'

'Did she name the hostel?'

'No.'

'She didn't tell you where she was staying. She didn't tell you her last name. Or her university, or the subject of her thesis . . .'

'No.'

'What *did* you talk about?'

'I mean . . . nothing.'

'Nothing?'

'Russia. How pretty Sergiev Posad is. Stuff like that.'

'Current events? Politics?'

'No.'

'Did you see the news, at any point, in her company?'

'No.'

'Did you see the police sketch in her company?'

'No.'

'Did you pass any soldiers or police in her company?'

'No. Well – maybe. Walking back to the hotel.'

'Did she react?'

'She took my arm, maybe. We'd talked about how it was scary, being a tourist, an American, with this travel advisory.'

'And . . .?'

'That's it.'

'Did she *seem* scared?'

'She *said* she was scared. She came back to my hotel with me. So she must have been scared.'

'And then she seduced you?'

Holt's face darkened. 'Come on, man.'

'During the night, she slept?'

'Yes.'

'You both slept?'

'Yes.'

'In the morning, did she say where she was going?'

'She was still asleep when I left. But over dinner, she mentioned some friends who had gone on to Penza. I got the impression she was going to join them.'

'Names?'

He shook his head.

'These were other students?'

'I guess so.'

'Did she give you any way to contact her?'

'No.'

Vlasov glanced at Ravensdale, who shrugged almost imperceptibly. 'If you think of anything else,' said Vlasov smoothly, 'tell the guard you want to speak with me. Senior Inspektor Piotr Vlasov.'

'But—'

'The wheels,' said Vlasov, 'are in motion.'

'But my—'

'The wheels are in motion.' He nodded at Ravensdale; they retreated.

'Come on! At least—'

The door clanged shut.

Back in the chilly corridor, the Inspektor offered one of his thin brown cigarettes. 'Are you a betting man? Because we'll have her, I wager, before the day is done.'

Leaning forward to accept a light, Ravensdale said nothing.

SERGIEV POSAD

Beneath the pebbled turnaround, a harried mother dragged a three-year-old wearing a snot-caked jacket toward a revolving door. A Japanese woman posed smiling before a skyline of minarets and cupolas. A valet listened to a couple's complaints and smiled non-committally. No one paid any attention to the man moving circumspectly into and out of the hotel's lobby via a side door, ferrying small bundles to a long yellow van parked just down the block.

Behind curtained windows inside the van, five lab-coated technicians shared cramped quarters with chromatographs, microscopes, spectrographs and thermal cyclers. As one team of techs swabbed blood from pillowcases – a surprisingly high percentage of linen recovered from any hotel's laundry will feature bloodstains – another carefully used tweezers to transfer strands of hair into reaction tubes. The tubes were inserted, four at a time, into a device the size of a small toaster oven. After a heated lid was locked, the temperature of a mixture inside the device rose and lowered in preprogrammed steps, separating and amplifying strands of DNA. Following amplification, a probe tagged with a radioactive marker bound itself within each sample to a complementary sequence. The resulting profile, displayed on a small green touch screen, consisted of three columns of alpha-numerical characters, with the leftmost identifying a genetic marker, the center 'Allele A', and the rightmost 'Allele B'.

At 10:45 a.m., the tech studying the screen gave a tight smile of satisfaction. After double-checking the results against a light-blue sheet of paper, he reached for a phone.

As his call went through, a lab-coated young woman four hundred kilometers away inserted an identical reaction tube into an identical thermal cycler. She initiated the amplification and radioactive probe, checked the resulting three columns of alphanumerical characters against her own light-blue sheet of paper. She gave her own cool smile and reached for her own phone.

SEREBRYANY BOR

'We have,' Vlasov announced, 'not two, but three matching DNA profiles.'

He paused, as if waiting for applause. Ravensdale wondered who he saw playing himself in the movie. In his chair before the hearth, Tsoi picked negligently at a callus on his left thumb.

'One,' continued Vlasov after a moment, 'constructed from the knit cap recovered at Turygino. One constructed from a hair found in Owen Holt's hotel room. And one constructed from a bloodstain found just two hours ago, in a vehicle in Novgorod Oblast. The odds of two different individuals possessing identical profiles, I might add, are approximately one in one billion.' He gave an arid smile. 'The vehicle is a rental car, in possession of a tourist family named Harris. They checked out of the Hotel Rodinki yesterday morning, just an hour after our Mister Holt. The phone of the teenaged daughter has served as a GPS; my men caught up with them this morning at Lake Ilmen.'

Elsewhere in the mansion Elena laughed, an innocent laugh, covering a full octave.

Vlasov crossed to a makeshift map table set up atop the harpsichord, thumped it with an index finger. 'I believe our quarry was a stowaway – the bloodstain was found on a swath of carpeting in the rear of the hatchback, where luggage would be stored – and the family had no knowledge of her presence. But, of course, they are being questioned even now.'

Ravensdale lit a cigarette, joined Vlasov by the laminated map. The asymmetrical Lake Ilmen was surrounded by a latticework of tributaries and meandering rivers. The only roads passing within shouting distance were the A-116, M-10, and E-105. Police checkpoints on the highways had been indicated by grease pencil. 'Open country out there,' he remarked.

'Indeed. Lakes and forests, the occasional provincial village. Last night the Harris family overnighted in one of these villages—' Another imperative thump of the index finger. 'Here, in Valdai. And sometime after dark, as it so happens, a Minsk motorbike was stolen from a parking lot directly beside their hotel.'

Ravensdale bent closer. 'Traveling by road, she would have hit a spot check by now.'

'I concur. Therefore, she has left the road. Traveling through this countryside on a Minsk, however, she could not average more than forty kilometers per hour. Last night the temperature dropped to ten below. Factor in the wind chill from riding a motorbike, and no human could have endured. We must assume she was forced to stop and shelter until sunup, and probably not too very far from Valdai.' The Inspektor's finger described a tight circle. 'The parameters of the search have been refined accordingly. The new description – American, dark-blue parka, scrape on the forehead, short hair streaked black – has been released to my people, along with the alias and cover story she used with Holt. But not to the media. No need to let her know we're on to her.'

Still picking at his callused thumb by the fireplace, Tsoi wore a faintly troubled expression.

'We have dogs and jeeps scouring the countryside. Helicopters and quadricopter drones, for difficult terrain. Thanks to FAPSI at the GRU, the use of a spy satellite. Of course, we maintain our vigilance at roads, railway, and bus stations. We focus now on the Minsk, but remain aware of the possibility that she has picked up, by hook or by crook, another ride. Within the next few hours, if she continues in the direction she has been going, we'll find her near Lake Seliger.'

Ravensdale nodded. Tsoi reached for his *khat* root. From someplace nearby the girl laughed again, musically.

SIX

LAKE SELIGER, NORTH OF OSTASHKOV

After relieving her bladder she walked a few paces from the Minsk, stretching her legs.

The sun was just cresting: a bright, cloudless, steely winter day turning on the axis toward afternoon. Her shadow had shrunk to almost nothing. In another few hours, she thought, twilight would come. The slush would refreeze, and the already-bitter cold would turn vicious. But by then, God willing, she'd be back in civilization.

She touched her toes, popping her vertebrae. Before climbing back on to the bike she spent a final minute soaking in the black pine and silver birch, the distant flat shimmering mirror of Lake Seliger. Under different circumstances, she might actually have enjoyed the view. The countryside was pristine, bold, starkly beautiful. Except for a single hunting blind on stilts, she had not passed any evidence of human habitation since morning.

Then suddenly the wind turned and she heard voices, dismayingly close. Ducking low, she rolled the bike quickly into the nearest copse of ice-dappled trees.

It came again: a murmur of conversation, sending a thrill of terror plaiting down her spine. A moment later they came into view, two figures walking not twenty-five yards away.

'When all of a sudden,' one man was saying. He looked six feet tall and nearly as wide, a descendent of hardy Russian peasant stock. He wore a thick handlebar mustache and fur trooper hat, and carried a double-barreled shotgun loosely in the crook of one arm. 'This dark-suited government functionary runs up and hands him a telegram. Stalin reads it and then says, "Comrades! A historic occasion! I have in my hands a telegram of congratulations from Leon Trotsky!"'

His companion – shorter, younger, more heavily bundled against the cold – listened intently.

'He opens the telegram and begins to read. "Joseph Stalin – you were right and I was wrong! You are the true heir of Lenin! I should apologize! Trotsky." The crowd goes mad. But then, from the front row, this little . . . tailor . . .'

Without warning the man took a knee, peering closely at the snow. Then he looked up, directly at Cassie's stand of pine.

Standing again, he raised a hand, beckoning the younger man to follow. He hefted the shotgun and came forward, heavy boots crunching. In the blink of an eye, he was almost atop her; she could either announce herself or be discovered.

She eased out of the trees, hands extended, not quite raised. The shotgun snapped up. '*Po'shyol 'na hui!*' the man exclaimed.

When he saw her more clearly, his stance relaxed. As he came forward again, she caught the scents of woodsmoke and beet soup. He was in his middle sixties, handlebar mustache flecked with gray. The other, thirtyish, was almost certainly his son – they shared the same wide forehead and anvil-like jaw.

'Where did she come from?' asked the younger. The elder only shook his head.

They were almost within arm's reach. She calculated odds. Two against one. And even the smaller man was twice her size. But, of course, size didn't matter. You hit first, and you hit hard . . .

'You heard him,' said the elder. 'Well? Cat got your tongue?'

'Hold on.' Canny, now. 'Does she look familiar to you?'

'Never seen her before in my life.'

'No; remember that picture? From the news.'

Papa Bear frowned doubtfully.

'It's her,' said the son. 'Who else would be out here, all alone?' His .22 rifle came up. 'You hold still,' he commanded, and then: 'We'd better—'

In no particular hurry, she reached for the shotgun's barrel.

Twisting it back, she pinned Papa Bear's index finger inside the trigger guard. Then all his bulk meant nothing; she tugged lightly, maneuvering him between herself and the youth, as he cried out. The empty lake threw back the sound.

The .22 barked. Papa Bear shuddered. Wrenching the shotgun free, she returned fire. The younger man blew backward like a dead leaf caught in a gale, rifle flying from his hands.

Then two men lay on snow turning red. Echoing gunshots bounced away through the forest, chased across the frozen lake.

The boy stared at the sky with wide, preoccupied eyes. She moved closer, kicked the rifle away. His gaze turned searchingly toward her. A light inside them flared, guttered, and died.

She turned back to Papa Bear. The side of his throat had been opened by the .22 slug. A tiny shred of skin puffed with each whistling, ragged breath. The index finger of his right hand had been torn almost free.

'You . . . devil,' he managed.

She socked the shotgun into her shoulder. Under the circumstances, it would be a mercy.

He coughed; a bubble of blood popped on his lips. He started to prop himself up on one elbow, fell back, rolled over, and sighed.

She watched for a long minute. He did not move again.

At last she lowered the gun. She waited, expecting remorse, or nausea, or redoubled rage at Quinn – more innocent blood now stained her hands, more innocent blood which would never wash out. But she felt nothing except a dull urgency, and in a way, that was worst of all.

Setting the shotgun carefully on the ground, she got her hands beneath the larger man's arms. But he proved even heavier than he looked. She had dragged him only halfway to the treeline before she needed to rest. Worse, the passage left a muddled bloody furrow in the snow. Until a fresh snowfall, the track could not be effectively concealed.

She gave up, went back to the Minsk, wheeled it out of the pines, climbed on board. Leaving the shotgun where it lay, she gave the dead men a last flat look and then kicked off.

Minutes later a helicopter appeared far off to the west. She hid again inside the forest. The chopper swept patiently back and forth, following lines someone somewhere had drawn on a map. At one point it flew directly overhead, so close that she could see a man in harness and aviator sunglasses hanging from an open bay. After a final pass it turned north, leaving her alone with whining wind and the coppery taste of fear in her mouth.

She drove on. The old Minsk's 125cc stammered and muttered. The gas gauge lowered steadily, but was not yet scraping bottom.

As twilight deepened, she reached the clearest indication yet of imminent civilization – silhouetted factories, houses, and a railway station breaking the line of the horizon. She came to another stop, letting the engine idle. Close now, she thought. Perhaps very close.

Time to risk the highway again. It would carry her quickly into the city. In an hour, she could be melting safely into anonymity on a busy street.

She eased around the town's perimeter, past dormant smokestacks, over spurs of railroad track. Beyond a low hillock she found the M-10, four empty lanes beneath the setting sun. She opened the engine. As she swung into a northbound lane, she switched on the Minsk's headlight.

On the paved road she bent low, trying to reduce the surface area presented to the brutal wind, and pushed the motorbike up to eighty kph. Power lines and signage and low buildings proliferated, blocking out the spokes of sunset fanning up behind the forest. Yet thanks to the strange vastness of Russia, she remained for a time the only vehicle in sight.

Then she passed a Skoda, then a Toyota. Then there came a sudden glut of cars, and she was forced to slow. A mixed blessing: her pace was compromised, but the wind chill decreased commensurately.

Threading her way between a Tiguan and a Vito, she registered the crunch of broken glass beneath the tires. After all the miles of rocky countryside, a flat now would be poetic justice. But the scrappy little Minsk met the challenge. The tires held. Pulling out of a clot of traffic, she gained speed again.

Clear sailing ahead. The city drawing ever closer. She gave her brave little chin a small uptick.

She was going to make it.

From twenty thousand kilometers above, a Persona satellite relayed an image etched on silicon to a Ministry of Defense sub-building on Arbatskaya Square.

The image was black and white, with an imaging resolution of five centimeters. It depicted a bird's-eye view of a north-western tributary of Lake Seliger: a wandering finger of ice, a fringe of black pine, and two prone figures sprawling in bloodstained snow.

The version relayed six minutes later to Tsoi's mansion on Serebryany Bor had been enlarged, with the prone figures tagged. Three men leaned close to study an image writ in over two million pixels. They could clearly make out two corpses, one face up and one face down, and a trail of gory snow where the second had been dragged a short distance.

'A hunting accident?' mused Tsoi.

The Inspektor looked at the timecode in the image's corner and shook his head. 'It's no hunting accident. These men had the bad luck to find our pretty before we did.'

'He's right.' Ravensdale indicated a smudged line. 'A rifle. Plausibly dropped by this one when he fell. But over here . . .' Another grainy smudge. 'A shotgun. Couldn't have ended up this far away by itself.

And look at the body. Someone tried to drag it into the trees, and
then gave up.'

Over the next four minutes, they examined twenty-two other images
collected by FAPSI. One, taken in Chudovo, south of Petersburg,
portrayed checkerboarded houses, factories, streets, railroad tracks
– and a small figure on a motorbike easing between them. Scowling,
they could discern the make of the cycle, the mud caking the license
plate, the auburn bell of the rider's hair.

'The Minsk,' murmured the Inspektor. 'The parka . . . Only, the
hair is not right.'

'She dyed it again,' suggested Tsoi.

Ravensdale glanced at the grandfather clock, then back at timecode. Eighteen minutes had passed since the image's capture. 'Nearest
checkpoint?'

'Thirty-five kilometers.' Vlasov lit a fresh cigarette. 'Outside
Petersburg. Assuming she continues north, she's heading right into it.'

The hollow thud of the helicopter's rotors came again.

This time the metal bird flew directly overhead, searchlight striking
off a tractor trailer to her left, briefly igniting the metal with white
fire. She almost obeyed a preconscious instinct to turn off the road,
hide again in the forest. But the memory of the freezing night, hardwired into her bones, kept her on course.

Just ahead, an orange construction barrier blocked the right-hand
lane. Funneled into a single channel, traffic slackened precipitously.
As vehicles crowded close, she chewed on her lower lip . . . but still
she continued forward.

Inside the parka she found a crumpled five-hundred-ruble note,
stolen from the purse in Sergiev Posad. *Left my license in my other
coat, officer. No big deal. Little something for your trouble, if you
wouldn't mind letting me through . . .*

The single-file line rolled slowly ahead. She breathed, trying to
gather the cool mist around herself. Up ahead she saw a chain of
fifty-five gallon steel drums, further narrowing the lane. Traffic slowed
again. A broken muffler a few cars ahead rattled her eardrums inside
her skull. Her tongue wet her lips. Still not too late to pull out of the
lane, she thought. Bounce across the sunken median, turn back the
way she had come. But she was nearly out of gas now. There would
be no turning back.

When she finally saw the blockade her stomach uncoiled in her
belly, poking at her insides like jagged bedsprings.

A scowling policeman was waving some cars through, directing others to pull into a holding pen created by traffic cones. Some vehicles allowed through were stopped at a second barricade, where passengers were forced outside at gunpoint. Parked off to one side: six Zhigulis and an army half-track. Even from a small distance she could make out a dozen soldiers wearing their requisite Kalashnikovs, another dozen *politsiya*, and a handful of men wearing the black berets and green-and-black camouflage of the OMON, the elite Interior Ministry counterterrorist unit which had as its motto '*We know no mercy and do not ask for any*'.

The line moved forward.

Stay easy inside. She could do this. No big deal. If she believed it, they would believe it.

Ten cars remained between her and her fate.

In just a few moments more, the scowling militiaman would direct her to pull over. He or one of his partners would demand identification. Cassie would hand over the folded-up bill and her lame excuse. And she would radiate calm, confidence, nothing-to-see-here-officer.

The line moved again. Looking down the queue, preselecting which cars to wave through and which to flag down, the glowering militiaman noticed her. He did a small but unmistakable double take.

The cool fog descending, cocooning her.

With a small gesture, the militiaman summoned an OMON agent to his side. Concentrating, she focused on his lips.

Once you get used to it, Quinn had said, *Russian is an easier language than English, and a far more logical one. In English, the five hundred most common words have an average of twenty-three meanings each. Ever seen a sign that says 'Slow Children at Play'?*

She had chuckled. Seated in front of the crackling fireplace in the red-brick colonial, aching pleasantly from a hard workout in the gym, it had all seemed entirely academic.

The Russian language is more precise. Its alphabet has thirty-three letters to English's twenty-six. Some letters in the Cyrillic alphabet sound just like their English counterparts: K like kitten, M like man. Then there are the tricksters, which look the same but sound different. B like V in vest. E like Ye in yes. Unlike English, where it might take two letters to make one sound – sh – Russian has one letter for each sound, period. Thus you can pronounce a sentence correctly even if you've never seen the words before. Don't look so distraught, my dear. A new language is like a hot bath. The trick is to settle in slowly . . .

'*Pasmatrl,*' the militiaman was saying without turning his head, using his chin to point out the Minsk – *look.*

Russian is also a far easier language to speech-read. English is full of homophones and sounds made in the back of the throat. Shoes, shoot, juice, chews, June, Jews – the lips form precisely the same shape in each case. Russian words, on the other hand, tend to be unique. Even better, they're spoken toward the front of the mouth, where you can see them.

The OMON agent replied, something she missed. Then the militiaman spoke curtly, and she caught it clearly: '*Patarapis'!*' – hurry up!

His compatriot trotted off, waving to a group of soldiers.

She looked behind herself. Only a few centimeters of space separated her from a UAZ truck.

She looked back at the militiaman in his crisp blue epaulets. He waved the line forward again. Now seven cars remained between her and the checkpoint.

No weapon; no escape.

The line rolled forward again.

Her instincts were screaming. She would not even get the chance to offer her folded-up bill and her lame excuse. As soon as she rolled forward another few meters, the trap would be sprung. They would come out with guns blazing, and that would be the end of Cassie Bradbury.

She tasted the concept, trying to titrate out paranoia and fatigue, to leave only the truth.

The militiaman directing traffic gestured: *Pull forward.*

For a moment more, panic gnawed at her with sharp fangs. Then the cool gray fog smothered it.

She turned the handlebars, pointing the Minsk out toward the median.

Hesitated for a final instant.

Twisted the throttle.

She clipped the car in front of her, shattering the Minsk's headlight, and snapped out of line, the snarl of the engine rising around her. Kicking up plugs of frozen grass, fishtailing as the rear tire struggled to find purchase, she rocketed across the icy dip of the median – the pit and roof of her stomach briefly swapping places; her teeth clamping together, narrowly missing the tip of her tongue – and spun back on to the macadam across the way, facing south.

The militiaman was yelling. Soldiers were running, holding automatic weapons. A first ugly rattle of machine-gun fire sounded. But by then Cassie had opened the engine again; the plucky old motorbike delivered, and within seconds the militiamen and the soldiers and their checkpoint and their ambush had all become pinpricks in the mirror mounted on her handlebar.

The engine whined. Her heart raced. The old bike rattled, felt as if it might fall apart at any moment. But it still performed, the trooper. Throttle pinned to maximum. Traffic in this direction was sparse, and she whipped easily around obstructions: a blue Volga, a compact black Zaporozhets, a Citroën van.

She careered down the highway, half-blind in the dusk with no functioning headlight, past slender birch and blunt oak, looping with dangerously little room to spare around a Pathfinder. Her fear behind the cool gray fog had become a kind of giddy ecstasy. If she hadn't turned, she thought, she would already be dead. It had been that close. *That fucking close.*

But now what? Heading away from the city, into open countryside, she would find nowhere to hide. She was almost out of gas. And they would come in force.

She was still holding the sweaty five-hundred-ruble bill, pressed tight against the throttle. Her cramped fingers loosened; the bill fluttered away in slow motion.

Ditch the road. Head back into the woods on the fleet little Minsk. But the sun was nearly gone. She would not survive another night in the wild.

Pushed to its limit, the 125cc engine was laboring. And another sound was climbing through the buzz – a sound which would haunt her dreams, the lazy *whonk-whonk-whonk* of helicopter blades.

In the mirror she found it. Military attack chopper, spotted with jungle camouflage, rising up from behind the checkpoint. Two bubble canopies glistened beneath a sky the color of fresh scar tissue. The thing was fully decked out, bristling armaments affixed to wings on the fuselage midsection. In a single desperate glance she saw eight AT-6 ATGMs, two fifty-seven mm rocket pods, and a machine gun turret.

The quality of the rotor's noise changed, speeding up – *whut-whut-whut-whut-whut* – as the chopper gained altitude. Taking a bead, she thought, and collateral damage be damned. To a country which had survived famines and public assassinations and pogroms and mass graves and systematic repression and crippling five-year-plans, what was a little more innocent bloodshed? And any second now another sound would climb over that of the rotors: the high keening scream of a rocket being fired, and that would be the last sound she would ever hear.

She heard the strident whistle of the rocket coming free.

She twisted the handlebars again, drilling back across the median as the whistle grew and grew. She caught air and for a moment was lost in exultation. Finally, a simple equation, two plus two equaled four, either she made it or she didn't, and her knuckles were white against the handlebars, and she was grinning a lunatic grin, and they said your life flashed before you at moments like this, but all she saw inside her mind was the little girl from Turygino. *Otkuda vy?* the girl had asked. *Where are you from?*

I'm an angel. Go back to sleep, honey.

The explosion lifted the bike almost gingerly, moving it a half-dozen meters through the air before setting it crudely down again. Behind her erupted a geyser of fire and steel and human beings, all screaming in agonized unison.

A boiling wave of flame; Cassie ducked, still twisting the throttle ruthlessly, adding her own scream to the chorus, struggling to maintain control. Then she was out of the worst of it, entering clear cold air. Road opened to the right, and she took it as all around debris pattered down like infernal rain.

The military attack chopper gave chase.

She raced down the highway, driving against traffic now, swerving out of the way of oncoming headlights. The pursuing helicopter suffered no such obstacles and stayed with her effortlessly, *whut-whut-whut-whut-whut*, trying to draw another bead with its remaining rocket. She twisted the handlebars sharply again, jounced back across the median. Overhead the copter wheeled, realigning itself. As she crossed two more lanes and hurtled toward dark forest

(*this is how it ends*)

another whistle began to rise

(*I regret nothing!*)

and climaxed in a huge gout of flashblind white fury.

She felt a strong hand made of air pushing her, flipping her. The sky and the ground and the sky rolled crazily. Lungs emptying, brain rattling. Her nose smashed against something, cracking audibly and unleashing a torrent of blood. The bike vanished from beneath her. She registered stuttering images: blood, flipping dark landscape, blood, a black cloud of smoke shot through with bright vermilion flame, blood. *Her* blood.

Somehow it ended, and she was upside-down, ass-over-teakettle, coughing violently, sirens cawing from somewhere, something dripping, and beyond it all, patiently, the idiot refrain – *whut-whut-whut-whut-whut* – of the hovering helicopter.

She began righting herself. Blood coursed into her eyes, stinging. The air was filled with thick rancid smoke and the stench of singed flesh, charred and sickly appetizing, the smell of backyards and Fourth of July cookouts.

A fusillade of secondary explosions ripped through the distance. The sirens grew louder, then cut off abruptly. She could not stop coughing. There were sharp pains and dull pains, racking coughs and blood, blood, blood. She managed to haul herself to her feet. She tried to run, and the world see-sawed tremendously, falling out from beneath her. She ended up face down again in cold dirt.

Another explosion; another blast of hot air; another coiling python of flame snaking up into the nightfall. Beneath the parka, downy hairs on her forearms stood on end. As quickly as it had risen, the explosion retracted, as if sucked back into the earth. Then there was a pillar of smoke and a dozen burning fires, small things that reminded her of birthday candles, and crackling everywhere, and below the crackling, the thin moaning and sobbing of wounded.

Fire extinguishers hissed. Rough hands wrenched her arms behind her back – another sharp flare of pain – and secured them there.

Boots and gun barrels and hoarse Russian surrounded her. The helicopter kept hovering. A veil of blackness descended, mercifully dark and quiet, creeping inward from the borders of perception, snuffing even the fog.

She reached for the darkness, drawing it close around herself, sinking gratefully into the abyss.

TVERSKAYA ULITSA, MOSCOW

Fletcher pressed the small parcel into Ravensdale's hand and then walked briskly away, footsteps rapping off decorative mosaics like gunshots.

After glancing at the plain brown paper wrapping, Ravensdale slipped the parcel into a side pocket and walked in the other direction. He passed a tiled triptych, a cluster of huddled *bomzhi*, a busker holding an acoustic guitar. He rode an escalator up, past windows stocked with perfume, cigarettes, flowers, jewelry, and phones. Stepping out from the Metro station beneath teeth made of icicles, he turned toward the floodlit onion-shaped domes of Saint Basil's Cathedral.

Even past midnight, Tverskaya Ulitsa was packed with crowds: couples passionately kissing, teenagers laughing and catcalling, a priest in a white collar vomiting into a gutter; punks and misfits, armed soldiers, and someone handing out leaflets while dressed, inexplicably, as a Teenage Mutant Ninja Turtle. All rushing to the next trendy café or underground casino, the next tapas or sushi bar, the next love affair or fist fight or business deal, determined to squeeze in as much life as possible before whatever dark tomorrow came careening around the corner.

Again came the odd sensation of doubling, of the old him and the new him moving side by side. He remembered these kiosks lining Tverskaya Ulitsa selling whitefish and cucumber salad, fermented *kvas* and hot *vatrushki*. Now they sold Diet Pepsi and prepaid calling cards and international editions of American news-magazines. But the deprivations and degradations which had lingered after the Soviet era, he reminded himself, were nothing to mourn. Nor was the confusion immediately following the fall of the Wall, when during the mad scramble to pick the flesh from the bones of the USSR he had seen the worst of people – including himself.

His hand moved of its own volition to touch the parcel in his side pocket; a tiny tic stitched the edge of his mouth.

As he neared Red Square, paved streets yielded to wine-colored cobblestones. A familiar smell cut through the diesel fumes and coal dust, making his nostrils twitch. Suddenly, he was back in his youth, watching his father stoke a bonfire in the small fenced yard behind their modest house. Dad had been burning leaves. Mingled with the scent had been composting brush and frozen loam. Soon it would be winter, time to dig out dusty ice skates from the front hall closet . . .

A sudden cross-connection to a day some years later. Ravensdale had become a teenager, absorbed in his own dramas. One night on his way out, he had neglected to close the screen door tightly enough behind himself. His cat Pepper had escaped. The next morning Dad had rescued the mangled corpse from the street, wrapping it in a black towel. They had conducted a funeral near the leaf-burning spot: Dad officiating, Mom crossing herself. Nestled inside a tattered red Kinney shoebox, Pepper had been consigned back to the earth from whence he'd come. Ravensdale had managed not to cry – but he'd been close, cheeks twitching, lips quivering.

After planting the box in the ground, his father had tossed aside the shovel, set one hand on each of his son's shoulders, and looked him straight in the eye. *It was a stupid mistake, Sean.* Close enough that Ravensdale junior could see every fold of sunburned skin in his father's neck, smell the Marlboros on his breath and in his hair. *A stupid mistake, and Pepper paid the price. There's no way around that. But everybody makes mistakes. You learn what you can from them, and you try to do better next time – and you move on. A man does his best. His best is all he can do.*

Not burning leaves, Ravensdale saw as he reached the edge of the square – burning flags.

A small, unruly knot before Lenin's tomb chanted, pumped fists, waved an effigy of the US President on a stick. Hand-lettered signs demanded retribution. A stars-and-stripes smoldered on the cobblestones. Ground Forces soldiers watched nervously, hands on the stocks of their weapons. Passers-by shot video with their phones. A surveillance drone buzzed far overhead, a small gray pinprick against the black sky.

Ravensdale watched for a moment, stroking his salt-and-pepper beard. Then he turned east, crossing before the brilliantly lit facade of GUM, *Glavnyi Universalnyi Magazin* – 'Main Department Store' – where the body of Stalin's second wife had been displayed after her suicide in 1932. He moved on to a wide side-street lined with car dealerships, jewelry shops, and upscale clothing stores. Approaching the driver's side of the parked Jeep, he chirruped off the alarm.

As he reached for the handle, a vehicle pulled up behind him, spraying slush. Doors opened. Something cold and hard touched the center of his back, dead center between the shoulder blades. A hand turned him around. He found himself facing three men, fortyish and heavyset, wearing woolen greatcoats and dead expressions. A flash of perverse satisfaction: no whitefish or *kvas* to be found on Tverskaya Ulitsa any more, but some things never changed. A KGB strongman by any other name . . .

Behind the men, the rear door of a black Lincoln Navigator yawned open. Two enforcers urged Ravensdale inside with hands on elbows. The third slammed the door behind him. The SUV jerked back on to the potholed street, and he fell into a seat rather than spill across the floor.

Seated beside him was a man of perhaps eighty years, with deep-set, luminous pale-gray eyes, a drinker's veined nose, a full head of wavy silver hair, a gleaming Imperial Eagle ring. When the man offered a hand, his grip was surprisingly gentle, with nothing to prove.

'Aleksandr Marchenko,' the man said. His voice was soothing, pitched low. Beneath a neat goatee, he wore the tranquil, indulgent smile of the career interrogator. 'And you, sir, have used many names. But the real one, I think, is Sean Ravensdale. You associate with some of the most infamous *mraz i slovoch*—' scum and swine – 'in our fair city.'

Ravensdale said nothing.

'Yes; so.' Idly, the man inspected his red, gold, and silver ring. His luminous eyes flashed. The only other occupant of the Navigator, the driver, focused exclusively on the road. 'What brings you back to Moscow, Mister Ravensdale, after so long away?'

Ravensdale said: 'Tourism.'

'Yes? And of course we are pleased to have you. But there is no record of your arrival. Somehow you seem to have missed customs.'

'You must be mistaken.'

'And your friend – Andrew Fletcher. Would I find a stamp in his passport, I wonder, were I to search his room at the Marriott?' In flashes of light coming through tinted windows, Marchenko's un-wavering smile looked like waxwork. 'Perhaps I can learn the true nature of your business if I ask the *vory* Otari Tsoi. Or Senior Inspektor Vlasov, of Bauman Street. A sad case, Inspektor Vlasov. Once, a fine investigator. But now he deals with the devil.'

Ravensdale held his tongue.

'I have a theory, sir, which explains your presence in Moscow better than tourism. You will humor me, yes? So. I conjecture that you have organized, with the *vory* Tsoi and the corrupt Inspektor, some sleight of hand. A little bird tells me, you see, that the Inspektor is en route to Petersburg even as we speak. He has made arrangements to take into custody the woman who killed your defector. Presumably, he will escort her back to Serebryany Bor . . . and then hand her over to you.'

They bounced across potholes, suspension creaking. Marchenko waited patiently.

'*Nyet faktov, tolko versii,*' answered Ravensdale at last. *There are no facts, only theories.*

'Ah.' The old man seemed pleased. 'It is true. At the moment, theories are all I have. But respectfully, sir, I believe that there *are* facts, in this case, and that I have named them.'

Ravensdale said nothing.

'So, I beg you. Help me to understand why I should step aside, let you and the corrupt Inspektor and the decadent *vory* work your sleight of hand. Something, perhaps, about the lesser evil, the greater good. Hm?'

Ravensdale said nothing.

'Or some penetrating insight about the wickedness of our government. New Russia becomes ever more like Old Russia. Compared to what the Kremlin gets up to – at the expense of her own people! – you and your friends are like choirboys. Hm?'

The bait sat untouched.

'You have one of those faces, sir, which is difficult to read.' Marchenko gave his ring an absent twist. 'Perhaps I have things all wrong. But lacking the benefit of your perspective, I fall back to the most obvious conclusion. This woman has committed a critical offense against *Rodina*. Once captured, she must be held to account.'

They turned a corner, hardly slowing. Two tremendous construction cranes loomed up into the night sky like gallows. A bus going the other way, running on an overhead wire, kicked up a sheet of dirty snow, shivering the Navigator with a wet slap.

'Americans, if you'll forgive me, are stupendous hypocrites. So much lip service paid to the ideal of freedom. Freedom, freedom, freedom. Yet you murder Blakely – for what? Did the genie go back into the bottle? No. The damage has already been done. And now, in trying to avoid getting caught with your pants down, what message do you send? The same one your country sends again and again: that you consider yourselves above your own rules. In my opinion, that is the true embarrassment.'

A blasting stereo passed outside: The White Stripes singing about a seven nation army. The Navigator recklessly turned another corner, shifting Ravensdale's weight in his seat.

'Managed democracy is a wonderful thing . . . for the managers. Its greatest strength is a free press, when "free" is defined by the leaders. But a simple man such as myself can't help but wonder: who is the true patriot – the one who sacrifices everything to preserve your precious First Amendment rights, or the one who blindly swallows doctrine?' The gentle smile was lulling, hypnotizing. 'You've done yourselves, with your handling of Blakely, a grave disservice. And now, with this sleight of hand, you will compound the damage. What's really needed is sunlight and fresh air. Throw open the windows and doors. Truth will out.'

Ravensdale said nothing.

For an instant, the pleasant smile flickered. Then it returned, widening enough to reveal a single gold crown. 'I consider myself a patriot, Mister Ravensdale, as you surely do. And I consider it my patriotic duty to interrupt your sleight of hand. I prefer the scalpel to the sledgehammer. But I use whichever proves necessary.'

They turned another corner.

'So. Of course, I might go head-to-head with the corrupt Inspektor. But then we risk your *vory* finding some other way to stir up trouble. Yes; so. I might easily deport you. Even more easily, arrest you. But neither guarantees that the woman will be held to account.' Marchenko made a show of thinking. 'So. I prefer cooperation. We must try to cultivate the habit, you know. Soon enough, we will find a common enemy in the Chinese.'

Ravensdale started to speak; Marchenko silenced him with a raised hand.

'Yes; so. When I realized that you were gracing us again with your presence, I made some inquiries. Seeking leverage; I will not lie. In response I received a report from a prison camp in Biysk, where a female detainee passed through eleven months ago. The description was right. The timing was right. The woman had since been moved to a location unknown . . . but it was encouraging.' The pale-gray eyes glowed with their crafty inner light. 'You will be skeptical, no doubt, because you've already made every effort to find your wife. But you, sir, work with *mraz i slovoch*. Everyone you know here is *mraz i slovoch*. And everyone knows them for what they are. And so, powerful though they may be in certain circles, their influence extends only so far.'

Ravensdale told himself: this was how it worked; the carrot and the stick. But something suddenly leapt inside him anyway, thudding painfully against his ribcage.

'To be honest, I was a bit skeptical myself.' They turned a final corner, heading back toward their starting point. 'But did I wonder, sir, whether I might be on to something? Whether the mother of your child might indeed be tucked away somewhere in Siberia – teeth rotting from her head, sanity fraying – so that she might be trotted out, at some point, as an example of what happens to traitors of the regime? And did I wonder what it might be worth to you to get her back?' He shrugged modestly. 'I did. And so I redoubled my efforts. A lifetime of favors, I called in. A long lifetime.'

From an inside pocket, he produced a phone. As the Navigator pulled to a stop, he thumbed a button and then handed the phone to Ravensdale.

On-screen: an image of a cramped, murky hallway. A phone on the other end of the connection was carried past drab fraying wall-paper, a drawn plastic curtain, the sound of a wooden spoon clanging in a metal pot. A hand worked a deadbolt. A door leaned open. Inside a room, a figure slumped across a bed. The brandisher of the phone twisted a goose-necked lamp, casting harsh light across her.

The thing inside Ravensdale's solar plexus gave a feathery flutter. For a few seconds he couldn't tell if Sofiya – emaciated, pallor like onion skin, hair cropped almost to the scalp, collarbones pronounced as coat hangers beneath the *zek*'s uniform – was alive or dead. Then he saw her chest shallowly rise and fall. Her eyes cracked open, revealing two milky crescents.

A newspaper was carelessly tossed; she flinched away. An imperative male voice instructed her to hold the paper toward the camera. She obeyed slowly, as if drugged. The broadsheet was the late edition of that day's *Izvestia*.

The connection went dark.

'Yes,' said Marchenko simply. 'So.'

Trembling slightly, Ravensdale moved to hand back the phone.

'Keep it. There is only one contact inside. When you are ready, dial again. I propose, as you may anticipate, a simple exchange. You bring me the assassin, after the Inspektor has delivered her, and I bring you your wife.'

For the smallest of intervals, Ravensdale hesitated.

Then he nodded.

VYBORG, NORTH OF SAINT PETERSBURG

Eight hundred kilometers north, a drama whose resolution would crucially affect both Sean Ravensdale and Cassie Bradbury was already under way.

Brushing long graying hair from his eyes, Sasha Kudryavtsev settled on to the couch beside Galina Ivanova. He pulled the coffee table closer, broke a rectangle of aluminum foil into two squares, and rolled one into a tube around a cigarette. After rolling the tube, he reached into dirty jeans, producing a cigarette lighter and a small plastic bag. He spread black tar on the remaining square of foil, poked the tube into his mouth, and flicked the lighter's wheel. Kept the liquid moving to prevent congealing, chasing the vapor with the tube, inhaling deep. Grinning dreamily, eyelids flickering, he passed lighter and foil to Galina.

And she took them. She ought not to – but she did. She worked the lighter, chased the vapor. And – there it came. She inhaled sharply. Oh, yes. There it came. Oh, yes, there it was. For just an instant, for just one beautiful instant, she was gorgeous and Sasha was gorgeous and all was right with this gorgeous, gorgeous world . . .

He took back the foil and the lighter. After smoking again, he produced another baggie, this one of fine powder, and helped himself to a generous snort. His body tensed; he shook his head, wobbling his cheeks. Then he grinned again and took another snort, even more generous than the first. So it was going to be one of those nights. *Good*, thought Galina colorlessly. When Sasha got wasted enough she was spared having to play his silly little fuck games, with the whips and the wig.

After he lay back on the couch, she took her own snort. She tilted her head back, noticing for the first time the view through the window: a wedge of moon, a brilliant sprawl of stars. There were more stars in the night sky, Sasha had once told her, than there were grains of sand on all the beaches of the world. He knew things like that. The moon and stars were backlit by shimmering green *aurora borealis*. Beautiful, she thought. Gorgeous. Looked as if Tinker Bell had floated past, sprinkling pixie dust on everything she passed.

Suffused by a terrific sense of peace and warmth and well-being, Galina curled up on the floor at Sasha's feet. Tingling, she listened to distant music. She sank deeper into a sweet, heavy bath. Then she kept sinking, through the floor. Nausea jetted sourly up from the pit of her stomach. She propped herself drowsily on to one elbow, looking for the baggie.

They took turns, smoking and snorting. When they were about to start in on a new bag, she decided to check on Kolya. Finding her feet, she wobbled from the living room. In heavy darkness she honed in on the floating words 'THIS ROOM BELONGS TO NIKOLAI'. Gently, she pushed the door open. Her son was breathing softly and evenly. Beneath a glow-in-the-dark Sputnik he slept coiled in a ball, clutching his blanket in two small fists.

She retreated. Back in the living room, Sasha had cracked open a bottle of samogon. He took a belt, passed the bottle to Galina, and then lifted foil and lighter.

She slid down next to him, weary eyes refusing to disengage from the flame. She gulped the moonshine. She listened to the whine of wind across the frozen bay, the measured breathing of her young son in the other room. The latter sound could make her shrivel up inside. Kolya deserved better than this. She should give him better. She should get away from Sasha. She should learn to be strong . . .

But the foil was coming her way again. She took another belt of samogon and traded the bottle for the lighter.

She sucked hard, holding the vapor in her lungs. Her heart scampered.

The *aurora borealis* climbed in through the window, flickering and dancing, coating the furniture with pixie dust. She reloaded the foil, worked the lighter's mechanism again.

Almost too mellow now to function. The tube seemed as heavy as the wedge of moon outside the window. But she managed to suck down one more tremendous hit. Then another gulp of samogon. Then she made a fist with her left hand, tapped powder on to the declivity near the bottom knuckle of her thumb, and inhaled.

Her heart shivered like a tiny bird with a broken wing. Her eyes rolled back. She slumped limply on to the floor, a weak papery breath whispering from between lips already turning blue. A final lurching beat, and her heart stopped. In her last instant of life, she could smell the ocean beyond the bay, salty, like tears.

PART TWO

SEVEN

SAINT PETERSBURG

Something was in Cassie's eye.

She blinked awake, trying to wipe at her face with the heel of one palm – but the hand caught fast behind her back.

Memories rose like popping bubbles. The world darkening from the edges inward; a shadow show of raucous voices and half-perceived images. She had been paraded, semi-conscious, before a line of men and women. Cameras and microphones, shouted questions, blinding lights. One woman behind a microphone had given her a complicated smile, tired and pained and somewhat sweet.

A ride in a van, slip-sliding in and out of reality. Armed guards on every side. Cuffs biting pitilessly into her wrists. Head throbbing, nose clogging. Struggling to draw each breath. At last, experience had vanished again, like a sheet of paper burning away, and for another stretch of time there had been only darkness.

Now she lay in a freezing concrete cell. Outside of a tiny barred window: night.

She groaned. Her nose felt broken and so thickly caked with blood that she could hardly breathe. The wound on her temple had reopened and then messily clotted again. Every rib felt painfully bruised, if not actually fractured. She had a mother of a headache. And some damned thing was still in her eye.

Shakily, she tried to stand. With hands secured behind her back, she couldn't balance; she rolled on to one side on the cold mossy floor.

Pursing her lips, she folded both legs at the knee. Wincing, she managed to pull booted feet up over the handcuff's chain. Then her wrists, though still bound, were in front of her. Leaning against a stone wall, she gained her feet.

Too much motion; her head whirled. She held perfectly still. Eventually, the dizziness retreated.

Cautiously, she pushed off the wall.

The cell was made of crenellated cement, extending six paces in one direction and three in the other. The only visible door was a narrow slot by the floor, blocked by a steel plate too small for human passage. The single tiny window was nearly opaque with a gleaming admixture of ice crystals and grime. In one dank corner, a fetid-smelling hole in the floor functioned as a latrine.

After a few moments' exploration, she slumped back down. The air was heavy with midnight chill. The cold was terrible, killing cold. At least the parka, filthy and smelling of smoke, remained essentially intact. But the pockets had been emptied; there was no lighter with which to start a fire, even if she could find something to burn, which she couldn't.

For a while, she stared vacantly into space. Then she shook her head. Hadn't she been in the middle of something?

Yes. Sluggishly, she had been trying to form a thought.

How did they put me in here?

Thrusting out her chin, she forced herself up again. She turned a slow circle, teeth chattering. The only visible entrance, the slot by the floor, was not even big enough for a cat.

She began a methodical search, using fingertips more than eyes. Feeling around the perimeter of the room, she found nothing but lichen and grime. Then she turned her attention to the low ceiling – cobwebby, mossy, and slimy. Straining until her calves felt the stretch, keeping her weight pitched forward, she walked her fingertips up and down the cinderblock. If there was a hidden door in the ceiling, she couldn't find it.

Focus proved difficult to maintain; her thinking skittered, a stone skipping across a pond. As she felt around the walls again, she became distracted by the thought that the moss might be edible. Squinting, she examined a patch closely. If nothing else, it might serve to moisten her parched throat. A moment later, she was chewing carefully. *Do like the monks who chew every bite a hundred times—*

She vomited.

Nothing in her stomach except bile. Spitting, dry-heaving, she clutched her head wretchedly. Now her thirst was awake – terrific, slavering, dwarfing the hunger.

She forced herself to keep searching.

At last she found a current of frigid air moving with more force than other currents of air. Apparently, an invisible crack formed a rough square around the steel grate, extending four cinderblocks up from the floor, two out to either side. She pushed, pulled, prodded, succeeding only in exhausting herself. Of course the mechanism to work the hidden door would be external – no lock to be picked, no visible hinges to be removed.

Now . . . she would get back on to the floor.

She got back on to the floor.

After a while, since nobody was watching, she allowed herself to cry. She cried silently, small tears leading to bigger ones, until her shoulders were chuffing and whatever was in her eye floated away. She wound down slowly, hiccuping, and then passed out.

The next time she swam awake, her cheeks were damp. She had continued crying in her sleep. *Stupid body*, she thought. *Wasting water.*

Her eyes closed again. A bee buzzed distractingly inside her skull. Her ears were popping. Her mouth tasted like pennies. Her head was on fire. Fever, she thought . . . She was on a raft, on a river, beneath a burning sun. She and Huck Finn were hammering out a deal in which she would exchange sexual favors for food. Above the cloudy river, mosquitoes floated in dense thickets. No wonder she had a fever. She had . . . malaria?

She felt both hot and cold, both flushed and empty. Her head was pounding, buzzing, thrumming. The base of her spine ached horribly. Her joints felt as if they had been emptied of cartilage and then refilled with molten steel. And the molten steel was beginning to seep out into her lungs – hot and thick, bubbling with every tortured breath.

Sick, she thought miserably.

She coughed. The cough started out dry and shallow and ended up deep, hacking, and wet. She was sitting up again, soaked in sweat. *Dying*, she thought.

She fell back with a congested, liquid sigh. Rallying, she tried again. This time she managed to gain her feet, propping herself against one wall to keep her balance. Woozily, she paused.

She listed to the window. One blunt-nailed index finger poked between cold metal bars. Slowly, she scratched a clean line on the grimy pane. Then another. Then a longer one connecting them, forming an *F.*

If you had a million years to do it, Holden Caulfield had said, *you couldn't rub out even half the 'Fuck you' signs in the world.*

On the heels of this came another memory, so time-worn that she wasn't quite sure it was a real memory at all. She had been a little girl, walking with her father, and they had come upon a snarl of red graffiti spray-painted on to the sidewalk. FUCK, the graffiti read. Cassie had sounded out the letters and then asked what they meant. Her father had chosen the words for his answer carefully. *It's a beautiful thing between two people, Cass, m'lass. It's when a man loves a woman and they make a baby together. Sometimes people use it in a different way; but it's a beautiful, beautiful thing. Don't ever forget that . . .*

She laughed aloud.

Unsteadily, she returned to the floor. Dizzy. Nauseated. Wretched. Funny how she didn't even feel the cold any more. Her breath was visible, yet she felt almost comfortable. Just like the Jack London story. And that was the most frightening part.

She drifted.

Sometime later, she woke with a small choked sob.

Still dark. Gooseflesh prickled her forearms beneath the parka. Her heart felt heavy and slow. If she didn't move, she thought, she would freeze to death.

She staggered to her feet again. Tottering, she paced. Every few seconds she paused to lean against the wall and let her head stop spinning. Her stomach was trying to eat itself. Soon that moss might start to look worth a second try.

Not yet.

She trudged on. The headache was terrible, crippling. Chills shivered from scalp to toes. With stupid determination, she kept pacing. She felt like crying or screaming. She rode the feeling, surfing, tingling, until the wave crashed. Then she was in weird territory, frightening but somehow familiar. *There's another place*, Fiver had said in a passage her father had highlighted in *Watership Down*, another of her favorite books – *another country, isn't there? We go there when we sleep; at other times, too; and when we die. It's a wild place, and very unsafe. And where are we really – there or here?*

Then, except for sore feet, she felt almost all right. Then a not-unpleasant but completely terrifying warmth bloomed in her extremities.

A tear ran down her cheek. She pictured a Denny's Grand Slam Breakfast: eggs, sausages, pancakes, hash browns gloppy with ketchup. A toasted everything bagel with strawberry cream cheese – the breakfast of champions, Michelle had called it. A frosty glass of orange juice. Granola with nuts and cranberries. Chocolate-chip Pop-Tarts. Banana waffles, sweet maple syrup. Cinnamon scones.

Breakfast, her father had liked to say, was the most important meal of the day.

Irritated, she swiped at her face.

She kept pacing.

For a time Quinn seemed to occupy the cell. He stood in one corner, wearing his crew-neck cotton sweater and brown loafers. Moonlight sparkled off his glasses, pooling in the cleft of his chin. His expression was expectant, mildly exasperated.

Eventually, a strange new thought wormed its way into her consciousness. For the first time she realized how comfortable a place to die this cell might be. The moss would yield, form-fitting. Agonies of hunger and thirst and fatigue would fade. She could close her eyes. Let go. And rejoin eternity.

Another feverish shiver. Groaning, hugging herself, she collapsed back on to the floor.

'Oh God,' she said aloud. 'Oh God. Oh God.'

An image from *Anna Karenina* lurched into her mind. When Anna had been pushed too far, when her exhaustion and loneliness and suffering had become too much to bear, she'd considered downing an entire phial of morphine instead of her usual nightly dose. And as she had lain back on her bed, the shadow from a single candle had danced across a stucco cornice. Suddenly, the shadow had spread, covering the entire ceiling, and other shadows had rushed to meet it, melting together and dripping over the room, consuming Anna as she lay shivering in her bed, thinking, *Death!* Only later had her tortured, feverish mind realized that the spreading shadows had been the result of the candle going out. But by then it had been too late; the seed had been planted, the dark urge had taken root.

Close your eyes. Let go. And rejoin eternity.

She moaned again, head swimming.

It's a beautiful thing between two people, Cass, m'lass. Sometimes people use it in a different way; but it's a beautiful, beautiful thing. Don't ever forget that . . .

Shuddering coughs wracked her body. Then, like Anna in her moment of extremis, she watched shadows spread from the ceiling corners, filling the cell, joining together, forming a single tremendous blot of darkness, and finally engulfing her.

COBBLER'S COVE: ONE YEAR EARLIER

'The world's most effective lock pick,' said Quinn, 'is a woman's charms.'

He was at his most pedantic: sitting with impeccable posture on the sofa beside her, speaking in a dry monotone. A professor again, not of comparative literature, now, but of biology.

'Kissing decreases cortisol, which lowers stress. Love-making floods the body with chemicals promoting calm and trust. Your most powerful weapon is nature itself. Spymasters have known this for centuries. Vide the "honey trap". Courtship begins with the exchange of non-verbal signs. "I am here." "I am female." "I mean you no harm." "You may approach." Crickets chirp. Humans wear bright colors, jewelry and watches that gleam during crepuscular hours, and beads and other geometric shapes that draw an eye evolved to find berries. Flowers lure us with fragrance as well as beauty . . .'

Why would he tell her this? If there was one thing she didn't need him to teach, it was how to seduce a man.

For the same reason hookers refused to kiss their johns, she answered herself: to remove from the transaction the personal element, emphasize the clinical. His sophism implied that she could sleep with someone as a tactic, with no emotional cost, no emotional investment.

Nor was he entirely wrong. As a little girl she'd pictured having a boyfriend as going shopping together for Christmas presents in the mall, arm in arm while carols played over the loudspeaker system. Or walking home from school, letting her suitor carry her books – talk about *quaint*. But she had spent a lot of time living in the real world since then. And in the real world she had already given herself to many men, and even some women, for many reasons besides love.

'Men,' Quinn was saying, 'puff out their chest like peacocks. Women drift past, announcing themselves. They've exaggerated their sexual identity to make their intentions clear: pigmenting their eyes, cheekbones, and lips. They emphasize the infantile schema by covering the nose with make-up. Welcome signs include the head-tilt-side, the palm-up, the shoulder-shrug, and the smile. Phase Two: validation of the signs sent out during Phase One. Acceptance signals include full body alignment, rapid blinking, flushing, submissive gaze-down, head-toss, postural echo, anxious self-touching, and shoulder-shrugging. Negative cues include gaze aversion, crossing the arms, or angling the body away – the proverbial cold shoulder.'

She would ensnare Oleg Zimyanin, Quinn had said, in the Moscow art gallery where he picked up most of his girls. She would use the oldest and most dependable of all trade-crafts. She would have no trouble, as the target's fondness for her type had been well-established.

'Phase Three: conversation. In many cases this also involves food, which engages the nervous system's parasympathetic division, shifting us from fight-or-flight toward relaxation and tranquility.

Ventromedial-nucleus circuits of the hypothalamus slow heartbeats, constrict pupils, warm and dry the palms. Sharing food, clinking glasses, and eating fortune cookies together stimulates bonding. Of course, alcohol always greases the tracks.'

He had shown her a long-lens photograph of Zimyanin, a man in his late twenties, in leather jacket and tracksuit and gold chains and ponytail, striking a faintly ridiculous pose – puffing out his chest, one hand cupping an elbow, the other reflectively stroking his chin – as he examined a painting.

'Phase Four. Overall, men prefer sloppy kisses, which pass chemicals, including testosterone, via saliva. Testosterone increases sex drive in both males and females. Oxytocin levels start to rise . . .'

Upon hearing the subject of her dissertation, Zimyanin would do a slight double-take. *The Bubnovy Valet school, really? Why, it must be fate. I have the finest private collection in the city. You'll have to come see it . . . but first, if you like, I know a wonderful restaurant just down the block. The maître d' is a personal friend.* She would dimple fetchingly, tucking a strand of hair behind one ear, tilting her head as she did so to catch the light.

'Phase Five: intercourse. Rocking back and forth while hugging stimulates pleasure centers linked to the ear's vestibular sense. Orgasm is triggered by nerve impulses traveling through dorsal aspects of the spinal cord's pudendal nerve—'

The next photographs, fish-eyed, as if taken with a hidden camera, portrayed a penthouse apartment as dapperly sleazy as its owner: framed erotica hanging on the walls, ornate Oushak carpets underfoot, a wall-sized window overlooking Moscow's Golden Mile. The bedroom featured a circular cherrywood bed and, comically, mirrors hanging on the ceiling, polished to a high gleam.

Once it was finished, she would excuse herself to use the ladies' room. In the study two doors from the bedroom she would find a spring-loaded, lever-fence Sargent & Greenleaf model R6730 lock, dial divided into a standard one hundred gradations, each marked with a white tick against a black background, with every tenth digit highlighted. Time and design flaws would have created slight inconsistencies within the mechanism that interacted with the drive cam to turn the lock bolt. By feeling the left and right contact points of the dial against the fence, she would quickly learn the lock's subtle but crucial flaws, and line up the gates under the fence by touch.

Inside the safe she would discover binders, maps, blueprints. She would not remove a single schematic; instead, she would memorize any information pertinent to the target dacha. *Like everyone, Cassie, you possess perfect eidetic recall. The only difficulty comes in activating the ability. I'll teach you some tricks to help things along. First, you'll find something like page numbers to serve as index points . . .*

And later, inside a small, anonymous hostel on Zhukovskogo Ulitsa, she would meticulously reproduce the documents she had memorized. Then, considering options and consequences, she would devise a method of incursion. She would have access to Quinn's bottomless bank accounts, his network of contacts. She would remember his lessons: that power mattered less than accuracy, that courage was resistance to fear, mastery of fear, not absence of fear. Once she had decided to go ahead, she would not hesitate.

Hesitation, Quinn said, would ruin her.

SAINT PETERSBURG

Awake.

Her ribs still ached. Her belly was still empty, her head still swimming. Still dark outside. She had been here for less than one night. It had been forever; but it had been less than one night.

Quinn was in the cell with her again, a suggestion of mirth etched across his face now – mirth at her expense, of course. He had tricked her, used her, and thrown her away. She would never get the chance to exact her revenge. She would never learn if his story had been all lies, or lies mixed with truth. She would freeze to death in this cell, or they would beat her fatally during the interrogation, or they would execute her after a show trial. She would cease being . . . but Quinn would go on and on, abducting other young people, tricking them, using them for his own nefarious purposes. She had not been the first – look how skilfully he'd played her; he had it down to a science – and she would not be the last.

She drifted again, down endless tunnels, past dim silhouettes, echoes of echoes.

Sometime later a new thought sparked, a dull ember floating through the darkness: break the window and she might use the glass to cut her wrist, and thus spare herself some suffering.

She let the thought drift right past. Unlike Anna Karenina, Cassie Bradbury was a survivor. If suicide had been an option she would have done it long ago, during some wintry, hopeless night on the streets of Manhattan.

Then another spark flared, brighter:

Use the glass to cut their throats, dummy, when they come to get you.

She stirred, lifting her head off the cold stone floor.

Pushing to her feet, she waited out a swirl of zigzagging black dots marring her vision. Gathering her strength, she maneuvered toward the window. The *F* she had scratched into the frosty grime had faded to a spectral stencil. Extending her index finger, she traced it again, contemplatively.

She tapped the glass with as much force as she could muster. Bars and handcuffs prevented her from getting her arm into it – but she managed to shiver the glass in its frame. If the handcuffs had been gone . . .

She examined the parka's zipper. The tab, a thin sheet of bent and sooty nickel, had seen better days. Clumsily, she brought her shackled hands into her sternum, closing thumb and forefinger around the tab, working it back and forth. Almost immediately, it snapped off. Then she was holding a centimeter-and-a-half of weak, flat metal. Not worth much by itself. But . . .

Finding the brightest available splash of moonlight, she experimented with the best angle from which to insert the tab into the lock of the handcuffs. Intended as only temporary restraints, handcuffs did not, as a rule, feature the most secure of locks. Just a matter of jigging the tongue back and forth, again and again, with increasing pressure and speed, building momentum, until—

The cuffs fell open, and then her hands were free. She weighed the manacles in one palm, considering.

She faced the window again. Using the spur of the cuff, she tapped the dirty glass. *Clunk.*

She tried again. *Crack*, and a hairline fissure appeared at the point of contact.

She tried again. This time she got the angle perfectly, and heat-treated carbon steel sliced neatly through glass: *kresssh.*

Freezing air whistled into the cell. Gingerly, she reached between rusted bars to pluck out the largest shard of glass on the sill, a wickedly curved slice almost eight centimeters long. Setting the shard and cuffs carefully aside, she recovered another fragment, two centimeters shorter but still adequate for her purposes. The rest of the big pieces had tumbled outside, out of reach.

Using two fingers, she greedily scooped up snow from the sill and shoveled it into her mouth. *Don't swallow.* Tiny pieces of glass. *Let it melt . . .*

Water. Ambrosia. Paradise.

She spat out a few fragments, aware of a brief tingling pain on her tongue, and went back for more snow. Cold, wet, refreshing, utterly delicious. Even the dirt seemed delicious: all part of Mother Earth's glorious, inimitable plan.

When she had consumed all the snow within reach, she sank back to the floor. Her last protection from the elements was now gone. She couldn't even zip up the parka. The temperature in the cell was dropping rapidly. But at least she had a chance.

She set the smaller shard within easy reach, closing the larger shard in her right hand, taking care to break neither skin nor glass.

And waited.

EIGHT

SEREBRYANY BOR

Ravensdale ran a hand gummily over his face, then put his legs over the side of the bed.

Still dark outside; not even a thin membrane of light glowed above the beach. His internal clock was hopelessly misaligned. The mansion slumbered around him. He felt a sense of dislocation: this might have been another dream, nestled within the night's uneasy complement like a *matryoshka* doll.

He visited the kitchen alone, moving past flat tops holding still as ice sculptures, and brewed a pot of coffee. After downing two cups, he carried a third back to his room. Sitting on the foot of the bed, holding the cup in both hands, he gazed blankly into the middle distance.

In his mind's eye he saw a cocktail party, more than four years gone, at Spaso House. The official residence of the US ambassador in Moscow had hosted its share of lavish soirées – most infamously the Spring Festival of 1935, immortalized by Bulgakov in *The Master and Margarita* – but this one had been tame, a standard week-night placeholder, less about diplomacy than about free food.

Ravensdale had stopped by with Jack Carlson. Fishing for recruits from their opposite number was part of the job, and word had come down that the FSB was dispatching one of its loveliest to the event for the same purpose. Upon entering the palatial Chandelier Room they found the young lady in question immediately, a striking beauty hovering near the buffet, décolletage on artful display. The *chargé d'affaires* told Ravensdale that her name was Sofiya Kirov, that she was a translator for a famed dramatist who was attending the party in search of material for a play. But the dramatist was locked in conversation with a diplomat, leaving Sofiya conveniently on her own, the better to find and recruit unsuspecting American targets, if they could not recruit her first.

Stationing himself behind a neoclassical column, Ravensdale took her measure more fully. Long black hair, high Tatar cheekbones, sable crêpe de chine, stunning emerald eyes. *I'd better watch myself*, he thought, *eyes like that.* She was in her early or mid-thirties. She looked around herself timidly, fingering the neckline of her dress, exuding anxiety – a calculation, if not an outright pretense. Showing her soft white underbelly, she invited approach.

He approached. '*Alë, garázh,*' he said ironically: *Hey, citizen.*

Fast forward to a rainy night fourteen months later. The exposure of a crucial Force Multiplication officer in Sicily had sent shock waves rippling through agents in the field. The possibility that Ravensdale might be withdrawn seemed very real. All that rainy night, whispering beneath the covers, he and Sofiya confessed star-crossed love like two teenagers. *O teach me how I should forget to think!* In Gorky Park, the next day, they put on the usual show for the usual telephoto lenses brandished by the usual surveillance teams on both sides. That night they rendezvoused at Sheremetyevo-2. Flew commercial, using cash, to JFK. Standing outside a Starbucks on the main concourse, surrounded by the zombies of three a.m., Ravensdale brushed aside a flyaway strand of her black hair (tinged, he noticed for the first time, with gray near the root) and kissed her neck. She responded with a small smile, edged with apprehension.

Ten months later he tried to follow the stretcher into the OR, but a young male nurse intercepted him, declaring that no family was allowed in the operating theater. So Ravensdale sat alone, in a waiting room of unyielding plastic, as the doctors worked to deliver the baby from his wife. Eventually, like expectant fathers stretching back into time immemorial, he paced. Outside was another rainy evening, a moody drizzle picking up and then fading away. At last the OR doors flapped open again. Stepping into the waiting room, peeling off skin-tight gloves, an aristocratic-looking doctor found his eyes. 'Ah; the doting husband. Your wife is resting comfortably. Your son is on his way to the nursery. If you'd like to meet him, now's the time . . .'

He blinked, came back to the present.

Setting aside the coffee, he reached into the night-table and took out Fletcher's parcel.

Not that I don't trust you. But the girl will not be released until your end of the bargain has been honored.

He turned the plain brown package over in his hands. The contents killed without discrimination. There might be innocent bystanders inside the restaurant. He had come here to put paid to past sins. What sense did it make to double down?

Something, perhaps, about the lesser evil, the greater good. Hm?

I prefer the scalpel to the sledgehammer. But I use whichever proves necessary.

He closed his eyes. Behind the lids he found Fletcher: *Being a good father means leaving your son a world worth inheriting.* And Dad: *A man does his best. His best is all he can do.* And Marchenko: *You bring me the assassin. I bring you your wife.* And Sofiya: sable crêpe de chine, dancing green eyes. A small smile, edged with apprehension.

SAINT PETERSBURG

A cinderblock moved, rasping.

In a flash she was awake, alert, back to the wall beside the meal slot, clutching the shard of glass. *Disable your target by slashing a muscle and he'll be unable to defend himself. Then you'll be looking for your fatal attack, your vein or vital organ . . .*

The cinderblock extruded a few more centimeters. Cassie held her breath. With a subterranean grating sound, four cinderblocks around the meal slot were vanishing. A shadowed figure was crab-walking through the low door and into the cell, pistol in hand.

Gliding up behind, she slashed a hamstring.

With a strangled cry, the man folded. Springing forward, she cupped his chin with her left palm, lifted it clear, and slit his throat.

Convulsing dreadfully, gushing blood, the man died. Another man behind him was charging forward, but his boot failed to find purchase against gory concrete. He slipped, and she was on him. The glass bit into the right side of his throat, severing the digastric, and he screamed a high womanly scream. The next slash opened his jugular.

With one foot, Cassie rolled him over. The uniform was the green-and-black camouflage of the OMON. The face was so ordinary as to defy description. For a brief moment, she looked into it.

One more for which Quinn would answer.

Then she moved again.

From the cell's floor she recovered a Stechkin machine pistol, with full twenty-round magazine. Switching to single-fire mode, she listened at the open door and then ducked out into a night filled with starlight.

She found herself in a yard spotted with free-standing cells, some half-buried, with only barred windows and cinderblock roofs showing above ground. The skyline was dominated by a tremendous glittering Russian-Byzantine church, with a huge gold-plated dome blotting out a background of stars. This, she realized after a second, was Saint Isaac's Cathedral. So she had ended up in Saint Petersburg, after all.

Before her was a large and blocky concrete building with an institutional air, the command center of the prison to which the isolated cells belonged. An attached structure jutted off to the right. Farther out, an oasis of electric light illuminated a parking lot and fleet of dark-blue tri-axle trucks. On the other side of the parking lot, she could just make out a high fence.

Turning, she looked past the cell in which she had been held, past another high fence, to a steep drop-off and icy river. Across the ice spread more of Saint Petersburg: obelisks and apartment buildings and broad squares and tall spires, and a population of five million into which she could vanish, if she could only reach them. Searchlights from both shores crawled irregularly across the river's frozen surface.

She looked wistfully back toward the trucks in the parking lot. Tempting. But in that direction would surely be dogs, and spike strips, and machine-gunners. The river it was.

Keeping to darkness, she approached the fence and the steep bank beyond. Four meters high, topped by razor wire, the barrier would have presented a challenge had she been in peak form, which she definitely was not. Still, adrenalin had given her a charge, clearing her head. If she moved quickly, she would have a chance.

Looping the Stechkin around one shoulder, taking two handfuls of cold wire fencing, she hauled herself up. Biceps and calves trembling, she repeated the motion. Then she had to pause, gathering herself for another upward push; suspended there, quivering, she felt a wave of faintness crash across her brow. If she passed out, she would wake up back in the cell . . . if she woke up at all. And never again would they be so careless as to give her any chance at escape . . .

Through sheer force of will, she heaved herself to the top of the fence and then over, cutting her left hand and nicking her right cheek on concertina wire in the process, but what were another few cuts and scrapes? Landing heavily, she took one knee and concentrated on remaining conscious. The tide of darkness lapped in . . . and in . . . and then pulled back out. After a woozy moment, she moved again.

Frigid sand slathered weirdly underfoot. The bank was sheer; she slid down heedlessly, letting gravity take her. Reaching the river, she tested the surface with one booted foot. By the shore, at least, the ice seemed perfectly solid.

Tentatively she extended her right foot without applying her full weight. After a moment she brought her other foot forward, ready to spring backward at the first creak. The ice held. She moved her right foot forward again and then took a few quick, shuffling steps across a thin layer of wind-blown snow. When she had gained two meters from the shore, she paused. From here she might still be able to leap to safety if the ice cracked. A few steps farther, though, would put her into the kill zone.

But the ice still held. So she took another step, and then – gingerly – another.

Freezing wind came keening down the river. Her teeth rattled like dice in a cup. But the ice still felt solid, and the closest searchlight had wheeled far off to the left. Keeping her eyes fixed on the far shore, she hazarded another few steps. Now she found herself reluctant to lift her feet off the ice at all; the following few steps were hobbles. The ice beneath her groaned complainingly. She might still reverse course . . . but she was already one-quarter of the way across.

Shuffling steadily forward, she soon found a rhythm. Keeping her weight evenly distributed meant remaining in constant motion. Like a shark, she thought. Stop moving and you die. *Story of my life.*

The muscles of her right calf cramped. Gritting her teeth, she came to an involuntary halt. Was it just imagination, or did the ice sag beneath her? If it was still groaning, she couldn't hear; the wind had grown deafening, a quivering glissando working up and down the river. Taking one knee again, she kneaded the knotted muscle of her calf. When her numb fingers proved ineffective, she used the cold barrel of the Stechkin. Eventually, the oxygen-starved tissue loosened. She held position for a moment, resting.

A new halogen searchlight blazed to life on the shore behind her.

Regaining her feet, she kept moving. The wind helled against her like an invisible buffer. The searchlight oscillated, coming within a yard of her, sending her heart into her throat, before reversing, sweeping off toward Saint Isaac's.

She shuffled resolutely on. Halfway across now; nearing three-quarters. The light was coming her way again. She debated turning and shooting it out, which might buy a moment. But doing so would reveal her position. And there would be plenty of other lights ready to replace it. Better to concentrate on hustling to the far bank. She could see it clearly now beneath the stark yellow quarter-moon: a pedestrian walkway leading to a park, bordering a residential block of domed churches and squat cottages.

An instant later came the sound of helicopter blades thrashing the night sky. *Goddamn it.*

She didn't pause to look up. She skate/shuffled across the ice, finding the rhythm again, never coming to a full stop. Just like cross-country skiing, she thought. A pleasant day in the countryside with friends. A roaring fire and hot cocoa waiting back at the lodge. Little marshmallows. Turtleneck sweaters . . .

Then she was nearing the walkway, the small park. The helicopter and searchlight had still not found her. The ice would be thicker here, nearer the shore; she began to run, knees pumping, tasting already the sensation of solid earth back beneath her feet—

—and watching in horrified disbelief as the ice buckled beneath her.

In the next instant, she was surrounded by churning water.

Even as every nerve screamed agony, she tried to pull herself back in the direction she judged to be up. But a jungle of living bubbles percolated around her. The light was all black and gray. Something thudded perplexingly inside her ears: her heartbeat, the helicopter blades, the drumbeat of narcosis.

Her kicks were dangerously close to thrashes, roiling the water to threads. She saw a delicate rill of blood, feathery in the water. Through a distorted cataract, she saw the hole through which she'd fallen. Driving for it, she miscalculated, missed by half a yard, ended up hammering impotently at solid ice.

A diffuse wash of light, as the helicopter passed overhead.

Turning, she swam back into blackness. Her body cried foul. Her side stitched. Her lungs would burst – yet she forbade herself to try again for the hole, despite the terrible pressure, until the chopper had passed.

The damned thing was hovering. Searching. She thrashed aimlessly, holding herself down. Darkness. Black waves rising. The cold was exquisite. The cold was boiling hot. The need to breathe would not be denied. She drove up with a pistoning kick, found the hole – *not yet for Christ's sake* – and despite her best intentions clambered out of glacial water, on to ice.

The helicopter had moved away, searchlight brushing farther down the river.

She drew a raking breath. Stumbling up, she turned in a circle, lost. Then she realized she need take only a few steps to achieve the pedestrian walkway. Upon doing so, she vomited a thin gray gruel across frozen gravel.

The Stechkin was gone. Her boots were gone. Waterlogged, the parka and blue jeans were doing more harm than good. Her teeth rattled fiercely. Yet she was grateful for the chattering, which indicated a beating heart. Good old body, always looking out for her. Why didn't she treat it better?

She staggered across icy ground. Her toes, clad now only in wet socks, clenched painfully. If she didn't lose a few, she would count herself lucky. But somehow she had made it across. That was what mattered. She had made it across.

Behind her, the helicopter's searchlight pinwheeled restlessly.

She stumbled across the gravel walkway, into the park. The only human beings in sight were unfortunate *bomzhi*, shivering beneath ragged blankets. The sudden stillness was pristine, dreamlike.

She crossed the park. On the other side, thin traffic flowed along a boulevard. She spied a blue-and-white Zhiguli prowler. Ducking back, she crouched. The cruiser passed, shining a light from the opposite window.

Her feet hurt; her ribs hurt; her chest hurt; her hand and cheek and nose hurt; her heart and lungs and brain hurt. But she lifted her chin, stepped from the park, and kept moving.

The old sleep poorly.

Rather than lie awake in bed, Mariya Zaslavsky cooked. She cooked ravioli called *pelmini*, and *perochki*, fried dough filled with meat, and sugar-covered *pishki*, and blini with apples and raisins. She brewed tea from loose *zavarka* leaves, and chain-smoked one Djarum Black clove cigarette after another. Had Ivan still been alive, he would have reprimanded her – for the smoking, the needless cooking (most of the food would go to waste; although Mariya still had a good appetite, there were limits), the giving up so easily on a good night's sleep. But of course Ivan was not around, and had not been for years, and so she cooked, and smoked, without fear of rebuke.

Once all her pots were bubbling, she carried a bottle and tumbler into the parlor, where stacks of handwoven carpets reached almost to the ceiling. Taking down her flat needle and harp-shaped loom, she settled into a chair upholstered with silk damask. Working by the glow of a single dim lamp, she added a row to the kilim on which she'd been working for the past week. Then she paused, to refill the tumbler and stroke at two white whiskers on the tip of her chin.

For twenty minutes, she wove and drank. Then she found herself gazing off philosophically into space, picturing Ivan in his youth, handsome and broad-shouldered and trim, wearing crisp Red Army fatigues. He flashed a sly, knowing smile. Mariya raised her tumbler in acknowledgement, although she knew she was only toasting a ghost.

An old woman's watery tear tracked down one cheek. She gave her head a small shake. Had Ivan truly been here, he would have shaken his head back at her. *You're still breathing, Mariya Zaslavsky*, he would have said. *As long as you're breathing, you have more to offer the world than carpets which never get sold and food which never gets eaten.*

Maybe. The Lord worked in mysterious ways. Even a fat lonely old widow, friendless, drinking too much, spending nights alone with a loom and a bottle and a stove and old memories . . . even she may have had something to offer.

She blinked. The pots, bubbling aromatically, needed stirring. The loom sat forgotten by one hand. Grunting, she pushed out of the chair.

By the time she doused the light, the small cottage had filled with the smells of meat and dough and cloves and ravioli and tea.

Sitting back down in the damask chair, she let her eyes close. The small radio she kept playing at all hours murmured weather, traffic, news. Mariya sighed, hardly listening. Clear and cold, traffic jams on the M-10 after the apprehension of a terrorist, a groundswell of political demonstrations, a rising star in women's tennis making waves with her skimpy outfits—

A window in the kitchen scraped in its frame.

Mariya's hearing was as good as her appetite – both had survived a long life with minimal wear – and she knew the sound of a break-in when she heard it. It had happened twice already, since Ivan's death, always during these early-morning hours after she finally turned off the lamp. Not for nothing was Saint Petersburg known as the Crime Capital of New Russia. Both times the intruders had been young drug addicts, looking for a few kopecks with which to score their next fix, more deserving of pity than of fear. Mariya had given the trespassers food, a few coins, and several items of warm clothing, and they had left humbly, guiltily, good kids at heart, as baffled by the twists of fate that had brought them to the mystifying present as was Mariya herself.

Without stirring from the chair, she watched the kitchen doorway, the food sitting on the table. A breath of chilly air wafted through the room. The window scraped quietly back into place. Furtive mouse-steps as the intruder crossed the floor. Then a young woman appeared, falling to the food. She was not much over twenty, dirty, with hair poorly cut and badly dyed. One of the *besprizornye*, thought Mariya – the countless orphans and waifs and runaways who lived in sewers and public urinals and cemetery vaults.

Moving carefully, Mariya found half-moon glasses on a fine gold chain around her neck. She took another, more careful look at the girl. Quite lovely, beneath the mess – but not at her best. A bit shaky. Dressed in a sodden coat, a bad idea in this weather. In fact, now that Mariya looked more closely, she saw bruises – and crusts of blood—

The girl collapsed across the table, spilling dishes, crumpling after them on to the floor.

SEREBRYANY BOR

Ravensdale's hands knotted into fists.

After a few seconds he made them loosen, leaving small bloodless half-moons printed across his palms. He looked at Tsoi closely. The gangster held himself erect, maintaining conscientious eye contact. The cast of the body wall suggested candor. But, of course, this, perhaps Ravensdale's closest living friend in the world, was a professional criminal, a man who lied for a living.

Nevertheless, Ravensdale trusted Otari Tsoi – more than he did Andrew Fletcher, and more, he reflected wryly, than Fletcher should trust him. The *Vorovskoi Mir* had forsaken State-given privileges, during the corrupt Communist regime, in favor of something more primal; they maintained their own community, enforcing their own system of justice and code of moral conduct. They kept a common fund called an *obshchak*, where profits were pooled and then distributed, not just among working thieves but among the families of those who were dead or in jail. In the Thieves' World, honor – a peculiar, selective, brutal sort of honor, but honor nonetheless – meant everything. By contrast, Andrew Fletcher and his ilk subscribed only to the eleventh commandment: Thou Shalt Not Get Caught.

'How?' asked Ravensdale finally.

'Broke a window in her holding cell. Used the glass to kill two guards.' Tsoi moved his shoulders helplessly. 'She was handcuffed; they got sloppy. No excuses. But Inspektor Vlasov remains in Pieter. He can supervise the recovery effort in person. And the Petersburg police are notoriously ruthless. She will not get far.' He sank on to the foot of the bed, let a moment spool away before adding: 'You have your own concerns here, *tovarish*.'

For an instant, Ravensdale thought he meant Sofiya; he felt himself flush. Then he realized that the gangster referred only to his own interests: the imminent *strelka*, the summit of organized crime leaders.

'Her escape,' allowed Tsoi after a moment, 'is a profound disappointment. But we have many balls in the air. The fumbling of one must not be allowed to disrupt all the others.' He toyed with a shiny black button on one cuff. 'To be honest, I considered not telling you. No need to risk distraction at this crucial time. And the problem will doubtless be rectified soon enough. But I've always been truthful with you. To a fault, perhaps.'

Ravensdale looked at his hands, closing again of their own volition into fists. He thought of Sofiya – sawdust complexion, blistered gray lips, hair shorn like an animal's, collarbones standing out beneath the *zek*'s uniform. He thought of the *pytka*, the torture, she had doubtless endured at the hands of interrogators after her return to the Motherland. Stainless steel cables, cedar splinters beneath fingernails, nerve bundles bludgeoned with truncheons. And the *pytka*, if he failed to rescue her, still to come . . .

He shoved the image away. Had not Orpheus ruined everything, right at the moment of truth, by turning to look back at his wife?

'The point is,' Tsoi said, 'you can believe me now when I promise you: *she will not get far*. You must concentrate, my friend, on delivering your end of the bargain.'

Tightly, Ravensdale nodded.

The restaurant created, in the center of Moscow, the atmosphere of a large country house, with exposed brick walls and rustic floor lamps. Now, on the leading edge of the lunch hour, a placard out front declared the venue closed for a private event.

Ignoring the card, Ravensdale knocked commandingly. He wore a suit of blended polyester and wool, procured by Tsoi, suitable for a mid-level *apparatchik*. Before leaving Serebryany Bor, he had inspected his reflection at length in a mirror. Looking back had been an anonymous government functionary, a long-time middle manager, whose face betrayed appropriate world-weariness, and nothing else.

The door opened. '*Ischezni*,' said a man rudely – *Get lost.*

Ravensdale showed his papers. The man leaned forward, heavy brow lowering. Moments later, a prim maître d' appeared behind him. 'Sir, we're closed for a private—'

'*Minsotsrazvitiye*,' announced Ravensdale: Ministry of Health and Social Development.

The maître d' stiffened; his Adam's apple worked.

Drifting through the doorway: soft canned Italian music, strings and mellifluous vocals, Ol' Blue Eyes crooning about strangers in the night. The smells of red sauce and cooking oil and Parmesan cheese. Glimpses of a coat check, fresh yellow flowers against robin's-egg blue tablecloths, framed oil paintings against ruddy brick walls.

The maître d' stepped closer. 'Come on,' he said reasonably. 'Karlo—'

'Karlo's been transferred. Now you've got me to deal with.'

'Let's be sensible. Right now is not—'

'Let me in, comrade, or you're shut down. Effective immediately. Sensible enough?'

'Come back at four o'clock.'

'And give you time to scour the kitchen? Forget it.'

'You must understand. Some of our—'

Ravensdale reached threateningly for a pocket. The maître d' stopped him with a quick hand, hissed: 'Go around the back.'

The alleyway was littered with ice-encrusted garbage. A trash can had fallen over, and Ravensdale told himself that he hadn't really seen the petrified body of a dead rat inside. The walls to either side of the restaurant's back door were sprayed with graffiti. The smells, thank God for small favors, were deadened by frost.

Upon stepping through the rear entrance, Ravensdale was stopped and searched by a crew-cut man wearing a sober dark suit. After losing possession of phone, wallet, and wristwatch, he was searched by a crew-cut man wearing crisp white and a red carnation in a lapel. Then by a crew-cut man wearing black leather, with flat, glossy eyes.

The maître d' stood by a stove, watching. Having run the gauntlet, Ravensdale arrowed toward him, asked hotly: 'These men work for the restaurant?'

'Private security. We're hosting an event.' A shrug, a hint of a sneer. 'I told you it was not a good time . . .'

'Off to a bad start, comrade. These gorillas are blocking escape routes, in case of emergency. And the outdoor area is not to be used for all-purpose dumping of trash.'

Raised eyebrows conveyed mild disbelief. 'We've never had a problem before.'

'Karlo cut corners. That's why he's gone. I'll need to see all past records of inspection reports.'

Walking the kitchen with the maître d' sticking close, Ravensdale scowled steadily, noting aloud inadequate ventilation, greasy floors, sharp corners, overloaded electrical sockets, soiled dish-towels. He counted nine flat tops in the kitchen. At least five remained at all times between him and the dining room. Civilians included three cooks, two waiters moving in and out, and the maître d'. Fifteen altogether, in addition, of course, to the five targets up front, and whatever guards and hangers-on attended them. And then there were the families back home: the sisters and brothers and children and wives . . .

The old Ravensdale would not have indulged this line of thought.

Drawing near the flap doors leading to the dining room, he paused to check the batteries in a smoke detector, sifting murmuring voices from the background noise of clinking silverware and cocktail jazz as he did so. Genrikh Volovich, the leader of the Balashikhiniski gang, was complaining about a shipment which had recently come through Pankisi Gorge. Grisha Chukin, of the Podolski, was suggesting that the Chechens took them all for fools. Aleksandr Vyshinsky, who had started as a *fartsovshchik* selling knock-off blue jeans and bootleg cigarettes on Moscow sidewalks, and was now considered a serious contender for the city's next mayor, was negotiating a trade: a share in Dmitri Tsereteli's lucrative MDMA trade for a slice of Vyshinsky's copper piping business, which although unglamorous could always be counted on to turn a tidy profit . . .

Ravensdale made himself move away from the flap doors, running a fingertip along a counter as if searching for dust.

The service bathroom was dirty. Wilting flowers filled a pencil vase beneath a sputtering fluorescent bulb. A notice on the wall proclaimed that 'EMPLOYEES MUST WASH HANDS BEFORE RETURNING TO WORK'. When Ravensdale stepped inside, the maître d' tried to follow. 'If you don't mind,' Ravensdale said.

Alone, he locked the door, dropped his pants, and settled down on to the toilet. Carefully, he worked the capsule free. Keeping the device concealed as much as possible in case of hidden cameras – you never knew – he flushed, rolled up his sleeves, and washed with soap and hot water. Then he unscrewed the capsule, found the needle, and punched through the tender white skin inside his left elbow. Naloxone entered his bloodstream in a hot rush. The used part of the capsule went into his front left-hand pocket.

The remaining half, containing aerosol etorphine, stayed concealed in his right palm. The synthetic opiate known to animal researchers as M99 caused respiratory paralysis, freezing the muscles of the heart and lungs. Death from hypoxia was nearly instantaneous. Efficacy was beyond question. When Spetsnaz commandos had pumped the substance into Dubrovka Theater in October of 2002, following the seizure of eight hundred and fifty hostages by Chechen separatists, one hundred theatergoers had perished along with the intended targets.

He rolled down his sleeves, fastened the cuffs, and reached to unlock the door. He was watching this moment from the future, from a safe well-lighted room he shared with Sofiya and his son, very far from here.

He stepped out into the kitchen and wandered back toward the flap doors.

The maître d' paced him. A waiter jostled past, opening the way to the dining room.

He triggered the capsule hidden in his palm.

Ol' Blue Eyes was inviting listeners to come fly with him. The maître d' was checking his watch. Something sizzled; the smell of pesto shrimp filled the kitchen. Aerosol etorphine, soundless and odorless, spread invisible deadly fingers. A droplet of sweat trickled down Ravensdale's temple. His testicles had drawn up tight. The urge to hold his breath was almost overpowering. But the naloxone would block his opiate receptors; he made himself draw a normal, easy breath. He was a man to whom killing came naturally, no matter how much he pretended otherwise. He was a husband and a father. He was a spy and a murderer. He was the old him and the new him and something else: another him still undiscovered. He was an animal – he could smell himself, a hot rank animal tang, his own brutish fear and excitement.

A waiter went down heavily, splashing pesto shrimp, and began convulsing. The maître d' spilled face-first across the greasy kitchen floor, cracking his jaw loudly against unyielding tile. The flat tops were collapsing too, like so many bowling pins: one, two, three, four, five, six, seven, eight, nine. Perfect strike.

Pocketing the capsule, Ravensdale pushed through the flap doors. From beneath a fallen flat top's coat he liberated a semi-automatic

Tokarev TT-33 pistol. He picked his way over corpses, some still jittering, and climbed three carpeted steps to the VIP area. The targets were already dead, expensive suits stained with expensive food. Faces mottled, sightless eyes staring blindly. Ravensdale shot them anyway: one, two, three, four, five head shots.

He picked up a linen napkin and, stepping over another corpse, went past the coat check and then out the front door. Cold fresh air hit him like a blessing. He turned down the sidewalk without hurrying, moving past busy and distracted Muscovites, wiping down the Tokarev and leaving it in a garbage can on the corner. He hailed a passing Sylphy – in Russia, any civilian vehicle becomes a gypsy cab in exchange for a few rubles – and gave the elderly man behind the wheel an address two blocks from his parked Jeep Commander.

As they pulled back on to the street, a muscle worked in his right cheek. Inside the pocket, he squeezed the spent half-capsule mechanically. His breath came fast and shallow. His testicles remained drawn up tight into his body, clenching.

A man does his best. His best is all he can do.

He set his jaw firmly, sat up very straight in the back of the Sylphy, and rode away from the restaurant without looking back.

NINE

MOIKA RIVER EMBANKMENT, SAINT PETERSBURG

The view through the window would have been of the Admiralty Building's gilded spire, had the glass been clean enough.

Inspektor Vlasov was kept waiting in an office furnished with blond wood, daguerreotype portraits of Lenin and Marx, and a chipped bowl of wrapped hard candies. After ten minutes he was fetched and led down a corridor to a heavy door, behind which he found a hastily-assembled war room: larger and higher-ceilinged than the office, but still relatively humble, and musty with smells of wet wool and stale tobacco.

Amidst younger men manning laptop computers and mobile phones, Inspektor Mikhail Bordachenko stood out. Six-four, with an athlete's shoulders barely contained beneath a straining sports coat, he towered over everyone else in the room, including Vlasov. His eyes were a vibrant hazel, his nose large and fleshy. 'So,' he said, guiding Vlasov to a quieter end of the room after shaking hands. 'It is an honor and a pleasure, sir, to welcome Moscow Sledkom—' *Sledstvennyi komitet,* Investigative Committee – 'to Pieter. Don't take this the wrong way, but I hope to send you happily on your way in the very near future.'

They pulled chairs out from a fading conference table lined with crème-colored telephones labeled VCh: *vysokochastoty* – high-frequency. Bordachenko proceeded to lay out a strategy along the lines Vlasov had expected. Having trumpeted the fugitive's capture, the Kremlin had now placed an embargo on news of her escape; therefore the use of *nashnik,* informants, would be strictly limited. But official agencies could pick up the slack, quietly and effectively. Police, military, and Investigative Committee agents had been watching transit hubs since early morning. Within the city, door-to-door sweeps had commenced, radiating outward from the girl's last known location near Demidov Bridge. Checkpoints had been put into place not only on streets but also on frozen canals and rivers. An impressive array of technical equipment (Bordachenko made an expansive gesture toward the young men and their laptops) was at their disposal. Photographs taken during the perp walk had been fed into state-of-the-art facial recognition software. Eighty nodal points of the assassin's face had been identified, a face print and 3D model constructed. Now the program was combing through vast amounts of footage gathered from countless security cams, drones, and mobile phones; any computer connected to the Internet could be remotely accessed without the owner's consent.

Vlasov lit a thin cigarette. 'Comprehensive,' he allowed. 'But if I may – the whole thing smacks somewhat of déjà vu. We should not find ourselves in this position at all.'

'In hindsight, we clearly underestimated her. But every factor must be taken into account. To all appearances, she seemed helpless.' Bordachenko's gaze did not waver. 'Rest assured; once the current situation has been resolved, heads will roll.'

Vlasov examined the glowing ember of his cigarette and said nothing.

'She is resourceful,' continued Bordachenko after a moment. 'But not in any condition that easily escapes notice. She's likely concussed from the incident on the M-10. On the run for over seventy-two hours, through bitter cold and harsh countryside. Broken ice on the Griboyedova suggests that she got a good soaking. Weak, dizzy, frightened, starving . . .'

'Perhaps frostbitten.' Vlasov smoked. 'Perhaps internally damaged.'

'Desperate. Getting off the streets will be her priority. She's hunkered down somewhere, out of sight.'

'Your city, Inspektor. Out of sight where?'

Bordachenko pulled at the tip of his fleshy nose with two fingers. 'Where does the tree hide best? In a forest.'

'The *besprizornye*?'

'My first thought. But it's too obvious. So she'll avoid it.'

They considered.

'Since escaping Moscow,' observed Vlasov, 'she has stowed away; she has latched on to an American tourist; she has stolen vehicles. But she has not tried to pass herself off as a native. Because her Russian is not fluent enough. Her knowledge of our culture is superficial. She cannot show up at a door and claim to be an old friend of an absent daughter.'

'So she's with foreigners like herself,' said Bordachenko. 'In a hotel.'

'Again, too obvious. We'll check hotels before anything.'

'A basement or an attic, then. Unknown to the true occupants of the residence.'

'Or she may have found someone she can threaten into silence. Someone isolated.'

'Or stupid. Or blind.'

'Or vulnerable. The American slut has seduced them.'

'Or greedy – she has bought their silence.'

A helicopter passed outside the window, rattling a loose pane in its frame.

'Concentrate on outcasts,' said Vlasov after a few moments. 'The fringe of society. Orphans, elderly, derelicts. Drunkards, foreigners. Anyone living alone. Also abandoned buildings, back alleys, heating grates.'

Bordachenko nodded pensively.

'We'll get her.' Vlasov funneled smoke out through flaring nostrils. 'She's just a girl with some set of *yaitsa*—' balls – 'far from home.'

VYBORG

Nikolai could work the remote control all by himself, just like a grown-up.

He restarted from the beginning his favorite episode of *Spokoynoy nochi, malyshi!*, in which the presenter, a pretty dark-haired lady, helped the puppets clean up their toys, and then together they screened

Adventures of Luntik. As he watched, he avoided turning his head to look at Mama, who slept on the floor at the other end of the living room.

He would leave her alone, he thought, and let her JUST SLEEP IT OFF. That was what she and Sasha were always telling each other to do. One would complain about a splintering headache or upset tummy, and the other would say JUST SLEEP IT OFF. The sick person would get left alone, and the one who was awake would yell at Nikolai to be quiet, didn't he know someone was sleeping, and when the sick person reappeared some time later, they would look pale and thin, but mostly better.

He watched the entire episode again. When the credits were rolling, he went to give Mama another once-over. Standing very close, right thumb hooked into his small mouth. She lay on her side, eyes closed. Her skin was the color of parchment. Something about her mouth seemed not quite right. It looked caved in, like a rotten piece of fruit. She held so still, he thought, that she didn't even seem to be breathing.

His eyes moved to the bottle lying on the floor beneath the coffee table. Her medicine, Mama called it, and the medicine-smell was very strong around her today.

Maybe he should try to give her another dose. Medicine made sick people feel better.

When he climbed down to retrieve the bottle, however, he saw that the last of the contents had already spilled out into the carpet. That was why the medicine-smell was so intense today, hanging over this part of the room in a cloud.

On hands and knees, inspecting the empty bottle, he noticed a gleam beneath the couch. Stretching out one arm, he managed to fish the item in question out into sunlight. It was a small plastic baggie, half-filled with chocolate drops. For the first time he became aware of his hunger – breakfast was often late, but never this late.

He stood again in front of Mama, holding the bag. After a few moments he began to sing lightly beneath his breath, hoping to wake her. *'The little bird cooks porridge,'* he sang tunelessly. *'She gave it to this one, she gave it to this one, she gave it to this one . . . but none for you! Why? You did not bring water. You did not chop fire-wood. There is nothing for you . . .'*

Mama didn't stir.

Looking straight into her face, he deliberately opened the bag. Dipping a finger inside, he dared her to wake up and scold him. *Kolya,* she would snap, *just because I'm sleeping doesn't mean you should eat candy you find on the floor for breakfast – can't you see that I'm VERY SICK?*

But she didn't move, even as he slipped a chocolate into his mouth and slowly chewed. It wasn't chocolate. It tasted like dirty socks and made his head spin unpleasantly, and after a few seconds he considered spitting it out. He chewed a few more times anyway. 'Yuck,' he said then and spat the half-melted glob on to the floor. Now his empty stomach was roiling. 'I've got a SPLINTERING HEADACHE,' he declared, 'and an upset tummy.'

No response from Mama.

He kicked the glob out of sight beneath the couch.

Leaving the baggie on the table, he went back to the TV. Now his head was throbbing, his stomach flipping miserably. A clench, a stitching cramp. He groaned.

He restarted the episode again from the beginning.

But he had trouble concentrating. Maybe because he had just watched the episode so many times in a row, and of course he'd already seen it a thousand times before. Or maybe because he was hungry. When you were hungry, Mama said, you didn't have energy. You had to keep your tank filled with gas, just like a car. Then you could run and play and jump. He had never before been so low on energy that he couldn't even watch TV. But as the pretty dark-haired lady helped the puppets clean up their toys, the screen seemed to turn gauzy. He daydreamed for a while – rockets slipping through the void of space, cosmonauts drifting on the ends of tethers – and when he came back to reality the puppets had already finished screening *Adventures of Luntik* and the credits were rolling again.

His stomach felt better now – just very empty. He almost wished Sasha was around, even though he never wished Sasha was around. Sasha might know how to make Mama feel better. At the very least, Sasha could give Nikolai some breakfast.

He cast a guilty look over his shoulder and then, leaving the television on its blank blue screen, went into the kitchen. For a time, he looked longingly at the cereal shelf. Nobody knew that he could reach it by himself. But then Mama would find the box half-empty, and he would get into trouble.

Instead, he helped himself to a juice cup from the refrigerator – he was allowed to help himself to drinks. He went into the bathroom and used the potty, getting a little pee-pee on his pants, but not too much. He flushed the toilet and washed his hands like a good boy. He went back to the living room, to gaze wistfully again at

Mama, hoping that his dutiful following of the rules would have changed something. It seemed to make sense. If he had somehow made her sick – by being bad, no doubt – then being good should make her better.

But she still didn't move.

His belly growled.

He went into his bedroom and fetched an armful of stuffed animals. Back before the TV, he lined them up – piglet, crow, dog, hare, and bear – and then sat, awarding himself a position of honor in the center.

He was crying now. Lower lip turned down; hot tears burning his cheeks.

Everything would be OK. No matter what he had done wrong to make Mama sick, everything would be OK. It always had been before. Eventually, she would wake up and make him breakfast and give him kisses and hugs and tell him she loved him and everything would be fine. Just a matter of time. Just had to let her SLEEP IT OFF.

His eyes dallied on the small baggie on the coffee table, filled with chocolate that was not chocolate. Maybe, he thought, he had just gotten a bad piece. Maybe another piece would taste better.

But he should be good. Being good was the way to make Mama better.

Snuffling, he restarted the episode from the beginning.

SAINT PETERSBURG

A group of men crossed a footbridge above a frozen canal.

After regaining cobblestones, Captain Nikita Loginov paused to get his bearings. Then, stamping his feet against the cold, he delivered orders: dispatching two men to check hotels upriver, and two down; two pairs to engage the derelicts and runaways who squatted beneath bridges and in alleyways behind cafés; a trio to visit the docks, to interview captains of restaurant boats, the only ships out on the frozen waters; four of his most stalwart and untemptable to visit restaurants and pubs (not for nothing was Saint Petersburg considered the beer, as well as the crime, capital of Russia); half a dozen to sweep through nearby tram, Metro, and trolleybus stations. With his remaining men he prepared to embark on further doorstepping, a process he would lead personally.

As the sun made its foreshortened trek across the winter sky, similar scenarios played out in every neighborhood in the city. Doors were pounded, photographs proffered, questions posed. North of Nevsky, the efforts encompassed public squares and gardens. On windy

Vasilevsky Island, they included the eighteenth-century campus of Saint Petersburg State University. As every one of Petersburg's five million inhabitants could not be visited, lists of likely suspects – the fringe of society – were assembled from interviews with postal and sanitation workers, meter readers and bartenders.

During the course of the afternoon, one hundred and twelve young women were taken into custody. The thirty most promising were delivered in person to the war room in Sledkom Headquarters on the Moika, where they were interviewed at length. Of these thirty, eight were deemed suspicious enough to be passed for further attention to an inner sanctum.

Here the young ladies found themselves facing a curious pair: a hazel-eyed giant of a man who gave as his name Inspektor Bordachenko, and a smaller man with short blond hair and a neatly waxed mustache, who offered no clue as to his identity, and in fact said nothing at all. By seven p.m. the last of the young women had delivered a detailed statement, convinced the pair that she did not merit further incarceration, and been released.

TAURIDA GARDENS, 7:25 P.M.

'Evening, comrade. Quiet night?'

'Could be worse. Just two brawls so far. But the night's still young. What are you drinking?'

'I'm on duty, comrade. You trying to corrupt me?'

'Sorry, sir . . . What can I do for you, then?'

'Have you seen this girl?'

'No, sir. We don't get many pretty young things in there. They know better. It usually gets rough for them.'

'Anything out of the ordinary? Regulars who haven't shown up, like that?'

'No, sir.'

'You'll keep your eyes open, though.'

'Yes, sir, you've got my word. Something to do with that terrorist out on M-10?'

'Mind your business, comrade . . . and keep those eyes wide open.'

KUPCHINO, 8:00 P.M.

'Cold night, eh?'

'That's what the flask is for, officer. Care for a nip?'

'And pick up your herpes? Not likely . . . Now, come into the light, buddy, and take a look at this picture. Seen this girl?'

'Not a chance. The girls who come through here don't look nearly so . . . clean.'

'Look closer. She'll have dirtied up a bit since this was taken. It would be just in the past day.'

'Haven't seen her. Only new girl's a *chornye* from Ichkeria. Dark but sweet, if you take my meaning. The darker the berry, I find, the—'

'Ask around. Whoever turns her in gets a nice reward. One thousand rubles, out of my own pocket.'

'I'll ask around, officer. Promise.'

VETERANOV LIGOVO, 8:30 P.M.

'Petro! Fancy seeing you out here. And jimmying your way into a locked car . . .'

'Lost my keys, sergeant, I swear to God.'

'Don't try me, Petro. Take a look at this picture. Seen this girl?'

'Never in my life. Wouldn't mind running into her, though. I could teach her a thing or two.'

'If you *did* run into her, you'd give me a call. Otherwise I might decide you were trying to steal this nice vehicle and run you in.'

'Sergeant! What about old times?'

'It's been a long fucking day, Petro . . .'

'OK, forget old times. I'll keep my eyes peeled. All right?'

SOUTH OF NEVSKY, 9:00 P.M.

Cassie stole glances from the corner of her eye.

The old woman was preparing tea by the stove. Seen from the back, she very nearly described the shape of a pear. After setting the kettle on a burner, she tidied up: whistling as she worked, affecting casual disinterest. But who knew what was actually going on inside that whiskered old skull?

As the water boiled, the babushka set out loose chunks of sugar to be held between the teeth when the beverage was sipped. Settling carefully into a chair, she lit the latest in an endless chain of fragrant, vaguely-anesthetic Djarum Blacks. A smile creased the seamed face, rearranging the wrinkles. 'Still hungry, dear?'

Cassie shook her head.

'So after the tea, you'll lie down and have another good rest. And I won't hear any argument.'

The babushka was old. Solidly built, but old; she would not put up much fight.

'You should see the look on your face.' The woman chuckled. 'As if you're considering murder, just to shut me up. That's the danger of robbing a lonely old lady, isn't it? You might get killed with kindness. My name's Mariya, by the way. Masha, to my friends.'

Cassie said nothing. Her head was thumping again. The tide of fatigue was rising.

'Not a talker, eh? That's all right; I can do enough talking for the both of us. When you've had enough of my voice, you just go lie down. I won't take offense. My husband did it often enough. Ivan, his name was. Masha, he would say, you could talk the ear off a brass monkey . . .'

With the Russian character, Quinn had said, *there is always more beneath the surface than meets the eye.*

Through an open doorway Cassie watched the silhouetted figure of the woman, slouched dozing in the damask chair.

Russian character encompasses European character, but it origi-nates in the Far East. Everything you think you know is therefore slightly, crucially, different. Russian mentality is not based on what we consider common sense. Spirituality trumps religion. Sophistication trumps formality. And suspicion of authority is deeply ingrained in a way that you – even you – cannot ever truly comprehend.

Before Cassie had removed herself, Mariya had talked at length – the propensity to ramble had not been exaggerated – about her dead husband, her arthritis, her problems with the tax collector, her favorite recipes, her tendency to overstock on dry goods. The old woman's loneliness was nothing less than pathetic. And yet it was a lucky thing. Food and a day's rest had paid some immediate dividends; the fever had broken, and Cassie thought she might manage to keep all ten toes. But now she needed real, sustained sleep. And until she could bring herself to throttle the life from the old woman, the babushka's loneliness offered her best chance at shelter. Suspicion of authority, solitude, senility, spirituality, all of the above . . . Who cared? Just so long as the tea and sympathy kept coming.

The radio murmured quietly, ceaselessly. The announcer reported a fire at a psychiatric hospital in Kolomna, a rising wave of anti-American demonstrations, a policy overhaul at the Central Bank, a brazen and fatal attack on five prominent Muscovites, one of whom had been considered a leading contender for the city's next mayor, at a popular restaurant in the middle of the day. No mention was made of her escape. Because that would embarrass the Kremlin, she thought. They would be looking for her on the sly – but officially, she remained in detention.

Maybe saving face would be enough for them. Maybe if she kept her head down for a couple of weeks, they would move on to other things.

Carpets and kilim hulked in corners like pillowy fortifications. The old woman dozed, propped in her chair like a sentry. The bedroom was cozy, agreeably redolent of cooking. Cassie could almost feel safe here.

Almost.

Even safer, she thought, to remove the old woman, leave nothing to chance.

Am I capable of that? Rodion Raskolnikov had wondered. *Can it be, can it be, that I shall really take an axe, that I shall strike her on the head, split her skull open . . . that I shall tread in the sticky warm blood, blood . . . with the axe . . . Good God, can it be?*

She blinked sleepily. The bed was comfortable, the flannel night-gown Mariya had lent her warm and soft. Eventually, her eyes closed and she slept – a deep, dreamless sleep.

THE MOSCOW MARRIOTT GRAND

'Sean?' An outthrust hand. 'Bill Benson! Christ – I don't even want to *think* about how long it's been.'

Ravensdale had never seen the man before in his life. He was about thirty-five, starting to go soft around the middle, but still clean-jawed and sharp-eyed. Clasping Ravensdale's hand, he leaned in and added with no particular emphasis: 'Andy's waiting.'

He led Ravensdale out of the lobby, through a sea of perfumed and bejeweled women, chattering about the late-night sushi joint they just had to try. Climbing into a taxi, he gave the driver an address two kilometers away. Several blocks later, he called an abrupt stop. They walked the length of an industrial side-street; he hailed a passing Combi. They rode another ten blocks, past round-the-clock construction projects lit by sodium glare. In the shadows waited a parked car, a black Opel. The man produced keys. They slipped inside and drove wordlessly to the eastern border of Sokolniki Park.

'He wants a game of chess,' remarked 'Bill Benson' as he discharged his passenger.

Before stepping over the park's threshold, Ravensdale cast a cautious glance around. At this hour on a Friday morning, Sokolniki's daytime crowd – joggers, tourists, and shoppers visiting the cash-and-carry warehouses – was nowhere to be seen. The night owls – homeless and *besprizornye,* dealers and junkies – circled the park warily, knowing better than to go inside after dark.

Ravensdale went inside. He crunched down a shaded path, past empty fast food stands, an ornamental fountain, a small dilapidated Ferris wheel. Built in 1931 as the city's second 'Park of Culture and Rest', the retreat during spring and summer was dazzling emerald, the color of Sofiya's eyes. Now it was buried beneath several centimeters of pristine snow. Narrow trails wound through thick, heavily shadowed woods of birch, maple, and elm.

Reaching the deserted central pavilion he paused again, squaring his shoulders, taking the lay of the land. A nearby Holiday Inn, white lit with green, towered over the treetops. But within the park was no sign of another living soul. In a small chess corner cloaked by snow-leaning branches, a handful of tables featuring built-in chessboards stood empty. A lone ivory clock left behind looked forlorn.

Dry branches rustled behind him; Ravensdale turned. 'Black?' asked Andrew Fletcher.

Ravensdale nodded.

'You sure? The Marriott's staked top to bottom.'

'I'm sure.'

'Let's walk.'

They walked: through patchwork shadow, straining to hear indications of human presence nearby. With the naloxone still lingering in his system, Ravensdale's opiate receptors remained blocked. He felt hypersensitive, tetchy. Even the wind stung.

'Like old times,' said Fletcher, less sardonically than one might have expected. 'Saw your *strelka* in the news. So where's our girl?'

Ravensdale made a two-fingered gesture: a bird flying away.

Creases of irony around Fletcher's mouth deepened. 'Tsoi double-crossed us.'

'No, she did it on her own. She's good.'

Distractedly, Fletcher took out a pack of cigarettes – Merit Lights, his old brand; did anyone, Ravensdale wondered, ever really quit smoking? – and lit one, puffing hard, inexpertly evening out the burn. 'So we're fucked.'

'Not necessarily. Honor dictates that he repay his debts. This afternoon I conducted *mokriye dela*—' wet affairs – 'on his behalf. At great personal risk, in such a way that the *muzhik* on the street can vouch that he wasn't involved. He owes me.'

'Honor among thieves.' Fletcher sounded skeptical.

'His man is in Petersburg, trying to make things right. I suggest we join him.'

'Why?'

Ravensdale looked at him narrowly. Tamped down his temper. For too long had the man held himself above the fray, letting others make the sausage. 'Whatever it takes, eh, Andy?'

'That's right. But what good will it do to have us there?'

Ravensdale grinned darkly. 'Because by now she's realized that you used her. She'll want payback. And that, my friend . . . that is how we are going to get her.'

SOUTH OF NEVSKY, SAINT PETERSBURG

Knocks thundered, jarring her from sleep.

Suddenly, she was upright in bed, ready to bolt. By then Mariya was out of her chair and the visitors were announcing themselves: '*Sledkom!* Open up!'

Through the open doorway, Mariya's eyes found hers. The old woman gestured down the hall, toward the rear of the cottage, and called in a cracked voice: 'I'm not decent.'

Cassie stole into the moonlit hallway, nightgown shushing around her ankles. At the far end, she faced a choice between a laundry nook and a closed door. The door led to a large closet, jammed with rolled-up and haphazardly piled carpets. Atop the nearest heap lay a half-unrolled kilim. She stepped forward, shut the door, clambered on to the kilim, and began to wind herself inside.

'Yes?' she heard the old woman say.

'Have you seen this girl?'

Cassie kept turning inside the kilim, pinning her arms tightly against her sides. She moved until she could go no farther. Then she could only wait, inhaling the odors of mothballs and slightly rotten fabric, feeling rough bristles against her cheek.

'Take your foot out of my door,' Mariya was saying.

'Answer the question first.'

'Are you NKVD? Because—'

'Madame, you are speaking with a Senior Investigator of the Ministry of Internal Affairs. Might I recommend that it would be in your best interest—'

'My best friend's son is an attorney. And his sister-in-law is a respected journalist. Might I recommend that it would be in *your* best interest to take your foot from my door.'

A long, fraught pause. Then came the sounds of boots cracking against wood, a door bursting open. Mariya gasped. Someone laughed crudely. Footsteps pounded into the cottage.

Cassie went cold.

If they had dogs, she thought, she was finished.

They thudded through the house, audibly overturning the mattress on the bed, the damask chair in the parlor. Books were swept from shelves. A piece of china shattered, very high and clear. The door to the closet creaked open. Something solid – the stock of a gun? – thumped into the kilim just beside Cassie's left ear. A mote of dust came free, tickling her nose. She bit the inside of her lip venomously.

The door creaked closed. Footsteps pounded away. The nascent sneeze prickled and itched in her nostrils; she fought it down.

'Next time,' a sarcastic voice told Mariya, 'don't fuck with us. Or you'll be sorry.'

Boots tromped from the cottage. Moments later, an imperious thudding sounded on the next door down the block. '*Sledkom!* Open up!' This time, it seemed, the homeowner obeyed without complaint.

Half a minute passed.

The closet door creaked open again.

'All clear,' said Mariya, and Cassie sneezed explosively.

ULITSA VARVARKA, MOSCOW

Sofiya Kirov looked desolately out the window, at a vacant lot nine flights below.

Beneath moonlight, snow blew in a lacy haze. A gray cat trotted along a splintered fence-top. A rusty shovel abandoned after some abortive attempt at construction leaned up against the fence, beside a cracked plastic child's sled. Otherwise, there was nothing to see.

She let the curtain fall closed again. A surreptitious tug, and the sash came free. Negligently, she twisted her wrist, gathering the ribbon up into her hand.

The door remained closed, the deadbolt locked.

Abstractedly, she wandered back to the bed. Spilling down again, she hid the sash beneath her body. A desiccated, despairing exhalation for the benefit of any hidden cameras. Woe is me, helpless woman.

She closed her eyes. Concealing the action beneath her body, she fed the sash up into the loose-hanging gray sleeve of the *zek*'s uniform.

When the moment came, she vowed, she would do it.

For Dima.

But she did not let herself think of Dima.

Instead, she thought about the man who brought her food: two solid meters of muscle sheathed in fat. He held himself in an alert, tense, vigilant way that threatened physical violence. A red dragon tattoo wound around a throat which looked tough as gristle. Strangling the man with the sash would not be easy.

Still, she thought, it was preferable to the other option: taking the light bulb from the goose-necked lamp, shattering the glass, and using that to slit his jugular. Easier to strangle the life from a man, she guessed, than to slash it away. In point of fact, she had never done either. She had come into the FSB via a desk job, working white collar crime. Upon showing an unexpected flair for seduction – first with her boss, and then with her bosses' boss – she had been promoted to field operations. Then she had been filched by counter-intelligence. In the years since, she had tumbled many a worthy adversary into bed, but nowhere along the line had she taken a man's life.

But when the moment came, she would do it.

For Dima.

But she did not let herself think of Dima.

She had not let herself think of Dima since the day, eleven months before, that she had bundled him up and headed out to the playground and heard the black van pulling into the lot and, glancing over, felt a whisper of the old apprehension, and then dismissed it – a woman in her circumstances had never been entirely free of apprehension – and gone back to enjoying the fresh air, to watching her son move a Tonka truck around the cold sandbox, to appreciating the lengthy hours of good sunlight even in February. And so they had surrounded her, silent and stealthy as death itself, until at last she'd realized what was happening, but by then it had been too late, and they had picked her up, clamping the sweet-smelling rag across her nose and mouth, carrying her bodily, kicking and biting, to the black van; and she had heard Dima screaming, and it had been at that moment that she had started shutting down, she had started dying, and now she did not think of Dima, now she never let herself think of Dima at all.

And all through the half-day flight which had followed, hooded and handcuffed on the cold steel floor of what seemed like a cargo plane, she had not thought of Dima. All through the ensuing UAZ ride over wild mountainous terrain, as the temperature plummeted to depths that killed men like insects, she had not thought of Dima. Eventually, they had taken off the black hood, because by then it had no longer mattered. By then there had been nothing to see except mountains and night. Then they had reached a valley filled with derricks and searchlights, guard towers and animal pens and motor pools, escarpments and ditches, latrines and barracks and guard houses. Two Kamov Ka-60s resting on a helipad near a huge drum of pressurized avgas; a Mil Mi-28 circling overhead, searchlight arcing. Being dragged over the threshold, through the gate, taking stock of her surroundings, she had understood immediately where they had brought her. This was the very essence of Nowhere. This was the place she would die.

She had been dragged to an office in the prison camp's center. Two caged light bulbs flickering in the ceiling; a dinged-up metal desk set diagonally in one corner. Atop the desk, a photograph of a cadaverous white-blond man, in full ceremonial military garb and red beret, standing beside Russia's president. Small windows set high in three of the four walls. In the fourth wall, above the desk, the mounted head of a small animal. Not a sheep, not a goat . . . Her gorge had hitched convulsively. Gray, shrunken, with wispy withered hair, the human head had lost both gender and age; it might have belonged to man or woman, adult or child.

The door leading outside had opened again, letting in the rattling whine of a generator. Slowly, the man had paced into the center of the office. White-blond hair standing on end; thin, petulant mouth. He had worn a greatcoat over what looked like pajamas. But his military bearing had been flawless, his professionalism undeniable. He'd absorbed Sofiya for a moment in silence. Then he'd reached out a hand, and she'd managed not to flinch. Gently, he had rotated her face, first left and then right. Standing straight, he had considered her down the aquiline line of his nose.

'Welcome,' he had said.

And all during the months of hell that had followed, she had not thought of Dima. As she'd learned to recognize the eager expression on the white-blond man's face which presaged another round of *pytka*, she had not thought of Dima. Every time he'd taken out the bottle of conductive lanolin used to intensify the electric current, the splints used to create a flawless and finely-hewn agony, the splintery board and bucket of ice-cold water used to simulate the experience of drowning, she had not thought of Dima. Eventually, she had signed the confession that he kept waving in front of her. There had been no point in resisting further. She had already died inside. Then the torture had ended, and she had joined the regular prison population: a different kind of torture. Fourteen-hour days of hard labor, mining ore by hand, inhaling punishing lungfuls of dust, digging with crude pickaxes the same mass graves they would end up inhabiting.

And even when the flight to Siberia had occurred in reverse – when they had taken her from the barracks in the middle of the night, hooded her and cuffed her, and loaded her on to another cold steel floor of another cargo plane – even as she had been unloaded here in Moscow, driven in darkness and syrupy fear through silent late-night streets, stuffed into the cramped grimy apartment under armed guard – even through this she had not allowed herself to think of Dima. Even as a glimmer of hope had returned – they would not have brought her here, after all, just to murder her; not when murder had been so easy, such a natural consequence of everyday life, in the camps—

(unless they wanted to make an example of you, show off your ruin, this new Vozhd)

(so you'd best get yourself out of here, my dear, and not wait around to see)

—even then she had not thought of Dima.

And she would not think of Dima now.

She would think only of the sash in her sleeve. The corded muscular neck with the dragon tattoo. The amount of pressure which might prove necessary.

She would think now of death, not of life.

Death, so that at last there could be life again.

Opening her eyes, she stared at the ceiling, and clutched the sash tightly, and waited eagerly for the chance to commit her first murder.

TEN

SOUTH OF NEVSKY

At a few minutes past noon, the old woman fixed a simple lunch of buns, mushrooms, and the thick noodle soup called *tokmach.*

As they ate at the kitchen table, the radiator twanged, the radio murmured. A dog barked on the street outside. A garbage truck farther up the block went noisily about its rounds. It was the soundtrack, thought Cassie, of a normal life. If she didn't watch herself, she would relax into it, letting down her guard – the very mistake she'd made with Quinn.

Once, she had lived for almost a year at a home in South Orange, New Jersey. Her foster parents there, Maddie and David Gunther, had been warm and funny; she a software engineer, he a real estate dealer. Their home had been a study in fawn-colored suburban generic, with beige carpeting, taupe Formica countertops, and plastic slip-cases covering the furniture. Some of Cassie's warmest post-Daddy memories involved sitting with the Gunthers on those dryly crackling plastic slip-cases, talking about SATs and extra-curriculars and student loans. Tedious things. But also comforting things. *Normal* things. Then one night Maddie had worked late; David had put down more wine than usual over dinner and developed a case of wandering hands. The next morning Cassie had crept out of the house before sunrise, heading to the bus station and New York City. Lesson learned. For her, there was no such thing as normality. Everything she cared for slipped right through her fingers . . .

'Like old times,' said Mariya around a mouthful of bun. She waved into the kitchen corners, where fragments of broken china still waited to be swept up. 'Never thought I'd miss it. I lived in fear of it; we all did. The knock at the door, the jackbooted thugs. The Black Marias – that's what we called the vans that brought you to the camps. But let's be honest. Even then we got a thrill out of it – bucking the system.'

Plumbing hissed behind walls; the radio droned soporifically. Cassie picked up a third bun, bit into heavy potato filling.

'I re-copied *The Master and The Margarita* by hand, my dear, no fewer than six times. Bitched about every word, too. That cheap carbon paper; ruined everything it touched. But nobody was holding a gun to my head.' A phlegmy chortle. 'To this day, I bet, I could quote you the entire book without getting a single word wrong. "Didn't you know that manuscripts don't burn?" Oh, but life is funny. I couldn't tell you what we had for breakfast this morning. But could I recite that book in its entirety, although I haven't read it for forty years? No question.'

The old woman paused. Absently, she lit a Djarum Black. When she spoke again, her voice was lower and slower. 'It was Ivan who got me into it.' She rubbed dry lips with one gnarled thumb. 'Always one to tip over the apple cart, my Ivan. Well, but it was only the right thing to do. You cannot imagine, I suppose, a state that bends over backwards to ruin the best of its own people. But we lived it. Every day.' She chased a black grin with a drag from the cigarette.

'Needless to say, my parents didn't approve of the match. Here I was, a cultured lady of the city; I fancied myself Kitty Alexandrova. Ivan was a troublemaker. A rapscallion. And a humble farmboy to boot, who grew up working a *kolkhoz*. But I married for love, of course. Never any question in my mind but that I would marry for love. Not that there weren't times I didn't regret it. Flat on my back in Vosturallag, one night, on a cold dirty cot, getting raped by a guard . . . And then, just a few weeks later, realizing that I was late. *Uvy*.' She shrugged and for a moment seemed about to laugh. 'Having the baby would have improved my life in the camp. The father might have taken me under his wing, finding me softer work. Sometimes women with child, *mamki*, were even given amnesties. But I did not want to have the wrong baby, for the wrong reasons, by the wrong father. I wanted to wait for Ivan. Sometimes you don't realize, when you're young, that a chance only comes around once in life. It's my greatest regret, never having had children.'

Cassie said nothing.

'Going through official channels to end the pregnancy was out of the question. My request might have been denied. Even if the authorities granted it, the father might have interfered. So in the end I took it upon myself. Brave, but foolish. I was young. Thought I knew everything. A handful of nails, a moment of determination, and—' The cigarette moved eloquently. 'There was a great deal of internal bleeding. I barely survived. But in the end, it did the trick.' Another shrug. 'You did what you had to do.'

Quiet, except for the murmuring radio, an advertisement now for auto insurance.

'Most of them, you know, were absolutely innocent. Not me. But most of the others. You could get thrown into the camps for telling a joke, for hearing a joke, for *thinking* of a joke. For saying that the sky was blue, that up was not down. If your neighbor wanted to fuck your husband and wanted you out of the way – watch out! One morning you would wake up and find yourself accused. The question of guilt was determined by the fact of your arrest. That's how Beria put it, and he should have known. And if you tried to argue, there was evidence of sedition. Off you went! And if you could not adjust, if you could not endure, you perished. Simple as that. No place for weakness. The labor was back-breaking: timber and coal. The diseases were terrible. The food was never enough. You were reduced to eating rats and garbage. You could shit yourself to death as easily as breathe. *Dokhodyagi*, they called us, the walking dead. Whatever principles one had, they vanished in a heartbeat. You turned against each other.'

She was gazing off into space, as if reading tea leaves only she could see. Suddenly, her head turned, and for an instant her eyes met Cassie's. 'If you ask me,' she said, 'this is why your Blakely was a hero. Because an outside enemy can always be fought. But once the rot takes hold inside . . .' Quickly, she looked away. 'Feh. Listen to me go. "For the love of God," Ivan used to say, "a true lady knows when to shut up and look pretty." Well; you can't say I didn't warn you.'

Cassie said nothing.

'Anyway. We've got to finish our sweeping. And fix that lock; they busted it. And I was thinking: if you could stay a bit longer, I could find other ways to take advantage of that strong young back. There's an outdoor market every weekend, you know. Once upon a time, my handiwork was in great demand. Now, you see, the kilim just pile up. Think about it. But first, give me a hand. These dishes aren't going to clean themselves.'

MOIKA RIVER EMBANKMENT

Inspektor Vlasov clawed for his phone. 'Vlasov.'

'Inspektor.' A moment of disorientation; then he identified the voice as belonging to the American, Ravensdale. 'I'm in Petersburg. Come meet me at the US consulate. *Kak mazho ckopee.*' ASAP.

A flare of anger – was Vlasov now at the man's beck and call? But the connection was already dead.

He pulled a hand down his face, levered off the camp bed. A quick toilette and he was on his way, making an excuse to Bordachenko (an 'intriguing lead') and boarding a *marshrutka*, a shared taxi, heading east alongside the sleeping ice-covered River Neva.

Wan daylight illuminated vast facades of gray stone interspersed with peach and lime. To the south-east, the dome and bell tower of Transfiguration Cathedral peeked sparkling above slanted rooftops. Truth be told, thought Vlasov as he rode, the city was far more enchanting than Moscow. Founder Peter the Great, the most far-seeing of czars, had not been afraid to leave behind the cold dark medieval ways accepted by most Russians as their due, to embrace Europe and move unencumbered into the future.

Inspektor Piotr Vlasov shared with his namesake this Eurocentric inclination. Like so many others, he had grown up a victim of the gray Soviet malaise – he was old enough to remember hoarding cheap brown soap, standing in line for hours just to get some rough toilet paper, staying up late listening to short-wave radios, hoping to hear on the BBC or Radio Liberty a snatch of a Beatles tune ('the belch of Western culture,' according to the Ministry of Propaganda). But when all this was finished, when the girl had been recaptured and the numbered account unlocked, Vlasov would move west and never look back. The French Riviera. He had visited once and fallen in love. There he could grow happily fat and old, indulging in fine food and expensive clothing and soft beds and rare tobaccos and high-stakes gambling and pretty women. The days would be warm and mellow, the nights long and sultry.

Midday traffic was heavy; the four-kilometer trip from the Moika took half an hour. At last the *marshrutka* turned on to embassy-rich Furshtatskaya Ulitsa. The American consulate was four stories, with a priapic American flag thrusting between ornate balconies above a tidy courtyard, and a Marine guard out front wearing crisp dress blue.

After submitting to a search, Vlasov accepted a badge and followed an escort into an elevator. The hallway into which they emerged was thickly carpeted, lined with doors, heavy with silence. They walked past flower arrangements and US Great Seals and furled American flags. They entered a conference room that was cleaner than the Sledkom war room and sleeker. A large monitor was mounted on one wall, at a right angle to a picture window overlooking a balcony. A row of clocks hung opposite, displaying the time in Tokyo, Paris, Stockholm, Beijing, Madrid, and Washington DC.

Sitting beside Ravensdale at a burnished walnut table was another American – sandy widow's peak, boyishly cleft chin, manicured fingernails. After a moment Vlasov placed him as Andrew Fletcher, the former chief of the CIA's Moscow Station. Fletcher gave the impression of having just come from an afternoon at a yacht club. He had never hoarded cheap brown soap, thought Vlasov, nor stood in line waiting for toilet paper.

'Close the door, Inspektor, have a seat. Thank you for coming so quickly. Julian Quinn; Senior Inspektor Piotr Vlasov, of the Investigative Committee. Inspektor Vlasov; Julian Quinn – a trusted associate from home.'

Vlasov shook the man's hand, said nothing about the alias. The palm was silky. The man smelled lightly of sandalwood and rose water.

'Inspektor Vlasov,' Ravensdale told the man he called Quinn, 'is our contact within Pieter Sledkom. He has the influence to get things done.'

They sat. Ravensdale took a moment to get his thoughts in order.

He pulled an ashtray close, lit a cigarette. 'We have reason to believe,' he said then, deliberately, 'that should Mister Quinn's presence in Pieter become known, our quarry might find the prospect of . . . making contact . . . irresistible.'

Vlasov said nothing.

'And so it would behoove us, once we've put appropriate measures into place, to make certain that his presence *does* become known. Also to broadcast that, after arriving as a special ambassador, he will not remain safely inside the consulate. Quite the opposite: he'll move regularly between quarters here and Sledkom HQ, where he'll lend a personal hand with your investigation. An unprecedented gesture of cooperation and goodwill between our two great nations. Of course, this means lifting the embargo on news of her escape.'

'*Za druzhbu myezhdu narodami*,' said Fletcher dryly. *To friendship between nations.*

Vlasov chewed on the inside of his cheek. 'The Kremlin will never sanction it.'

'Let me handle the Kremlin. Can you get Bordachenko on board?'

'And how, may I ask, will you "handle" the Kremlin?'

'I have a friend.'

Both Fletcher and Vlasov looked at Ravensdale, who casually spat out a wayward flake of tobacco.

'Listen. We want her. You want her. Bordachenko wants her. This is how we are going to get her. A well-publicized convoy moving between here and Sledkom, twice a day – morning and night – until she takes the bait. Undercover agents and snipers all along the route. But we're out of our home territory, Inspektor. The lion's share of the manpower will need to come from you.'

'From Pieter Sledkom, you mean.'

'That is what I mean. So I ask again: if I handle the Kremlin, can you handle Bordachenko?'

Several moments passed. The Inspektor slowly nodded. 'Not without promise,' he concluded. 'I can try.'

VYBORG

Nikolai lay awake, picturing the box of Kosmostars sitting on the cereal shelf in the darkened kitchen.

He shifted uneasily in his bed. His lips worked soundlessly. Tears stood in his eyes.

He must not take the cereal. He must not take the cereal. He must not take the cereal.

He left the bed and went into the kitchen. Tongue creeping from one corner of his mouth, he dragged the step stool to the light switch. He switched on the overhead, then spent a moment pondering. Behind him, illumination spilled into the living room. Mama was still SLEEPING IT OFF.

Towing the stool across the floor again, he climbed to the cereal shelf. Scared, guilty, but most of all hungry, he took down the box of Kosmostars. Just one handful – and nobody need ever know—

But the cereal proved too delicious, his hunger too great. Standing on the stool, he wolfed down one handful after another. Only when the box was empty did he look around, shamefacedly, at the scattered fallen pieces on the floor testifying to his transgression.

He replaced the box, got down on hands and knees, and ate cereal off the linoleum. Then he took his juice cup from the refrigerator and drained it.

But he was still hungry.

His mind turned to the chocolate-that-was-not-chocolate. Bad enough, though, that he had eaten the cereal without permission. Eating the candy would just compound the damage. Only if he ate some supper, some *real* supper, something that would make him grow big and strong, would Mama not be angry when she woke up.

After shooting an aching glance toward the living room, he climbed back on to the stool. In a cabinet he found a cardboard box of noodles. Tongue poking again from the corner of his mouth, he tried to recall exactly how Mama did this. She put the noodles in a pot, added water, and put the pot on the stove. Turned on the burner. Told Nikolai to play a little longer until supper was done. Then the noodles were ready. She poured them into a sieve, draining the water. She dumped them on to a plate and then put butter and salt on top.

Simple enough.

He found a pot beneath the sink, tipped the box into it, added water, set it on the burner. Found the knob and twisted. A *tick-tick-tick* came from the stove. So far, so good.

He went back to the refrigerator and took out the butter. Then he found the salt and set both on to the ledge by the sink. After some searching, he found the sieve and set it beside the salt and butter. He spent a moment looking at his handiwork and then nodded, satisfied.

Now he had only to wait.

He went into the living room, avoiding looking toward both his mother and the chocolate-that-was-not-chocolate. Usually, he played with his toys while supper was cooking. It would be best, he thought, to do everything just the way he usually did. He assembled his stuffed animals and toy rocket ship. Everybody went to the moon, and while they were there some aliens landed. The aliens were bad guys who shot lasers. In the end, piglet snuck up behind them and bit one on the leg, scaring the aliens back into their flying saucer. The good guys won. Everybody was happy. They had a party to celebrate, with lots of cake and soda.

Supper should be done by now.

He returned to the kitchen, very proud of himself now for what he was doing – the biggest-boy thing yet, in a life ever more filled with big-boy things. But as soon as he approached the stove, he knew that something had gone wrong.

Nothing obvious. But there was that *tick-tick-tick*, coming from the stove, which didn't happen when Mama was cooking. And there was no fire beneath the burner. There was also a weird smell in the air, like old eggs, or farts.

He climbed on to the stool and looked inside the pot. The noodles looked just exactly the same. They had not cooked at all.

His lip began to tremble again. He had failed, and now he would start to bawl, just like a baby. He would cry and cry and never be able to stop. And Mama would never get better. And Sasha would never come back, and nothing would ever be the way it used to be, and it would be all his fault—

He bit his lip, hard.

After a moment he climbed down from the step stool. He left the kitchen, with the burner still going *tick-tick-tick*.

He walked to the front door, reached for the knob.

The night wind waiting on the other side was fresh and cool. Only once it had come in and run around the house, stirring things up, did Nikolai realize how extremely funny the cottage had come to smell. There were rotten garbage smells, like yucky spoiled hot dogs. There was the old eggs smell coming from the stove. And beneath it all was another smell, sort of like the smell of the beach during summer, when the temperature got up high and the seaweed began to decay; salty smells, meaty smells, *sick* smells. And were they coming from Mama's direction? Yes. Because she was very sick, he thought, very very sick, indeed.

Standing in the doorway he looked down the hill, at Mister Rawicz's house.

He could make it there, he thought. If he put his mind to it, he could. Farther than he was allowed to go by himself, yes, but not farther than he *could* go. If he pretended he was a soldier or a secret agent or a spaceman on a mission of vital importance, he could be brave and fleet and strong, and he could make it without getting lost or getting in trouble. He knew he could.

But Mister Rawicz was JEWISH. He looked harmless enough, it was true, with his bulbous nose and his rubbery ears and his halo of white hair. And he seemed kind enough. Once he'd given Nikolai a gingerbread cookie dusted with cinnamon. But he was not to be trusted. Nikolai didn't know just what JEWISH meant, but he knew it wasn't good.

At length, he nodded slightly to himself. Mama would wake up, he thought as he shut the door again. Either that or Sasha would come back. One way or another, everything would be all right. Delivering himself to Mister Rawicz was a risk not worth taking.

He walked to the kitchen – *tick-tick-tick* went the burner – and switched off the overhead light. He used the potty, then crawled back into bed. Then he did cry, staring at the dimly fluorescent green Sputnik hanging from the ceiling, until at last his wet eyes closed, lashes sticky from tears, and he coasted down a greased rail of exhaustion, into darkness.

SOUTH OF NEVSKY

Mariya's reedy snoring drowned out the soft gabbling of the radio; the news came through only during the brief pause following each inhalation and exhalation.

The Sports Ministry was protesting a proposed audit on . . . *zzzZZZZzzz* . . . ending a postal industry subsidy for newspaper and . . . *zzZZZZZzzz* . . . Old New Year's being celebrated across Russia with intimate gatherings before the solemnity of Lent . . . *zzZZZZZzz* . . .

Cassie felt very close to safe.

They had already come and searched. Finding nothing, they would not be back. So long as she stayed here in Mariya's cottage, where old but not unpleasant cooking smells always lurked in corners, where the snores of an elderly woman spoke of a dependable barrier between herself and the outside world, she had little to fear.

. . . *zZZZZZzzz* . . .

Of course, she must manufacture an excuse not to visit the outdoor market, which would be all too public. But that should not be difficult. The old woman already suspected the truth – that quick shrewd glimpse when the subject of Blakely had come up confirmed it – and would not push too hard.

. . . *zzzZZZZZZzzzz* . . .

A vision pressed itself upon Cassie with sudden clarity: making coffee in the morning as Masha slept. Then the cottage would smell fresh and sharp and wide awake, and in some minor and inoffensive way her claim to the territory would be staked as the coffee-smell mingled in the corners and curtains with the old cooking smells. And somewhere farther down the line would come other smells, medicinal smells. Tinctures and baby powder. Rattling pill bottles, warm dry calloused hands. When the old woman ailed, Cassie would find at last the chance to repay some of her kindnesses . . .

A nice fantasy. Yet no different, at root, than the fantasies she'd once entertained of going Christmas shopping in the mall with some faceless boyfriend. Fantasies, she thought, were just another form of denial. In the real world, everything she ever cared for slipped right through her fingers.

. . . *zzzZZZZzzzz* . . .

The cause of an airplane crash in Japan had yet to be . . . *zzZZZZzzzz* . . . tainted chicken was spreading salmonella across . . . *zzzZZZzzzz* . . . a special envoy from the United States had arrived at the American consulate to assist with the continuing . . . *zzzZZzzz* . . .

Then a familiar voice piped through the old radio. All at once Cassie was sitting up in bed: struggling to breathe, heart threatening to burst through the shallow wall of her chest.

'My presence in Russia,' Julian Quinn was saying, 'acts as a symbol of the importance we attach to US/Russian ties and indicates the commitment of the United States to preserving the bond of trust and—' . . . *zzZZZZzzz* . . .

Quinn.

In Saint Petersburg.

Now.

FURSHTATSKAYA ULITSA

The wall-mounted monitor came to life, displaying a satellite map of Petersburg, zooming in on a top-down view of the building they currently occupied.

'In just a few hours,' said Ravensdale, 'Mister Quinn will step out through the front door and into a waiting limousine: a reinforced ZIL-4112R from the embassy fleet, which can withstand anything up to and including an RPG attack. An official pilot car will precede the vehicle. A rear guard will follow. But we can't make the motorcade too daunting. We must supply the illusion of accessibility. Additional escort vehicles must remain undercover. Ideally, four at all times – two in front, two in back, each carrying a driver and two agents.'

Bordachenko nodded. 'I've spoken with the *ispravnik*. You will want for nothing.'

Vlasov let a wisp of smoke trail from his nose. 'Will he wear a vest?'

'He will. But that's cold comfort against a head shot. And so we should, if possible, prevent her from getting close enough to shoot. In fact, we assume her access to materiel will be strictly limited. But—' with a sidelong glance at his compatriot – 'she does have the capability to improvise. We must therefore take every precaution.' He worked the remote. The image on-screen zipped closer to the court-yard. 'She may well be tempted to make the attempt as he gets into the car. But here she has no clear route of escape; only Furshtatskaya itself. Too many guards, too many guns. Still . . .' The image zigged. 'I'd like to see shooters posted along Chaykovskogo.' The image zagged. 'And Kirochnaya. Far enough away that she won't spot them, but close enough that they can take the shot if necessary.'

Bordachenko and Vlasov traded a look. The former nodded.

'The car will travel west, three hundred meters down Furshtatskaya, before turning south on to Liteynyy Avenue. Then west on to Ulitsa Pestelya, and across Fontanka Canal. As they cross the bridge, we've got Summer Garden to the north and Saint Michael's to the south – favorite tourist destinations. The combination of crowds and ready access to escape routes, at the confluence of the Moika with the Fontanka, make it a likely spot.'

'It is,' said Bordachenko, 'the very spot at which Karakozov tried to assassinate the czar in 1866.'

'My point. So. We'll need additional men – plain clothes – on both sides of the bridge. A sniper here . . .' Zig. 'And here.' Zag. 'Once we're across: left on Sadovaya. Then over another, smaller bridge crossing the Moika. Too much open space here, I'd think, but again, we err on the side of caution. Plain-clothes agents here, and here. Snipers here, and here. Continuing down Sadovaya, we reach the intersection with Italyanskaya. Another prime location: multiple escape routes, cover to shoot from, heavy traffic. Again, we need men close enough to act, not so close as to scare her off. Here. And here.'

Bordachenko pooched out his lips, nodded.

The image zipped to Prachechnyy, on the bank of the Moika. 'Then on to Nevsky. When he leaves the car, she'll have trouble getting close; plenty of uniforms in the area already. But she might turn that around on us. Come up with a disguise we don't anticipate, strike where we least expect. We need to be ready for anything.'

'Whilst giving the appearance,' said Bordachenko, 'of being ready for nothing.'

Ravensdale smiled mirthlessly and nodded.

SOUTH OF NEVSKY

Cassie selected ingredients, keeping one ear cocked to make sure the old woman's snoring didn't pause.

Behind cleaning solutions and detergents she found potting soil and fertilizers, seeds and bulbs, bleach and lye, pesticides and mousetraps, ammonia and drain unclogger, batteries and antifreeze. She began taking down bottles, lining them up on the washing machine.

A Molotov cocktail, Quinn had said, *is the world's simplest firebomb. Any highly flammable material in a large glass bottle will do. That means lighter fluid, ethyl or methyl alcohol, gasoline, kerosene, turpentine . . .*

She arranged her ingredients with grim satisfaction. *But Molotov cocktails are just a start. Should circumstances conspire to keep you from your contacts – should you find yourself unable to get your hands on Pyrodex or plastique or any of that good stuff – you can whip up something nearly as effective using the contents of any ordinary house. The secret to explosives? In a word, combustion. Combustion requires oxygen, hydrogen, a spark of energy, and a carbon source. So; we'll start small. Take a common bathroom cleanser, which contains ammonia, ethyl or methyl alcohol, and various additives in trace amounts. Then take a little piece of aluminum – aluminum foil, a can, some wiring with the insulation stripped. Drop it in and close it up and back away, because your aluminum will be reacting with your ammonia, creating hydrogen gas and azide, and pretty soon you can apply the Ideal Gas Law, which says that if the temperature is high, the pressure will be in direct correlation . . . To give you an idea of the kinds of temperatures and pressures we're talking about here, Cassie, this is the same principle that drives the space shuttle, which uses hydrogen gas for rocket fuel.*

She poured the contents of a bottle of disinfectant into the sink, then half-filled the bottle again with fertilizer. She shucked a large battery from a flashlight, dashed it against the concrete floor with a grunt.

But your ammonia-and-aluminum-foil bomb is a firecracker compared to, say, ammonium nitrate. That's what Timothy McVeigh used in Oklahoma City. Ammonium nitrate is powerful, but insensitive. That means it's not going to explode until you want it to. You can transport it without worrying about losing a finger. The flip side is that when you do want it to go off, you're going to need to help it along – using some kind of priming charge.

Biting her lip, she tipped the leaking battery, trickling liquid into the bottle. Her hands shook slightly, slopping out acid on to the floor. Each time a drop fell, she braced herself. In a chemistry lab this all would have been done with rubber gloves, collective flasks, safety goggles, stabilizing compounds . . .

Slow and steady.

A clammy sweat had sprung up on her brow. She paused to wipe it off, then kept pouring.

Gently, she mixed, using a circular, soothing motion, dredging up in the process a memory of trying to mix a very full glass of chocolate milk without a spoon, the Nestlé Quik Bunny grinning loonily at her from a box on a countertop. She had been a very little girl.

She mixed faster. Not being as careful as she should. In a hurry to get this done, to get at Quinn while she still had the chance. What kind of man took advantage of a girl who'd lost her parents? He had led her, under false pretenses, down a dark and bloody road. *All the perfumes of Arabia will not sweeten this little hand.* The miseries he'd put her through, the cold and hunger and danger and fear, all for his own selfish purposes. *What's done cannot be undone.* The machinations, the manipulations. *Overall, men prefer sloppy kisses, which pass chemicals, including testosterone, via saliva.* She was going to be sick—

She paused, swallowing hard, pressing down rising bile.

She blew sweaty hair off her forehead. After a few moments, she returned to the task at hand.

When the precipitate had mixed to her satisfaction, she felt a sudden urge to pour the concoction down the drain. She could slip back into bed and, in the morning, continue her new life with Masha, pretend none of this had ever happened. Nothing was preventing it . . .

Instead, she carefully set down the bottle on top of the dryer. She turned back to the washing machine, to make another selection. From the damask chair down the hall the old woman snored steadily, all unknowing.

ULITSA VARVARKA

Yuri Antsiferov watched closely as the prisoner cleaned her bowl.

Months in the *katorga* had melted any superfluous ounce of flesh from her frame. Close-shorn hair revealed every lovely contour of her face and skull. Even starvation and filth could not compromise her air of status, of prestige. As Yuri understood, she was a very important asset, a Director's case run straight from the top floor of Lubyanka, a veteran of the *Federal'naya sluzhba bezopasnosti* herself, now awaiting a vital and top-secret prisoner exchange. But she possessed a natural regality which went beyond station and circumstance, which was inherent and inviolable.

When she handed back the bowl, their eyes met.

As a younger man, he had been accustomed to the attention of beautiful women. At twenty-two he had become the Russian Professional League's undisputed master of bare-chested, full-contact kick-boxing; his nickname had been the Dragon. Females had fawned over him, fought over him. But many years had passed since. He had lost, one at a time, the things that attracted beautiful women. Now women only ever looked at him to see what they could get from him.

This one, too, only wanted to get something from him. Captive and captor, he reminded himself. So let her make eyes all she wanted. Cozying up to him would not mean an extra ration, nor even a kind word. Yuri Antsiferov was not a man to fall prey to the manipulations of a beautiful woman. He had seen his mother manipulate his father too many times to ever let it happen to him.

When he turned toward the door, she said: 'Wait.'

He looked back. She held herself meekly – but her meekness was unconvincing, a facade with which she tried and failed to conceal her tremendous natural beauty.

'What are they going to do with me?' she asked.

He thought about it, shrugged, and reached again for the knob.

'Wait,' she said quickly. 'Please.'

He looked back again, dully.

'I need a bath,' she said. 'Some clean clothes. Can you—'

He shut the door on her. Shooting the deadbolt, he frowned. She must think him a very easy mark, indeed.

In the kitchen, a neglected skillet was sizzling on the stove. At an old trestle table, Viktor Samsonov was examining a fan of cards from below heavy-lidded eyes. Yakov Pikhoya sat across from him, crossword puzzle propped on his ample belly, frowning dourly at his own hand. Both men wore over-the-shoulder holsters equipped with PSM pistols, as did Yuri himself.

'Any day now,' Yakov was saying as Yuri came into the room.

'I'm thinking,' Viktor answered. At thirty he was the youngest of the group and seemingly too nice for the business in which he'd ended up. He would have done better finding a simple girl and moving somewhere out of the city, thought Yuri, and taking up something harmless, like farming.

'It's not brain surgery, kid. But take your time. No hurry.'

'Shut up,' Viktor said. 'There's no time limit.'

'Yeah, but your eggs are burning.'

Yuri Antsiferov fell into a chair without comment. Viktor studied his cards.

'It's not rocket science,' Yakov wheedled.

'I'm *thinking*.'

'No. If you were thinking, I'd be smelling the smoke. All I smell are burning eggs.'

Viktor threw down his cards, flustered, and pushed back from the table. At the stove, he looked into the skillet and muttered a curse. He scraped eggs into the garbage. 'Someone's got to go to market.'

Yakov and Yuri both said nothing.

Viktor sighed. '*Blyad.*' He set down the skillet with a bang and, grumbling, stormed off to find his coat.

Yakov squared his cards on the table, went back to his crossword puzzle. Yuri turned his head a bit, catching a glimpse of himself in the door of the oven. In the dim reflection he could see only rough shapes – the heavy jaw of his face, the solid block of his shoulders – and no fine detail. Without the wrinkles and sagging pouches, he could see the man he once had been. The Dragon.

His mind circled back to the woman . . . if it had ever really left her. She must, he thought again, consider him one hell of an easy mark. But in playing with him, she was playing with fire. The Dragon, after all, was a force of nature. His opponents in the ring had learned that lesson the hard way. Push the Dragon too far and a veil of black rage fell over his eyes, and he did not come back to himself until the referee was pulling him off a limp, bloodied mess on the canvas.

And if the woman pushed too hard, she would regret it. Because a man had needs. And he had not been with a female since a wild night with two *prostitutki* the year before. If she kept batting her eyelids at him, she would find out just what happened when a beautiful woman took a man for a fool one time too many . . . just as his mother had eventually learned from his father.

'Mirror, mirror, on the wall,' cracked Yakov.

Yuri looked quickly away from his reflection, flushing, and then kicked out the chair from beneath the man, guffawing rudely as his partner spilled down to the dirty floor.

ELEVEN

FURSHTATSKAYA ULITSA

The man calling himself Julian Quinn climbed into the limousine; a Marine slammed the door behind him.

The ZIL-4112R pulled away, sandwiched between pilot car and rear guard, riding low on puncture-proof tyres thanks to military-grade armor doors. After navigating a narrow access road fronting the row of embassies, the limo merged on to the main avenue heading west . . . and then, in the bumper-to-bumper sludge of Saturday morning traffic, drew immediately to a stop.

'Clear at beta,' said a voice in Vlasov's ear.

'Clear at gamma,' said a second voice.

'Clear at alpha,' said Vlasov into his collar.

No gunshots had sounded; no explosions had shaken the block's windows in their frames. Yet the Inspektor felt an intuition, a vibrating instinct. Their quarry, he thought, was nearby. Invisible in the crowds, sizing up the situation, developing a plan of attack.

He looked up the wide avenue, checking faces, and then down. He saw tourists and chauffeurs and bodyguards, diplomats and secretaries, soldiers and couriers, traffic cops and construction workers. Tour buses and private cars and police cruisers and limousines, delivery vans and taxi cabs and a single lumbering backhoe. Horns blared; exhaust blew everywhere.

No sign of the girl.

The limousine crept glacially forward with the rest of the traffic. Vlasov strolled down the sidewalk ahead of it, making better time on foot than the ZIL made on the street. Reaching the end of the block, he came to a stop. To cover his lack of motion, he lit a thin brown cigarette. Drawing deep, he looked around again.

Here came the limo, turning left on to Liteynyy, still moving at a crawl. His lips brushed the collar microphone. 'Trapdoor on Liteynyy. All clear.'

'Clear at Chaykovskogo,' said another voice.

'Clear at Kirochnaya,' confirmed a third.

The ZIL edged south. Maintaining a distance of about ten yards, Vlasov followed.

Four kilometers away, Inspektor Bordachenko listened to the voices in his earpiece.

A sudden sharp report made him fall into a crouch, reaching beneath his coat. But it was just a sooty Moskvich, backfiring as it put-putted down the road before the Admiralty Building. Bordachenko straightened sheepishly, withdrawing the hand from beneath his lapel.

No civilians seemed to have noticed his reaction. Students from the nearby Art and Industry Academy rushed to catch trolleys. Two girls walking with hooked arms laughed merrily. A slender, bearded teenager struggled with a heavy black viola case. German tourists bartered aggressively with a street vendor; an old woman urged a poodle to piss in a gutter; a young family pitched coins into the dry fountain of Alexander Garden. Even the contingent of *politsiya* posted before Sledkom headquarters paid no attention. Only the undercover operatives – a pair on the nearest corner, another on the corner beyond – exchanged taut, loaded glances.

Bordachenko smoothed down his coat, stood straight, and checked his watch. She would not show herself, he thought.

He tugged anxiously on his nose. Just seventy-two hours before, life had been easy. There had been no escaped girl, no demanding Inspektor from Moscow, no slippery Americans, no dangerous political rip-tides to be avoided. Of course, at the time he had not appreciated his good fortune. Instead, he had worried about his mistress, his love handles, the irregular mole on the back of his neck. Such was life. You never knew what you had until it was gone.

He looked up the street and down. She would not show herself, he thought again.

Ravensdale stood on a corner, facing east.

Wind blew a light skim of snow along the sidewalk. Three women walking past engaged in animated conversation. Across the street, two men leaning in a doorway ate pastries out of tightly-clutched waxed paper. A traffic light at the nearest intersection changed. A motorcyclist cut off a truck driver. Angry words were exchanged.

Down the block, a clutch of off-duty soldiers lounged outside a cellphone store.

A girl was threading her way through the crowd: shoulders closed, head lowered.

His eyes followed her. Early twenties, dark hair. Yellow silk scarf, face tilted down. Poised on the balls of her feet. Hiding something beneath a dun-colored cloth coat.

She came to a stop on the corner, standing behind a bald man wearing a blue windbreaker and a gym bag over one shoulder. Sidling closer to him as they waited for the light to change.

A traffic policeman blew his whistle, glanced toward the corner. The girl turned away from the man in the windbreaker, wandered a few aimless paces.

Ravensdale watched her.

She was half a head too tall. But she might be wearing lifts. He checked his watch. The motorcade would be along any minute. She was less than five yards away, hovering.

Better safe than sorry.

He dropped his cigarette and moved forward.

Inside the limousine, Andrew Fletcher exhaled shortly. 'Can we get some fresh air back here?'

The driver, a young Marine in midnight blue, glanced over his shoulder, adjusted the climate control, and refocused on the traffic.

Fletcher wiped his brow. His hand continued inelegantly – the range of motion compromised by the Kevlar body armor beneath his dark Ermenegildo Zegna suit – to check his breast holster. Listening to the voices chattering in his earpiece, he leaned back and heaved another sigh.

Once upon a time, he thought, it had not been such an uphill fucking climb.

Once upon a time they had all been idealists, bright college boys who knew that they had right on their side, who knew that America stood for everything good in the world, that it was a privilege to spend one's days trouncing her enemies. Now it was all opportunists like Blakely and Ravensdale, looking out for number one; backstabbers treated by the twenty-four news cycle like brave saviors because they dared to 'buck the system' – really, because they dared to be selfish, and because the maw of the media had to be fed. Leaving men like Fletcher, who cared only about what was right, who saw the lasting simplicity of the equation, to pick up the slack, to bend over backwards, and now to place himself squarely in the center of a cross hairs. Had Benjamin Blakely not been a turncoat, had Charlie Bent not proven incompetent in Beliy Gorod, had Sean Ravensdale delivered on his promises with Tsoi, Fletcher would not have found himself here. He would have been back in his office in Washington, doing good on a wide scale, putting into place the components of a new operation, instead of risking his life to mop up a messy spill before it spread.

Ah, but there was a saying about that: something about spilt milk. Despite everything, he grinned.

As Ravensdale drew close, the girl broke into a run.

He lunged after her, diving between two well-dressed businessmen, pushing aside a kid with a balloon. He almost got hold of the tip of the yellow scarf; then she spun on one heel, pivoting away . . . and plowing into a wall of matronly flesh. Then he had her. Pulling back, using his bulk as an anchor, he tightened the silk around her throat, stopping her dead.

From farther up the block, the off-duty soldiers watched. Across the street, the two men in the doorway paused their breakfast. But nobody roused themselves to interfere. The girl had gone limp on the other end of the scarf, playing dead, or something like it. She was younger than Ravensdale had thought in that first glance; sixteen, seventeen. Long attenuated eyelashes. Frightened mouth like a small pursed apricot.

Reaching beneath her coat, he found items tucked into large, loose pockets: two wallets, three phones, a key ring, a guilloche gold cigarette lighter.

An ordinary pickpocket.

He stepped back, releasing her.

Looking at him bright-eyed, snarling, she vanished.

Women in Petersburg, thought Vlasov, were sexier than women in Moscow.

Both were beautiful, of course. But the women in Moscow, with their flawless make-up, gym-toned bodies, and sleek tight black clothing, all seemed cut from the same cloth. Nothing was left to chance. A machine might have mass-produced them. Here in Pieter was more variety and seemingly less effort. Tall, short, wide, narrow, full-bodied, slender, blonde, brunette, redhead: he saw every flavor of which a man might dream. Many emitted an artsy vibe completely unlike the mercenary air one sensed in Moscow. Girls like this, he thought, would be open to experimentation.

But some were *too* artsy. A young woman, for example, who flickered through the corner of his gaze as she walked down Liteynyy Avenue, who might have been pretty had she not tried so strenuously to make herself ugly. She was emaciated, for one thing, with face and eyes as hollow as a skull's. Her nose was slightly misshapen, as if she had gone a few rounds with Nicolai Valuev. She wore an ill-fitting old Red Army jacket and had shaved her head down to gleaming white skin, piercing her nose and ears with safety pins.

Their eyes grazed; she turned away, heading north.

Absently, Vlasov smoked. He came to a stop, looking after the limousine slowly approaching Ulitsa Pestelya. The first of the under-cover vehicles had already made the westward turn.

He looked back after the girl with the shaved head.

Too intense-looking; too thin.

But . . .

No.

But . . .

Maybe.

She had already lost herself in the crowd.

'Possible suspect,' he murmured into his collar. 'Height one-point-six meters. Slight build, shaved head, piercings, green army jacket. Heading north on Liteynyy.'

Sometimes you'll just get a feeling about something, Quinn had said. *You're picking up on body language, unspoken signals. When in doubt, trust your instincts.*

She walked quickly, not looking back.

The man, she thought, had recognized her.

People send a wide array of unintentional messages. There are easy things to see, the so-called negation and aversion behaviors: touching the face or hair, leaning away, crossing the arms. Then there are more subtle things, like pupil dilation, pore size, skin flush, breathing, muscle tone changes. The study of non-verbal behavior is called kinesics. You probably won't even realize consciously what signals you're picking up. But when you're out there – with a descriptive gesture indicating the world beyond the red-brick colonial, the Williams-Sonoma decor, the warmly crackling fireplace – *follow your gut.*

He had recognized her. And now – she saw by turning her head a few degrees – he was following her.

And he was talking into his collar.

Self-recrimination rose in a bitter flood. The oldest, most obvious of all tricks – a baited trap – and she had fallen for it. She had delivered herself into an ambush. It had been naive to think that a few childish precautions – a shaved head and some piercings and Masha's dead husband's old Army jacket – would protect her.

She found a reserve of the chilly gray mist, gathered it around herself, using it to cool the rising emotion, to remain in control.

She refrained from looking around again. If it was indeed a trap, the route followed by the motorcade would be studded with agents, snipers, cameras. But put enough distance between herself and the path linking the US consulate to Sledkom HQ, and she would have a chance.

She walked. Impassive facades rose on every side; no cross street to duck into, no alley, no escape until the next block. She moved faster, shoving her way ahead. Pigeons took wing, fluttering up on to power lines. A fat man snapped a reprimand. She ignored him, hurrying ever faster.

The man had recognized her. More: she had recognized *him*. But how? In the back of her mind blinked a newspaper photograph: a gaunt, well-dressed man with a pretty little mustache, addressing a crowd of reporters. *With the help of our faithful and watchful citizenry, the cowardly criminals responsible for this heinous act will soon be flushed from the sewers like the rats that they are . . .*

'Motherfucker,' she whispered beneath her breath and hastened even faster.

'Got her,' said the sniper. 'Heading north, toward the embankment. Moving fast. Should I . . .?'

'Negative.' Bordachenko used two fingers to hold the collar microphone closer to his lips, as if that would amplify not just his voice but his authority. The last thing he needed was an overeager kid opening fire on a crowd because of a mistaken identity. '*Negative* until we've got positive ID.'

'I'm still with her.' Vlasov's voice was pitched higher than usual, slightly breathless. 'I've got her.'

'I want backup.' Bordachenko summoned a composure he did not feel. 'Who sees them? Someone on foot.'

Radio silence.

'For the love of – *who sees them?*'

'I've got her,' said Vlasov again, panting. 'She won't lose me.'

Bordachenko swore, reached with his free hand for his phone. Time for the whizz kids in Sledkom to deliver on their promises.

Shunting aside pedestrians, Vlasov reached beneath his coat and loosened his gun in its holster.

Now she was falling into a flat-out run. He stepped into the street, avoiding the crowds but placing himself in the path of a motorbike. The driver blasted his horn. Dodging the bike, Vlasov started sprinting. But he had smoked too many thin dark cigarettes; his snug-fitting tailored white suit, ideal for making an entrance to an underground casino with a pretty lady on his arm, was not so good for chasing a fast young girl through the streets of Saint Petersburg.

As he ran he drew his Makarov automatic, racked the slide to chamber a round. Someone saw the gun, and excitement hissed through the crowd. As one they gasped, shrinking back. A good thing; for as they withdrew, they exposed the running girl. He might shoot now and take her down. But that would require stopping, taking aim. And she was almost at the corner. She was *turning* the corner. He was right behind her—

Smooth-soled Italian calfskin shoes lost purchase, sliding across sooty cobbles. She melted out from somewhere to his left, liquidly, graceful as a ballerina, and something bit through his coat and into his side, a very strange and terrible sensation, of violation and hard cold steel piercing soft supple flesh.

His legs turned suddenly to air. As he folded, she charged off again. The blade she had used clattered into a gutter. He struggled in vain to raise the Makarov, even as a few bystanders managed to get their phones up and start shooting video, the fuckers.

She ducked behind a parked car and was gone.

The bystanders filmed Vlasov.

He coughed, spat, put his head down. Blood was pulsing out his side, pooling beneath him in a dark sticky puddle. The swine were still filming him. Not a one moved to help, nor to stop the girl.

He looked up, into the blank goggling lenses of half a dozen smartphones. '*Yob tvoyu mat*,' he said amiably to the assembly – *Fuck your mother*.

'Got her,' said the tech manning the drone. 'Heading north on Mokhovaya.'

He sounded no older than Bordachenko's youngest son. His piping voice should have been begging for kissel, not offering the best information they had at a crucial junction of a vital manhunt. Bordachenko said hopefully: 'Inspektor. Still with us?'

No answer.

'Inspektor.' The hiss of an open channel. '*Inspektor.*' Bordachenko grappled for the name of the drone's pilot. 'Efrussi. Where's Vlasov?'

A painfully long pause. 'No sign,' said the young voice at last. 'Should—'

'Negative. Stay with the suspect.' Closing his eyes, Bordachenko consulted a mental map. 'Durasova and Negretov – to Chaykovskogo. Post-haste. Sitko, call your friend in the River Police. We need a cordon blocking the embankment. Mister Ravensdale, move up to Gangutskaya – and stay ready. She's heading your way.'

Andrew Fletcher listened to his earpiece.

She was finished, he thought.

She had gone as far as she could go. A noble effort it had been – much more successful than anyone had anticipated – but she was finished at last.

But she had surprised him before. And if she escaped again, it would be his own goddamned fault. He had trained her too well. Blakely had made her necessary, Bent had fumbled the disposal, Ravensdale had failed to deliver on his promises . . . but Fletcher himself was the one who had chosen her, motivated her, molded her into what she was.

A man, he thought, should finish what he started.

After a second's hesitation, he threw open the reinforced door of the ZIL-4112R. Before the driver could react he was out on the street, clawing for his breast holster.

She ran.

Past a string of parked cars, a hotel courtyard, an inoperative fountain surrounded by granite figures from Russian fairy-tales: The Armless Maiden, Ivan the Fool, Ruslan and Lyudmila, Koschei the Deathless.

She pounded around another corner, nearly colliding with an OMON agent brandishing a weapon – facing away. She slipped her left arm around his throat, moving on autopilot; inserted the other arm behind his head, locking her fingertips just behind his left ear. Her right knee drove into his spine between the fourth and fifth vertebrae. Extending the fingers of both hands, she shifted her weight sharply back, neatly dislocating the skull from the spinal column. One more. God willing, the last one.

She dropped the body. As the crowd gawked, she worked the weapon from stiff hands: a 5.45 mm PSM pistol.

She ran again, stumbling, pulse thundering in the hollow of her wrist, the PSM in one hand. Lungs burning, legs wobbling. Deathless, she thought. Deathless. Her heart tried to climb up her gullet, out her throat. *Run!*

Ahead on her right: the frozen river. Across the water: a dazzling minaret. From everywhere at once, or so it seemed: rising and falling sirens. Beyond them, distantly but growing closer: the laconic thud of helicopter rotors.

A pair of dry gunshots sounded behind her. She turned down a narrow brick alleyway, heart doing cartwheels and somersaults. An iron ladder led up. *Options multiply as they are seized.*

She climbed recklessly, briefly flashing back on to another fire escape, a year before and miles away, outside the hang-out pad in the East Village. *Police! Don't fucking move!*

On the rooftop she laid flat, chest down, six stories above the city. *Coup d'oeil* was the French term: literally meaning *stroke of the eye*; in military terms meaning the ability to discern, in one glance, the tactical advantages of terrain.

A crosswind buffeted her, snapping the collar of the jacket against her cheeks. She ignored it, focused. From her new vantage point she could see the river to the north and roads clogged with traffic, with tiny model cars, to the south, east, and west. Blaring sirens drew the eye, pressing her way, but snarled by traffic. The majority of ant-sized pedestrians ran instinctively away from the gunshots. Those running toward her stood out: policemen, undercover agents, elbowing through the crowds. She found snipers, small with distance, posted on rooftops. The helicopter hovering above the body of the OMON agent, a block behind her current position. Floating almost directly overhead, less than thirty yards away: a quadricopter drone.

She rocked back on to her haunches, took aim. The drone danced mockingly through the sky. She fired; missed.

She was about to move again – to leap to the next rooftop and scale quickly back to street level – when something made her look southward.

One of the men coming toward her, running all-out, had clicked some switch in her mind. He wore no uniform. He moved clumsily – wearing armor beneath his clothes, she thought – but the gait was nonetheless recognizable.

She had spent a full year training beneath Julian Quinn in the red-brick colonial. She knew intimately his carriage, his bearing, the shape of his stride.

Julian Quinn was racing in her direction, holding a gun.

She raised the 5.45 mm PSM pistol. It would be almost too easy.

Don't get cocky.

Clear day, no wind, just about fifty paces . . . a moving target. She led off. He kept coming. A lamb to the slaughter.

The drone ceased to exist. The policemen, the howling sirens, the pounding helicopter ceased to exit. There was only the gun. The man in her sights.

He had lied to her. Betrayed her. Ordered her death.

Focus on the target. Then refocus on the front sight, so it comes into sharp focus, keeping your forearms and the gun level . . .

In the last second, he seemed to understand what was coming. He slowed, eyes searching the rooftops.

She licked her lips.

'Fuck you,' she said aloud.

Her finger hesitated against the trigger.

COBBLER'S COVE: ONE YEAR EARLIER

She sat before the fireplace, poring over photographs.

The first pictured her father wearing military camouflage, standing beside Julian Quinn on what looked like a target range. The next pictured her father at a cocktail party, standing beside a former President of the United States. The two men seemed to be sharing a joke – heads bent together, shoulders almost touching, eyes twinkling. A US Great Seal hung in the background, above a white brick hearth.

Fake, she had insisted.

Real, he had answered with conviction.

Here was her father, shot through a telephoto lens, standing in a large public square beside a man with a receding hairline and muscles going to fat . . . in Moscow, according to Quinn. Then her father on a hillside, squinting up at the camera from a gun he seemed to be cleaning, looking almost unrecognizable in a thin mustache and flak jacket. Her father shaking hands with someone who seemed vaguely familiar, a face she knew from movies – or maybe a politician, a congressman she'd seen in the newspaper or on an interview show. Then her father wearing a turban, not in some kitschy carnival side-show where he'd placed his face into a cardboard cut-out of a cartoon Arab, but against a backdrop of craggy dark mountains. Holding an automatic weapon. More turbaned figures, also holding automatic weapons, milled behind him. Beyond them, a dark saw-blade of rock bisected a pale sky.

Tell me, Quinn had said. *How did your father die?*

Car accident, she'd answered.

'Mechanical failure', right? The brakes bombed on his Subaru, and he went into a lamp post at sixty miles per hour? He had shaken his head. *The bad guys killed your father, Cassie. That man in the public square is a* mafiya *kingpin. He buys or steals raw fissile materials – uranium, plutonium, deuterium, heavy water – and then sells them to the highest bidder. Your dad was building a case against him. Your dad was going to shut the whole operation down.*

He worked, she had protested, *in consulting.*

Business restructuring? With a specialty in Russia and Eastern Europe? Another shake of the head, gentle but firm. *A cover. He worked for us. He did vital things for this country.*

She flipped back to the photograph of the man in the public square. Tilted her head, studying the face. This, according to Quinn, was the man who had caused her so much pain. Receding hair, layered fat. The banality of evil.

Believe me, Quinn had said. *Once you learn the whole story, you'll be glad I found you.*

And he had been right. Because otherwise she would never have learned the truth. She would never have learned that this was not a world in which God made you an orphan just because He felt like it, just for the hell of it. Instead it was a world in which Daddy had been a patriot, a hero. Killed In The Line of Duty. And now Cassie would take his place. Avenge him. And Make Things Right.

SAINT PETERSBURG

On the other side of the sight, Quinn searched the rooftops, trying to find her.

Her finger curled tighter. She would do it. Not only for herself, but for all the others he had doubtless used, would doubtless use again.

And there's no need to ask him anything first. Because he'll just lie again – and you know the truth already. Daddy was no spy. Daddy was a book-lover and a consultant and a lousy cook and a great father and a man of peace and now Daddy is dead and Quinn made you into a monster and you might as well accept it, already. Daddy would be so disappointed if he could see what you've become, but he can't, he won't, he won't ever, because Daddy is dead Daddy is

*dead Daddy is dead, and Quinn lied, he lied, he lied, finding your
weakest spot and playing on it, pretending the world makes sense but
really it doesn't, nothing makes sense, nothing means anything,
nothing matters, and Quinn lies, lies, lies—*

She fired.

Half of Quinn's head vanished in a red mist.

'Found Vlasov,' said a gasping voice in Bordachenko's ear. 'He's
down.'

'Quinn's also down,' said the drone's pilot. 'Suspect on the move
again.'

Bordachenko covered his eyes, already closed, with one hand.

Keeping in a low crouch, she climbed swiftly down the fire escape,
aware of the drone buzzing in her wake.

The park pacing the River Neva was peppered with old-fashioned
lamp posts. Beside a strip of frost-covered greenery ran a thin road,
less congested than the wider boulevards in the center of town. A
sky-blue Lada Kalina idled at a stop sign, waiting to turn on to the
river. Cassie made for it, ducking reflexively at the sound of more
flat, curiously unemphatic gunshots.

Her feet slapped against cobblestones, thud thud thud. Gnats
whizzed past, zip zip zip. As she reached the Kalina, a bullet shattered the driver's side window. She saw the driver's head whip forward
and sideways. Bright rosettes of blood pattered across the windshield's
interior. The woman rolled bonelessly back, eyes showing only white.

Cassie tore open the door, shoved the driver across the parking
brake, slid behind the wheel, gnashed gears, and jerked out on to the
riverside boulevard. Glancing into the passenger seat she saw a slack,
pretty, lifeless face, and weakening freshets of blood.

Her eyes skimmed to the rear-view. A stranger looked back: bloodshot eyes, safety-pin piercings, shaved head.

A police Zhiguli-8 appeared, racing across an intersection, *ramming*
her, the crazy fuck.

The Zhiguli crunched into the side of the Kalina, tossing her head
painfully on her neck. The rear windshield exploded. She wrestled
again with the gear shift. The Kalina was drifting, being pushed across
the road toward the frozen river. She lifted her foot from the accelerator, popped the car into reverse, and then spun the wheel hard.

She hit the gas again; with a torturous scream of metal the Kalina
disengaged, ripping away from the Zhiguli. Back into second. Then

she was jouncing forward again, with cold wind filling the car. Something was dragging from the undercarriage. Her neck blazed pain. The entire left side of the Kalina seemed to be crumpled in. Distantly, she was amazed that the car was still moving. In her rear-view the Zhiguli was turning in a circle, trying to orient itself to give chase, looking like a wounded insect. And a black sedan was looping around it, engine opening up. And the drone was still with her, buzzing maddeningly.

Finished, she thought.

Not yet, god damn it.

She shifted up to third.

Sirens ahead. A flock of flashing lights. Fragmented in the remains of her side-view mirror, the black sedan.

The helicopter soared up from behind rooftops, arcing high, blades pounding, *whonk-whonk-whonk*, the sound that would haunt her dreams.

Finished, she thought again.

She twisted the wheel, smashed through a kiosk, clipped a stand-pipe, twisted the wheel again and veered to the right, bounced up over an island of grass – whatever was dragging from the under-carriage caught hard and tore free – and landed on pavement again.

Before her, a checkpoint had been hastily assembled. She swerved again up on to the sidewalk, passing over a spike strip, losing all four tires, plowing a stop sign off its post. Riding on rims, kicking up sparks. Past a marketplace, a Chinese restaurant. The helicopter and drone had stayed with her.

She laughed.

Ravensdale heard the car before he saw it.

Calmly, he drew his gun, flicking off the safety.

He held the weapon steady, focusing on the vanishing point just beyond the sight. In his earpiece, Bordachenko was warning him to stay ready. And here came the helicopter. And here came the whine of the revving engine. And here, he thought, came the car. Any time now. Any time now. Any . . . time.

He saw it: an unwieldy hunk of metal and shredded rubber, slaloming on and off the sidewalk, around stalled traffic, through kiosks and carts and road signs, sending pedestrians scattering; a collapsing ruin of a car, steaming, fragmenting, punctured tires flap-ping, engine laboring into higher and higher registers. Two faces loomed behind a windshield freckled with blood. One was deflated with death. The other was strained and white and intense. As he took aim, the latter gave its chin a small obstinate uptick.

Ravensdale held his breath and fired.

The windshield starred, spiderwebbing with cracks.

Blinded, she hit the brakes. The Kalina plowed into a street vendor's table – tortoiseshell and copper and plastic sprayed – and then into a brick wall, *pow*. And then the mad dash was over. Her neck was aching, and everywhere was steam and screaming and the stink of spilled oil. A few pieces of junk jewelry slithered down the ruined glass, clung to the windshield wipers.

The dead woman in the passenger seat rolled slowly forward, striking her head against the dash with a meaty thud. Lights flashed, distorted through the webbed glass. Sirens cried. People yelled. Steam fizzed. Cold wind blew. Helicopter blades pounded. Drones buzzed. Oil dripped. Something was pressing against Cassie's ribcage. She wondered dreamily if she had impaled herself on the steering column. Her hands slipped beneath the loose-fitting Red Army jacket, exploring. The explosives she had devised in Mariya's laundry nook were still there, still intact, duct-taped to her stomach.

She tore the smaller bottle free from her belly, unscrewed the cap. Found the fleck of aluminum foil in the right-hand pocket of the jacket. Dropped it in, screwed the cap back into its grooves. Inside the bottle, toxic gases began to build pressure. She tore the larger bottle from her torso, jammed it beneath the wheel well, leaned the smaller bottle against it.

The steam billowing around the car was colored, now, by a tongue of orange flame. For one more eternal instant she paused, watched inky black smoke start to swirl.

Steeling herself, she reached for the door.

Ravensdale advanced with the gun held two-handed, straight-armed.

As he drew near the burning vehicle, an instinct came into play. He slowed, reluctant to move closer. The licking flame, the stench of petrol . . .

The driver's side door seemed to crack open. But black smoke rose in thick billows, confusing things. Ravensdale risked another step forward, scowling. His hands were shaking.

There came a thud; from every side at once, from above and below, traveling through the ground, beneath the street, toppling him. He felt his eyebrows singe. He began to crawl away, back the way he had come. After crawling for what seemed a long while, he looked over his shoulder. The flaming metal carcass of the Kalina was flipping up, spinning with dreadful slow-motion majesty. Swirls of fiery ash, lariats of dark flame; a melting tire, a soaring steering wheel, and a blackening human cadaver, all caught in a timeless frieze.

The Kalina came down hard.

A pipe burst; water scintillated into the air.

He coughed . . . and vomited.

Found the gun, aimed it back into the inferno. The Kalina was a skeletal husk, shot through with fire. He saw the charred corpse. As he watched, the corpse curled, flaked, and disintegrated.

TWELVE

FURSHTATSKAYA ULITSA

On the wall-mounted monitor ran footage captured by helicopter, drone, and private camera-phone: the Kalina rocketing around a checkpoint, right side crumpled in, tires punctured, hood lolling, rear fender barely hanging on—

Vlasov's phone rang. Propped in a chair, eyes hazy from opioids, jacket open to allow his bandage to breathe, he seemed not to hear.

Ravensdale paused the footage. Another ring. Vlasov started, answered; listened, grunted, hung up. 'The genetic material,' he reported, 'shows it's not her.'

Bordachenko and Ravensdale said nothing. Vlasov slipped the phone back into his pocket. The footage ran forward again. Ravensdale's own figure made an appearance, advancing straight-armed, firing. The Kalina's bloodied windshield starred. The vehicle plowed through a vendor's table, sending costume jewelry spraying. Then into a brick wall. Smoke thickened. Ravensdale switched feeds, to a new angle provided by the drone. Brackish black mushrooms provided the driver ample opportunity to escape – and from this vantage point they could see the route she must have followed, down an alley beside a donut shop. Then the cataclysmic explosion, the momentary white-out. Chaos and confusion.

Vlasov thumbed open a vial, swallowed another *oksikodon*.

Ravensdale skipped back to just before the helicopter joined the chase. The girl ran north on Mokhovaya, loose jacket flapping.

Moments before, off-camera, she had stabbed Inspektor Vlasov with a knitting needle, which had been recovered from a gutter. Moments from now, she would fatally shoot Andrew Fletcher in the head, providing, as it happened, a simple and decisive conclusion to one of Ravensdale's agendas . . . but not all.

A sudden memory: Andy Fletcher not as a runner of agents, but only as a man. Ten years before, at a dinner in Georgetown, his first wife, three margaritas deep, had started boasting about her walk-in closet full of mink. Fletcher had shot Ravensdale a quick look – embarrassed, beseeching – more vulnerable, in that moment, than he would ever be again. For the first and probably last time, Ravensdale had felt for the man a pulse of genuine sympathy.

He focused. Fletcher was gone. But Sofiya was still here. Switching feeds again, he enjoyed the clearest view yet of their quarry's latest incarnation. Shaved head and hollowed cheeks reminded him of the corn-husk scarecrow that had once been Sofiya. Flat blunted affect and expressionless set features reminded him of nothing so much as himself.

He froze the image. The three men in the conference room considered the small girl swimming in the tattered Red Army jacket.

Ravensdale tapped his chin thoughtfully. 'Where did she get the coat?'

He switched to yet another angle, from which insignia on the epaulets were plainly visible: red stripes, gold stars.

'Standard infantry insignia,' Bordachenko said, 'dating from World War Two. Thirty-five million men served during the Great Patriotic War. The coat might have come from any veteran, any second-hand store.'

'Or,' said Vlasov, 'from any war widow.' Tenderly, he indicated his blood-spotted bandage. 'Who would be more likely to have a knitting needle.'

The clocks on the conference room wall counted off the fleeing seconds.

'How many veterans are left?' asked Ravensdale. 'How many war widows?'

'And how many in Petersburg?' wondered Vlasov.

'And . . .' Ravensdale turned to Bordachenko. 'How can we find them?'

SOUTH OF NEVSKY

Except for a single light burning in the parlor, Mariya's cottage was dark.

Coming through the front door, Cassie paused. She could see the old woman in her usual place, propped in the damask chair. She could hear the usual ceaseless murmur of the radio. But there were no cooking smells tonight, not even the smell of clove cigarettes.

'. . . initiated the high-speed pursuit. But what is beyond question is the cost it has inflicted on the city of Pieter. Seven dead, many millions in property damage. No fewer than six agencies were apparently involved. Despite such resources, according to sources directly involved with the investigation, authorities ultimately proved unable to . . .'

With a single charged glance, as Cassie entered the parlor, Mariya stopped the younger woman in her tracks.

'The incident began at about seven fifteen a.m. According to eyewitnesses, the object of the pursuit was a young woman with a shaved head, green Army jacket, and heavy piercings. The fugitive initially led authorities on a desperate chase through the district between embassy row and the embankment. Helicopter and drone—'

For the first time in Cassie's experience, the old woman snapped off the radio. '*Ischezni,*' she said tonelessly: *Get lost.*

Cassie shook her head.

'It's not a request.'

'Masha—'

'I count to five. Then I call the police myself.'

'They didn't follow me. I spent all aftern—'

'One.'

'It won't happen again. I won't go out again.'

'Two.'

'Masha – please.'

'Three.'

'*Please.*'

'Four.'

They regarded each other.

'All I do for you,' said Mariya darkly. An involuntary grimace twisted her face. 'And you bring trouble to my doorstep. This old fool should have known better. You can't ever trust a thief.'

Cassie blinked. Eyes shining, she nodded.

As a necessary side effect of the parabolic microphone, the low frequency lacked fidelity; the treble was spiky, the mid-range spotty.

Marrying you was a mistake, said a tinny female voice. *I'm not making any excuses. I did a stupid thing.*

Don't get defensive, a man answered. *I'm just saying—*

You try to turn everything around! I was actually looking forward to spending some time together after you retired. That's how stupid I am . . .

The gray van rolled ahead; the voices faded, faltered, and died. The master sergeant suppressed a sigh. Running a finger down the list in his hand, he found the next address, two blocks ahead.

As they moved, his headphones transmitted a child's laughter, a patch of black silence, the sound of running tap water; a lone classical guitar, a flushing toilet, a whistling tea-kettle. Nearing the target address, the driver slowed. The tech working the thermal imager nudged his joystick, taking aim, conjuring on his screen swirls of roiling pinks, purples, and yellows.

Inside the apartment, a solitary figure sat on a couch, watching TV. A second swirl of heat became evident: a smaller figure curled up on a floor on the other side of a wall. The sergeant leaned forward. A fugitive, hidden in a crawl space . . .?

The figure rocked on to its back, rolling over. A tail unfurled, lazily wagged. A dog.

The master sergeant leaned back, consulted the list in his hand, and read to the driver an address on the next block.

They drove. The microphone listened.

. . . interested in hiring people who can rise to the challenge, who can fill whatever position needs to be filled at the moment . . . they do employee reviews at six-month intervals, and the sky's the limit. Well . . . You know, Mother, a little support once in a while never killed anybody . . .

Past blaring rock music, a television laugh track, passionate sighs. Then:

How do you know you're the one with the problem? Pause. *I'm just saying. Until you talk with the doctors, you don't really know, do you? He smokes a lot of—*

The van turned a corner. A clicking keyboard, a creaking hinge, a squalling baby. Then:

. . . the start of last summer. And I didn't even realize who they were. But Feodor did. We actually argued about it. He said: Do you know who that was? And I said, yes, I know, we just met them, she seems very nice. And he said, no, that's Anastasia Leskov. *And I said, no. She seems so down to earth . . .*

A popping cork, clattering silverware. Then:

Should I stop? Does it hurt?

*Yes . . . it feels good. Yes, Kostya, yes. Put another finger in me.
Oh, Kostya.*

Say my name.

Konstantin. My baby . . .

Not the neck. Don't leave a mark.

At the next address on the list, they found a sole figure sleeping
silently in a bed.

At the next: a woman sitting at a table, whisking out playing cards
while squabbling with someone working in the kitchen. *V zádnitse.
I knew the day I hired a Vietnamese that I was fucked . . .*

At the next: an old man humming to himself, the same two thin
cracked notes over and over again.

At the next: a pair sleeping heavily.

At the next: a figure sitting alone in a parlor, listening to a radio.
The van rolled on.

FURSHTATSKAYA ULITSA

Ravensdale cracked his neck, stretched the cramped muscles of
his shoulders, ground his cigarette into an ashtray, pushed back his
chair.

In a restroom down the hall, he washed his face. Then he visited
the small communications room on the embassy's first floor. After
pulling rank with the sleep-deprived PFC on duty, he enjoyed his first
unsupervised access to a secure connection since arriving in Russia.
He dropped into a creaking leather seat and dialed. Pings echoed as
the encryption took hold. After thirty seconds came a hollow buzzing.
Two rings, three . . . 'Hello?'

'Tess.'

'Sean!'

In the background: 'Whozit?'

'It's your daddy, honeybun.'

'*Da-deeee!*' The phone scraped mysteriously. 'Daddy,' said Dima
breathlessly. 'When I was baby, I din like pizza. Now I big boy, I real
like pizza.'

The voice sounded different – more mature, even after just a few
days apart. Ravensdale smiled. 'How you doing, champ?'

'I playin', Daddy! I dream, dream 'bout cookies an, an, an, planets
and stars and Cap'n Hook!'

'I miss you, buddy.'

'I don' cry at all and I see birdies way way up high and I read
Hungry Cat'pillar with Miss Tess. OK, 'bye!'

Tess came back on the line. 'I trimmed his hair,' she said apologetically. 'It was getting in his eyes.'

'I trust your judgment. How's he treating you?'

'He is,' she said with unmistakable satisfaction, 'a very good boy.'

'I a *big* boy,' piped Dima in the background.

'We only had pizza once,' she said. 'Mostly, we're eating healthy.'

'Sleeping OK?'

'Like a doll. Kids can adjust to anything.'

'I shouldn't be much longer. I owe you, Tess.'

A pause, slightly too long. She had been interested in Ravensdale, he suspected, ever since Sofiya's disappearance, and perhaps even before. 'My honest pleasure,' she said carefully. 'He's a joy.' In the background, the joy screamed bloody murder. 'Don't chase the cat,' said Tess quickly.

'I'm sorry to do this, Tess, but . . . there's something else.'

'Name it.'

He closed his eyes for a few instants, then opened them again. 'You've got my key. There's a shovel in the mud room. Out back, past the porch, there's an old oak with a fork in the middle. If you go past it, there's a rock face leading down to the lake. Careful; it'll be slippery.'

'No worries.'

'At the lake, turn right. You'll find Indian kettles back there. Each a few inches wide except for one, about two feet. Shaped kind of like Texas. Can't miss it. Filled with natural clay. You've got to dig down maybe two, three feet. Won't be easy, this time of year.'

Another pause. 'What am I looking for?'

'A lockbox. Take it. Then take Dima. Go to the Radisson in Newport.'

Silence.

'Register under the name . . . Let's say Parker. I'll call as soon as I can. Might still be a few days. Then I'll come get Dima and the box, reimburse you, and—'

'Sean: that's crazy. I've got obligations here.'

'I'm sorry, Tess. I didn't want to put you in this position. But I'm afraid I have.'

'Am I . . . in danger?'

'Not if you do what I say.'

'Jesus.'

'Don't drag your feet. You've got to go now.'

'What *is* this?'

He said: 'Give Dima a big kiss for me.'

He hung up.

Closing his eyes again, he pinched briefly at the bridge of his nose.

Dialing Serebryany Bor, he listened to the encryption kicking in.

A man answered. Ravensdale asked for Tsoi. Waiting, he looked at a tasseled American flag hanging by the door. His fingertips explored the singed remnants of his eyebrows: a curious sensation.

Tsoi came on the line, displaying his usual easy bonhomie. '*Tovarish*. Luck?'

'Not yet. But I'm looking ahead.' He laid out his request. When he had finished, static fizzed briefly over the line: another pause slightly longer than it should have been.

'Let me see,' said Tsoi then, 'what I can do.'

FINLYANDSKY STATION

She had come full circle: another half-empty train station, another cluster of shivering homeless, another bird-shat statue of Lenin.

She stood before the schedule board, pondering. She might ride the high-speed Karelian train to Helsinki in style. But trying to cross the border without first improving her disguise, in light of the description she'd heard on Masha's radio, would be unwise. She had traded the Red Army jacket for a pea coat and fur-lined *ushanka* hat stolen from a vendor's stall, but the camouflage would not resist any except the most cursory inspection.

That left the drab commuter trains, the *elektrichka*. One was heading to Vyborg in twenty minutes. Just thirty kilometers south of the border, the town would make a fine staging area for the endgame.

She bought a ticket. On the platform, she circled around the questing gaze of a security camera. The train was drafty, redolent of cabbage and fish. Most of the passengers began dozing the instant they slumped awkwardly into their second-class seats.

She found an empty row behind a woman reading a paperback with a garish four-color cover. Somebody near at hand began working their way through a steaming Thermos of soup. The wafting fragrance – noodles, vegetables, chicken broth – made her think of Mariya's kitchen. That roused her appetite and a commensurate wave of self-pity. The self-pity brought up in turn the cool gray mist, comfortably numbing.

Politsiya and soldiers walked up and down the platform outside the train: looking at tablets, looking into windows, looking away. A whistle blew. The train began to move. Gaining distance from the

station, the carriage fell into a comfortable rattling rhythm. Recessed
lights tucked beneath the luggage rack came on. Cassie leaned back
in her seat, exhaling.

She felt nothing.

The door at the near end of the train opened. A *provodnik* came
in, dressed all in black like a mourner. 'Tickets,' he called.

He moved down the aisle, punching tickets and handing them back.
When he had gone, Cassie closed her eyes. She was back in Mariya's
cottage, begging to be allowed to stay. (Pathetic. She regretted it
already.) She was climbing again into the Kalina, shoving the dead
woman across the parking brake. She was sighting on Quinn's face
as he slowed, scanning the rooftops, seeming to realize what was
coming. *Fuck you.*

She felt nothing.

She was slitting the OMON agent's throat with a shard of broken
glass. She was shaking Owen Holt's ringless hand in the bar in Sergiev
Posad. She was winging in toward the dacha, aiming for the peaked
roof beneath stringy clouds. She was watching herself in the mirror
on Zimyanin's bedroom ceiling as he violated her. *It's a beautiful
thing between two people, Cass, m'lass. It's when a man loves a
woman and they make a baby together.* She was lying in a soft bed
in the red-brick colonial, thrusting out her brave, determined little
chin. *The bad guys killed your father.*

The train rolled into a turn, shifting her balance. She was accepting
the gun Quinn had casually produced from his waistband. She could
have turned it on him right then, ended all this before it began. *Could
have, would have, should have.* She was licking her lips, taking a
running jump between rooftops in Alphabet City. She was spending
her first ever night in a homeless shelter, forbidding herself to cry
– if others sensed weakness, she was done for. She was sitting on a
plastic slip-cover in the Gunthers' fawn-colored suburban living room,
debating which made for a stronger transcript: foreign languages or
athletics. A normal girl. A regular life. The road not taken.

She was walking with her father, coming upon a snarl of spray-
painted red graffiti. She was mixing a glass of chocolate milk while
a radio played on the countertop. Mommy and Daddy were both alive,
and she felt safe, she felt warm, she felt loved.

The door at the end of the carriage opened again, as if by a ghost's
hand; a blast of cold air and noise swept in from the vestibule.

She looked vacantly through her own wavering reflection in the
window, at dark frozen earth rocketing past in a blur. Eventually,

the clanking rhythm of wheels across track slowed. Not far ahead, illuminated by a few straggling lights, a train station appeared.

'Vyborg,' said the *provodnik*, coming again through the car. 'Last stop. Vyborg.'

Muddled passengers filed out on to a cold platform. Cassie walked with the throng. Inside the terminal she passed shuttered ticket windows, magazine stalls, and a currency exchange. In the parking lot, she kept walking. Centuries-old towers shared a skyline with ribbed construction scaffolding. Rows of small cottages paced a frozen bay. Snow-covered gabled roofs glimmered beneath a smoky yellow moon. The air smelled of saltwater, sawdust, metal, and tar.

Closing the pea coat's top button, she walked on. Behind lighted windows, Saturday-night revelers drank and laughed. Icy wet wind swept off the bay. Northern lights shimmered behind the moon. She was moving, without having made a conscious decision, uphill, toward a red-and-white lighthouse.

When she reached the tower, she kept going. Houses were increasingly isolated up here, the town rambling behind her. She felt colder, and hungrier, than she'd realized. Fatigue was a crouching beast, ready to pounce. Soon she would need to choose a door, take a chance. Not yet.

She left the road, veering on to a winding path. Hill steeper, breath coming harder. Like a shark. Stop moving and die. Story of her life.

She was heading for a house set apart from any neighbor. Low gate, frozen mossy front walk, shambling woodpile. No driveway, no light inside, no sign of inhabitation.

The gate was unlocked. She walked a quiet circle around the cottage, sniffing the air. Something rank drifted on the night wind. She thought of brimstone and sulfur, of Quinn's revenant haunting her.

Around back: an old screen door. She touched the latch experimentally. The door creaked open.

Holding her breath she walked forward, into darkness.

PART THREE

THIRTEEN

MOIKA RIVER EMBANKMENT

Exiting the car before Sledkom HQ, Ravensdale paused briefly to look around the city at midnight.

The pallid streets were stunningly quiet. Such quiet, in the center of a city, was somehow unnerving. The traffic that had slowed Fletcher's limo to a crawl during the bustling morning had left no trace. The only visible vehicles were a single street sweeper, a solitary garbage truck, and an idling Italian Fiat, whose driver had pulled over to argue with a pretty woman in the passenger seat. A tremendous stone statue of Nikolay Przhevalsky, bearing more than a passing resemblance to Joseph Stalin, seemed to look back at Ravensdale challengingly.

Inside the marble lobby, he and Vlasov submitted to the *de rigueur* search. Six minutes later they stepped into a warren of body odor and close air and wreaths of smoke, of clicking and tapping and artificial light. Ravensdale accepted a cup of coffee, set it aside with a grimace after the first sip. Russians, he thought, would always be a tea-drinking people at heart.

Bordachenko led them to a laptop operated by a young man with wild black hair and three days' worth of beard. 'Four hundred and eighty sites, investigated in just shy of six hours – and nothing whatsoever to show for it. A waste, in the end, of time and resources. Thus we've given up on veterans and war widows, and redoubled our efforts with drone, security, and civilian footage. Of course, the facial recognition software is imprecise; a human eye is required for verification. Some potential leads on which I'd value your insight . . .'

As the first images ran – surveillance drone footage, exposing night-vision-green girls stumbling tipsily across bridges, relieving themselves in alleys – Ravensdale's belly crawled. *There is something squalid and rancid*, Stephen Fry had said, *about being spied on.*

He took out a cigarette, held it without lighting it, and tried to focus.

Across the laptop's screen moved dozens of young ladies, many filmed without their knowledge, all possessing the same basic facial structure, or close enough for the computer's purposes. Surveillance cams revealed belligerent young women filmed during traffic stops, intent young women inspecting shelves during late-night grocery runs, coquettish young women letting men light their cigarettes outside restaurants. Video remotely recovered from unsuspecting civilians' phones showed a girl wearing a headscarf sitting cross-legged on a floor in a dark room, a naked nice-looking blonde flipping a middle finger at whoever was filming, a brunette trying on lipstick in a bathroom mirror. Moral qualms aside, thought Ravensdale, the technology at hand created an operational challenge. There was just too much data. The mammoth security apparatus at their disposal threatened to sink beneath its own weight.

Drone footage again: a prostitute propositioning a client inside a stopped car, a young woman huddling on a park bench beside a man who had either fallen asleep or passed out. Security cams again: in convenience stores, bank vestibules, parking garages. Private video: girls orchestrating dance routines, girls reading magazines, girls emoting into microphones in nightclubs and karaoke bars, girls conducting video chats in various stages of undress.

An empire which accrued total power among the ruling elite, he thought, eventually used it.

In the Central Avtobus station on Gorokhovaya, a young woman boarded a green-and-white *avtobus*. On a platform at Moscovsky Station, a girl boarded a red-and-gray train. On a platform at Finlyandsky, a woman moved around the very outer edge of the frame, face averted. Dark pea coat, fur-lined *ushanka*, small but determined chin . . .

Ravensdale leaned forward, tapping the screen. 'What train was this?'

The figure froze. The young tech scowled. 'The . . . ten thirty-eight to Vyborg.'

'Has it arrived yet?'

The image minimized. From a checkerboard of icons, the tech made another selection. Moments later they were looking at another railroad platform, this one deserted. Moments after that, an *elektrichka* pulled in. The timecode pegged the event at just over an hour before. Passengers filed off, half-staggering with fatigue. In the midst of the throng walked the young woman in pea coat and *ushanka*, head lowered.

For an instant she looked up, almost directly into the lens of the security camera.

The tech froze the image, then magnified it.

The unlit cigarette in Ravensdale's hand snapped in two.

VYBORG

A bar of eerie moonlight slanted through a doorway.

She approached obliquely, still holding her breath. Even without inhaling, she registered disturbing smells on the air: charnel sewers and constipation, swampland rotting beneath plump dragonflies, a decomposing mouse stuck in the gullet of a snake.

She reached the doorway. As she regarded the living room, brackets appeared on either side of her mouth. After a moment of cognitive dissonance, her brain caught up to her eyes with a thud. She was looking at stuffed animals, arrayed in a line near a darkened fireplace before a dormant television, beady eyes gleaming as they soaked in the blank screen.

A dead woman lay nearby, swollen tongue lolling purple from one corner of the mouth.

A sound came from deeper in the house: a low hissing, a stealthy clicking, like bones or dice.

Several long moments later, Cassie moved again.

The darkened kitchen reeked of gas. She honed in on the burners. Strays pieces of food, cereal and raw pasta, crunched underfoot as she crossed the linoleum floor. She twisted a knob and the hissing-clicking bones fell quiet.

She opened a window, letting in cold air. After refilling her lungs and taking a moment to shove back the dark shadows collecting inside herself, she searched the rest of the house.

She found two small bedrooms. One was decorated with stuffed animals, a glow-in-the-dark Sputnik, board books, coloring books, crayons, action figures, wind-up robots. Painted rocket ships marched in cheery colors around the wainscoting. A wooden plaque hanging on the door declared that 'THIS ROOM BELONGS TO NIKOLAI'. The little boy in question, perhaps four years old, sprawled across his bed, tangled in a blanket. He had tousled greasy hair, rumpled clothes, and delicate eyelashes lying against creamy cheeks. He was still breathing, lightly but steadily.

The other bedroom featured quilts and pillows, bottles of perfume, paintings reminiscent of Georgia O'Keeffe. A bookshelf was lined not with books but with small china and glass figurines: cats and horses and rabbits and lambs, scale-model Eiffel Towers, Christs-on-crosses. A low-ceilinged closet was filled with casual inexpensive women's clothing. A small chest on the closet floor contained not jewelry, as Cassie expected, but an impressive selection of sex toys: vibrators and plugs, lubricants, a laced leather bustier, a short riding crop, a coarse blonde wig.

There was a single bathroom, stocked with feminine and juvenile toiletries, body wash and bubble bath. Inside the medicine cabinet Cassie found a man's deodorant, shaving cream, and safety razor. Her mouth quirked.

She went back to the kitchen. A pot on the stove contained uncooked pasta. An empty salt shaker sat on the counter beside a decaying stick of butter. With the gas stench dissipating, other odors of spoilage and death grew ever stronger.

Returning to the living room, she picked her way around the dead woman, opened another window, and let fresh air blow through. Then she stood appraising the scene, constructing a chain of events to explain what she was seeing.

The elements near the dead woman – a bottle on the floor, a stain of spilled liquid soaked into the carpet, a fleck of blackened tin foil – were key. The only thing missing was the junk itself. In the next instant she found it: a baggie on a coffee table near the fireplace. So. The lady had probably started with a few belts from the bottle – something home-brewed, judging from the lack of label, and likely very strong. Then she had chased the dragon. Had she been alone, or had the owner of the men's personal effects in the medicine cabinet joined her? The question could prove crucial. The former, and Cassie might expect company when the mystery man came home. The latter, and she could conclude that the man, in the time-honored tradition of men everywhere, had hastily decamped when something had gone wrong.

The baggie contained black tar. The blackened foil suggested that, indeed, the woman had been smoking. But where was the lighter? Cassie looked beneath the couch, around the fireplace, and then, after bracing herself, beneath the dead woman. She found a rolled tube of foil, a scorched cigarette butt. But no lighter.

The man had taken his lighter with him.

He had probably also, then, taken another baggie. No needle tracks on the woman, so she must have been snorting. Overdose from smoking alone was nearly impossible; one passed out before ingesting a fatal dose. So the mystery man had cleaned up. Why had he left behind the black tar?

Because it had been lost. Beneath the couch, or under the woman.

And the man had, understandably, been in a rush. And then the little boy had found it, moved it on to the table. She thought of the hissing gas range, the spilled food, the pot of pasta, the empty salt shaker. With Daddy gone and Mommy dead, the little boy had been left to fend for himself. He had filled a pot with pasta, turned on the gas range, and passed out.

The brackets around her mouth deepened.

She went back to his room. Crouching, she put her face very near to his. From slightly-parted lips puffed a soft breath.

She straightened again, cultivating a clinical sense of detachment. She had left Mariya alive . . . and look how that had worked out. The boy slept the sleep of the innocent. He would feel no pain. With Mommy dead and Daddy gone, he would actually be better off. She could vouch for that personally.

She opened her hands, closed them again.

It would not be easy. Not with those angelic eyelashes, that cupid's bow mouth.

She stood considering, looking down at him, opening and closing her hands.

ULITSA VARVARKA

Watching Sofiya eat, Yuri Antsiferov had discovered within himself a previously-unsuspected vein of poetry.

He reflected on how the most potent phenomena in nature were personified as women: full moons and seas and death, and even *Rodina* herself. He realized how much the gentler sex shared with a clear spring day, a babbling fresh brook, a fall of autumn dusk. How much the prisoner's eyes resembled emerald and turquoise, jade and blood-stone, and her skin alabaster, ivory, pure mother's milk—

When his gaze moved to her Tatar cheekbones, he caught himself. All at once he remembered an aphorism he'd heard as a child, about the first Roman army to enter Tartary. A legionary captured a Tatar and announced as much to his legatus but, upon being told to deliver the prisoner, was forced to admit: 'The Tatar won't let me.'

Sofiya scraped the inside of the bowl with the spoon. She licked her lips – her tongue a small pink blossom against the blistered gray – and then, looking up at him, stood.

She handed back the bowl with a supplicating half-curtsy. He paused, waiting for the inevitable request for a bath or clean clothes.

But she said nothing.

Instead, she drifted closer, so subtly that he couldn't have said which part of her moved. All he knew was that suddenly they were nearer each other than they had been a moment before. He caught her smell: unclean and overripe, vaguely disgusting and yet strangely arousing. He became aware of the position of the others in the apartment: Yakov grabbing some sleep on the threadbare couch in the front room, Viktor cleaning up in the kitchen. Something could happen between Yuri and the prisoner, right now, and neither of the others would ever know.

And she came closer again, in that way she had, where he couldn't even say how she had done it, so natural and inviolable was her grace, her femininity. The color high in her cheeks. Her breath came short and fast. And would it be hot on his cheek, that breath? It would. All he need do was reach out and draw her to him, and he could discover just how hot. And why shouldn't he? Was he not still the Dragon? Did he not have absolute power over her? And did not women respond to powerful men? And if something happened between the two of them, right now, in this room, what would be the harm? It would be the most natural thing in the world, for something to happen between a beautiful woman and a powerful man alone together in a room. It would mean nothing, and nobody need ever know. When it was done he might feel ashamed by his own decadence. But in the moment he would feel strong again, young and powerful, and now she was drifting still closer, into his arms, and without thinking he turned to set down the bowl by the goose-necked lamp, and that was when he heard the sound, *whhhssk*, soft and sibilant as a butterfly's wings, and then something feathery touched his neck, closed around it, and drew tight.

He straightened, grunting with surprise.

She jumped on to his back, weighing less than a blade of grass, less than an afterthought. He reached around, closing one massive hand around her twig-thin throat, and plucked her free. Brought her around front, where he could see the thing in her hand. A ribbon, a belt . . . no. The window sash.

And then he understood.

He flung her across the room, into a corner, where she struck her head and then lay helpless and whimpering, exposed for the betraying little whore she was.

Now the dragon was awake, the dragon that had made Yuri undisputed champion in the most brutal of sports, the dragon that would not rest until the woman was so much bloodied pulp to be scraped off the floor, which would teach her, yes, it would teach her the wisdom of biting the hand that fed you. When your captor decided to slip you an extra ration, just from the goodness of his heart, just because he was a decent fellow who took pity on a helpless bitch, you should not take advantage. She would learn.

'*Pizda*,' he muttered. *Cunt.*

Footsteps pounded down the hall. Yakov and Viktor burst into the room as one. Yuri's veil of rage lifted momentarily; he saw them exchange a look and then move forward, each reaching for one well-muscled arm, struggling to restrain him.

Then the veil fell again, and he flung them clear, one in each direction. He turned back to the woman, huddled crying in the corner. The fallen sash with which she had tried to strangle him beside her on the floor. He felt a new wave of sympathy for his dear departed father. The philanderer, they had called him, and everyone, all the aunts and sisters and second cousins, had clucked about what a bad man he had been, what an unfaithful husband and lousy Papa. But had they ever once thought that maybe Mother had brought it on herself? Maybe she had stroked Father's ego, leading him on, just as this bitch had done to Yuri, only to jump on his back, to try to strangle him, metaphorically or otherwise, the instant his guard was down? Had they ever put themselves in Papa's place? A man tried to be generous, and what did he get in return? Betrayal.

Growling, he advanced. The dragon was awake now, and nothing, nothing could stop him—

A gun spoke harshly.

Yuri sat down, hard.

The fury drained away, replaced by pain. He drew a long, hard, shuddering breath. He looked over at Viktor, the whelp, holding a PSM pistol in two shaking hands.

The boy had shot him.

The woman was still crying softly.

Shades of gray washed across the room. Yuri touched a corner of his mouth. His fingers came away red. His heartbeat was a fading mutter. The dragon was curling up, refolding vast leathery wings.

He looked at the woman. Their eyes met, and for an instant he read something in hers – something sad and victorious and furious and hopeless all at once.

He took one more breath, shuddered it out, and lay still.

Yakov stood unsteadily. He moved to Yuri, poked him with a toe. No response. He looked at Viktor, and then at the woman.

'You,' he said darkly. 'You had better be worth it.'

VYBORG

Nikolai opened his eyes.

For a long time he lay looking passively at Sputnik, not moving. Something rattled in the center of his brain, thud-thump-thunk. He recognized that thud-thump-thunk from the year before, when he'd taken a bad spill on the ice out on the bay. At the time, he hadn't known he'd taken a bad spill. One minute he'd been skating along faster than a race car, faster than a rocket ship, screaming laughter. The next he'd been on his back, looking up at a livid sky partly blocked out by a circle of concerned faces, with that syncopated beat pounding in the back of his head. In the days that followed, a tender lump had risen on his skull. Mama and Sasha had argued about whether he had suffered a SEVERE TRAUMA (Mama's words) and needed a hospital. Sasha had insisted that the boy would be OK, if they just left well enough alone, and sure enough, Nikolai soon had been.

But now the ragged pounding headache was back. Looking at the simple geometrical shape of the glow-in-the-dark Sputnik, he tried to figure out why that should be. Had he taken another fall on the ice? No. Something else had happened. And it had been something bad. The headache was just the start of it. His belly was empty. He'd apparently wet his bed – he was lying in a sticky puddle – but that, too, was just the start of it. Not only was *something* wrong, he realized then. *Everything* was wrong. Everything he'd ever taken for granted, everything that made the scary world OK—

It came like a thunderclap:

Mama was sick.

Mama wouldn't wake up.

Mama might be—

He climbed out of bed, groaning. After pausing to let the sour sloshing in his stomach abate, he started toward the living room . . . and then came to an abrupt stop.

A woman stood in one corner of his bedroom.

Watching him.

She was pretty, with creamy skin beneath a fur-trimmed hat. Standing motionless in the platinum morning light, she looked like a mannequin.

Nikolai's thumb moved to his mouth. For a small eternity he looked back at the woman in silence, trying to puzzle out the implications of this latest development. At last he called uncertainly toward the living room: *'Mamochka.'*

No reply, except the winter-whine of wind coming off the bay.

'*Mamochka*,' he called again.

'Nikolai,' the woman said.

He stared at her.

'Your Mama went to see the doctor. She asked me to look after you. Do you understand?'

Mutely, he nodded.

'If you do everything I say,' she said, 'we'll get through this fine. And your Mama will come home, and everything will go back to normal. But in order for that to happen, you have to do *everything I say*. OK?'

He nodded again, glazed.

'And if you don't . . . Well. We don't even need to talk about that, do we?'

He shook his head.

'Good.' She touched his tacky clothes. 'So. *Baushki-bau*. My name's Katya. Let's get you washed up.'

Before drawing a bath, she stripped off his pee-stained shirt and pants. Nikolai accepted without resisting. His head was still pealing rhythmically; simply remaining on his feet required effort.

In the bath, he zoomed and swooshed toy boats around, splashing, as she lathered him up. The warm water made the ringing in his head recede, and he became lost in the play. The boats were riding not through water but through space. The wooden boats were aliens, and the plastic boats were good guys, outnumbered but brave. Many laser guns were fired, many waves of attackers repelled. In the end, the aliens soared up into the sky, heading back to their home planet, defeated.

The woman's ministrations were inexpert. The water grew too cold, and then when she tried to correct it, too hot. Nikolai got soap in his eyes, which stung. But he managed not to cry. He would not be a baby. He would be a big boy and do everything she said, and then Mama would come home and everything would go back to normal.

After toweling dry, they returned to his room. She helped him struggle into clean clothes. 'Hungry?' she asked.

He nodded.

He sat at the kitchen table, watching, as she did something at the stove. This time there was no snake-like hiss, no *tick-tick-tick*. After a few minutes, the smell of cooking food filled the house. After a few minutes more, she did something at the sink with the sieve. Then she poured noodles into a bowl. Adding a jar of sauce from the cupboard, she mixed. It did not taste like Mama's cooking. It was overdone and too salty. Nikolai was hungry enough that he cleaned his bowl anyway. Then he asked for seconds.

West of town, a search party moved slowly across rutted ground.

Junior Lieutenant Golod of the Saint Petersburg *politsiya* placed his boots with care amidst loose boulders and snowy mud. On either side, dogs snuffled busily, pausing every few moments to resample the scent brandished by their handlers.

Suddenly, Golod tripped over a gnarled root, sprawling down with a curse. Someone laughed harshly. Golod regained his feet, face burning. Not his fault, he thought angrily, that he wasn't uncultured, *nekulturny*, like some of the men in the search party, country bumpkins accustomed to negotiating such uneven ground. Not his fault that he was used to sidewalks, pavement, the fruits of the modern era.

They moved again, through trees, scrub brush, wilderness, separated by a frozen estuary from civilization, from the red-and-white light-house, the toy-sized town. A faint cold breeze rustled pine needles. The sun in the sky was dull, utterly lacking in warmth.

Leading the procession, a soldier abruptly raised a clenched fist. The motley group – a makeshift collection of city and country police, civil and military agency – stumbled to a disorganized stop. In the vanguard, machine guns thumped into gloved hands. A troika of men fanned out, prodding the undergrowth.

Beside Golod, a man from the PG's Office narrated the latest development to someone sitting in some warm comfortable room back in Pieter. 'Called a stop, sir. No, sir, not clear yet why. No, sir, still no indication . . .'

Whatever it was, it proved a false alarm. They moved again. Before they had covered another hundred meters, a dog emitted a low, pained whine and then strained forward, tail whipping. A rabbit, driven above ground by hunger, bounded away with two terrific hops, leaving the dog to bark impotently.

Golod covered a sneeze. Coming down with something. The icing on the cake.

The search party moved forward again, pounding the brush.

FOURTEEN

With the boy safely installed before the television, Cassie conducted another search, this time with the benefit of late watery dawn breaking outside the windows.

The small house had given up most of its secrets the night before. But there remained a few discoveries still to be made – more evidence of the mysterious vanished man (mud-caked boots in back hall, forgotten clothes in dryer), a cache of food beneath the sink (canned soup, pickled fish, bottled mushrooms, and *varenye*, a condiment made from berries), and, of most potential value, a computer in the master bedroom, half-covered by a carelessly tossed blanket.

The computer was a mutt – Chinese tower, Russian keyboard, bootleg American monitor. A few years old, but not a bad set-up, considering. Camera, photo printer, functional Internet connection. Cassie woke it up, spent a few querulous moments acquainting herself with the Cyrillic keyboard. She opened a browser and reconfirmed what she already knew about local geography. Finland was just thirty kilometers away. Googling the Vyborg customs station, she found an official website.

For the next twenty minutes she read closely, chewing on one thumbnail. The passage, technically at Nuijamaa, was the second most traveled along the lengthy international border. Each year, eight hundred thousand vehicles carried over one million passengers across. The station was well documented in attractive color photographs. There were six lanes for cars and busses, and one devoted exclusively to rail. The Finnish side boasted an institutional-looking white building, a simple blue-and-white flag, a tidy sign proclaiming 'FINNISH CUSTOMS AND FRONTIER GUARD'. The Russian side was smaller, darker, grayer, with heavy spruce forest crowding in close on every side. The comments section shed light on the nature of the average border-crosser: Finns pouring east every weekend to take advantage of cheap booze, and Russians going the other way, hunting for inexpensive duty-free goods.

After perusing the website, she moved to the window. Fingers of light streaming through a clear blue sky illumined a picturesque morning, a postcard-perfect view of a town compactly arranged on a narrow peninsula. The bay was dazzling azure farther out, where the ocean's hoarded warmth beat back General Winter, but ice-white near the shore. Skiffs were frozen in place against docks piled with piping, cables, and drums. A medieval castle rising from an islet competed with the red-and-white lighthouse for the privilege of watching over the small gabled cottages, the cobblestoned streets, the shipyard and decaying sawmill.

As Sunday morning brightened, she thought, the Finns would bestir themselves slowly after a night of hard drinking. They would swallow aspirin, drink multiple glasses of water, find heavy greasy breakfasts to soak up the alcohol in their stomachs. Then they would head back to the customs station. They would have passports already stamped with visas, which they would carry in handbags and fanny packs. Foggy from hangovers, they would make easy pickings. But she did not speak a word of Finnish. To be useful, any documentation she stole would need to be Russian.

From the living room, the boy chuckled at something on his TV show. His laugh was nearly as beatific as his eyelashes and cupid's bow mouth. Nothing was more innocent, she thought, than the laughter of children.

And nothing was more virtuous than the mother of a young child – or so people tended to think.

Her brow creased.

She went to have another look at the dead woman's wardrobe. After a few moments, she assembled an outfit: modest, cheery, respectable. An upstanding mother's outfit, the kind of outfit to make a chivalrous man reach to hold a door.

Facing a mirror, she moved the coarse wig forward on her scalp, then back. She used a heavy layer of foundation to fill out her cheeks, petroleum jelly to change the shape of her eyebrows. Muted red lipstick, a pair of faux-pearl earrings. Small sunglasses perching near the tip of her still-disjointed nose. She admired her reflection: blonde once again, but now an older, grown-up version of herself. Maddie Gunther, Junior, ready to strike off and sell some real estate. *Good morning, ma'am. Notice all the direct light. The kitchen has been completely remodeled, and the school system is really very excellent. But there's another offer on the table, so we want to move quickly . . .*

The road not taken.

She took off the sunglasses and the wig, pulled on the *ushanka* again, and went to check on Nikolai and see about starting some lunch.

As Train #7017 prepared to leave the station, nine men materialized from shadow.

One moved toward the engine, hailing the conductor. Three others spread out along the platform, readying automatic weapons. The remaining five moved toward a door in the first passenger car, which after a moment hissed open.

The team of Spetsnaz Alpha, *Spetzgruppa 'A'*, swept through the car, brandishing weapons threateningly, peering closely into faces of startled passengers. Reaching the end of the carriage, they checked the bathroom. Before moving into the space between cars they paused to look, listen, and switch the forward man.

In this manner they checked the entire length of the train in less than four minutes. Reaching the last car, they returned along the tracks on the far side from the platform, using mirrors mounted on long elbow flashlights to inspect the roof and beneath the undercarriage.

All clears were exchanged. As train #7017 pulled out of the station, ten minutes behind schedule, the Spetsnaz melted back into shadow.

'I'll be right back,' Cassie said. 'You stay put.'

Seated before his second DVD of the day, Nikolai didn't answer.

Outside, echoing church bells hung on cold sunny air. Far out in the bay, distant running lights drifted. After spending a moment orienting herself, she began picking her way down the hill.

In town she mingled, window-shopping, seeking in reflections the perfect targets. As she did, she became aware of a covert surveillance presence overlaying the town like a foul-smelling blanket. They were being cagey about it – they had learned subtlety. There were no *politsiya* blatantly consulting tablets, no machine-gun toting soldiers, no buzzing drones or noisy hovering helicopters.

But low profile or no, they were here, and in greater force than a small border town could justify. A kid braving the icy streets on a bicycle was, on second glance, not a kid at all, but a raw-boned young man with roving eyes. A woman shopping across the way had invisible antennae vibrating like tuning forks: a mirror image of Cassie herself, slyly taking it all in while seeming not to. A man lighting a cigarette on a bench . . . another eating brunch alone at a window behind a newspaper . . . another hawking small souvenir replicas of

Vyborg Castle, making change clumsily, as if he'd never done it before . . .

She kept moving.

A couple with two young children, boy and girl, were heading into a bar-restaurant called Nordwest. Following them inside, Cassie picked up a tourist map of the town. Smiling vaguely, she told the hostess she'd be meeting someone. At the bar she ordered a diet soda, watching the family in the mirror. This far north, the physical differences between Finns and Russians were hard to distinguish; everybody was tall, slim, square-faced, fair. But as minutes passed, she picked up snatches of the family's speech, more cadences than words. The tempo was musical, modulated – lilting Finnish, not square-footed Russian. And so the family was useless to her. She left the restaurant just as two undercover cops came in, all hunched shoulders and sweeping eyes.

The day was warming. Melting ice dripped from gutters. Plangent wind slipped off the icy bay. As clouds scudded across the sun, ingots of light and shadow alternated on the cobblestoned streets.

In the town square, by a statue depicting a rather squat Lenin, a thirtyish father chased a boy who rode a bicycle with training wheels. 'You're getting it,' the man said in Russian; 'you're getting it; you're getting it!' The boy screamed laughter.

Cassie loitered within earshot, cleaning a smudge off her sunglasses, glancing at her wrist as if considering a watch. After ten minutes, the man and his son rolled off down a narrow street. She followed. Referring to her map, noting the cottage into which they disappeared. She might return after dark, allow herself entrance, and see what she could find inside.

On the next block, she found herself walking behind another family of four. The mother and father bickered in the flat, equivocal way of parents trying to conceal a quarrel from children. A boy of approximately six held a squeeze packet of apple sauce in one hand, a book featuring a picture of Cheburashka on the cover in the other. A baby was expertly crooked in the mother's muscular arm.

'Just that if you've seen one,' the mother was saying, 'you've kind of seen them all.'

'So if you don't want to go, just say so.'

'It's not even the real cathedral, is it? It's only a few years old.'

'So if you don't want to go, just say so.'

'It's just that Danya gets heavy.'

'So. If. You. Don't. Want. To—'

'I don't want to go.'

'There. Was that so hard?'

Their Russian, with its hardening of final soft labials, placed them as tourists from the south. The father wore a hipster's scraggly beard and thin sideburns, a denim jacket insufficient for the weather, and a distinctly unhip fanny pack. The mother wore a stylish hooded cape, a short bobbed haircut, and a harried air.

'So,' said the father, 'you want to just get on the train?'

'Maybe find something to eat first. Then hop on in time for his nap.'

'Where do you want to eat?'

'Anywhere. The closest place.'

'Right here.'

As they clustered around a menu under glass, a crowd of Finns came up the sidewalk. Jostling ensued. Interposing herself between the Finns and the Russians, Cassie let herself be pushed up against the hipster and his fanny pack. Under cover of the press of bodies, she used her stomach to hold the bag against his waist, maintaining pressure, as her fingers worked the zipper. Wallet, phone, loose cash – passports. She nimbly plucked out four red booklets, left the pack unzipped, and melted away down the block.

A white Bukhanka van, windows tinted far beyond the legal limit of seventy percent VLT, cruised slowly down the opposite side of the street. Averting her face, slipping the passports into the folded map, she walked smoothly on.

On the next block she turned into a restaurant which awkwardly combined Irish leitmotifs with Asian, Mexican, and Native American. Inside a locked bathroom stall, she examined her haul. The family's name was Reznikov. The mother's and boy's passports were several years old – the woman, Raisa, looked like a different person, fresh-faced and rested and optimistic; the boy, Maxim, was a baby, chubby-cheeked and tow-headed – and included no biometric chip. The father and infant had newer documents, including chips. She tore the latter two passports into shreds, flushing the chips down the toilet, leaving the remaining scraps in a trash bin so as not to risk clogging the plumbing.

Outside again, she headed back toward the lighthouse, taking note now of cars parked along the cobblestones. She would wait to steal one until tomorrow morning, so as to give no time for an alarm to be raised. She would make certain that the numbers at the end of the license, which identified the oblast from which the vehicle harkened, matched her cover story. Plenty of tourists in town; no shortage of vehicles from which to choose.

She walked past a homeless woman whose raggedy clothes looked suspiciously fresh, as if recently distressed by hand. A man lackadaisically moving a wide push-broom across a sidewalk, who paused to watch her go by. Another selling saffron pretzels, following her with incisive dark eyes. She ignored them all, looking pointedly straight ahead, putting one foot mechanically in front of the other, and climbed the hill, past the lighthouse, back to the waiting cottage.

In the rear of the white Bukhanka van, Ravensdale held tightly to an armrest.

Leaving behind the cobblestoned streets, they see-sawed across dirt roads, ditches, and darkening snowy fields. As the local representative of the Ministry of Internal Affairs delivered a never-ending monologue about the houses they passed, the techs handling the equipment – both imported from Petersburg – exchanged derisive glances. Ravensdale couldn't tell if the disdain was intended for the unfortunates under discussion, for the IA representative, or for himself.

'And here we have the Platonovs. She spreads her legs for anyone with a kopeck and a bottle of *Troinoi Odekolon*. He responds by begging all the more cravenly for her affection. Let's listen, you'll see . . . Well, evidently they are taking a break at the moment. But if we swing by again later, after the booze has loosened them up, we'll get an earful, I promise you. Vasya: up the hill now. Here we have the lighthouse. The keeper is a man named Amalrik. A decent enough old fellow, Amalrik. He knew my father. He's lived alone since his wife died, almost twenty years ago now. He's *zastenchivyj*.' Timid, shy. 'Keeps out of trouble. No chance he would ever harbor a fugitive. But just up here, a different story. Yes, a very different story. A Jew – and not just any Jew. His forefathers, they say, helped to write the Protocols themselves. Vasya, slow down; we'll want to take a close look here.'

They creaked to a stop behind a stand of taiga. The techs sat up straight and, despite their city sophistication, trained their parabolic mics and thermal imagers as if they had caught a serious lead. Scratch a Bolshevik, Lenin himself had said, and find a chauvinist.

'This one, Rawicz – I always keep my eye on him.' The thermal picked out a single blotch of color within the cottage: seated, arms slightly raised as if reading a book. The microphone picked up only a discordant howl of wind. 'He is studying, I gather. They are always plotting . . . but they are patient. Well, he doesn't have our fugitive with him. So he lives to plot another day. Vasya: the Ivanova woman now.'

The hill grew steeper. They neared an isolated cottage: low gate, icy front walk, snowy woodpile. 'Galina Ivanova. Another embarrassment to our fine town. Such a talented skater, as a girl, that they talked about competition in her future, even the Olympics. But then – what else? – drugs. See, there she is, and there's her boy.'

Two swirls of hot pink – a small child propped in the lap of an adult – sat before a cooler swirl of purple, a television or a computer. As the parabolic microphone came into range, a woman's voice piped through the headphones: *Come on*, baushki-bau, *you can do better than that. A real smile, OK?*

'Vasya: To Olga's now. One of our more decent citizens, Olga Purizhinskaya. Runs the account ledgers at the shipyard, and mostly keeps out of trouble. But she has bad taste in men. And she likes them rough. On a Sunday evening, she's likely alone, recovering from the weekend, but if we're very lucky we might get ourselves a show . . .'

Cassie juggled the boy on her lap until his face lined up again with the camera. 'One more,' she commanded.

He grinned obediently, and she snapped the shot. 'Now go play.'

He wriggled down without arguing, ran back for the living room at full-tilt. A moment later he was happily absorbed again in his game, in which rocket ships and dinosaurs fought a battle royale against stuffed animals and police cars, all to a soundtrack of a grim little song about a bird denied porridge.

She resized and cropped one photo of each of them, and printed both. With a kitchen knife, she carefully carved out rectangles of the necessary dimensions. Brow ruffling, she used the tip of the blade to scrape the old pictures free of the stolen passports. Two tiny dollops of household glue fixed the new ones in place.

She laid several items across the bed: sewing kit, scarf, sunglasses, mid-length dark hourglass coat, strip of teal ribbon. Shrugging on the coat, she inspected her reflection in the full-length mirror. The same respectable mother character she had contrived earlier gazed steadily back. The road not taken.

She shrugged off the coat, reversed it. With needle and thread, she attached the sand-colored scarf to the hem of the coat's sturdy beige lining, and then slipped it on again. The longer, lighter garment made her look both taller and wider, and several years older.

From the bay, the long, lowing bass note of a ship's horn sounded dolefully.

She reversed the coat again, rigged up her ersatz hem with two safety pins. She experimented with the wig – removing it altogether, which revealed her gleaming bare scalp; tucking the back beneath the collar of the coat; tying it up with the ribbon on one side.

Two distinct women were emerging in the mirror. One was a younger and sportier Cassie – correction, Raisa Reznikov, from Kursk – with sunglasses, a half-ponytail, and a short dark hourglass figure. The other, almost an entirely different person, came into being after she popped the lenses out of the sunglasses, turned the coat inside-out, and released the hem and ponytail: an older, taller, wider version, with full bell of blonde hair, long light coat, and bespectacled academic mien.

The younger, sportier model was the woman who would pass through customs during the morning rush-hour crowd. But if something went wrong – coat inside-out, hem released, lenses popped out, ribbon untied – this woman would vanish, and the other woman would take her place. *Presto.*

Practicing, she got the change down to ten seconds.

Nine.

Eight.

Eight.

Eight again.

Eight was as good as it would get.

She locked eyes with her reflection. *We're going to meet my husband in Helsinki. We've traveled together from Kursk, but decided to split up for a few days.* Must strike just the right note of sullen hostility. There had been a marital spat here. The prying of a nosy customs official would not be welcome. *He's coming by train with our daughter, through Imatra. Got this idea into his head that she'd like to see the dam. Of course, it's really* he *who wants to see the dam. He's an overgrown boy, when you get down to it.* If the customs agent was female, she might add one last dash of conspiratorial sorority. *You know how they are.* But there she would stop. Must not overplay her hand. And must not touch her face or wig, cross her arms or lean away . . . And must not equivocate. No *I guess*es. No lengthy over-complications to put her gawky Russian on full display. In and out; decisive. *Yes is the better answer.*

She rehearsed again, timed herself changing disguises again. She had lost a second, bringing her back to nine.

*   *   *

'Here,' she said and patted her lap.

Nikolai climbed up unquestioningly. He wore his favorite space-themed pajamas, with the snug booties built right in, and held a plastic cup of juice with a flexible straw. (Mama would never let him drink juice right before bed. There were advantages, he was deciding, to having Katya as a caretaker.) Settling in, he looked expectantly at the row of bedtime books arranged on the dresser top. Maybe, as Katya was unfamiliar with Mama's rules, he could convince her to read more than the usual two. Maybe three, or even four . . .

'Once upon a time,' she said gravely, 'there was a little bunny rabbit named Nikolai.'

Mama had never told him a story which didn't come from a book. But Mama was still at the doctor's office, and hence nowhere to be seen, and Katya was the grown-up. He blinked and gave her his full attention.

She rumpled his hair affectionately. 'And Nikolai lived with his mama. And there was a nice lady bunny rabbit who lived with them too, named Katya. Their best friend.'

He laughed. 'But that's *our* names.'

'So they are.'

It was a silly story she was telling, about bunny rabbits with the same names as real people. But the look on her face was not silly. It was the look grown-ups wore to indicate that something very serious was under discussion, that *I am not playing a game here, Kolya.*

She paused for a moment, looking at him intently, making sure he appreciated the gravity of the story he was about to hear. And despite the brightness of the room – the overhead bulb burning, the colorful well-lit rocket ships marching cheerily around the wainscoting – a shiver trickled liquidly down his spine.

'Now in the world of bunny rabbits, you know, cats are really bad. Cats like to attack bunnies, and scratch them up, and bite them, and sometimes even eat them. There was one cat who was the worst of all. The king of all evil cats. His name was Koschei.'

Nikolai nodded somberly. Every child knew of Koschei the Deathless, the ancient and hideous monster who might come after you if you didn't eat your vegetables or go to sleep on time. Koschei could not be killed the way a man could. Unless one could track down his soul, he was immortal. And his soul was not easily found. It hid inside a needle, which hid inside an egg, which hid inside a duck, which hid inside a hare, which hid inside an iron chest, which was buried beneath a green oak tree, which grew on a mysterious disappearing island . . .

'There was only one rabbit who scared Koschei. This was a very special, very magical bunny rabbit named Maxim. And do you know the funny thing? Maxim looked *just like Nikolai.*'

'Just like him?'

'Just exactly like him. So. One day, Nikolai and his Mama and Katya were out in the garden, eating breakfast. They liked to eat carrots and lettuce and cabbage and peas and potatoes and onions and chives. There they were, happily nibbling away and minding their own business, when all of a sudden the evil cats conducted a raid. Do you know what a raid is?'

'It's when the police come search your house and look around and arrest you.'

'Exactly. And when the evil cats came, Katya grabbed Nikolai, and they ran and hid in their underground hole. But Nikolai's mama moved too slow. So the evil cats nabbed her and took her away.'

Another dramatic pause. He licked his lips, waiting.

'Well, every bunny rabbit knew where Koschei took his prisoners – to a jail on the other side of the colony. Nikolai and Katya realized right away that they would need to go and rescue his mama, fast, before anything bad could happen to her. But this was a dangerous time to travel through the bunny rabbit kingdom. Because the evil cats had guards everywhere. And these evil cat guards loved more than anything to arrest bunny rabbits and put them in the jail. And sometimes, when the cats got hungry in the middle of the night, they would go visit the jail and just choose a bunny rabbit at random and then eat them. Munch munch munch.'

'No,' he said hoarsely.

'Yes. So, as they were getting ready to go, Nikolai had an idea. He realized that since he looked *just like Maxim*, the one bunny rabbit all cats were afraid of, he could play a very smart trick! He could pretend he *was* Maxim. And he could say Katya was his mother, so the evil cats didn't hurt her either, because they would never dare to hurt Maxim's mother.'

'But where was the real Maxim?'

She paused. 'Nobody knew,' she said after a moment. 'Nobody knew, honey. They'd spent their whole lives waiting for him to show up, but he never had. Some bunnies had decided he wasn't even real at all. They thought he was just a story.'

'Oh.'

'But the evil cats believed in him – that was what mattered now. Because Nikolai and Katya hit the road that very night, heading to the jail, to rescue his Mama. And just as they feared, they didn't get very far at all before a cat guard pulled them over. "Who are you, and where do you come from?" the guard demanded. And what did Nikolai say?'

'He said, "I'm Maxim, and this is my mama, and you better let us through or you'll be in serious trouble!"'

'Exactly! And what do you think happened next?'

'The cats let them through.'

'They did.' Her soft, strong hand stroked hair off his forehead. 'They did. Because those cats were even more afraid of Maxim, you see, than they were of Koschei. They let the bunny rabbits right through. So the bunnies went on a little longer, along the road, and then some more cats stopped them. "Who are you, and where do you come from?"'

'"I'm Maxim, and this is my mama, and you better let us through or you'll be in serious trouble!"'

'Right! Except they were so scared of him, he didn't even need to say that part about getting in trouble. He just said, "I'm Maxim, and this is my mama." And that's all he had to say, and the cats let them through.'

Another solemn nod.

'So then they got to the jail. And there were so many cat guards that Nikolai got scared. He wanted to turn around and run back home and hide in his underground hole. But then he knew he would never get his mama back, and some hungry cat might come in the middle of the night, and choose her, and eat her! So even though he was scared, he kept going. He and Katya rolled right up to the front of that jail, to a gate surrounded by evil cats. And what did Nikolai say?'

'"I'm Maxim, and this is my mama!"'

'That's right. And you know what happened?'

'The cats let them through.'

'That's right. And then the bunnies saved Mama. And then word went around the kingdom that Maxim had come back, so the evil cats packed their bags and went somewhere else. And everybody lived happily ever after. The end.'

Nikolai considered. 'I like how the bunny had my name.'

'He sure did.' She levered him down on to the floor. 'Need to use the potty before bed?'

'No.'

When he climbed beneath his blanket, she killed the overhead. Night lights blinked on, dappling spidery illumination across the painted rocket ships. 'OK?' she said.

'OK.'

'We're going to go get your mommy tomorrow, Nikolai.'

Relief flooded through him, so overwhelming that he nearly burst into tears. Silently, he nodded.

'We can play a game when we go. We'll pretend we're the bunnies from the story, and you'll tell everyone you're Maxim and I'm your mommy. OK?'

He nodded again.

'Sleep well, *baushki-bau*,' she said and started to remove herself.

'Katya?'

'Yes?'

'Leave the door open a crack?' he said hopefully.

'OK, *detka*. And don't be scared. I'll be right outside.' She paused, and then added: 'I'll take good care of you.'

Lying in the dead woman's bed, she ran restive eyes across a dark ceiling.

In the morning they would wake, breakfast, and dress. Ordinary clothes for him; short dark hourglass coat, shades, and half-ponytail for her. She would leave Nikolai alone while she went to, ahem, fetch the car. And just thirty kilometers later, they would reach the check-point. Ten minutes after that she would be in Finland at last, where the entire state security apparatus would not be bent on finding her. And then this would all, finally, be over . . .

Outside, the snarling wind cranked briefly up into a shriek.

In the grip of that wind, drifts of snow would be massing against the woodpile beside the house. Inside her crude coffin of logs, Nikolai's mother would by now be crusted with ice. But so it went, in the end, for everyone. For Quinn. For Blakely. Eventually, for Cassie herself.

But not yet.

She breathed, slowly and steadily. Consciousness oscillated in time with her respiration, turning deep and then shallow, shallow and then deep. If she couldn't sleep, she could at least rest. Tomorrow she must be ready. Tomorrow was the last hurdle. In which the brave and resourceful bunny rabbits eluded the evil cats. *Chapter six*, she thought dreamily, *in which Eeyore has a birthday and gets two presents . . .*

In which Nikolai and Katya elude the evil Koschei and escape scot-free. And little does young Nikolai realize that in fact Katya is Cassie and Cassie is Koschei, or the closest thing this particular story has to Koschei. Cassie is the bad guy here, because Cassie is doing to young Nikolai exactly what Quinn had done to her. Putting him at risk for her own selfish purposes. Taking him to run a gamut of stupid, brutal men with big guns and itchy trigger fingers. *Using* him, not to mince words. Using his naivety, his trust, his love, and his hunger for his missing parents – just as Quinn had done to her.

It was the way of the world. The older and stronger took advantage of the younger, the dumber, the weaker. You didn't have to like it. But you did have to be on the right side of the equation. Otherwise you suffered. As *she* had suffered.

No longer.

Now the fog had truly lifted. Now she was truly awake. Now she saw clearly at last.

In the real world, it was every man for himself.

Distantly, an owl hooted. A wolf howled a mournful reply – almost just outside the window, raising the hair on the back of her neck.

FIFTEEN

The little bird cooks porridge, she gave it to this one, she gave it to this one, she gave it to this one . . . but none for you! Why? You did not bring water. You did not chop firewood. There is nothing for you . . .

Eventually, he slept. In the dream he was inside a car, leaning up against a door, and the door popped open; or perhaps the rest of the car fell away, but the door remained in place; or perhaps it was the world itself that fell apart, the air and the light which held the door and the car together that failed. In any event, the integrity of the vehicle deteriorated, the door opened, and Nikolai and the speeding car parted ways. He was falling. Katya had not kept him safe. Grown-ups lied: about that, about everything.

His eyes were half-lidded, and he looked at his glowing Sputnik. He half-dreamed, half-listened as the stuffed animals clustered around him whispered: *Don't trust the grown-ups. Grown-ups lie. Grown-ups always lie.*

It was true. Mama had lied about whether or not Papa would come back – so long ago that she thought Nikolai had forgotten. But he would never forget. She lied about whether she went to bed right after she put him to sleep. (She very rarely did.) She lied about whether Sasha hurt her when they hugged hard. Sasha lied too: about whether or not he would play with Nikolai, about whether or not he would still be at the house in the mornings. (He very rarely was.) Sometimes he lied without even lying, which was like a double lie. He told Mama she looked pretty, she should have another bite of cake, but with his eyes glinting in such a way that indicated he didn't really mean it. Nikolai saw; he saw it all. Adults were confusing and horrifying and contra-dictory. If you could count on one thing about them, it boiled down to this: they lied.

In this shadow world of half-sleep, piglet became a sage, a sooth-sayer, a general the others would follow into battle without hesitation. You would never guess it to look at him, but piglet knew a lot.

Don't trust Katya because she's a grown-up and she lies.

But what else was he supposed to do? She was the only grown-up around. He needed her. At least until Mama came home . . .

He tossed, turning over, closing his eyes tightly. *Go away, piglet. I don't want to listen to you any more.*

In the morning, he bounced out of bed eagerly, consumed by a single thought: today was the day they would go get Mama.

As he crossed the room, he felt a penetrating gaze on his back. He turned. Piglet lay slumped crooked on the bed, small black eyes accusatory. A rill of the previous night's fear trickled across Nikolai's happy mood, like a storm cloud moving across the sun.

'Breakfast,' called a merry voice.

He slowly turned away and went to have breakfast.

Vegetable soup, stale bread, and *varenye* waited on the table. The discontent he felt at the meal was balanced by the fun of having routine so blithely upended – whoever heard of soup for breakfast? He ate a few polite bites and drank water. Katya drank tea. After the meal she set him in front of the TV – another violation of the rules, so early in the morning – and then went into Mama's room. Minutes later, she disappeared through the front door.

He watched an entire episode of *Spokoynoy nochi, malyshi!*, was just starting again from the beginning when he heard the front door open again. He listened as she packed a bag in the bedroom. Then she came out and turned off the TV. Nikolai blinked, hardly recognizing her. For the first time in his experience, she had no *ushanka*; he could see her blonde hair, tied up on one side with a ribbon. She wore sunglasses balanced on the tip of her nose, and make-up, and a small purse, and a short dark hourglass coat.

Crouching before him, she looked levelly into his eyes. 'We're going to go get your mommy now, sweetheart. Just like the bunny rabbits in the story. And if anyone asks . . .'

'I'm Maxim,' he said.

'Such a smart boy. You're Maxim, and I'm your mother.' Smiling, she reached into the purse. 'You won't have any trouble,' she said, 'because you look *exactly like Maxim*. Look what I found.'

She produced a small booklet and opened it. Nikolai saw a photograph of a boy who looked, indeed, very much like himself. Puzzling out the letters below, he put together the first name: M-A-X-I-M.

He grinned. 'Cool.'

'Right? I found one for myself, too.' Back into the purse went the passports. Out came Nikolai's winter hat, with ear flaps and a tassel. She tugged it on to his head. 'So just remember: if we run into trouble you say, loud and clear, "I'm Maxim, and this is my mama!" And we'll get your mother back. And while we're at the doctor's office, I bet you'll get a special treat – a lollipop. Sound good?'

'What about you?'

'What about me?'

'Where will you go, after Mama comes back?'

She looked at him. 'I'll come play with you again real soon, *detka*.'

'Promise?'

She squeezed his hand. 'Cross my heart and hope to die.'

She buckled him into the back seat, slid behind the steering wheel, and pulled away without a backward glance.

Gripping the wheel tightly, she tried to clear the flight decks in her mind. Just an ordinary mother with child. Ordinary tourists, occupying an ordinary Toyota Alphard minivan. She'd had an ordinary fight with her ordinary husband. *He's coming by train with our daughter, through Imatra.* If she believed it, they would believe it. *Of course, it's really* he *who wants to see the dam.*

The Alphard's suspension expertly absorbed the road's small rolls and dips; the ride was smooth and silent. The stillness, somehow malign, did not help to ease her nerves. She almost reached out and switched on the radio, just to drown out the quiet. But then she risked tuning into a news report at just the wrong time. The boy might hear the wrong thing. She left the radio off.

She would ditch both kid and van, she thought, somewhere in Helsinki. He would survive. She had. Things were tough all over. In the real world, it was every man for himself.

Before trying an airport, she'd lay low for a while, and then steal another passport. And then . . . somewhere new. Out west, maybe. Once she'd known a guy named Bogie, who had gone to seek his fortune in LA. Maybe it was time to look him up, see what there was to see out in La-La Land. She'd thought her days of wandering were over. But she'd made that mistake before. Reality always came back around.

A glossy black crow sitting on a fence post watched the van pass. Eyes rimmed red in the cloudy, dreary light. *Once upon a midnight dreary, while I pondered weak and weary . . .*

Towering snowy pine and spruce. The sky gray, flat, and low. The only other vehicle in sight a truck, just vanishing beyond a low hill ahead. The road should have been more crowded. She was counting on a crush at the customs station to help ease them through. Why wasn't the road more crowded?

Still ten kilometers, at least. Time enough for a crowd to develop.

A train appeared on the right, hooting. In back, Nikolai sat up straighter. 'Look!' he yelled, so vigorously that her heart staggered in her chest.

'I see!'

'Look! It's so fast!'

'I see!'

'I hope it's the good guys!' he cried happily. 'I hope it's the good guys coming to help us and not the evil bad cats and evil Koschei trying to get ahead of us because they're going to win. Look how fast they're going!'

'I think it's the good guys!' she said.

'I think so too! I hope so! I really hope so! They're going so fast! But we've got to get Mama and so it really better be the good guys because if it's the evil cats we're really in trouble!'

'It's the good guys! But if it's the bad guys, what do we do?'

'I say I'm Maxim and you're my mama!'

'Such a smart boy!'

Traffic thickening now, thank God. And even more ahead; slowing down, bunching up. A sign announced in multiple languages the imminence of the border crossing. The road branched into multiple lanes. And here came the clog of traffic, with a vengeance. The minivan drew to a stop behind a wheezing bus.

They idled.

He's coming by train with our daughter, through Imatra. He's coming by train with our daughter, through Imatra. He's coming by train with our daughter, through Imatra.

They crept slowly ahead. The customs station looked just as it had on the website, with one lane for the train, which had come to a stop, and six for motorized vehicles. Trunks were inspected, passports scrutinized, windows leaned into, paperwork filled out. Certain travelers were invited to pull over into stalls, leave their cars, and accompany border guards into a low gray building. On the other side of the border, the Finnish apparatus hummed along: bigger, brighter, cleaner.

They pulled up to a white line. A guard wearing a clipboard and holding a beret approached her window. 'You're Maxim now,' she told Nikolai. 'And I'm your mama.'

In the rear-view, she saw him nod soberly.

The guard leaned down: early twenties, dirty blond hair, air of profound disinterest. At the same moment the cool gray fog descended, thicker than ever, enveloping her. She felt tremendously calm, tremendously in control, as if she watched herself, watched an entire scene already scripted, from the outside.

'Anything to declare?' the guard asked.

'No,' she said, handing over the passports.

'Tourists?'

'Yes. We're going to meet my husband in Helsinki . . .' She almost said more, bit her tongue. *Don't try too hard.*

'Fruits and vegetables?'

'No.'

He leafed through the passports, handed them back, then passed over the clipboard. A form on top, a ballpoint pen on a chain. 'Fill this out.'

She did, providing Helsinki as their destination, tourism as their purpose, and a home address in Kursk. As she handed back the clipboard, her eyes flicked past the guard. A dozen yards ahead, the customs operation fed into a brief no-man's land. Then, beyond a Tigre APC with a light machine gun mounted on a rooftop turret, was Finland.

'I have to go potty,' Nikolai announced suddenly.

A cold hard wind picked up, blowing the cool mist to shreds.

She thinned her lips, looked back over her shoulder. 'Can you hold it?'

'No. I need to go now.'

The guard was watching. She had no choice. 'OK,' she said.

He directed her to pull forward again, park in a stall bordered by waist-high slats of Plexiglass. Before stepping out of the van, she looked around, noting the position of mounted cameras, dogs sniffing at the ends of leashes, a helicopter passing overhead. A tourniquet was closing around her chest, squeezing her heart.

She might still floor the accelerator. But on every side of the stall beyond the Plexiglass barricades, the minivan was penned in; vehicles in front, vehicles in back. She might piledrive one or two out of the way, but she could not plow through them all. And even if she could manage to get beyond them – even if she could manage to part the terrific metal sea – she would find emergency measures instantly implemented, spike strips and armed guards, and beyond those, the Tigre APC. And, of course, the helicopter. Always a damned helicopter . . .

Nothing for it but to leave the van, take the kid to the bathroom, and pray.

She closed her eyes for a split second.

She opened them and reached for her door.

Junior Lieutenant Golod sneezed.

Miserably, he flicked a wad of snot from his fingertips. Then he dug a tissue from his tunic. From the far side of the border, two members of the Finnish Customs and Frontier Guard looked at him askance. Supercilious bastards, thought Golod, with their spotless blue-and-white uniforms and their snotless noses. But their precious manners came at the price of virility. Just a matter of time until *Rodina* kicked their ass again on the battlefield, reabsorbing them into the great Russian Empire.

Closer by, a handler and his Caucasian Mountain Shepherd watched, with hints of both humor and concern, as Golod gave his nose a terrific honk. Almost daintily, the junior lieutenant repocketed the sodden tissue. He gave the handler a challenging stare. The man turned away, finding the fragment of cloth with the quarry's scent and offering it to the dog again. The powerful tail thumped twice.

A waste of time, thought Golod as he watched the canine team snuffle on. They would all catch their death of cold for nothing. The woman would never try to pass right in front of all these cameras and guards and helicopters and dogs. She was not a *samoubiystvo*, a suicide waiting to happen, or she would not have lasted nearly this long. Probably, she had gone south long before, and this was all a wild goose chase.

His nose was already running again. Nothing out here but cold and wind and trees, it seemed, and the carbon monoxide of a thousand idling vehicles. No wonder his body was breaking down. Even the dog was shivering . . .

. . . and growling, low and thick.

Straining forward, ninety kilos of muscle pulling the leash tight, and then looking back to see its handler's reaction.

Not shivering, Golod realized suddenly.

The dog was quivering with excitement.

He followed the line described by the taut body.

A trio had just walked past: a guard, a young child, and the child's mother.

Golod absorbed the woman from the back. Blonde, proper, responsible. Nurturing, if still a few years from conventional thick-waisted matronhood. A far cry from the shaved-head young punk they were seeking. And in the company of a child and a guard, which elevated her almost above suspicion.

But the quivering dog, now arrow-straight, said otherwise.

Golod drew his threaded SIG Mosquito semi-automatic pistol with ten-round magazine and, holding it loosely by his side, exchanged a glance with the dog's handler.

As they walked, Cassie bent away from cameras under the guise of wiping Nikolai's nose with a tissue. She said, 'Make sure you wash your hands after you use the potty.'

'Yes, Mama.'

'Soap and water.'

'Yes, Mama.' He looked up at the guard. 'I'm Maxim,' he said guilelessly.

The man grunted.

'Halt,' someone was calling.

Cassie ignored it.

They kept moving.

'Hold it. You there. *Halt.*'

This time there was no pretending she had missed it. The man escorting them had heard it too; he turned his head. And others were picking up on the spoor in the air, the frisson of unfolding developments.

The guard who was issuing the command – ten, twelve yards away, a few years older than her, thickset, red-nosed – had drawn his gun.

She turned on her heel, heading back toward the van, dragging Nikolai along. On her left a dog arrowed toward her, quivering at the end of its leash as its handler fought to hold it back. She nudged Nikolai around to her other side, a mother protecting her brood. 'Need to go potty,' he said weakly.

They were almost back to the minivan now. But the guard with the drawn gun was advancing. Another was coming up behind the Alphard. By then she had the door open. She hiked Nikolai into the back seat. She closed the door and moved to cross around the rear fender, but the man there was unlimbering his holster. She reversed, went to cross instead in front of the hood, and nearly collided with the one holding his gun.

She found a friendly smile. Cocked her head lightly, communicating gentle surprise. *What's the problem, officer?*

He paused, still pointing the SIG Mosquito uncertainly toward the pavement. She reached unhurriedly for his gun-hand, her body language conveying the opposite of urgency. Almost tenderly, she pressed her thumb into the ulnar nerve. The collateral ligament released; she plucked the Mosquito from unresisting fingers.

The one holding the dog dropped the leash, hissed a command. The beast tensed, preparing to leap, haunches bunching, lips peeling back, and she put a bullet between its eyes.

Turning on the one whose gun she had taken, she shot him in the chest, sending him falling back.

Weapons were coming around, berets and pointed caps. Voices shouted. She ducked inside the minivan. A gun fired, *zwing*, and glass shattered, and then an aerating red vapor filled the air, throbbing from a victim Cassie couldn't see. *Oh fuck*, she thought. She was twisting the key. The key seemed to weigh a thousand pounds. *Oh fuck, I fucked up royally.*

'Hold on,' she told Nikolai mildly, without turning to look at him.

She jammed the van into gear. Beyond the Plexiglass barricade was a lane of stopped traffic: the front fender of a blue Latvija, the back fender of a red Trabant. Not enough room for the minivan to pass through. But behind her the traffic was even more clogged, so she aimed forward, wrapped ten white knuckles around the steering wheel, and floored the gas. In the rear-view she vaguely saw Nikolai's head rock loosely on his neck as the car sprung forward.

The barrier splintered. The front of the van plowed into the Latvija and Trabant, moved them a half-yard each before the engine stalled. A tattoo of automatic weapon fire sent more glass flying. She ducked, not in time to avoid a shard which sliced open the side of her face.

A circle of men advanced. A few cars away, someone was crying. Woozily, she blinked. Scents of primex and smoke thick on the air. Gun still in her hand. She raised it. But why? These men were innocents. Dupes, like her.

She tossed the gun on to the passenger seat. Twisted the key in the ignition again. The engine coughed, sputtered, and reluctantly fired.

Something *whishhhhhh*ed. For a fraction of a second she sifted through surreal impressions – a hot-white shooting star cutting toward her, a blooming white flower – and then a great percussive *whomp* rattled her brain inside her skull, and she entered the formless stuff of dreams.

She came back. The van was filling with haze. Something was spitting and rolling and hissing and rattling. A CS grenade, kicking around the back seat.

She reached over the saddle between seats, found the boy's hand. It would be OK, she wanted to tell him. It was over now. They would take him away before she could do any more harm. It was finished, at last.

The hand was limp.

The face was white – except for a shocking welt of red where a fragment of glass had opened the throat.

She stared at him.

The clouds of gas rose. Her eyes burned. The mist closed in. *You are telling me that he is asleep?*

Suddenly, then, she remembered the quick change she had devised. Somehow, in the heat of the moment, she had forgotten. She reached for the door with one hand. Not too late. She would become someone else, someone new, someone uncompromised. Someone innocent. She would be gone like the wind. Deathless . . .

Even as her hand touched the latch, it fell. Misty brightness faded. Pain and sorrow faded. And then there was only darkness.

SIXTEEN

LUBYANKA SQUARE, MOSCOW

Aleksandr Marchenko's office in FSB headquarters was cramped but clean, featuring parquet floors and pale-green walls, a glass-covered desk, a secure white phone on a credenza, and a view of Solovetsky Stone across the square. The sight of the stone, which was intended to honor the victims of political repression, irked him. The irony of placing it at Lubyanka, home of every secret service from the Cheka onward, was undeniable. Of course, it was just a bone they had thrown the dogs. But it would be nice, for once, to receive praise and thanks for the burdens they took upon themselves, to be encouraged to stand up proudly and say: *We do this for* you, *fucking* suka, *all for* you.

An unfocused mind: a peril of old age. Look, by comparison, at the young technician hunched on the other side of the desk, wearing headphones, working the dials of his signal receiver with utmost concentration. Foxy dark face, mole beside his mouth tugging down with his frown. A serious young man, thought Marchenko with approval. So long as the Motherland kept turning out serious young men like this, she would be in good hands; the elder generation could go gently off into the good night without remorse.

The young man was snapping his fingers, indicating a pair of headphones on the desk. Marchenko leaned forward – creak – picked them up, slipped them on.

'—regular doses of midazolam and sevoflurane. Also, five armed guards will ride on-board the chopper, ready to take action should sleeping beauty so much as stir.'

That was the corrupt Inspektor. The fidelity was remarkably clear, as if the man shared the room with them. Marchenko's agent – the same Internal Affairs representative who had accompanied Ravensdale in the van the previous day – must have aimed the parabolic microphone very skilfully indeed.

When the American answered, the voice was softer but still easily audible. 'And in Moscow?'

'She's expected at Lubyanka, of course. But a switch will happen en route from the airport. A traffic jam, an extra ambulance . . . She'll end up in Serebryany Bor. And then it's out of my hands.'

The flick of a lighter's wheel, followed by a muted cough. The ensuing silence was so long, so conclusive, that Marchenko glanced at the fox-faced young man, raising his brow interrogatively.

'All these *myshynava voznya*,' remarked Vlasov at last. 'All these mice games. But here, at last, it ends.'

A bolt of static. Then more silence. Then Ravensdale said: '*Dobriy vecher*, Inspektor. Until next time.'

Marchenko made arrangements.

First and foremost came the trade. *Za dvumya zaitsami pogonish'sya ne odnogo ne poimaesh.* Run after two rabbits, and you'll catch none. Only once the assassin was safely in hand would he risk complicating the situation. Time enough to regain possession of Ravensdale and wife, at an airport or a border crossing, after the prime objective had been attained.

He ordered Sofiya Kirov not only delivered to Lubyanka, but cleaned up. Watching the feed he noted a fierce beauty, largely in the quarrelsome emerald eyes, which had survived the prison camp and the tussle between her keepers – one man was now dead – and now survived the fire hose and delousing. He could see why counter-intelligence had dispatched her, way back when, to develop Ravensdale. He could see why Ravensdale considered her worth any sacrifice. He felt a thump of something wistful, something long dormant. His own wife was twenty years gone, and he never thought of other women. Almost never.

Behind his desk again, he readied his ranks. To assume that Ravensdale would allow the initiative to remain with the FSB was naive. So he put into play six mobile units on the street. Four drones – quieter than helicopters – overhead. He designated code numbers on encrypted channels; backup plans, backups to backup plans. Then he sat, phone by hand, and waited.

The call came at ten minutes before nine p.m. He let the phone ring twice as the fox-faced young tech started the trace. Then he answered. 'Marchenko.'

'Ivanovsky Convent,' Ravensdale said. 'Twenty minutes. Just you and Sofiya.'

'No. Smolenskaya—'

'Don't play games.' The line went dead.

The tech shook his head. Marchenko sighed, pushed back from the desk.

Fifteen minutes later he sat with the woman – handcuffed, hooded – in the back of an unmarked high-top van outside the domed katholikon of Ivanovsky Convent. They shared the van's interior with two guards wearing standard MP-443 Grachs. The fox-faced tech crouched on the floor between low benches, working his equipment.

The phone rang again. '*Sanduny banya*,' Ravensdale said. 'Twenty minutes.'

'Comrade. Let us—'

The connection was dead.

'He's moving,' said the tech. 'But not with a cellphone. Something harder to trace. A two-way radio.'

'*Sanduny banya*,' Marchenko told the driver. Was it his imagination, he wondered as they pulled back into motion, or did the cant of the woman's head beneath the black hood indicate amusement?

They had driven only three minutes before the phone rang again. 'Next right.'

Before he could answer, the line cut out. 'Next right,' he told the driver and gestured at the tech, who sent a coded burst on an encrypted channel.

They bounced past a darkened culvert, turned down a potholed residential side-street. Rows of double-parked windowless vans lined both curbs. Ten, twelve, fifteen vans, high-top, low-top, gray, white, black, and green vans. A gaggle of vans, a kettle of vans, a murder of vans. All windowless.

The phone rang. 'Stop,' Ravensdale commanded.

Marchenko waved a stop.

'Out. With Sofiya. No one else.'

Marchenko stood – creak – taking hold of the chain between the prisoner's wrists. One of the guards ratcheted open the rear door, letting in cold wind and fine black dust. Marchenko climbed down, pushing the woman before him.

Fire escapes. A few lighted windows. A few bare-limbed trees. Dirty snow piled in gutters. A cell tower on the next block. Near the corner, a young couple walking with heads together, moving away. And everywhere, the windowless vans.

'Walk forward,' said the voice.

Marchenko walked forward, holding the phone in one hand, the handcuff chain in the other. No sign of the watchers, the drones, the mobile units with PKMs capable of pumping out 750 rounds per minute. But they were there, close by. Let the American have his game. Get the rabbit in the snare. There would be time enough, time enough . . .

'Stop,' said the voice.

Marchenko stopped.

'Take off the hood.'

He took the hood off the woman. She looked around, blinking, bruised, narrow-eyed, swaying on her feet.

'Send her forward. By herself.'

'Not until I have mine.'

'First send her forward.'

'First give me mine.'

A second passed.

Five seconds.

A side door on one of the vans slid open.

Ravensdale climbed out, leading his own thin woman, wearing her own manacles and black hood. He held no firearm. Of course he didn't. It was still a gentleman's game. No intelligence agent had intentionally harmed an opponent, on the playing field, since World War II. Once the Americans were in the basement, strapped to tables, it would be a different story – but for now, here, they were all gentlemen.

Ravensdale came forward, positioning the girl in front of him, using her, perhaps unconsciously, as a shield. She wore a billowing coat that concealed her figure, and beneath the hood something chunky, possibly a mouth guard. She took small, restricted steps, indicating that her ankles had also been manacled.

Three steps away, Ravensdale stopped. He looked at Sofiya. '*Alë, garázh*', he said: *Hey, citizen.*

She gave a weak smile.

He whipped the hood off his captive, exposing a shaved head. Nose and ears pierced with holes; hazy drugged eyes beneath glitter-coated lids. As expected, the bottom half of the face was covered by a leather restraint mask. Up close the girl looked even smaller, even younger, than Marchenko had expected.

Behind and around Marchenko, a dozen engines turned over.

A van pulled up beside him. A side door banged open. A flat top reached out expectantly.

Marchenko's eyes met Ravensdale's.

He released Sofiya, who was pulled into the van. In the same instant, Ravensdale pushed the girl forward. She stumbled, and Marchenko moved to catch her.

Ravensdale vanished into another van. Then vehicles were pulling away on every side, moving in different directions. A starburst, a stampede, designed to overload the watchers. Marchenko hardly cared. Up now to the drones, the mobile units. Out of his hands. *In* his hands, at long last, he had his prize: the American assassin.

She was still anesthetized, legs loose, eyes muddy. His own unmarked van pulled up, brakes squealing. He handed her inside, climbed after. They pulled away, nearly colliding with another vehicle which had executed a sudden *rybolovnyi krjuchok*, fishhook reverse.

They gained speed, reached the end of the block, turned on shrieking tires. He snapped his fingers before the girl's overcast eyes. No reaction. For an instant, panic consumed him. The cold-blooded American had poisoned her. Marchenko would be denied his prize, even now . . .

. . . no. Just anesthesia. Already, her eyes were starting to clear.

A muffled groan. Beneath the leather mask, her jaws were trying to work. Marchenko told himself to wait. But it was Christmas Day. He was five years old again. He must open his present.

He reached behind her head, worked the straps on the leather mask. Instants later, it fell into her lap. She opened and closed a pasty mouth.

'*Chyort.*' Thickly. '*Chyort . . . voz'mi.*'

Not the voice he had expected. A younger voice; the voice of a native Russian. And she was not emaciated, he saw now, so much as willowy. Her head had been shaved and her face pierced, but . . .

. . . the mask had hidden her jaw. Slimmer than the assassin's. Younger, slighter.

'*Ambal?*' she said muzzily. '*'Tchyo za gàlima?*'

Marchenko leaned closer, glowering – and then leaned away, cursing bitterly.

The official State Residence of the President of Russia, called Nogo-Ogarevo, was a refurbished nineteenth-century manor surrounded by a six-meter wall, tucked into a dense forest of pine and black fir west of Moscow.

Following a duty vehicle down the long driveway, Marchenko found himself thinking – how could he not? – of the old days. No lack of officers had found themselves, back in Stalin's time, beckoned to late-night meetings in remote dachas like this one, to receive their sentences from Uncle Joe. Most had probably quaked in fear. But Marchenko was not afraid. Unlike Stalin's treacherous and cowardly inner circle, which on a fateful night in March of 1953 had delayed medical assistance in a dacha very like this, Marchenko cared more about *Rodina's* future than his own. If a scapegoat was needed, he would gladly offer his resignation – or his head.

The anteroom into which he was led echoed like a tomb. Moonlight bled through mullioned windows. He followed a skeletal man down a twisting corridor, past bodyguards, to a private study. There he found a solemn President, standing still as a mountain, gazing philosophically into a hearth in which a tasteful fire crackled softly.

The escort removed himself. Marchenko put his heels together, achieving full height, and said without preamble: 'Bad news.'

Only a flicker of reflected flame inside the cold blue eyes moved.

'The American switched the girl. We have lost the assassin . . . and gained only the gangster's whore.' He tipped his chin up proudly. 'I accept full responsibility.'

A long minute stretched out. Marchenko could feel his fate drifting this way and that, a tattered flag caught in a capricious wind.

At length, the President gave a thin smile. 'We should,' he declared, 'drink to our worthy opponents. And a game well played.'

At a sideboard of Burmese teak, he splashed Platinka into tumblers. They drank together. Yet Marchenko took nothing for granted. Uncle Joe had also served his victims drinks – although he himself had usually abstained, preferring to keep his faculties for whatever may come.

'In your estimation,' said the President casually, 'our chances of recovering the assassin before she crosses a border . . .?'

Marchenko scanned for hidden meanings. Inconclusive; he shrugged. 'Tsoi has clearly thrown his full weight behind Ravensdale. He will find some shady back alley through which they might escape. And if that proves impossible . . .' He gestured with the tumbler. 'The American has only to kill the assassin, rather than let her fall into our hands. And so I would say: not good.'

'Comrade Tsoi has pushed his luck too far.'

Marchenko said nothing.

'But right at the moment, he is the most powerful man in Moscow. The *shpana* respect him. Action now creates problems we don't need.' A knot popped in the fireplace, sharp enough to echo. 'The future will bring more opportune chances. Unless, that is, you see something to be gained by moving now . . .?'

'I'm afraid I don't.'

'We will content ourselves, then, with executing his whore.'

Marchenko gave a somber nod.

'Don't stuff a rag into her mouth before feeding her to the dogs. Let her scream. And make sure word gets out.'

Marchenko nodded again.

The President downed the rest of his vodka in a simple peremptory draft. He seemed considerably less troubled than Marchenko had expected. The equanimity was perhaps explained by his long history in the KGB. The man still relished the game. And, of course, he still had Blakely's cache – spoils whose true value would become clear only in time.

Or perhaps it had more to do with those judo-thickened shoulders. Although the West could not help picturing the Kremlin's spymasters as they had during the first Cold War, chess players hunched over a board looking five moves ahead, this President played not chess but judo. He was accustomed to the long patient wait for the perfect opening, the period of watchful inactivity preceding the sudden critical strike.

'And the corrupt Inspektor?' Offhandedly, dispassionately; an afterthought. 'Will he, too, commit treason against us with impunity?'

'Here, at least, I have good news. Inspektor Vlasov was picked up trying to board a flight at Pulkovo, with false documents, three hours ago. He will be arriving at Lubyanka even as we speak.'

The President's thin smile flickered back. 'One must admire his technique.' It took Marchenko a moment to realize he meant not Vlasov but the American, Ravensdale. 'Like watching a monkey play the violin.'

Nodding, Marchenko polished off his own vodka.

'Brings to mind the good old days.' The President poured himself another drink. 'Don't look so glum, comrade. It is the battle, not the war. Glory waits just around the corner.'

'Yes, sir.'

'We will eviscerate them,' said the President cheerfully. 'The wily old monkeys. We will bury them alive as they cry for mercy. We will drink wine from their skulls, feed their eyes to the birds.'

'*Vechnaya Slava*,' said Marchenko warily – *Immortal Glory.*

The President offered a hand. When Marchenko reached to take it, the Imperial Eagle ring caught the firelight, sparkling.

ULAN-UDE, BURYATIA

Six thousand kilometers to the east, a small terminal huddled in low mountains.

Descending a stairwell from a Tupolev Tu-95, three passengers paused on the tarmac to look off for a moment at the surrounding landscape, ice-bright beneath a new day's sun.

The turboprops of the Tupolev, the world's loudest military aircraft, thundered deafeningly, but as the passengers crossed the single short runway, the noise dissipated quickly behind them on the weird thin air. An industrial clock inside the deserted terminal announced the time as just past seven a.m. At a grimy ersatz café – a few chairs, two metal tables, and an electric heater – the three passengers and their escort, one Chief Marshal Uimanov, breakfasted on tomatoes, cucumbers, smoked fish, and strong black tea. Uimanov then led them past two snoozing customs agents, outside again, to a rack of rusted bicycles and motor scooters. A dark young boy pushed himself off a low stone wall. The boy's cheekbones were lower than those of Muscovites, his coloring closer to Mongol, his straight black hair almost Chinese. The Chief Marshal barked a few words, and the boy unchained from the rack three prehistoric Uralmoto motorcycles, with battered helmets hanging from handlebars. At Uimanov's guidance, the boy affixed extra petrol and water to handlebars and side-racks.

Uimanov grinned, revealing slanting tombstone teeth. '*Neplokho*,' he said. Ravensdale shook his hand and the man turned, trotting again into the airport. The boy leaned back against the wall.

Settling on to a bike which lowered dangerously, Ravensdale reached into a pocket of his knee-length black leather jacket and consulted a magnetic compass. He clamped on the helmet and drew on gloves. His fellow travelers followed suit.

Before they started, he spent a moment considering them. Sofiya's pallor was deathly; her cheekbones stood out in sharp relief beneath the helmet; her blackened eye was mottled and swollen. Fatigued and ashen though she was, however, he nonetheless picked up a glimmer of her old self, a touch of obstinacy in her gaze and her wide-set stance. She would make it – for Dima's sake, if for no other.

The girl was harder to read. Beneath the helmet, her face was set, expressionless.

They pushed off, heading south, Ravensdale in the lead.

The initial path from the airport followed a dirt track. Soon the motorway bore east; the travelers continued off-road, bouncing over hard-packed steppe. After an hour they reached the banks of the Reka Selenga, which they followed past foxes and thatched yurts, and one elderly woman wearing a shawl, too busy at the riverbank to turn even at the racket generated by the ancient motorbikes.

Fifty kilometers on, they reached a small cluster of gabled red buildings. Dismounting, Ravensdale stretched his aching back, massaged his right shoulder and left knee; the ride had given new color to old injuries. The village's few occupants assembled to gawk. They were not Russian but Buryat, nomadic Siberian aboriginals. Sofiya handed a silver kopeck to one child, a protein bar to another. Then they were welcomed into the largest of the buildings, where they ate *shchi*, cabbage soup.

By the time they moved on, a dark note had crept into the afternoon light. Harsh winds drove down the already-frigid temperature. A hawk circled before the emerging moon. Shivering now beneath their leather jackets, they continued south. The few hints of life they glimpsed beneath the rose and violet skies were as they might have been tens of thousands of years earlier: goats, yurts, tribesman, camels, and sheep.

Full night brought a starry sky, which was awesome, disconcertingly grand. The night wind leeched away body heat – but also, thought Ravensdale, prevented the old Uralmotos from overheating. They stopped again, refilled gas tanks, ate protein bars, chased them with melted snow. Spending some of the precious charge of the GPS, he corrected course slightly.

They continued. Beneath gloves and boots, hands and feet grew numb. A distant owl hooted desolately. Once, a helicopter passed several thousand yards to the west. They rolled the bikes to a halt, killed engines and headlights, and watched. A spotlight swept in wide searching arcs. The helicopter disappeared. They drove on.

Half an hour after the helicopter, Ravensdale looked back to find that one of the bikes had drifted far behind. Not the girl, who was sticking close. Sofiya. They stopped, giving her a chance to catch up. When she did, she looked whiter than the snow. One of her eyes was bloodshot. Her stance was less sure than before; she teetered on her feet. He put his helmet against hers. 'We can't stop here,' he said. 'We'll freeze.'

'I'm all right.'

'We'll rest for a few minutes.'

'No. I'm all right.'

He put her in front, where he could keep an eye on her. Her balance was off; as she rode, the motorcycle pitched and yawed. Sometime in the smallest hours of the night, her left footrest clipped an icy rock, and she almost went over, almost spilt out her brains across the tundra. But she righted herself, and he swallowed his heart, and they drove on.

At sunrise, Ravensdale consulted the GPS again. They turned south-south-east.

When they reached the Tuul River, they celebrated with the remaining protein bars. Ravensdale smoked his first cigarette in twenty-four hours. By his math, they had crossed the border into Mongolia sometime around midnight, roughly when they had seen the helicopter.

They refueled for the last time and followed the banks of the river, and at half-past nine, exhausted and frozen and trembling with lassitude, crested a shallow hill and saw spreading before them a modern metropolis: Ulan Bator, the capital city, population one million.

He looked at Sofiya. Beneath the helmet, she was smiling.

He looked behind himself; the girl was gone.

SEVENTEEN

The Institute for Advanced Strategies – INTERDEPART-MENTAL MEMO – EYES ONLY
From: HG
To: Roger Vaughn
Date: 21 January
Re: PROJECT MATCHMAKER

Dear Mr Vaughn,

Permit me to acknowledge receipt of your letter of January 19th, which was forwarded to me by Paul Gastmeyer. I read your proposal with great interest, and invite you to visit my office at your earliest convenience to discuss the endeavor directly.

Your letter is being retained on file for possible future reference.

Sincerely yours,
Howard Gibson
Director

*

The Institute for Advanced Strategies – INTERDEPART-
MENTAL MEMO – EYES ONLY
From: HG
To: Roger Vaughn
Date: 22 January
Re: PROJECT MATCHMAKER

Dear Mr Vaughn,
    Regarding our discussion during your visit: I am setting the
necessary paperwork in motion, and we can go from there.

Sincerely yours,
Howard Gibson
Director

*

The Institute for Advanced Strategies – MEMORANDUM FOR:
THE RECORD
Subject: PROJECT MATCHMAKER Subproject 50
Date: 22 January

1. This memorandum is written to record the purpose of
   Subproject 50, the reasons for establishing it, and the
   mechanics by which it will be administered.
2. The purpose of this subproject is twofold: (1) To determine
   the location of former operative XXXX-XXXXXXXXXX
   (Subproject 32); and (2) To determine the location
   of former asset XXXXXXXXX-XXXXXXXX
   (Subproject 4).
3. The reasons for establishing the subproject are to conduct
   debriefing re: PROJECT MATCHMAKER.
4. As Project originator XXXXXXX-XXXXXXXX is
   deceased, general management of the Project has transferred to XXXXXX-XXXXXX, and the subproject will
   be handled under the stewardship of XXXXX-XXXXXX.
   As expenses are incurred and upon presentation of
   vouchered proof of expenditure, requests will be made
   in the amounts expended. Subproject 50 will be closed
   out upon completion and cash on hand returned to
   Finance.

Distribution:
Orig – IAST/CD
1 – Chrono (b)

*

The Institute for Advanced Strategies – MEMORANDUM FOR:
THE RECORD
Subject: PROJECT MATCHMAKER Subproject 50
Date: 29 March

1. In this subproject, procedures have been implemented to
   fulfill the following criteria: (1) To determine the location
   of former operative XXXX-XXXXXXXXXX (Subproject
   32); and (2) To determine the location of former asset
   XXXXXXXXX-XXXXXXXX (Subproject 4).
2. PROJECT MATCHMAKER, in which operative
   XXXXXXXXX-XXXXXXXX (Subproject 4) gained access
   to XXXXXXXX-XXXXXXX for purposes of neutralization,
   was successfully completed on 9 January XXXX (N.B. See
   Subprojects 3 – 49) but remains open because two key elements (Subprojects 4 and 32) remain unavailable for debriefing.
3. Development of Subproject 50 has proceeded to the
   satisfaction of this office. Balancing time and budget restraints
   against the demands of the project, XXXXX-XXXXXX has
   implemented surveillance on select known associates and
   financial holdings of XXXXXXXXX-XXXXXXXX,
   XXXXXX-XXXXX, and XXXXXXXXX-XXXXXXXX.
4. Another review should be conducted on 1 May, or when
   expenditures reach $500,000.

Distribution:
Orig – IAST/CD
1 – Chrono (c)

*

The Institute for Advanced Strategies – MEMORANDUM FOR:
THE RECORD
Subject: PROJECT MATCHMAKER Subproject 50
Date: 1 May

1. In this subproject, procedures have been implemented to fulfill the following criteria: (1) To determine the location of former operative XXXX-XXXXXXXXXX (Subproject 32); and (2) To determine the location of former asset XXXXXXXXX-XXXXXXXX (Subproject 4).

2. A tax payment filed on April 1st for the residence of XXXX-XXXXXXXXXX (Subproject 32) in Ticonderoga, NY, was administered through a bank located in Schenectady, NY, where a cash deposit was made on 21 February by one 'XXXX-XXXXXX'. Inquiries suggest that 'XXXX-XXXXXX' is a manufactured identity. SS# was assigned following a personal interview in the Schenectady Social Security office conducted on 6 October XXXX, during which 'XXXX-XXXXXX' presented a Delayed Certificate of Birth, NY State Photo ID Card, and supplementary evidence in the form of Visa credit card bills. Delayed Certificate of Birth was obtained on 28 January XXXX via the Office of Vital Records of the New York Department of Health, following a request for search of records which resolved inconclusively. All efforts to trace 'XXXX-XXXXXX' to listed addresses and credit card companies have failed.

3. To avoid the risk of putting subject XXXX-XXXXXXXXXX (Subproject 32) on alert, subproject manager XXXXX-XXXXXX has determined that the bank should be kept under surveillance. As subproject costs to date are rapidly approaching $500,000, a request to extend the budget has been filed and awaits approval.

4. The payment of the tax on the Ticonderoga property indicates that XXXX-XXXXXXXXXX cannot afford to let the property foreclose. The likelihood that he will attempt to orchestrate a sale in the near future, using the Schenectady bank and the 'XXXX-XXXXXX' persona, are high, and this should be taken into account when the budget extension is considered.

Distribution:
Orig – IAST/CD
1 – Chrono (c)

*

The Institute for Advanced Strategies – INTERDEPARTMENTAL
MEMO – EYES ONLY
From: HG
To: Roger Vaughn
Date: 7 May
Re: PROJECT MATCHMAKER Subproject 50

Roger,

Permit me to inform you personally that to my great pleasure
the request for budget extension has been approved.

And just in time, as I understand from our conversation this
morning that your hunch was correct, and as of yesterday the
Ticonderoga property has been put on the market.

As you close in your quarry (one of them, anyway), I want
to thank you for your insight and your brilliant, focused labors
over the past several months. Never doubt the value of your
contribution to our national security.

I want also to note how much I have valued the chance to
get to know you, for the first time, as a friend.

Let's celebrate with dinner this weekend? Claire requests that
Laurie bring some of her wonderful New England Cranberry
Pie.

HG

PS. Go Yanks!

*

NEW YORK CITY

Cassie sat on a bench in Tompkins' Square Park, watching the late-
night Saturday crowd evolve slowly into the early-morning Sunday
crowd.

She sat beside a relief which showed a woman and child gazing
forlornly out to sea, a commemoration of the 1904 sinking in Long
Island Sound of the *General Slocum*. Her eyes moved steadily across
chess boards, dog runs, flaking benches, wire trash baskets, winding
paths; misfits and drunks, pervs and junkies, blurry-eyed bridge and
tunnel kids, and families done up in their Sunday best. Somewhere
in this park, she thought, was someone who could put her on to
Michelle's trail. She planned to sit right here, soaking in the faces,
until she found them.

Some faces were old, some new. Nothing ever changed out here, not really. The *dramatis persona* shifted as people followed mild weather or went to rehab or went home; then it shifted again as they failed at rehab, failed at home, and showed up back in the park. Only very rarely did someone disappear forever . . . and most of those, Cassie suspected, met a bad end. For everyone else, life on the streets formed an endless Möbius strip. Exhibit A, Cassie herself: right back where she had started.

She scratched absently at one arm. Her clothes were dirty; they itched. Her hair, cropped short and dyed black, felt filthy. Four days spent on a Greyhound bus had left her feeling grimier than four months spent in LA . . . and LA had left her feeling pretty goddamned grimy.

Footsteps crunched up on her right. Turning her head, she felt only dim surprise at the sight of Michelle. Nothing ever changed out here, she thought again; not really.

'Hey,' Michelle said, dropping down on to the bench. 'Long time.'

Her companion – Xavier Dark, Cassie remembered, although his given name had been Steve, Scott, something like that – remained standing, gazing at nothing. The past sixteen months had taken a toll on Xavier, who looked cadaverous and wasted. But Michelle looked essentially the same, if a bit older, a bit leaner.

'Where you been?' Michelle asked.

'Boston,' Cassie said. 'Then LA, for awhile. How about you?'

'Ehh.' Michelle gestured loosely, inclusively, at the park around them.

They sat for several moments without speaking. A few pigeons strutted importantly past the bench, pecking at air. Xavier swayed on his feet. From a black denim jacket he took out rolling papers and a pack of Drum tobacco and began to assemble a cigarette, still swaying. As he rolled the cigarette he started nodding, chin jerking down to his chest and then up again.

Cassie examined Michelle, trying to figure out if she was using too. But Michelle's eyes were clear. She was rubbing chapped lips, then examining the flecks of dead skin on her fingertip. 'So what's going on up in Beantown?'

'Nothing much,' Cassie said.

'Out in LA?'

Cassie wrinkled her nose. 'Sketchy out there.'

'Missed you, Cass.'

'Missed you too.'

'Where you staying?'

'Nowhere. I just got here.'

'You're outdoors?'

'I'm outdoors, man,' Cassie agreed, and they both laughed.

'We got a place, few blocks away. Section Eight. Except it's kind of a dry spell so everybody's got to bring something. Food or whatever. But you're a special case. I can probably talk to Jesse; he's the alpha there . . .'

'I've got cash,' Cassie said.

'No problem, then.'

'Enough cash,' Cassie said, 'to really get a place. Like, legit. Like, just you and me, if you're interested.'

'No shit.'

'But I've been in some trouble. So I don't want to, like, put my name on a lease.'

Michelle looked at Cassie alertly. But she didn't say no.

The railroad-style Section 8 flat had uneven splintered floors and water-marked ceilings. Stepping through the door, they were intercepted by a kid of around fifteen, rail-thin, with spiked hair and a triple-pierced lip. 'Moo ha ha ha,' the boy said. 'That's my evil laugh. MOOOO ha ha ha ha!'

'Fuck off, Matt,' said Michelle kindly.

A girl holding a bong lay on a couch, watching a Steve Carell movie on an old TV. A chubby freckled brunette wearing a flowered scarf sat on the floor before the couch. A tall rangy man dozed in a corner, near a small-boned hip-hop kid, Asian or maybe Spanish, who read a tattered paperback. An overweight black-and-orange tabby prowled between sprawled legs and empty bottles and full ashtrays, tail switching.

'This is Cassie,' Michelle informed the assemblage. 'She's staying here a couple days.'

Nobody reacted.

In a tiny adjoining room, they found a dirty bare mattress. The walls were covered with pornography featuring under-aged-looking models in pigtails and schoolgirl uniforms. Michelle paid the decor no attention. She took out a phone, tilted it, trying to find a wireless signal. After a few moments, she gave up. 'Gonna grab a paper,' she said. 'Hang tight. Lie down if you want. If Jesse shows up, tell him you're with me.'

She left. Cassie spent five minutes lying on the mattress, looking away from the porn, at the warped bleary glass of a window facing an air shaft, before wandering back into the front room. The girl on the couch offered the bong. Cassie took a small, polite hit and passed it to the freckled brunette. Someone made strong, fragrant black coffee with a French press. Outside, kids played on the street two floors below, running and screaming.

Michelle returned, bearing a stubby library pencil and a copy of *Our Town Downtown*. Sitting in a column of sunlight by another warped window, she and Cassie circled eight possibilities. The doorbell rang; pizza was delivered. Cassie chipped in five bucks and ate two slices.

The bong made another round. Michelle and the freckled brunette gave the hip-hop kid a shampoo with pediculicide in the kitchen sink. More strong coffee was brewed. Cassie circled five more possibilities in the real estate listings. Xavier Dark materialized, used the bathroom, and vanished. Michelle smoked a cigarette, staring at the ember. Matt and the freckled brunette went into the next room. The sound of their love-making came in fits and starts, as if they kept falling asleep.

Cassie went to sit on the fire escape. She inhaled the fresh air, held it in her lungs. She closed her eyes, squeezed them tight, conjuring flashes of light.

She went into the apartment again. A new player had appeared on the scene: a squat young man wearing a tank top, about five-seven, with broad shoulders and stout forearms. As Cassie entered, he was bumping fists with Michelle. '*As-Salāmu Àlaykum.*'

'*Wa Àleykum As-Salaam.*' Michelle turned. 'Cass, this is Jess. Jess, Cass.'

He regarded her critically, as if grading a piece of meat, and grunted.

He had brought a twelve-pack of PBR. They drank and smoked. The overweight cat snored. A shadow crossed the sun outside.

A white girl with bad dreadlocks arrived. She smoked pot, stroked the cat, told a disjointed story. 'One time? My sister was out of weed? She knew this guy at camp who set her up? And Buddy, that's her cat, was playing with a catnip toy? And my sister said that catnip and pot have, like, the same active ingredient? Like, she learned it at camp? So we tried smoking the catnip? And I think it worked?'

'You *think* it worked,' Jesse said. He had one arm around Michelle and one around the freckled brunette. Cassie could see downy underarm hair beneath his tank top, thin and wispy, like a teenager's.

'Resin, too,' said the hip-hop kid, 'gets a bad rap. But believe me—' and he laughed a strange, high-pitched laugh – '*believe* me, take my *word* for it, you can get *high* from resin.'

'One time?' started the girl with dreadlocks, and then lost her train of thought.

Michelle pushed up and went to use the bathroom. Cassie followed. When Michelle came back out, Cassie took her aside. 'Michelle,' she said, 'I gotta get out of here.'

'Come on, Cass. It's temporary. We're looking at places tomorrow.'

Cassie hesitated.

'Fuck's sake. Chill out.'

After a moment, Cassie reluctantly nodded and followed Michelle into the front room again.

Sometime later she lay down on the couch, closing her eyes. Jesse and Michelle and Matt and the freckled brunette sat on the floor around her, talking. Someone lit a cigarette. The smell of burning tobacco commingled with stale beer and old pizza and skunky marijuana and body odor and kitty litter. Cassie's stomach turned lazily. So long away, and nothing had changed. Almost as if she had never been gone at all. *Shouldn't have come back*, she thought. But where else could she go? Any port in a storm.

Eyes closed, she listened to stoned and rambling conversation, and drifted.

She should count her blessings – part of her had been afraid that Quinn's people would be watching the park, would arrest her again as soon as she showed her face – and not complain.

The brunette was telling a story about the Slender Man, who she maintained was based on someone from her hometown. She was within a few years of Cassie's own age. But the discrepancy between their life experiences was wider than the Grand Canyon, vaster than the known universe.

How? thought Cassie. How could she have survived everything, only to end up right back where she had started? What kind of sense did that make? What kind of half-assed God was running things, anyway?

No kind of God. That's what kind.

Nothing made sense. Nothing meant anything. Nothing mattered.

I felt so depressed, Holden Caulfield had said, *you can't even imagine.*

Michelle told a story about Polybius, the video game that drove people insane. Once, in Portland, she'd met a man who claimed to have designed it. One night, not long after telling his story, he had vanished from the local scene, never to be seen again. Some people said he'd played his own game and his mind had snapped . . .

Thank God Michelle had not borne a grudge. Sure, they had been friends once – best friends – but that had been eons ago. And it had not ended well. Cassie remembered fumbling the window up, with Michelle behind her, breathing hard. *Hurry.* Slipping into the night, dimly aware that her friend hadn't made it out behind her. Not her fault, of course. But still.

Where had they brought Michelle, that night? To one of Manhattan's countless precinct station houses? To the Tombs, or Juvy? Or had she, like Cassie, been brought to a remote safe-house in the countryside? No. Cassie had been chosen. Michelle . . . Michelle was ordinary.

'I knew this guy once?' the brunette was saying. 'He was, like, home alone with his dog? And he was, like, listening to the radio? And he heard this report of, like, an escaped mental patient?'

But just suppose, thought Cassie.

Just suppose that Michelle *had* been tapped by the agency. Not the way Cassie had been tapped – Cassie was more physical, more resourceful, and frankly smarter. Michelle was more of a go-with-the-flow kind of gal. But, of course, the agency would have use for girls like that too. Informers, in a word. As Benjamin Blakely had shown, the differences between Russia and twenty-first century America were not nearly so pronounced as one might have assumed. The agency would need plenty of people like Michelle. Go-with-the-flow types.

The room was growing quiet. Final cigarettes were ground out in ashtrays. Someone belched reflectively. Someone else started snoring, from the floor beside the couch.

Just suppose, Cassie thought again.

Just suppose that Michelle was still working for the agency. Putting them on to other girls like Cassie, for starters – disposable assets, they might call them. And perhaps . . . probably, even . . . keeping out an eye for Cassie herself, who they knew might eventually come back to Manhattan.

And just suppose that when Michelle had slipped out to get the newspaper, she had called someone. And then she had come back and plied Cassie with booze and weed, lowering her defenses. And when Cassie had sensed something wrong and tried to disengage, Michelle had placated her. *It's temporary. We're looking at places tomorrow.* And then more aggressively: *Fuck's sake. Chill out.*

Because sometime in the middle of night, when they all slept, the incursion team would make their move. They would attack with military precision, and Cassie would never see them coming. Then Michelle would get her pay-off, her thirty pieces of silver, and Cassie would be back in their clutches. They might murder her, as they had tried to do in Beliy Gorod, tying up loose ends. Or they might compel her to do still more violence, still more harm, on their behalf. Finishing Blakely, the hero whistle-blower, had been just the start. They would not let her rest until she had crammed their agenda down the throat of every so-called enemy of the state in the world and, in the process, murdered every innocent child who crossed her path. She could never let down her guard. She could never trust anyone. Everything she cared for slipped right through her fingers . . .

Paranoid.

Yet suddenly she was sitting up, wide awake.

Sleeping bodies covered the floor. The cat's tail slowly switched. And mice were rustling in the walls; that was what had woken her.

Except, they weren't exactly *in* the walls, were they? They were in the hallways on the other sides of the walls. And they were in the ceiling, and they were on the fire escape balcony. But when she shot her gaze toward the warped window she caught only a drifting shadow, quickly melting away.

She stood, stepping over slumbering figures. Put her back against the wall to the left of the door, sucking in a deep breath and holding it, straining to hear past the thud of her heart.

Something hissed quietly. She triangulated. Probably Semtex 10SE, rolled on to a spool and then wired to the wall – that was how she would have done it. Three-second fuse. When it fired, sledgehammers would pound through the weakened gypsum. Then all hell would break loose.

Michelle called them when she left to get the newspaper.

Three . . .

Waiting for me to show up again. Waiting all this time. Stabbed me in the back.

Two . . .

Fuck it. CONCENTRATE.

One.

The hissing turned into an angry fizz. And here came the first sledgehammer, spraying bits of drywall. In the same moment, two windows shattered. A wickedly sizzling grenade rolled into the apartment, clattering out of reach beneath a radiator.

The front door burst off its hinges. Two mirrored gunstocks poked through like animals' snouts. She grabbed the nearest one, pulled, and wrenched. Backing away toward the bedroom she stepped on a hand, eliciting a squawk.

On the filthy bare mattress Jesse and the freckled brunette sat naked, clutching each other fearfully. No sign of Michelle. Cassie slung the gun around her neck, slid the window open. Wind ruffled her hair. *Déjà vu.* She squirmed out, dropping lightly down to the litter-and-pigeon-crap-strewn floor of the air shaft ten feet below – and losing her balance from even that short fall. Out of shape, out of practice.

Out of luck.

Shaking her head, she was up again. Smashing a window across the shaft with the stock of the Heckler & Koch, sweeping the frame clear, climbing into a first-floor apartment, toppling flowerpots and figurines. She found herself standing in a tiny room, near a woman cowering in a bed. A mound of laundry piled in one corner, a glass of water resting on a night table. The apartment followed an inverted blueprint from the one across the way. A few steady strides brought her through the living room, to the front door. She worked multiple locks, fumbling in the darkness.

Before moving into the hallway, she used the mirror mounted on the H&K's stock to scan the shadows. A dull metal banister, a winking Judas hole, a scatter of takeout menus . . . and two looming spherical silhouettes. For one confused moment she thought they were hanging mobiles, like the Sputnik dangling over Nikolai's bed in Vyborg. Then she realized that they were helmets.

Boots crunched against the floor of the air shaft; the woman cringing in her bed screamed.

Cassie tilted the mirror again. *Concentrate.* At least two men, maybe more, waited in the shadowed corridor. Black body armor, chitinous black helmets, black boots. If she came out fast and dropped low, she might get them before they got her.

Glass crinkled as a first man scrabbled into the apartment behind her. *Go!*

She held her breath again.

She went.

Falling on to her knees, skidding on takeout menus, wheeling and firing, lighting the darkened corridor with a surreal flash. One man jerked away, grunting, as another returned fire. A white-hot poker grazed her temple. Someone fired again, and a mule kicked her squarely between the breasts, driving the breath from her lungs, knocking her flat on to her back.

She had lost the gun. She tried to wheel around, to hook a pair of feet with a scissor-kick and tumble one man into another. But she was out of shape, out of practice, out of breath, out of luck. She kicked a shin, missed finding a grip. A gun barked again, sending fire bolting down her backbone. Yet she still lived. The ricochets lacked a biting edge. *Rubber bullets.*

Even as she tried to raise her hands to protect herself, another projectile hammered excruciatingly into her ribs. More dark boots flooded the hall – from the apartment behind her, from the foyer around the corner – and surrounded her, pooling like black water as she curled, limp and mewling and gasping, into fetal position.

EIGHTEEN

SWIFTWATER, PENNSYLVANIA

The siren whooped twice.

Ravensdale pulled over, crunching gravel beneath his tires. The police cruiser swung on to the shoulder behind him. The cop – gray wool uniform, tan Stetson, black Gore-Tex jacket – took his time in coming out. Then he approached on the passenger side, slowly. After giving the Fiesta's interior a long look, he crossed behind the rear fender and came up on the driver's side. Beneath the brim of the Stetson his eyes were flinty brown, cheeks gaunt, chin sharp. 'License, registration and insurance.'

Ravensdale had them ready. 'Was I speeding, officer?'

'Going to ask you to step out of the vehicle, sir.'

'Why?'

'Just leave the key and step out of the vehicle, sir.'

Ravensdale sifted through possible responses. He had been within five miles per hour of the speed limit. His inspection sticker was up-to-date. His tail-lights were unbroken. But if this was what he feared, they would already have staked out the house. One way or another, better to deal with it here.

He climbed out. With one hand in the small of his back – surreptitiously checking for a weapon – the trooper urged him toward the cruiser. As they walked, gravel rasped underfoot. The sun was down, but the sky was still light. An industrious woodpecker in the nearby woods worked, paused, and worked again. Nearing the car, Ravensdale was unsurprised to recognize the man waiting in the back seat.

'You,' said Howard Gibson as Ravensdale slid in beside him, 'are a hard man to track down.'

The trooper closed the door, popped a toothpick into his mouth, and wandered off. Overhead, a first splinter of silver moon had appeared, shining faintly against the gathering dark.

'Shaved the beard.' Gibson examined him clinically. 'Suits you. You look ten years younger.'

Silence.

'Relax, Sean. I'm here as a friend. Got an offer, in fact, that might interest you.'

Up the road, the trooper found a purple sticker-bush in which to pretend absorption. He leaned forward and then abruptly drew back, slapping at a forearm.

'I don't pretend charity, and I don't ask for it. This is win-win. Deputy Director of IAS. You'll report directly to me.'

Ravensdale couldn't mask his surprise. Gibson chuckled. Wrinkles around the man's eyes made him appear to be smiling even when he was not; when he laughed, his whole face came together. 'Don't blame you for looking that way. Last year, to be honest, I wouldn't have gotten within spitting distance. But . . . well, sir, I won't lie. We shit the bath pretty good. Martyred the bastard, is what we did. More popular dead than he ever would have been alive. Now every able man's got to grab a bucket and start bailing.'

Ravensdale said nothing.

'Once in a lifetime opportunity.' Gibson's southern roots came out in his flattened, drawling vowels. 'You ride in on a white horse. All past indiscretions forgiven and forgotten. And you get to sock a little something away for a rainy day while you're at it.' A lazy shrug. 'Like I said: win-win. The Ticonderoga house bought you some breathing room, I guess. But life is long. Kids need college. And I can't really see you or the wife pumping gas.'

Ravensdale said nothing.

'And those guys in Lubyanka, they've got long memories. Eventually, they'll turn over the right rock, the way I just did. Long run, you'll sleep better at night this way . . . How is she, by the way?'

Ravensdale said nothing.

The setting sun painted chiaroscuros across Gibson's face, exaggerating the laugh lines, making him look positively whimsical. 'Fair enough,' he said unconcernedly. 'So. You need the security detail, and you can use the paycheck. I need someone I can march before a senate subcommittee and say, "This man does not go with the program. Fact is, he keeps trying to retire." Symbolic.'

'Gee.'

'That's my pitch. What do you say?'

Ravensdale said nothing.

Gibson shifted position in his seat, looking mildly pained, as if suffering from a gas bubble. 'Also,' he added after a moment, 'we picked up the girl.'

Ravensdale's brow knit.

'We invested too much to just let her go. And she's damned good, isn't she? Ruined for Eastern Europe, of course, but I bet we can find someplace she'll come in handy. Problem is, she doesn't trust us.' Another laid-back shrug. 'But you . . . you had her dead to rights. And instead of handing her over to the Kremlin, you took her across the border. She'll trust *you*.'

Ravensdale shook his head. 'Ditched me the second she found the chance.'

'She'll settle down, once she sees the light. Lead by example, I always say.'

'We finished, Howie? Because I've got milk in my trunk.'

Gibson paused. He indicated Ravensdale's breast pocket. 'Spare one of those?'

Ravensdale took out his cigarettes. He handed one over, took one for himself, lit both. Without a key in the ignition, his window refused to lower. He cracked open his door instead.

'If you ask me,' said Gibson deliberately, 'you've earned some peace. You're a good man – close enough for government work, anyway. Left to my own devices, I'd let it be. But . . .'

Ravensdale waited.

'The buzzards are circling. So. I didn't want to go here, but if you force my hand . . . we're looking at an entirely new round of Title Eighteen. The guys in legal have it all worked out. They're raring to go.'

'What's the charge?'

'Sedition, of course.' Gibson exhaled smoke laconically. 'You got off easy the first time, between you and me, because Andy Fletcher vouched for you. But now Fletcher's gone. The fact remains that you fraternized with the enemy. So if we need to play hardball . . .'

Coolly, Ravensdale exhaled a clockspring of smoke.

'Be flattered, Sean. I want you on our side so much that I'll get down in the mud to make it happen. So. Duty calls, soldier. Go home; put your milk in the fridge; put your kid to bed. Have a talk with the little woman. And when you're ready, we'll be outside. Sofiya can head down tomorrow, the next day, look at some rentals. We'll pick up the moving expenses.'

In the darkening forest, the tops of the trees blushed red. Long fingers of shadow stretched out toward the parked cruiser. A whip-poorwill gave a lilting cry. The woodpecker replied urgently, *tap-tap-tap-tap-tap.*

'The easy way,' said Gibson, 'or the hard way.'

Ravensdale smoked, exhaled. 'His master's voice.'

The house was a white wooden four-square, sun-gold in the last of the day's light.

The foyer was decorated with a wicker umbrella stand and a bowl of wax fruit on a low table. From the dining room wafted scents of *sirniki* pancakes and sour cream. From the kitchen came the clattering of a dishwasher being emptied.

In the living room, Dima was watching TV in his pajamas. Coming in, Ravensdale ruffled his son's hair. 'How you doing, kiddo?'

'Ka-CHOW!' Dima said without looking up. A mustache of dried chocolate milk on his upper lip. On-screen, Lightning McQueen was accepting a compliment. *You've got more talent in one lugnut than a lot of cars has got on their whole body . . .*

Ravensdale glanced through a window. The police cruiser was just pulling up out front, dousing its lights.

In the kitchen, he pecked a kiss on to the back of Sofiya's neck. 'See the car on your way in?' she asked.

'What car?'

'*My* car. This guy stopped right in front of me, and I hit him.'

'Anybody hurt?'

'No. Just a – what do you call it? Bender fender. We exchanged insurance.'

'Dima in the car?'

'Thought it was the funniest thing he'd ever seen.'

Ravensdale unpacked groceries, putting milk into the refrigerator. 'You eat?'

'We both did. Yours is on the table. I'll put him down.'

'Let me.' A beat. 'Then we need to talk.'

She turned from the dishwasher. Her black hair had grown shaggy, almost but not quite long enough to cut and style. Her cheeks had filled in, both flesh and color. Her green eyes were cloudy, hard to read. After a moment, she turned away again. 'Should I be nervous?'

He put hands on to her shoulders, pecked another kiss on to the nape of her neck. 'We'll be fine.'

In the living room, he snapped off the TV. Holding Dima's hand, he climbed the stairs. After brushing teeth, the boy – heavier every day – climbed into Ravensdale's lap, carrying the book he had chosen. 'Mommy hit a car,' he announced.

'She mentioned.'

''Nother car stopped, and Mommy crashed into it. Boom. She said bad words.'

'But nobody was hurt.' Ravensdale opened the book. 'That's what matters.'

'Oh,' said Dmitri, settling in.

'Frog and Toad were caught in the rain. They ran to Frog's house. "I am all wet," said Toad. "The day is ruined."'

Dmitri snuggled up; a thumb found its way into his mouth.

'"If you stand near the stove, your clothes will soon be dry. I will tell you a story while we are waiting," said Frog.'

We picked up the girl. Problem is, she doesn't trust us.

So Fletcher's private game had been not so private after all. And now Ravensdale would inherit it. In the end, he would do the opposite of dismantle the man's work; he would perpetuate it. Run it.

'"When I was small, not much bigger than a pollywog," said Frog, "my father said to me, 'Son, this is a cold, gray day, but spring is just around the corner.' I wanted spring to come. I went out to find that corner."'

Maybe it was necessary. Justice was the act that produced the greatest overall benefit for society. Lesser evils were necessary in the name of the greater good.

It might have been Andy Fletcher talking. From beyond the grave the man had bequeathed Ravensdale not only his prize agent, it seemed, but also his ethos. *Whatever it takes.*

'"I went around the corner to look for spring. There was only some wet mud and a lizard who was chasing his tail. I was tired, and it started to rain . . ."'

Still – Dima deserved a world worth inheriting. Good men could not content themselves with bread and circuses, no matter how tempting.

'"I went back home. When I got there," said Frog, "I found another corner. It was the corner of my house. I went around that corner, too. I saw the sun coming out. I saw birds sitting and singing in a tree. I had found the corner that spring was just around." The end.'

He closed the book. 'Another story,' Dima said.

'Next time, champ. Bedtime.'

For several seconds, the only sound was the droning cry of the wind outside. Dima's emerald eyes – Sofiya's eyes – glinted with the consideration of challenge. 'Next time?' he asked at last.

'Into bed, kiddo.'

A man does his best, he thought wearily. *His best is all he can do.*

Dima climbed into his Lightning McQueen bed. Ravensdale covered him with a blanket, leaned over, pecked a kiss on to the button nose, and accepted one on his cheek. 'Night, champ.'

'Night, Daddy.'

'Sweet dreams.'

'Sweet dreams, Daddy.'

On his way out, he switched off the light.

JUST LIKE JACKIE

just

like

jackie

LINDSEY STODDARD

HARPER
An Imprint of HarperCollinsPublishers

For
Nana and Pop
&
Grandma and Grandpa

chapter I

Before I know it I have Alex Carter's nose blood on me. My fist is tingling and his blood is squirted up the right sleeve of my sweatshirt. Everyone is crowding around, and Alex is crying like some tiny baby.

"She's crazy!" he screams and points right at me. "She punched me!"

He shouldn't have called me Robin. Maybe his face would be all in one piece and he wouldn't be sobbing like a weenie if he knew when to shut his mouth.

Baseballs drop to the hard-packed snow and all the players rush to third base, where Alex is crying and I'm standing over him. Everyone else is abandoning their snowmen and games of tag and running fast to surround us. "Fight! Fight! Fight!"

They're probably all thinking it's about time Alex Carter got popped. And they're right.

Derek's fumbling over now too, as fast as he can, and yelling, "Robbie! Wait!" but his feet are too big and he's the slowest kid in the grade and he'd be no help in a fight anyway. Too scrawny.

The teachers are sprinting across the yard to get between us, but I'm in ready position. Right fist up to strike if I have to. Left hand inside my baseball glove, blocking my face. I should have known Alex wouldn't do anything but cry and bleed in the snow. He's the biggest bully in the fifth grade, but I shut him up good. He's not laughing at me now and flapping his arms and calling me a motherless Robin bird.

A splatter of red is drying on my sleeve, but I don't give a crap. Tough people look tough. That's why Alex has long flowy blond hair like feathers and baby-blanket-blue eyes. And why my knuckles have his blood on them.

And he was calling *me* a bird. I don't have any feathers, nothing soft like that. My hair is blond too. But *dirty* blond. Not all white and fluffy, and I don't wear it loose and flowy like he does. Mine is pulled back in two thick braids under my Dodgers hat. The braids aren't perfect either because Grandpa doesn't always pull them tight enough. So by the end of the day all my curls give up on being good and start popping out left and right. I know how that feels.

Alex is blubbering now, and spraying snotty blood from his nose like it's going to kill him. It splatters like spilled transmission fluid, red splotches across the white ground. Grandpa taught me how to seal transmission fluid leaks under the hood of a 1999 Honda Civic at the garage. But I'm happy to let Alex sop up his bloody nose with the sleeve of his sissy-boy snowboarding jacket. There's no sealing up a kid that's gone that bad. I should know.

"What's wrong with her?" he screams. White puffs of sad, sorry bully breath escape from his crying mouth.

The first teacher that gets there is telling him to tip his head back and pinch his nose and asking if he's all right and making a big deal.

Derek's still running and yelling, "It's not her fault!" which feels pretty OK because it's true and no one else will believe me. But Derek does.

Then Mr. Danny has me by the shoulders. "That was *not* very ladylike," he says all mean and close-jawed and under his breath like he's sick of me but also maybe secretly glad someone finally gave that pest Alex what he deserved.

"What kind of ladies are you talking about?" I say. "The prissy, snap-in-half kind who let stupid boys call them names?"

He pushes me away from Alex and toward the front door of the school, and all the kids who are out for recess are staring at me with their jaws hanging open.

Derek's following behind us now and he's out of breath. "Not . . . her . . . fault . . ." Mr. Danny shoos him off. "Let . . . her—"

But no one can hear the rest of what Derek is stammering because Alex Baby Carter yells out, "That's why people need moms! Or they'll end up like her!" He's crying at the same time, so he sounds all pathetic, but I'm not letting him get away with that crap.

I try to wiggle out of Mr. Danny's hold, but he tightens his grip on my shoulders. So I whip around and shout back, "You turned out mean and weak and pathetic! What does that say about your mom?"

"Robbie!" Derek exclaims and pumps his purple fleece mitten in the air. And I can't tell if he's cheering me on or trying to get me to shut my mouth so I don't get in any more trouble than I'm already in. But either way I know he's got my back.

The rest of the kids in the yard are still just standing around with their mouths hanging open. Mr. Danny nudges me across the yard toward the school.

No one talks about my mom. Not even Grandpa. Not ever.

I would listen to Grandpa if he talked about my mom,

and not get all mad. But he doesn't. Maybe because he forgets, the way he sometimes forgets why he folded his winter jacket and put it in his underwear drawer, or what goes first, socks or shoes. Or maybe he doesn't forget my mom at all. Maybe he just doesn't want to remember. I do, though. But I can't. Not without Grandpa. And every time I ask he closes up tighter than a rusted bolt.

The front door slams behind us as Mr. Danny walks me into Principal Wheeler's office. I pull away and slump in one of the office chairs. No other kids are here. No other kids are ever here because this is a school of chickens. I don't even know why they have so many chairs in the office. They just need one. Mine.

"You'll have to call Robinson's grandfather," he tells Ms. Burg, the office lady. She sighs like this is old news and picks up the phone. "This time we'll need him to come in."

"Come in?" I sit up fast. "My grandpa's not coming here. You can just suspend me and I'll walk to his garage and help him work on the cars."

Mr. Danny puts his hand on my shoulder and I shake it off. "That's not how it works, Robinson. What you did today is really serious."

Ms. Burg dials and holds the phone pinched between her ear and shoulder and I'm staring at the big clock on the wall above her head. It's afternoon already, which

means Grandpa could be all turned around and confused, and if someone like a stupid office lady named
Ms. Burg pulls him out of his routine it could be even
worse.

"You don't have to call—"

"Enough, Robinson," she cuts.

"While you're at it, you better call Alex Carter's mom
too," I say. "Because he's blubbering real hard out there.
I'm pretty sure I heard him cry for his mommy."

"Robinson." Ms. Burg looks at me over the tops of the
green frames of her glasses and shakes her head. And
I'm wondering if she got named Ms. Burg on purpose
because it sounds like *bug* and she looks exactly like one
with those dumb green glasses. Plus all she does is bug
kids all day.

Then my grandpa must pick up the phone because
she puts on her fake nice voice and chimes, "Yes. Is this
Mr. Hart? This is Ms. Burg from Robinson's school. She's
fine, she's sitting right here with me, but we'll need you
to come down to the office. There's been a little incident."
Then she swivels in her chair so I can't hear the rest.

Mr. Danny sits down in one of the bad-kid chairs
next to me and looks right in my eyes. "Why did you do
that?" he asks. "I just don't understand."

"I told you. He wouldn't stop calling me a little Robin
bird, flapping his arms and acting like he's all funny. I

warned him to stop." I look down at the blood drying on my fist, then punch it twice hard into the worn leather pocket of my baseball glove.

Mr. Danny doesn't say anything else, just blows a gust of disappointed air out of his nose.

"No one calls me Robin," I remind him. "How many times do I have to tell him that before it gets through his thick skull? My name's Robinson and I'm sick of his crap."

Mr. Danny shakes his head like I'm a lost cause and I'm good with that. Lost causes get suspended and work in their grandpas' garages for the rest of their lives and that is A-OK with me. Plus the ground is thawing and the sap is running and Grandpa could use my help collecting it from the maple trees we tapped, then boiling it into syrup. School just gets in the way of the stuff worth doing.

"Her grandpa is walking over now," Ms. Burg reports, pushing her glasses back up her nose and dialing another number.

"Hi, Mrs. Carter?" she chirps. "So sorry to have to bother you. I know this is a tough time—" She swivels her chair again so I can't hear the rest, but I bet it's all full of sugar because nothing Alex does is ever wrong and it's always my fault.

Then Alex Baby Carter comes in the office and they

sit him in a chair way on the other side, far from me. Good idea. He's holding a big wad of white gauze over his nose, the kind Grandpa and I have in our first-aid kit at home.

Ms. Burg tells him that his mom is on her way. "She's going to take you right to the doctor to get that nose checked out." He nods. Then she pokes her head into Principal Wheeler's private office. "Mr. Hart is on his way."

"Nobody calls me Robin," I tell Alex, slamming my fist harder into the pocket of my glove and staring right at him. Now I'm mad because it's Alex's fault that Grandpa has to walk over here by himself and it'll be his fault if Grandpa takes a wrong turn and ends up searching the shelves for something he can't remember at Dean and Walt's country store.

Alex sniffles and winces when he takes his hands off his nose. The blood's all dried up. "What kind of girl only wants to be called Robinson, Robbie, or Son?" he asks.

"The kind that just pounded your face."

"Robinson, that's enough," Mr. Danny cuts in.

It better be enough. Enough to shut Alex up for good.

The office door swings open and Grandpa hobbles in. His legs are shaped like he's been riding a horse all his life instead of fixing up cars and tapping maple trees. He moves more side to side than forward. His navy jump-suit from the garage has his name, Charlie, stitched over his heart, and I wonder where his jacket is. It's cold out.

He takes one look at Alex's gigantic wad of blood-soaked gauze and says, "What in God's name . . ." with a voice that's as deep as the lines that run across his dark forehead. I shoot a glare at Alex that says, *You better not say a thing about how he can't be my real grandpa, or how I bet I wish my mom wasn't dead. Or else.*

Grandpa takes a long look at me, then down at the blood squirted up my sleeve, and he shakes his head. I hate making Grandpa shake his head.

"Mr. Hart, the principal is waiting to speak with you," Ms. Burg says, and she gestures toward the door that says *Principal Wheeler.*

I stand up to walk in with him, but Mr. Danny stops me. "This meeting is just for adults, Robinson." Then before I know it Ms. Gloria is there too and Mr. Danny is opening Principal Wheeler's door and telling me to sit back down.

"Shouldn't I be—"

But the door is closed and my grandpa is gone, into the principal's office like he did something bad and not me. And he doesn't even like to talk too much unless he's under the hood of a car, or splitting wood for the pile, and all these adults talking about their stupid school stuff will make him confused, and he didn't do anything wrong except get given a bad kid.

I almost wish I could take it back. Pull my fist out of Alex Carter's face and count to ten instead, like Ms. Gloria taught me. Count to ten, take three deep breaths, or repeat baseball stats until that's all I could think about—*Career leaders. Batting average: Ty Cobb, .366. Hits: Pete Rose, 4,256*—until I got calm again. Then maybe Grandpa wouldn't have to shake his head and go to the principal's office, and I wouldn't be such a pain in the butt, like a trailer that's too heavy for his small frame to tow.

chapter 2

When Principal Wheeler's office door opens and they all come out, the grooves on Grandpa's forehead look deeper.

Ms. Gloria sits down next to me and says, "We all agree that you need to go home with your grandpa today. Tomorrow we'll discuss some next steps about a behavior plan that will help you manage your anger in school."

"Tomorrow?" I shoot up from my seat. "I'm not suspended? What kind of school is this?"

"Robinson . . ." Ms. Gloria's got that voice she uses when she's trying to calm me down, soft and low and serious. But I don't care.

"Isn't it illegal in this state to punch someone in the face? Didn't I break a Vermont law? What kind of message are you sending, letting me stay here?"

Grandpa puts his hand on my shoulder and pats it three slow times. "You're lucky now, Robbie," he says with that deep voice all full of gravel and split wood. "You'll come with me today to cool off and get your head straight, because this is unacceptable."

Grandpa thanks Mr. Danny and Ms. Gloria. And then, as if things could get any worse, Alex's blond, flowy-haired mom shows up in black stockings and clicky high heels and a long black coat with big buttons. She looks like one of those prissy, snap-in-half-type ladies, but she has the same deep forehead lines that Grandpa does. I didn't realize people as young as regular mom and dad age could get those.

"I'm sure you'd like to apologize before you go," Mr. Danny says.

"No way—" I start, but Grandpa squeezes my shoulder hard like he's tightening lug nuts.

"Sorry." But I say it more to my untied Nike Air Griffeys than to Alex. "If you don't call me Robin anymore, I won't punch your face again." I cross my fingers behind my back just in case.

Grandpa tightens the lug nuts on my shoulder. "Try again."

This time I just mumble, "I'm sorry for what I did." But my fingers are still crossed.

Mrs. Carter looks up from her sniffling sissy Alex

and studies Grandpa's hand on my shoulder for a quick second that she thinks no one notices. "You're Robinson's . . ."

"Grandpa," I say. But I know what she's thinking. That we don't match. That Grandpa is the dark color of a motor oil leak and I'm light as power steering fluid on my darkest summer day. But it's none of her business.

"That's . . . very nice." But she raises her eyebrows when she says it, like grown-ups do when they're on to something, and it makes me wonder if she can see into Grandpa's tired memory and if she knows that sometimes he leaves his keys in the refrigerator and the milk by the door. Because that's nobody's business except Grandpa's and mine. But her raised eyebrows and long look make me feel hot and nervous, like we've got to get out of here fast because if someone finds out, they'll make it a huge deal like grown-ups always do. Then what?

Mrs. Carter looks straight down at me. "Keep your hands off my son." And when she's walking away with her arm around Alex, I hear her mumble "old man unfit to raise," but I can't catch the rest. And even though it makes my fists clench tight and I think that she deserves a nose to match her son's, before I know it I'm pulling Grandpa out the office door and away before he can mix up his words and anyone else raises their eyebrows and sees into our secret.

●●●

On the walk to the garage I stay one half step ahead of Grandpa so he just has to follow along in case his memory gets tired. I do that to him sometimes, make his memory tired. Whenever I'm bad he forgets more. That's why I have to try to be better.

"You can't be using your fists, Robbie," he tells me. "You're better than that."

"Alex deserved it," I say, because he did. "And not just for calling me a Robin bird. He's mean to everyone all the time behind teachers' backs, then acts all innocent when they're looking again."

"That doesn't make it right. Violence will get you . . ." But he's drifting off. And I know he means that violence will get me nowhere fast but he forgot the end of his sentence. And he's shaking his head again. I hate that so much.

I wait for Grandpa to tell me about Jackie Robinson like he always does when I do something bad. But he just goes along, saying nothing, and it doesn't feel right all quiet like that, so I tell it to myself in my head:

The man you're named for was a great ballplayer. The first black player in the league. People taunted him all the time, but he didn't pay no mind. He couldn't. Even if they called him names, he just let it roll right off. He had to.

And that's how I know I'm not much like the real Robinson. But Grandpa wishes I was.

He tells me about Jackie Robinson because he wants me to realize I have to do better. And that even when people are rotten, I shouldn't fight back.

But he's not even telling me today. He's just walking quiet, side to side, side to side, on his bowed legs. Maybe he doesn't know what to do with me anymore and he's giving up. Or maybe he's forgetting about Jackie Robinson too.

I want Grandpa to tell me about when he was five years old:

It was the first World Series televised in color and Jackie Robinson and the Dodgers beat the Yankees in seven games. The only World Series they won in Brooklyn.

But we just keep making small steps down the sidewalk.

Grandpa's hand is swinging there beside me, and I kind of catch it for a second in the pocket of my baseball glove and squeeze. He looks down like he's surprised I'm there, like he'd forgotten.

"I'll be more like Jackie Robinson, Grandpa."

He smiles at me and we walk on to the garage through the new falling snow.

chapter 3

As soon as we get to the garage I see Harold's feet sticking out from under a Toyota Tacoma. I give his boot a kick and he drops his wrench on the cement floor and slides out from under the truck.

His hair is thick, dark brown, and wild. He lets it stick up all over his head like he just woke up, and that's only one thing I like about Harold.

"What do we have here?" he asks, standing up and wiping his hands on his jumpsuit. "Shouldn't you be in school, Robbie?"

"Got in trouble."

"Trouble is no place to be," he says.

"Better than school." I sit on the stool that has the one shorter leg that I can always get rocking really good.

From here I have a perfect view of all four bays, and right now each bay is full. And each car has something wrong with it, and I bet I could figure out as fast as anyone how to fix every last one.

"Got busy here this afternoon," Harold tells Grandpa.

Harold is my grandpa's left-hand man. That's because everyone knows I'm Grandpa's right hand. But left-hand man or not, I don't want a lecture from him about school and working hard and being good. He sometimes does that, pulls up a stool and sits down next to me and looks at me right under the brim of my Dodgers hat, right in my eyes, and tells me how I need to get through school and be my best self. Grandpa says it's because Harold and his husband, Paul, are adopting a kid and he's practicing being a dad.

Harold is regular dad age. I bet he hopes when he and Paul get their kid she's not like me. Someone who doesn't get all red hot inside, who doesn't punch stupid boys' noses, even when they deserve it, someone who doesn't make him shake his head for anything.

"So what happened?" Harold asks.

"Had to take care of this boy and his crappy attitude."

Harold tugs one of my braids. "I thought you were working with that counselor at school on not getting so angry. Counting to ten and stuff like that."

"Her name's Ms. Gloria. And I am working on it." Harold was there when Grandpa signed the papers to let me start seeing a counselor at school. That was the last time Grandpa was in the office, and I promised myself I'd never make the school drag him back there. Stupid Alex Carter. "But even if I counted to ten today I still would've slugged him."

He hits the brim of my Dodgers hat, which I usually hate but don't really mind when Harold does it. "Always my little spark plug."

And I know what Harold means, but I'm not his little spark plug. I'm all Grandpa's. He's the only person I'm related to, which is maybe turning out to be a raw deal for him.

Harold throws his arm around my shoulders. "Listen, kid." And I know he's going in for the whole practice dad talk. "When you're out there in the world, you're representing your family. And I know you weren't raised to be fighting."

I nod my head and keep teetering on the stool, hoping that Grandpa has a job for me.

"Little spark plug like her . . ." Harold starts.

"From an old codger like me," Grandpa finishes. That's one of the jokes they're always saying. Like who could ever believe that I came from my grandpa?

We still get that from time to time, even in a town

this small, where almost everyone knows us. Long looks and scrunched-up faces trying to solve our family puzzle.

Sometimes Grandpa reminds me that I'm one-quarter black, even though you can't tell by looking at me. "And that one-quarter comes straight from yours truly," he says, jamming his thick thumb to his chest. It doesn't matter that you can't see it right off, he tells me. That one-quarter is still in me, beneath my surface, deep at my core.

When I was little and didn't understand, I used to picture a shiny, silver twenty-five cents quarter deep in me, next to my heart. Most grandpas pulled quarters from behind little kids' ears and let them go to Dean and Walt's country store for penny candy, and it made me feel better to think that Grandpa's quarter was somewhere deep in me, and worth something more than candy. Worth keeping.

"Up off your duff, Robbie." Grandpa claps his hands twice to get me moving. "We've got work to do."

Harold gives me a fist bump, picks up his wrench, and slides back under the truck. Grandpa tosses me my work gloves, which are just like his but smaller, and points in the direction of the closest bay. I nod and toss my baseball glove on the stool.

"What we've got this afternoon is a 2003 Toyota

4Runner," Grandpa says. But I know that without any-one telling me. I know cars like I know baseball.

I pull on my gloves and Grandpa shows me a box of replacement headlight bulbs.

"You remember how to do it?" he asks.

"Yup." And I know Grandpa remembers too, because even if he sometimes forgets that he already had his morning cup of coffee, or that it's winter so he'll need his jacket, he never forgets cars. That's one place where his memory isn't tired at all. And that's a good thing because I don't need Harold raising his eyebrows and looking long at Grandpa. Harold's too busy to notice any-way. He's always under a car or thinking about his new baby coming soon.

"Ready?" Grandpa asks.

"Ready," I say.

I slide my fingers under the hood of the car and find the lever. When I pull on it, the hood pops up fast like it's been waiting to burst all day. I know what that's like.

Grandpa tests me on the basics before we get started. This is our warm-up. He points. I name.

"This one." He's pointing to a round cap in the middle.

"Check and change oil."

He moves his finger to the right.

"Transmission fluid."

"And here?" His finger points toward the back and I have to stand up on my toes and lean in far to see.

"Washer fluid."

I know them all.

Grandpa pulls on his gloves too, which means we're ready to start the job.

"First?" he asks.

I turn my Dodgers hat backward and look into the hood. I see the connector lock release. "Disconnect the light," I say. Then I do it. Pressing down on the lock release makes a small pop like a short bunt, and I like that. When I pull at it a little, it disconnects from the old, burnt bulb.

Grandpa's hovering over me, making sure I do it right. "Good," he assures me. "Now what?"

"Retaining ring." I stick my head in closer to find it. The faint smell of plastic and metal and oil rise up to my face, and I like that smell. When I find the ring I twist it to the left and detach it from the headlight assembly. Then I take the burnt bulb from the retaining ring and give it to Grandpa. He throws it in the trash.

"Good, Robbie."

I still have the retaining ring around my finger. Grandpa puts the new bulb in my other hand, and I put it exactly where the other one was in the headlight assembly. Then I twist the ring back and it's in. It feels good when everything pops in and fits just right.

"Last?"

"Plug her in!" I shout and reach for the connector socket.

"Ta-da!" Grandpa cheers. "A-plus." An A-plus from Grandpa in the garage is better than any other A-plus ever.

"Now the other one," he says. And I do it all over again, but this time Grandpa doesn't say anything because I know the steps by heart.

When I finish, Grandpa squeezes my shoulder, but in a *good job* kind of way this time, and Harold comes over to start the car and turn the lights on. "Looking bright, Robbie," he says, and reaches out for another fist bump, which is kind of our thing.

I'm not feeling all hot and mad and like I could burst anymore.

In the bay next to us, an intern from the technical high school down the street is working. It's his last day, which is good because he's taking my jobs. Right now he's jump-starting a Honda Accord. I know how to do that too. That's even easier than changing headlights. Grandpa doesn't let me use the word *easy* in the garage, though. He tells me it seems easy because I'm good at it. "If it was easy, why would all these people bring their cars in here to have us do it for them?" he says. I guess that makes Grandpa a genius, then. And me too.

Sparks shoot from the Honda's battery like little tiny fires, and Harold rushes over to help. I know that the little fires mean the intern attached a negative to a positive by accident. Either that or he didn't connect the jumper cables to the dead battery first. Grandpa says that's really important and that those sparks can catch fast. I know how that is too.

But right now I feel pretty OK. Far from Ms. Burg and Alex Carter and his clicky-heeled mom.

There are only three places in the whole world that make me feel like this, like I'm not sparky at all. Third base, where Jackie Robinson played; our sugar maple trees in the backyard; and in Grandpa's garage, fixing something that's broken.

chapter 4

"What do you bet the sap's running?" Grandpa asks when we're walking home from the garage. I bet it's running fast because the conditions are perfect. I also bet he already forgot all about Alex Carter, and about me getting in trouble at school today.

"I think we should be ready to collect," I say. And as soon as we get to our house I throw my book bag and baseball glove on the porch, grab the empty milk jugs from the shed, and shove my feet in my big Bogs boots that come almost up to my knees.

Out back, we have twenty sugar maples that are bigger around than Grandpa's hugs. A few weeks ago we drilled two holes in each, hammered in taps, and attached metal buckets for the sap to drip down into. It started running as soon as we drilled the holes, like the trees had been waiting to burst. That's what happens when you tap them at the exact right time. When it's freezing at night but sunny and warm during the day.

As soon as we get out to the backyard I can see fat drops of sap falling from the taps into the buckets.

"Time to empty." Grandpa hands me a cheesecloth.

We have to filter the sap from the metal buckets through a piece of cheesecloth to collect all the bad stuff so it doesn't get mixed in.

We run the sap through the filters and collect it in the old plastic jugs. Once they're full, it's my job to half bury the jugs at the edge of our yard and pack them tight in the snow to keep the sap cool.

Grandpa says we'll boil soon.

"If you promise to be good at school tomorrow, you can help me split," he says.

I don't technically say I promise, but I know I'll be good enough to keep Ms. Burg from calling Grandpa in. I don't want anyone else asking him questions and telling him how bad I've been and making him shake his head and rub his temples. No way. I can be good enough to keep Grandpa away from all those adults and all their concerns.

I run back to the shed for our work gloves and protective glasses and Grandpa's ax. The snow in the yard is halfway up my boots, and I like the way it feels to sink in all the way to my rolled-up jeans as I walk back to Grandpa. He only lets me hold the ax with the head down and with two hands, and only if I walk.

It's my job to put the big pieces of wood on the old stump chopping block. I have to place them perfectly so they don't wobble at all. It's Grandpa's job to swing the ax and split the wood along the grain into smaller pieces that'll fit in our outdoor fire pit for when we start to boil the sap down into syrup.

Grandpa always breathes out a big "Ha!" when he swings the ax down on the wood, like an umpire calling a strike. Then the wood cracks like a broken bat, split down the grain. Sometimes it only takes one hit like that and the wood just falls apart. Sometimes it's a little tougher. Like if the wood has a big knot in it, the ax can't get through it right off and Grandpa has to take lots of swings and then pry it apart with his hands at the end.

"Couple more," Grandpa says, and I know he's getting tired because he's not pulling the ax up as high over his head as he did the first time. But his memory's not tired. Not out here. He never forgets what he's doing at his chopping block, like his brain is hardwired. Hardwired to fix broken cars and split wood out by our sugar maples.

And I sometimes wonder if he remembers other things out here at the chopping block while his memory isn't so bad. Like my mom. And the way her voice sounded and if I look like her or what happened that made him shut up so tight like his tongue forgot how to say her name.

And I'm thinking about asking him. Trying again while we're out here at the chopping block. I run my work glove against the rough bark of the next piece of wood and open my mouth, but I know he'll just shake his head and change the subject. Like he always does.

"OK, Robbie," he says. "That'll do for tonight." He lowers his ax and I lob the new split pieces on the stack under the eaves of the house.

The creases are deep across his forehead, and I hope that he is remembering all that stuff out here by the sugar maples, because no matter how deep I search, no matter how hard I think, or how tight I close my eyes and try to see, I'll never be able to find any memories. And I'm scared he's forgetting his. Then I'll never know.

I make footsteps in the snow for Grandpa to follow, and I wait behind him on the porch as he struggles with the key to the front door, pushing the wrong one in over and over even when it doesn't fit. "Goddammit!" he grunts. "This stupid . . ."

I put my hand over his. "This one, Grandpa." I point

to the silver key hanging on the chain. "That big one's for the garage, remember?"

"Of course I remember that," he says.

I smile up at him and know that even if I try to ask now, it's too late, because he's all jumbled up and confused. But there's no one else to tell me about her, so I help Grandpa up the steps and into the warm house.

chapter 5

When I get to school the next day everyone's looking at me funny. They always kind of do because I'm the only girl they know who wears boy clothes and kicks everyone's butt at baseball, but today they're looking at me extra funny, like Alex's blood is still sprayed up my sleeve or something. I hop over the wooden fence into the schoolyard and don't pay them no mind. Just like Jackie Robinson.

"They let her back here?" I hear one girl scoff.

"No way." It's Chelsea and Brittany. They're completely pink from their Uggs all the way to the gum they're smacking with every stupid syllable they say. They're also the girls who hang off Alex Carter like he's some god or something.

"I can't believe it. Did you see what she did to Alex?"

"Shouldn't she be suspended? Her grandpa came and picked her up. If that even is her grandpa."

My hand makes a fist, but I just let the words run right off, like Grandpa says. And I try to count to ten while I'm searching around for Derek because I usually hang with him until the doors open for school. I put my baseball glove up over my mouth like I'm talking secret messages on the mound with my pitcher and catcher and blow hot air in the leather pocket. Each breath warms up my face before it fades back to cold.

Then I see him running across the yard and yelling my name. "Rob!" Derek looks so funny when he runs that he's making me laugh right out loud into my glove. He's stick skinny and short and his ears kind of poke out, but his feet are so big that he looks like he might trip over them at any second. He can tell I'm laughing at him too, but he doesn't mind because he knows we're cool. Ever since I peeled off the *kick the midget* Post-it that Alex Carter stuck on his back in third grade, he's been kind of hanging around. And that's OK with me.

"Rob! Rob!" He's yelling and waving his hands over his head.

He's not named after Derek Jeter either. He didn't even know who that was when I asked. He doesn't know anything about baseball. Watching him running over toward me, I'm thinking we should switch names, Derek and me, because he's as soft and small as a Robin and I'm as hard as a Derek. That *k* like the crack of a bat. *K* for *strike*. I'm hard like that. He's the one that's like feathers. I guess that's why we're friends.

He's all out of breath by the time he gets to me. "Did you get in trouble?" he huffs.

"Not enough. I'm still here, aren't I?" I punch my right fist into my third baseman's glove.

"I've been wanting to see that kid get slammed since first grade." He's still breathing hard as anything. "His nose exploded!"

"I know. I'm the one who exploded it," I remind him. "No one calls me a motherless Robin bird."

Derek goes quiet, and I know that means he's sorry Alex was such a jerk. "What did your grandpa say?"

"Same stuff my grandpa always tells me. That I have to be more like Jackie Robinson." Even though Grandpa didn't say anything about Jackie Robinson to me at all this time, like it didn't matter anymore who I was named for.

"Well, Alex Carter deserved to get popped." He looks around the yard. "Think he'll come today?" he asks.

I shrug my shoulders. "Doubt it. He was crying like a baby."

Derek gives me a high five as the bell rings and

everyone runs toward the big double doors of the school.

Principal Wheeler is directing us into our class lines in the lobby while we wait for our teachers. We get in the back of Ms. Meg's homeroom line, and I'm looking for Alex, but I don't see him, which is kind of too bad because I want to see what his nose looks like after a day of bruising. I bet it's purple and yellow and gross. I want everyone to see what a nose looks like after you call me a motherless Robin bird.

"Hey, Robinson." It's Candace, a girl from our class, and she's tapping me on my shoulder. She's a little pink too, but not the gum-smacky kind of pink that Chelsea and Brittany are.

"You OK?" she asks. "I saw the whole thing, how Alex was making fun of you yesterday even after you told him to stop."

"I'm fine," I say.

She starts kicking the snow out of her Bogs, which are the same boots I wear sugaring except hers are pink and mine are black. Then she says, "I think Alex is a huge jerk. I just wanted to tell you that. And no one ever stands up to him and I'm glad you did."

Candace looks up from her boots and is smiling really big and holding her hand up for a high five like Derek does sometimes. I give it to her and it feels pretty OK.

"Are you grounded or anything?" she asks. "My mom would have died if she knew I hit someone."

The words stick in me sharp, a fastball in the gut, and I can tell she feels bad the second she says it because she looks down at her Bogs again.

Derek grabs my wrist. But I shake him off. I'm not a touching kind of person like that.

I imagine shoving Candace. Just a little maybe so she remembers not to complain about her mom around me because at least her mom isn't actually dead, but I shake the image out of my head and start counting to ten instead.

"I'm not in trouble," I mutter.

"I'm glad," Candace says to her Bogs.

Then I turn around fast and hope the line starts moving down the hall to Ms. Meg's room.

"You wanted to punch her, didn't you?" Derek whispers.

"Shut up or I'll punch you," I whisper back, but Derek knows I'm not serious because I wouldn't ever have to punch him.

"She was trying to be nice, you know," he says.

And I do know. That's why I didn't shove her. That's why I counted to ten like Ms. Gloria taught me and remembered some baseball stats. *Career saves: Mariano Rivera, 652.*

Finally Ms. Meg shows up and we start walking to homeroom. Derek nudges me. "Remember. What would Jackie do?" and that gets him cracking up right away. He always laughs when he says that, like it's the funniest thing he's ever come up with. It is kind of funny, I guess, but not too funny because I actually have to ask myself that sometimes.

Today, Jackie would just stand in line and get through the day. So that's what I'm going to do.

chapter 6

Ms. Gloria's been pulling me out of class for counseling once a week on Wednesdays almost the whole year. It started as soon as Ms. Meg and Mr. Danny noticed that I boil over easier than a pot of sap. But today's not Wednesday, it's Friday, and she's knocking on Ms. Meg's door and I know even before she pokes her head in that I'm going to have to go with her right now anyway.

"Robinson?" She waves me over.

Ms. Gloria's hair is wavy with curls and already turning white. She pulls it back in a loose small bun at the back of her head, but the curls creep out and spill down the sides of her face. Her eyes are blue. Not baby-blanket wussy blue like Alex Carter's, they're windshield-washer-fluid blue. Like they could scrub-the-streaks-and-smudges-and-bird-crap-right-out-of-you blue. And when she looks straight into your eyes and uses her no-nonsense voice, there's nothing anybody can really do but what she says.

"Bring your stuff," Ms. Gloria tells me. When she turns away, I roll my eyes and try to take three deep breaths because when I bring my stuff that means it's not going to be quick, and next period we have recess and that's the best period of the day and I'm going to have to spend it reading with Ms. Gloria. Or talking about my feelings. Which is about the opposite of a game of snow baseball.

I drag my book bag behind me along the classroom floor and walk as slowly as I can because more time walking means less time talking about my feelings. I look back at Derek and he gives me a goofy grin. Candace's head is down on the desk and I wonder if she still feels bad about telling me her mom would die if she hit someone, or if there's something else making her head heavy. But she picks it up and half smiles too and sends me a little secret thumbs-up. I half smile back. Maybe quarter smile.

"You're going to have recess with me today," Ms. Gloria says as we walk down the hall, like it's some prize. "And we're going to chat about taking some responsibility for your actions."

"Are you going to have recess with Alex when he comes back, to tell him to stop being a huge jerk?"

"Alex will have consequences for his own behavior."

"Yeah, like a broken face."

"Robinson." Ms. Gloria's using her no-nonsense voice, and she stops me right there in the hall and makes me turn my Dodgers hat around backward so I have to look straight into her washer-fluid-blue eyes. "I'm not saying Alex was right. But I am saying you were wrong." Then she starts walking again and calls over her shoulder, "And *keep* that hat out of your eyes. I don't want to suggest to Principal Wheeler that we revisit our hat policy."

What would Jackie do? I ask real quiet in my head, and it's kind of hard because I think he might run down the hall to join his class lining up outside Ms. Meg's room to go to recess. I think he might tell Ms. Gloria that she couldn't stop him because he had third base to protect and a batting average to raise up.

"Can't we do this after—"

"Nope," she answers and opens the door to her small room. It has space for one long table, six chairs, Ms. Gloria's desk in the corner, and lots of posters on the walls about feelings and "accountable talk" and "I statements" and other warm fuzzy stupid stuff, and a couple of bookshelves with bins full of books. I sometimes take books from the bin that says *sports*. Ms. Meg says I should read all different kinds of books, but Ms. Gloria says I can read whatever I want in her room.

I sit down where I always sit, staring out the only window into the yard and I can tell Ms. Gloria is looking right at me because my hat is still turned backward and I know if I try to pull it back over my face she'll make me turn it right back around, or take it until the end of the day, or even tattle to Principal Wheeler. So I just forget it. But that doesn't mean I have to look at her.

"Tell me about what happened yesterday."

At first I stay shut, but I know that doesn't work with Ms. Gloria because once she waited me out all the way through lunch and recess. I had to eat this gross brown bag lunch brought up by the cafeteria lady with an icy milk and smushed jelly sandwich that didn't even have peanut butter because Alex Carter is allergic so no one can have peanut butter in our school ever. He ruins everything.

So I grumble, "Yesterday was fine."

She just keeps waiting, which means that my answer isn't good enough, so she'll wait until I say something that she calls "real."

"Robin isn't my name," I say, and even thinking about Alex Carter jumping around me and flapping his arms is getting me all mad again and my fists clench up. "I told him to stop. I told him to call me my real name and that I'm not any feathery little Robin bird. I'm Rob-inson, and my grandpa gave me that name on purpose, so he better shut up."

"Do you want to tell me about your name, or about your grandpa?"

I cross my arms over my chest and sit back in my chair, staring down at my rolled-up jeans and Nike Air Griffeys. "No."

"Then let's look at this." Ms. Gloria pulls out a piece of paper with my name at the top and *Behavior Plan* typed out in big letters, a list of directions, and a picture of a baseball diamond with all the bases.

"Ms. Meg, Mr. Danny, and I put this together so you can track your own behavior and start joining your classmates again for recess."

"Is Alex getting one of these?"

"His business is not your business," Ms. Gloria says. "You can only change your own behavior."

She taps her finger on the behavior plan. Each base of the baseball diamond is supposed to be a part of the school day. Morning is first base, lunch and recess are second base, and afternoon is third base. Ms. Gloria explains how Ms. Meg and Mr. Danny will give me a score for each and my goal is to make it to home base every day.

Stupid.

Through the window I can see the other kids in my class roll the bodies of snowmen across the yard. Mr. Danny is handing out baseballs and bats, and a couple of guys throw down their black book bags to make visible bases for snow baseball. It's not fair that they're playing when no one in this school would have even had the idea to play baseball in the winter if it weren't for me, and I'm stuck in here because I showed a bully what happens when you're mean to Robinson Hart.

"Robinson." Ms. Gloria snaps her fingers and points at the behavior plan again. "On the top of the page is a reminder list of all the things you're working on." Then she makes me read my goals out loud.

"One: use appropriate language for school. Two: count to ten, take three deep breaths, or recite baseball stats in my head to calm down when I'm feeling angry. Three: socialize with others by asking them questions about themselves," I mumble.

"What do you think?" Ms. Gloria asks. And I want to tell her that this piece of paper isn't going to make any bit of difference at all and that I belong at recess hitting real home runs out in the snow and not fake home runs on this dumb baseball diamond drawing.

But because I hate missing recess and I don't want Grandpa to ever have to go to the principal's office again or Harold to have to give me another practice dad speech, I say, "It's fine." And for a second I think maybe from now on I can just make up my mind to be good.

"You had a big strike yesterday," Ms. Gloria reminds me. "I expect a home run from you today."

Then I see Alex through the window. He's running across the yard toward the snow baseball game. I lean forward trying to see what his nose looks like. I can't tell from this tiny room, but he's high-fiving Ronald in left field and hustling to take his place in center.

"What the—Alex is here?" I blurt.

"OK, let's think of a strategy for reentering your class this afternoon," Ms. Gloria says. "Especially since your favorite person has arrived."

She's trying to be funny, and I'm trying to come up with a plan, but all I can think about is Alex in the outfield and how no one is making him stay in from recess even though he started everything, and how it really isn't Candace's fault that she mentioned her mom like that and how I should be nicer to her.

And I'm trying to listen to Ms. Gloria, but really I'm thinking about how Derek is just sitting off to the side of the baseball game outside, blowing on a snowball he made, watching it melt between his mittens like he always does, and I have to be inside and he isn't even playing. We shouldn't just switch names, we should switch lives, because he'd probably love to stay inside and talk about his feelings with Ms. Gloria instead of going to recess, and then I could beam a line drive right in the hole between Alex and Ronald in the outfield.

Ms. Gloria raps her knuckles on the table in front of me. "Robbie, can you tell me what I just said?" The words didn't stick at all. I was trying, I swear, but my mind was running the bases somewhere else.

And then Alex catches an inning-ender fly ball and is pumping his fist and trotting toward home. He nudges Ronald, who's running next to him, and points toward Derek, who is still sitting on the sidelines, not paying attention to the game because I'm not playing, and there's no one else for him to hang with. Then Alex nudges Ronald again and points and jogs up close to Derek, and lobs the ball right at Derek's head. It glances his cheek and shocks him half to death because he grabs his face and rolls backward like the stick-skinny little kid he is and I'm pretty sure he's crying because he hates sports and scares easy. And Alex and Ronald are laughing and pointing at him and making it worse, so other kids laugh too.

And Mr. Danny is blowing his whistle, not because he saw what Alex did and is calling a foul, but because recess is over and it's time for everyone to run through the doors to the lunchroom.

And before I know it my fists are clenched and my

jaw is locked and I'm sprinting away from Ms. Gloria and her little room and the baseball diamond behavior plan and flying through the big double doors, down the hall-way, and into the lunchroom. And I'm trying to count to ten or take three deep breaths, but it feels like jumper cables are clamping down hard, positive is attaching to negative, and sparks are about to fly.

And before I know it, I'm locked up arm in arm with Alex Carter and pulling his stupid soft feather hair hard and pushing him down to the lunchroom floor. He's try-ing to get away and swinging punches toward my face but he's not strong enough and I've got him pinned, staring at his ugly bruised-up nose, and I'm thinking that I'm glad Ms. Gloria made me pull my hat around backward because now I can get even more up in his face like when the coach springs from the dugout and argues with the ump. And I want to punch him again hard for what he did to Derek at recess because Derek is small and never did anything to hurt anyone, but I don't want Grandpa coming back here. So just as I'm trying to think of baseball stats—*Hit by pitch, Alex Rodriguez, 175 times*—and realizing that Alex Carter is just like Alex Rodriguez, acting all tough and perfect but really such a sissy-boy cheater, Mr. Danny is blowing his whis-tle and pulling me off Alex.

Chelsea and Brittany are standing with their lunch

trays pressed against their stupid pink sweaters and their mouths are hanging open, staring.

Kids are circling around and Mr. Danny's trying to keep me separate from Alex and get me to walk toward the lunchroom doors. "What do you think you're doing?" he's shouting.

And Derek is running up and yelling, "She was helping me! See what he did?" and showing off the red mark on his cold skin where Alex lobbed the ball at his cheek. "Alex is a bully! No one ever sees it!"

And Alex Carter is crying on the floor and holding his head and acting all innocent.

I try to shake out of Mr. Danny's grip because his voice has gotten softer and serious and he's talking right to me. "Why did you do that? Robinson, why did you do that?" He's all up in my face. And I don't like him all up in my face like that, and I don't like that Ms. Gloria rushed to the lunchroom too but is kneeling down by Alex and helping him up when she's supposed to be on my team. So I stomp hard on Mr. Danny's foot and tell him to back off and that he doesn't know crap about me. But he doesn't loosen his grip. He drags me off to the principal's office and points to the same chair I was in yesterday and says to Ms. Burg, "Bring in her grandpa again."

Derek's outside the office door and I can see him

through the window and he's trying to explain to Ms. Gloria what happened and he's pointing to his cheek. She pats him on the shoulder, sends him to the nurse, comes in the office, and looks straight at me with her stern, disappointed face. And before I can tell her that I remembered a baseball stat instead of punching Alex Carter in the face again even though he deserved it, she says, "Strike two, Robbie."

chapter 7

This time when Grandpa hobbles his side-to-side walk into the office Harold is with him, which means Grandpa is going to shake his head and I'm going to get a practice dad talk. And I wish Harold would just save it for his own kid because I didn't do anything wrong.

Grandpa's mad. He grabs my arm hard and squeezes until I can feel my heart beat in his hand. "What were you thinking?"

I'm not used to seeing Grandpa mad, and it looks all wrong on him.

"Let go," I say and yank my arm away. I've never been mad at Grandpa before either, and that feels all wrong too, but he was squeezing my arm and glaring at me like I was in big trouble and he never even asked me what happened.

"You have some explaining to do," he says.

"Whatever," I mumble.

That makes him glare harder, so I pull the brim of my hat down and he says, "Not whatever."

Harold is shaking hands with Ms. Gloria and Mr. Danny and if they didn't already know better, everyone would think he's my dad because my family's so messed up and I don't look like anyone or act like anyone I know and everyone just shakes their heads and wishes I belonged to someone else.

Principal Wheeler opens her office door. "Please come in," she says. "We only have a few minutes before the teachers need to get back to their classrooms."

Then everyone's walking past me and into her office. Ms. Gloria, Ms. Meg, Mr. Danny, Grandpa, and Harold. They'll all say how frustrated they are with me and come up with some plan as brilliant as a baseball diamond drawn out on a piece of paper. This time I scoot to the chair closest to Principal Wheeler's door so I can press my ear up and try to hear what crap they're saying about me, and if Grandpa's finishing his sentences, because it's afternoon and I'm making him stressed and his memory might get tired. And I can't have anyone looking at him long and wondering if he's unfit to raise a girl like me. Because he's not.

"Robinson," Ms. Burg huffs and motions for me to move away from the door, but I stare at her like no way am I moving just because she told me to, and she looks the other way and shakes her head too.

It's hard to catch everything, but I can hear Grandpa saying he's sorry over and over. And I don't know if it's because he's really that sorry or if he forgets he already said it. And it's not even him who should be sorry. Alex Carter should be in there saying sorry over and over for being so mean to kids half his size. And calling me Robin and motherless, then acting all innocent.

I can hear Mr. Danny's tone through the door, which is mad and annoyed, probably because both times I fought Alex Carter have been when he was in charge of the yard, so it makes him look pretty bad. But no one could've stopped me, so he shouldn't even really feel that bad either.

And I hear Ms. Gloria saying, "We need to hold on to her. I'm worried. It has to be a group effort."

And I hear Ms. Meg saying, "A suspension site would be horrible for Robinson right now." And all this other stuff about hearings and legal representation. And it's starting to seem pretty serious. I want to be suspended, but suspended to Grandpa's garage to figure out what's wrong with all the cars, and suspended to our backyard to help Grandpa split wood and boil sap. I don't know what a suspension site is, but it sounds bad.

I slide my Dodgers hat back around over my face and press my ear closer to the door.

Harold is asking, "If Charlie signs this, what exactly is he agreeing to?" And Ms. Gloria's talking about how she pulls me out on Wednesdays for counseling already and something else I can't hear. And something about anger, and my goals, and talking.

And then it's kind of quiet and I picture them all shaking their heads. Grandpa says he's sorry again and Harold says thank you to everyone. And I quickly move back to the other chair so it doesn't seem like I was spying.

"Robinson, please come in here." It's Principal Wheeler's voice. When I walk in, Grandpa can hardly look at me, which is fine because I still have my hat pulled down far.

"Turn that hat around." Ms. Gloria means business. She'll wait me out, so I just do, but I make a big huff about it because I like my hat the way I like it.

"We are all really worried about you, Robbie," she says. I hate that crap. No one needs to worry about me but myself. "Your behavior is unacceptable. It's troubling, we don't like it, and it can't happen anymore." Ms.

Gloria is using her no-nonsense voice. "We're going to be watching you like a hawk and trying to get to the bottom of this. Ms. Meg's going to be watching, Mr. Danny is, your grandpa will be too, and you know I'll be watching you."

"Me too, Robbie." Harold pats my shoulder. "I've got my eye on you too."

He's trying to be all practice dad. And I want to tell everyone that the only one who needs to be watching me is Grandpa because I'm his and no one else's.

"So I'm not going to be suspended?"

"No," Principal Wheeler answers.

They're just going to make my life here crappier by being up in my business.

"The first thing you'll do is figure out a way to apologize to Alex. Consider it your weekend homework," Ms. Gloria tells me.

"You can't be serious—"

"Very serious, Robbie. Your actions were very serious and now we are all very serious."

"Are you going to make him apologize to Derek?"

Then Grandpa reaches across the table and grabs my arm again, but not hard. Like he's just holding me still for a minute. "You'll apologize." He takes a deep breath. "And you'll do what . . ." And I can see Grandpa's searching for his words and I hate the look on his face when that happens, like he's wandered off and gotten lost and can't find his way back to what he was saying.

". . . what Ms. Gloria says," I finish. "I'll do what Ms. Gloria says." And it kills me to say that because I don't want to do what Ms. Gloria says, but it kills me more to leave Grandpa hanging in the middle of his sentence with everyone watching.

Ms. Gloria starts explaining about how I'm still going to be seeing her but with a small group of other kids, and I want to yell that there's no way I'm doing that but Grandpa's hand is there holding me still so I remember some stats until Ms. Gloria is done talking and Harold is shaking everyone's hand again.

"Let's go," Grandpa says. He keeps holding my arm as we walk out of the school like I might run if he lets go. And even though running fast and hard across the yard right now would make me feel better, I'd never run from Grandpa.

Harold is walking a half step ahead of us, and it's not until then that I realize they must have closed the garage because of me, and now there are going to be so many cars to catch up on. At least I can help with that.

That's when I hear the clicky heels approaching down the sidewalk. "It's Alex's mom," I whisper to Harold, and I pull my hat back around to cover my face.

"Mrs. Carter?" Harold reaches out for a handshake,

but she doesn't even look at Harold, she looks straight under the brim of my Dodgers hat with those grooves carving deep across her forehead.

"I'm Haro—" he tries, but she cuts him off quick.

"I thought I told you to keep your hands off Alex."

Grandpa gives my arm a squeeze. "What do you say, Robbie?"

"Sorry," I mutter. "He was bullying my friend, and I couldn't let that happen."

"Don't put this on him," she spurts. "He has enough to deal with. Next time you go near him I will be pressing charges." She clicks off into the school and down the hall toward the nurse's office, where I'm sure Alex is playing his innocent-pretty-boy routine.

"What's pressing charges?" I ask.

"Lawyers. Lawyers and big trouble," Harold explains.

And that shuts me up fast because I don't need other people's moms and teachers and definitely not lawyers sticking their noses in our business.

"You've really done it this time," Grandpa mumbles and nudges me down the street.

Harold shakes Grandpa's hand and tells me that we have a big talk coming. Then he turns toward the garage and Grandpa points the other way down the street toward home.

"We're not going to the garage?" I ask. But he doesn't

even answer me or tell me one crap thing about Jackie Robinson and how hard it was for him to stay calm when everyone was acting terrible. He just keeps holding my arm and walking as fast as his side-to-side legs can go.

"I can help with all the extra cars from today—"

"That's enough, Robbie," Grandpa cuts me off, and keeps on walking.

When we get home and go up the steps Grandpa tries two keys that don't fit, the one for the garage and the one for the truck. I don't help him or say a word because I'm so mad we're not at the garage sealing transmissions or replacing brake pads.

When the right key finally slides in, Grandpa goes straight to his office, where the mail is piled up, brings out a piece of paper and pen, and tells me to sit at the kitchen table.

"Write your apology to that boy."

"Alex? No way." I shove the paper away. But Grandpa's not even listening because he's mad at me just like I'm mad at him.

The door slams and Grandpa's gone out in the yard. I can see him through the kitchen window, and I can't believe he's collecting sap in the jugs without me. And he's putting the big pieces of wood on the stump chopping block by himself and swinging the ax up high and down hard to split them through the middle, and he does each piece in one fast swing. The two halves just break apart, easy as that.

I crumple the blank paper and cross my arms over my chest. But I can hear each hard thwack of the ax and each "Ha!" that Grandpa grunts when he makes contact, and every one makes me grit my teeth harder because I want to check how many gallons we got and I want to throw the split pieces on the woodpile.

And before I know it, dark is creeping up outside and I can't hear him thwacking anymore. I'm looking out the window and I can't see him at the chopping block or the sap buckets. I stand up and peer around to the woodpile, but he's not there stacking either. All the split wood is just lying around the stump where it fell.

I'm shoving my feet in my boots and not even zipping my jacket because something feels wrong. Grandpa never gets mad and he never leaves chopped wood scattered, and a bad feeling is sitting hard in my stomach.

I swing open the door and yell, "Grandpa!" I can hear my voice echo off the sky through the woods. I run past the stump chopping block and our gallons of sap packed in the snow, following Grandpa's side-to-side footprints right past the metal hanging buckets and dripping sap and into the woods. "Grandpa!" My breath is hanging in the dark, cold air. "Grandpa!"

I'm wondering if he decided to go on our favorite hike on the Appalachian Trail that runs behind our yard and up to the hiker shelter, where we stop to eat lunch on summer weekends. But he wouldn't go without me. And he wouldn't go at night or in the winter. Without the first aid kit and without a headlamp.

My heart is beating fast because maybe he forgot it was winter. Or maybe he forgot where the trail goes. Or maybe he's that mad at me, and he's running away.

I hear a crunch of snow and I trudge after it, following his prints farther into the woods. "Grandpa!"

And then he's calling back out to me. "Robbie?" With that voice full of gravel. "Here!"

And he's just standing there, leaning against the trunk of a tree, and his eyes are big like when we catch a deer in the headlights of the truck. Like he's scared.

"Grandpa?"

"I guess I just got a little turned around," he says. "I thought we tapped some more maples back here, no?"

"No, Grandpa." I walk up to him slow like he really is a deer who might scare off easy and forever if I'm not careful. I take the ax from him and hold it head down and with two hands like he taught me. "Follow me," I say and make him hold on to my shoulder as we tramp back through the woods toward the house until we get to the yard.

I can't let the chopped wood stay all scattered in the snow. And seeing it like that makes me wish I could take it all back again. Like Grandpa could pull the ax out of those pieces he split, and put them back together, and I could pull back my shove from Alex's shoulders and run back into the room with Ms. Gloria and just talk about my feelings because if I had then I wouldn't have weighed down Grandpa's engine like that, I wouldn't have made his memory tired, and he wouldn't have wandered off without me.

Grandpa and I pick up the pieces and stack them with the rest, and I promise myself for real this time, I'll be more like Jackie Robinson.

chapter 8

It's Monday and I have a blank copy of the baseball diamond behavior plan so I can get around my bases by the end of the day, and I'm all ready to start fresh and let things roll right off and stay out of everyone's face, especially Alex Carter's, when Ms. Meg says we're going to do a project about our family trees.

She can forget about that right now, because I'm not doing it. No way.

Alex starts whispering something to Ronald, and I bet it's something mean. They're laughing and Ms. Meg gives them a look, so they stop. But when she turns away Alex goes back to whispering and laughing and he's rolling up tiny little paper balls and tossing them into Oscar's dark curly hair in front of him. It's making me all hot and mad because he doesn't have some stupid baseball diamond plan out on his desk to help him not be a jerk.

Already I regret writing him an apology this weekend, even though I wrote it as a haiku, which Ms. Meg told us is the earliest form of poetry. But that's not why I chose it. I chose it because it's short.

Alex, I'm sorry.
That is all I have to say.
That was the last time.

Ms. Meg also taught us that you can interpret poetry in lots of different ways, so while most people think the last line means I won't hit him again, you could also interpret it to mean that I won't apologize again.

But watching him laughing now with Ronald I'm wishing I never crumpled the apology haiku and tossed it in his cubby this morning because he doesn't deserve to read it and he isn't sorry about anything at all. And neither am I.

I ask to go to the bathroom and maybe when I come back I'll have missed the whole project and everyone will be done and presenting their family trees to the class and Ms. Meg will say, *It's OK, Robinson, you don't have to do it because we're moving on to the next thing.* Then we'll just go on to a different project and I'll keep on being cool and letting things roll right off like Jackie Robinson and I'll get through the morning just fine and Ms. Meg will draw a smiley face on first base and send me off to recess with Mr. Danny.

Even though I take extra long in the bathroom and make laps around the fifth-grade floor, peeking my head in other homerooms to see if they're doing stupid family trees too, which I can't tell, when I get back Ms. Meg is still just explaining the project.

"You get to create your family tree however you want," Ms. Meg tells us. Brittany and Chelsea are whispering about papier-mâché at the table behind me, and I picture sticking it across their mouths and letting it harden so all their stupid words are stuck inside their mouths forever and they can never giggle at Alex Carter again.

"Today we'll start by doing a little writing just to get some ideas flowing about our families."

Everyone is unzipping their book bags and taking out their notebooks like they're excited to get started. Except me. Ms. Meg says my name and gives me a look like she's trying to remind me that I'm only one strike away from serious trouble. I yank hard on the zipper of my book bag. My notebook is tucked in the pocket of my baseball glove, which makes me even more mad because

I wish it were recess.

Candace has her head down on the table again, which is weird because she doesn't seem like the head-down-on-the-table type of kid. I guess this project is so stupid that even the good students like Candace don't want to do it.

Ms. Meg makes her way over and pats Candace on the back.

She sits up fast and whispers, "Sorry."

Derek nudges my elbow. "Rob, you OK?" He's really good at knowing when something's wrong. "I can help you—"

"I'm fine," I say, because he can't help. Not with this.

Ms. Meg has her notebook projected up on the Smart Board. It says *Family Tree: Quick Writes.*

Quick Writes are basically writing prompts Ms. Meg gives us. They're usually not so bad because we never have to write too much or for too long, but these ones will be bad.

Derek nudges me again and looks at me like he wants to know if I'm really OK, and I shake him off because I'm trying my best not to be mad at him just because his family tree will probably be easy to make and have lots of branches.

"Number one. I want you to write a list of three people who are important in your family," Ms. Meg says.

I clench down hard on my back teeth and try to remember as many baseball stats as I can. *Career leader, stolen bases: Rickey Henderson, 1,406. Single-season leader, home runs: Barry Bonds, 73, 2001.* But Ms. Meg is giving me that look, so I start writing really slow:

Important People in My Family:
Grandpa

"I have seven so far," someone whispers. And I'm trying to let it roll right off. I can see Derek's list growing longer and longer in my peripheral vision, like I'm a pitcher and he's got a good lead off first base.

"Next question," Ms. Meg announces finally. "This time we'll write for two minutes without stopping." Kids moan, not because they only have one family member, but because they don't want to write for two minutes straight.

"Number two," she says. "Jot down any details you know of your birth. What have your family members told you about the day you were born? Ready? Set. Write." And she starts the timer for two minutes.

Most career ejections of a MLB manager: Bobby Cox, 158. But it doesn't work because before I know it I'm standing up and about to turn the whole table over because this is such crap and I'm not making some stupid family tree project. And everyone is biting their pencils and writing their stories and sketching these gigantic trees with moms and dads and cousins and branches sticking out everywhere and I wish I had Grandpa's ax, because I'd raise it up high over my head and chop them all down in one big swing.

"Robbie." Derek's tugging on my arm, trying to get me to sit back down before I do something stupid.

But then the door creaks open and everyone looks and it's Ms. Gloria, and it's the first time I'm hoping she takes me, because if she doesn't I'm going to break something.

"Robinson," she says calm and low. "You look ready." I'm thinking, *Perfect timing*, when she calls out, "Also, Candace, Oscar, and Alex. You'll be coming with us too."

chapter 9

This has to be some kind of joke. Like a really bad, unfunny joke.

We're all sitting around Ms. Gloria's table in her little room. Alex is across from me. Kicking distance. Candace is next to me, and across from her is Oscar. His hair is still full of those little balled-up pieces of paper that Alex was throwing at him in Ms. Meg's room. Ms. Gloria sits at the head of the table.

"You can't keep me in here with her." Alex pouts and points at me. He has a Band-Aid across his nose.

"Scared?" I ask.

Ms. Gloria's giving us that look that tells us to cut the crap. "You done?"

Alex and I both cross our arms and slump back in

our chairs. Ms. Gloria gives me the sign to turn my hat backward, so I jerk it around hard.

"Good," Ms. Gloria says, all no-nonsense. "Then we can start."

She holds a wand in front of her that has purple and silver glitter floating slowly from the top to the bottom, then she turns it back over and the glitter starts falling again slowly, top to bottom. "This wand holds a lot of power," she tells us.

I'm waiting for someone to break through the door and say they've made a mistake and that I don't have to sit across from Alex Carter ever again in my life and that Ms. Gloria is not about to put a spell on us with some stupid sparkly wand.

"All the students who have ever participated in Group Guidance have held this wand when they speak up and share their feelings in the conversation," she explains. "That's why it's so powerful. There are a lot of words and emotions and bravery captured in here."

"Group Guidance?" I scoff.

Ms. Gloria tells us how we'll be meeting in this group at least three times a week and how the wand is the talking wand and no one speaks unless they are holding it. I want to grab it from her so I can say, *Is this for real? You put me in a group with Alex?*

Ms. Gloria can make me sit here, but there is no way

I'm sharing any words or emotions or bravery or whatever else. If I just stay shut and refuse, maybe they'll
rethink my suspension so I can go do something worthwhile like help Grandpa in the garage.

Ms. Gloria rips off a piece of chart paper and uncaps
a black marker. I can smell its licorice from here. I hate
licorice. "Before we begin, we have to make some rules
together. Then once we make the rules, we have to promise to stick to them."

She writes *Group Guidance Norms* across the top of
the chart paper.

"Ideas? Anyone?"

Candace starts. "Don't talk unless you have the
wand. Respect the wand." I roll my eyes even though
I'm trying to be nicer to her. Why does she need to be
in Group Guidance anyway? Because she puts her head
down on the table sometimes? She's probably the nice
kid they threw in with us so we wouldn't fail. Teachers
always put a good kid in every group. Otherwise crap
never gets done.

Ms. Gloria writes down *Respect the wand!* on the
chart paper.

"Respect each other too," Candace adds. "No laughing at what someone says."

Ms. Gloria writes that one down. "Anyone else?"

I look at Oscar and realize I don't think I've heard

him say one word since Ms. Meg introduced him to our class the day he moved here from Brooklyn. That's where the Dodgers are from, but when the Dodgers moved they went to Los Angeles, not to Vermont like Oscar. I don't know why he has to be here either. Maybe every group needs a good kid who raises her hand a lot like Candace and a quiet kid like Oscar who will balance everything out.

Alex is the bully. And I'm the kid who won't let him get away with it.

"Robinson?" Ms. Gloria asks. "What do you think is important to a group conversation? Can you add to our list?"

I want to tell her that I don't think group conversations are important at all, but I just sit there.

Ms. Gloria would wait me out forever because that's what she does, but Candace jumps in. "Eye contact!" Ms. Gloria writes it down.

By the end we have a list. Candace basically created the whole thing, but Ms. Gloria makes us read it over together and sign it on the bottom, which means that we agree to stick to the norms. The list looks like this:

GROUP GUIDANCE NORMS
1. **Respect the wand!**
2. **Respect each other. No laughing at anyone else.**

3. Use eye contact when someone is speaking.
4. Be present. Listen to what others are saying even if you're not sharing.
5. Everything we say stays in the room.
6. Passing is OK.

alex carter
Candace Barnes
Oscar Oates
Robinson Hart
Ms. Gloria

Number six was mine. I mumbled it out when Ms. Gloria was capping the licorice marker. That way I won't have to say stupid crap.

"Today we'll just do a group check-in, and next time we'll be able to have a longer conversation."

Ms. Gloria explains how we'll pass the talking wand around and each say how we're feeling today on a scale of one to ten. If we want, we can say more about why we're feeling that number.

Candace starts. "I'm a five."

She's looking down at the wand. I'm wondering how someone so nice can only be a five. And then I'm wondering why she isn't saying more about why she feels like a five. She likes to share. But she isn't.

Then Alex laughs and mumbles something under his breath. I'm pretty sure I hear what he says and I think it's how Candace is chubby so she could never be a ten, and my fists tighten into balls, but Ms. Gloria speaks up while I take three deep breaths and loosen my hands.

"Are you having trouble with the norms already?" Ms. Gloria asks. "You just laughed at someone else and talked without the talking wand." She keeps staring right at him with her no-nonsense look. Finally it's Alex Carter that gets that look instead of me.

Candace passes the wand to Ms. Gloria, who says she's an eight. "There are a couple of things troubling my mind, but overall I'm really happy to be starting this group today." Then she passes the wand to Oscar.

"Five," he says, but it's almost like a whisper, so I still don't even really know what his voice sounds like.

"What?" Alex jumps in. "No one can ever hear you."

And I should be taking three deep breaths and waiting for the talking wand, but I can't. "Maybe he'd be more than a five if you weren't such a jerk," I snap.

Ms. Gloria glares at Alex like she could cut him with her eyes, and I wish she would. Then she glares at me too like I did something wrong, which I didn't, except talk without the stupid purple glitter wand.

"Robinson—" Ms. Gloria tries, but even her

no-nonsense stare won't stop me, or the fact that I don't have some talking wand.

"Ms. Gloria, Alex threw those balls of paper in Oscar's hair in Ms. Meg's room!"

"Did not!" Alex screams like the baby he is.

Oscar shakes his head back and forth and runs his hands through his hair. It's raining paper balls on the floor beneath him.

"I watched him do it!" I never tattle on people, but I'm so mad at Alex and I'm sick of him getting away with everything.

"I saw it too," Candace says, quiet and nice and to her hands, and now I'm starting to feel OK because even Candace is breaking the norms.

"See?" I shout.

Ms. Gloria almost never raises her voice, so when she does we all go paralyzed.

"Enough!" she yells. "Alex, if this is true, I think it's time for a little meeting with your mom." He tries to whine something back, but she talks right over him. "And I want you all to look at your signatures. You signed this list of norms." She takes a deep breath and points at where we signed the chart paper. "Unless your word and your name mean nothing, I expect you to follow them."

And I want to yell back that my name does mean

something, which is why people better say it right, but that's against the norms, and *Robinson Hart* is written right there near the bottom of the list.

Oscar passes the talking wand to Alex.

"Nine-point-five," he says with his prissy little mouth, like he's better than everyone else and his life is so perfect.

Then he passes the wand across to me. I'm about to say that he'd be a ten if his nose didn't look like a tie-dyed green-and-purple monster bulging out from his face. But I don't because I think it breaks norm number two, and I don't want my grandpa coming in here today to shake his head for anything at all. But Alex deserves it.

I'm really feeling like a two, but I say, "Pass."

It's nobody's business how I'm feeling, or that I can't forget my grandpa's scared face when he wandered off and that we have to do this stupid family tree project, which is making me feel more like a zero.

And I know what Ms. Gloria is trying to do. She's trying to push us to all get along and bond and be nice and make friends because she's like Grandpa and she thinks that there's sweetness at everyone's core, like a maple tree. But there's not. There's definitely not sweetness at Alex's core and not at mine either. I don't know what my core is made of except maybe Grandpa's one-quarter, but it's not all syrupy sweet, that's for sure. It's not like the center of a perfect sugar maple. It's tight like a knotted piece of firewood, gnarled and hard to chop through.

chapter 10

Once school is out, I'm close to a ten because I'm at the garage and Grandpa says I'm on my own with the 2012 Dodge Grand Caravan that's driving in right now. He's never let me talk to the customers on my own before. That's always been him or Harold, but Harold's at the hospital because the baby he's adopting is due this week and he's going with the birth mother to her doctor's appointment.

Grandpa's already busy working on a Subaru, so he points to the Dodge Grand Caravan and says, "All yours," and I think he might be giving me a test to see how I do.

"Hear carefully," Grandpa says, and I know he means listen carefully, but sometimes he changes his words around so they sound wrong, and I wonder if that's why he's letting me talk to the customers now instead of him. Because I can keep my words straight. And before I know it, I'm not a ten anymore because I'm thinking of him getting all mixed up and turned around and how it's probably my fault that I'm making his memory more tired.

I pull on my work gloves. "I got it, Grandpa," I call over my shoulder because I'm already walking out to the parking lot to greet the customer. That's what Harold would do. He says the customer is always right, even when they're not, and you have to be nice and put your best foot forward.

As soon as the van parks, the back door slides open and three little kids tumble out and rush past me. They're all bright, feathery blond and having an imaginary sword fight, dodging between the parked cars in the lot. Their jackets are unzipped and falling off their shoulders, but they don't even seem to notice.

"Get over here!" their mom screams, and slams her door. First I see her leather high-heeled boots making pockmarks in the old melting snow like a freshly aerated outfield, and before I look up and see her flowy blond hair I know it's Alex's mom. She adjusts her scarf, sees me, and says, "Oh Jesus. You've got to be kidding."

That's exactly what I'm thinking.

Of course the first time Grandpa lets me talk to the customer it has to be her. And I'm not sure I have a good foot to put forward here, but I can't run in and get Grandpa because then he won't let me help him fix the car, or worse, he won't remember Alex's mom, and he'll get embarrassed and let his words wander off, so I just have to try.

"Hi, Mrs. Carter," I say. "What seems to be the problem with your car?"

"You can't work here," she huffs. "Aren't you ten?"

"Eleven." But what I want to say is what the crap does it matter how old I am if you can't fix your car and I can? "I've been fixing cars since I was six."

Now her kids are jumping up on the bumper of the van and launching themselves as far as they can into the parking lot's melting slush. She tells them to stop, but they don't listen. Guess no kid in that family knows how to listen. And I'm wondering where Alex is and why he isn't with them, not that I'm complaining. He probably went home to ice his busted nose.

"The last time I brought my car here I worked with a nice man named Harold."

"He's not here today. But I am, and I'd like to get started diagnosing the problem with your car, if that's all right with you." I put my fists on my hips and start counting to ten so that only nice things come out of my mouth.

She crosses her arms, huffs again, and juts her chin toward the Caravan. "The check engine light is on."

I think about what Harold would say next. "I'd be happy to take a look at that for you. Do you mind moving it into the garage so I can begin working?" Even though I know how to drive all kinds of cars, even standard shift, no eleven-year-old has a license, so I can't let Mrs. Carter know that Grandpa sometimes lets me. Then she'll think he's even more unfit to raise me, which is bull because I'm a better driver than half the adults on the road.

She sighs and mumbles, "You've got to be kidding me," again, then shoves her kids back in through the sliding door of the van and backs out of the parking space. I push the automatic door opener, and she drives in through the big garage doors to the first bay, where I have everything I need to figure out what's wrong with her car.

The kids tumble back out and I tell Mrs. Carter she can wait inside in our lounge. "It should only take a minute."

"I want someone else to check your work," Mrs. Carter tells me. "I'm not relying on some eleven-year-old."

I clamp down hard on my back teeth as she pushes her monster children through the doors to the lounge inside, where I know they will bounce off the couches. Two of the kids are identical twins. The third one is smaller. All boys. All blond and flowy and not listening.

I want to yell after her and say that her car is in good hands, even if they are eleven-year-old hands, that my hands can fix anything, including her stupid son's stupid attitude, and if she wants me to readjust another one of her kids to just send him on out. Instead I take a deep breath and turn toward the van.

Grandpa's installing new windshield wipers on the Subaru Outback across the garage, and he walks over when Mrs. Carter takes her kids inside. "Good job, Robbie," he says. "What'd she say was the program?"

I know he means *problem*, not *program*. Since he wandered off into the sugar maples, his memory's been more tired than usual, even during the day, and I wish he would just rest so everything could come back to him.

"Check engine light is on."

"Know what to do?" he asks.

"I got it, Grandpa."

The scan tool is black and yellow and looks like a big cell phone with a long wire attached. When I plug it into Mrs. Carter's van, it will give me a code and tell me exactly what's wrong.

I open the driver's door of the van and slide into Mrs. Carter's seat. It feels weird to be in Alex Carter's car. It's sort of like when I see Ms. Meg or Mr. Danny or Ms. Gloria at Dean and Walt's country store and it feels all wrong, like I'm peeping in on a part of their life that I'm not supposed to see.

White towels line the backseat, and they're covered with muddy paw prints and black hair, and that makes me hate Alex Carter even more because he has a dog and I've always wanted one, but Grandpa says no, he doesn't need one more thing to take care of. Alex will probably put his dog on his family tree.

When I turn back around to plug in the scan tool, I knock a plastic bag from the console and it spills all over the passenger floor, and I'm thinking this is exactly when Mrs. Carter is going to come out and check to see how the eleven-year-old is doing with her car, so I shove everything back in the bag fast. A huge pack of M&Ms, some kind of makeup with a big black brush, and lots of bottles of pills that rattle when I pick them up and look like the kind of bottle I got when I had strep throat. I want to look closer and figure out what's in the bottles and why there are so many but I know I'll get caught peeping where I don't belong, so I put the bag back on the front seat and try to forget about it.

I keep my eye on Grandpa in the next bay while I

plug in the scan tool and wait for its code. The new windshield wipers are on the Subaru, and now Grandpa's head is under the hood. I know I shouldn't be worried because his brain is hardwired for cars. Just like mine. But I keep thinking that he might just drift off again.

The tool beeps and I read the code. It's something with her gas cap, which is the best-case scenario and should be an easy fix. I pull the lever down by my feet and the gas tank door pops open. I'm sliding out of the driver's seat to go check out the tank when I hear Harold's voice.

"What're you working on, Robbie?" He's got on regular clothes, not his navy blue jumpsuit with Harold stitched over his heart.

"What are you wearing?"

He hits the brim of my hat, laughs, and tells me he didn't want to dress like a schlub when he was going to see his baby's birth mom in the hospital. "I don't want her to think her baby's going to some greaseball."

"But you *are* a greaseball," I kid him.

He looks at me like I have a point and says, "She doesn't have to know that." Then we laugh together.

"When is the baby coming?"

"Any day!" He beams, and he's crossing his fingers.

"Cool," I say, but I'm already sick of talking about baby stuff. "I have to check out this gas tank."

Grandpa makes his way over and shakes Harold's

hand as I open the gas tank door.

"Easy!" I shout because I love when I've solved the problem, when I figure out what's wrong and how to fix it. It's that snap-into-place feeling. "The gas cap is missing."

Harold gives me a fist bump and Grandpa nods his head. "A-plus, Robbie."

Harold comes with me when I go inside, where Mrs. Carter is waiting with her kids, but he lets me tell her what I found out about her van. The twins are doing a cartwheel contest across the lounge, and the littlest one is wrapped around Mrs. Carter's ankle and crying.

It's kind of hard to talk, or think, because they're so annoying, but I focus on the deep grooves that run across her forehead, the grooves like Grandpa's, and I tell her, "It's an easy fix. Your gas cap is missing." I'm trying to tell her how important something so small as a gas cap is because it helps maintain pressure within the fuel tank and how she's probably not getting her best gas mileage because she's losing fuel through evaporation, but she doesn't even care. She cuts me off.

"Oh, good God. I bet I left it on top of the car last time I filled up."

Harold goes to find a replacement cap and says it's on the house.

"Thank you," she says to him. "I don't think I could

have handled one more bit of bad news." And I see those lines on her forehead cut deeper.

Then she walks out, lugging her youngest kid with each right step while the twins run past her and push through the doors to the lot, where Grandpa is parking her car.

We're watching Mrs. Carter shove her kids in the sliding door and scream at them to buckle up. One of the twins keeps popping out of the door and dancing wild in the parking lot. When she finally gets everyone in and buckled and drives away, I remember the bag of pill bottles rattling across the floor of her car and I wonder again what they're for.

"You sure you want kids?" I ask Harold.

He puts his arm around me and says, "Yeah. I'm sure." And if he still wants a baby after seeing those crazy monsters, then he must *really* want a baby.

We're looking out the window and watching Grandpa walk back from the parking lot, and I want to tell Harold about how Grandpa wandered away Friday night and almost got lost up in the woods. And how I think Grandpa's check engine light is on and I don't know how to figure out what's wrong. But I hope it's something as easy as a missing gas cap. And that we can get a new one, on the house, and drive off all fixed.

But I don't tell Harold because what if it's something

more serious? Not just a missing gas cap, but he's got too many miles on him, or tough terrain has worn down his struts. So I just stay quiet and let Harold put his arm around me and keep thinking about how Grandpa's the only branch on my family tree and how we don't even look like we belong in the same orchard, and how Harold will be getting a kid soon. One he asked for.

Then Harold's husband, Paul, pulls up in his 1958 green Chevy pickup truck. I call her "She Roll" because the *V* and *T* are missing across the back hatch where it says *CHEVROLET*, so it looks like *CHE ROLE*. It's kind of our thing.

"There's my ride," Harold says and I walk to the parking lot with him.

Paul hops out of the front seat. "She Roll!" he calls as soon as he sees me.

"How's she rolling?" I ask, which is my favorite question to ask Paul because his truck is so old you just never know when it's going to putt-putt-putt and sputter to a stop.

"Still rolling like the queen she is." He pats She Roll on the hood. Then he gives me a hug before he hugs Harold, and even though I'm not a touching kind of person it feels pretty OK.

Grandpa comes over too, and we wave good-bye as they drive off.

It's already getting dark and my stomach is growling. I help Grandpa pull down the big garage doors and watch him search for the right key to lock up. He tries two wrong ones before he slides the right one in and we can start walking home.

On the way I tell him all about Alex Carter's mom and how she doubted me because I'm eleven, and how I'm actually not so bad at talking to the customers, so I could do that again if he wants. I can tell he's listening because he pats my shoulder, but he's not saying anything. I sometimes wonder if he's getting quieter and quieter because he knows he fumbles his words and gets embarrassed and shakes his head, and I hate that. And I'm thinking how if he gets too quiet I'll never be able to finish my stupid family tree project because I don't even know what my mom's name was. And every time I've tried to ask, he snaps shut fast.

And just when I think I'm getting the guts to try to ask him about my mom, he pats my shoulder again and says, "You did a glued job, Robbie."

So I just reach up and touch my baseball glove against his hand and say, "Thanks, Grandpa."

When we get home Grandpa looks out back toward the sugar maples. "This weekend we'll boil the sap," he says. "You can invest your friend."

And I know he means *invite*. And I know he means Derek.

"OK, Grandpa." Then I take the keys from his hand and find the silver one to the front door and let us in.

Inside, he sits down on the bench by our front door and bends over to pull off his boots. I try to help him with his jacket, but he shakes me off.

"I'm not a hundred years old, you know," he grumps. And I know he's not a hundred years old, but when it gets later in the day he always looks older than he did that morning.

He starts toward the kitchen. "Let's see about some breakfast."

"Dinner," I say. "I'll help, Grandpa."

He opens the cupboard and takes out a box of mac and cheese. "I'm fine. You must have some schoolwork to do."

I unzip my book bag and take out a worksheet that Mr. Danny gave us during gym class about heart rate. I have to find my pulse and time it for ten seconds, counting each beat, then multiply by six to figure out my beats per minute. Then I'm supposed to do the same thing after I run in place for a full minute. Then I have to write four sentences about what I notice about my heart and exercise.

I'm sitting at the table, searching for the pulse on my

wrist, but really I'm keeping an eye on Grandpa in the kitchen.

He fills the pot with water and turns on the burner.

I find the thump-thump in my wrist, and I'm trying to count but I can't because I'm watching him hold the box of mac and cheese like he's not sure what the next step is. He takes a knife from the wooden block on the counter and my heart jumps faster. He starts sawing open the box.

I rush over. "Grandpa, like this." I carefully take the knife from his hand and show him how to open the cardboard box.

Then he pours the pasta shells in the pot, and even though the water isn't boiling yet, I don't say anything. He stirs it with the knife, and I don't say anything about that either.

After the water gets to boiling I dip in a wooden spoon and try one of the shells. "They're done," I say and turn off the burner. The bubbles die in the water and he looks down like he's lost something in the pot. I keep waiting for him open the cupboard and grab the strainer, but he just keeps staring down in the pot until I can't watch him look anymore.

I fling open the cupboard and get the strainer myself. "Almost my turn for the cheese squeeze," I say.

The cheese squeeze was my part for as long as I can

remember. Grandpa always let me cut open the top of the silver pouch and squeeze all the orange cheese on the hot shells and mix it up. Then I'd lick the spoon. He would call me for dinner by hollering, "It's time for the cheese squeeze!" and I would come running. I used to have to stand up on a stool to reach the pot, but I don't need that anymore.

I do almost all the parts now. Not just the cheese squeeze.

"My part, remember?" I touch Grandpa's arm, and he moves away from the stove. The pot of mac is heavy and this has never been my part, but I get it over to the sink and pour it perfect into the strainer without even one of the shells missing and falling down the drain.

"You didn't have to . . ."

"It's OK. I like cooking, Grandpa." Which isn't actually true, but it comes out anyway.

I pour the shells back into the pot, and it feels so good to squeeze all the orange cheese out of the pouch. I slide my fingers down both sides and it comes out smooth and all in one big melty, snakey glop. Then I squeeze the pouch hard in my fist to get all the last bits out. I grit my teeth and crush it and squash it and pretend it's Alex's stupid face when he calls me Robin, or when he says, *Why don't you call your mommy? Oh, wait! You don't even have one!* I crush and squeeze and get it all out. Then I stir it all up. But I don't lick the spoon anymore like I did when I was little.

Later in bed I listen through the wall to Grandpa's room, and wonder if he'll open his door in the middle of the night to go find those sugar maples he said he was looking for out back. Or hike up to the Appalachian Trail shelter without me. I listen for the springs in his old bed when he turns over, and I listen for his snores. And I wonder if his memory is going to be rested tomorrow because if he can't remember that we only tapped the front twenty sugar maples in the backyard, or how to open a cardboard box of mac and cheese, how will he remember to tell me who my mom was and how she died and if I'm like her?

I'm trying to count my heartbeats like Mr. Danny taught us, but my brain keeps wandering and before I know it, I'm trying to think of a haiku for Grandpa. It's hard to count out all the syllables in my head without a pencil to write it down, but I think I have one.

Grandpa, sorry. Don't
wander away. Promise I'll
be just like Jackie.

chapter 11

The next morning, Ms. Meg says, "Happy Tuesday!" like it's some special day even though I know we're just going to work on our stupid projects. Then she tells us to share with our table groups everything we've written in our notebooks about our families so far and that soon we're going to start making our trees. Derek opens his notebook. Candace does too, but she makes a big annoyed sigh and puts both elbows on the table with her face pressed between her fists.

"Tell us about your grandpa," Derek says. "And how he knows all about making maple syrup and how I get to come over and help when you boil the sap and we eat sugar on snow and how your grandpa can fix anyone's car."

He's trying to make me feel better because he's my best friend and because his page is full of a million family members and all I have written down, still, is *Grandpa*.

"You share," I tell him.

"But no one in my family is as cool as your grandpa." Even though he's trying too hard, that does make me feel kind of better. But I'm still not sharing because this project is stupid and I'm not making a family tree anyway.

Ms. Meg is walking toward our table, which means we have to get on topic or else she'll sit down with us and then we'll all have to share before she moves on to make sure another group is on task.

"Fine. I'll start," Candace says when she sees Ms. Meg approaching. "My mom is a professor and my dad does something with computers." She tells us how every once in a while her mom gets to travel with her class to London and how she gets to go with her this summer.

Ms. Meg walks by our table. "I'm also really close to my aunt Jane," Candace continues. "She lives an hour away, but we see her on the weekends." Candace keeps talking about her aunt Jane and her three cousins while Ms. Meg passes by. That's why you always need someone like Candace in a group.

"I also have a sister," she adds. Then as soon as Ms. Meg pulls up a chair at another group's table, Candace sits back in her chair and stops talking like she doesn't have one more word to say. I'm about to ask her if her sister is younger or older just so I don't have to share my stupid blank notebook but Derek asks her first.

"She's older. And she reminds me of it all the time." Then she puts her head down on the table again. I nudge her, but she just stays like that, so I look at Derek, and shrug my shoulders and tell him it's his turn to start talking.

He's telling us about his mom when Ms. Meg announces to wrap up our conversations, that it's time to share out with the whole class. Candace doesn't pick her head up, and I kind of want to tell her she should before Ms. Meg notices because she's not supposed to be a head-on-the-table kind of person. But I don't know what to say or how to get her attention without touching her, so forget it. I see Ms. Meg looking at Candace and she crinkles up her forehead and jots something on her clipboard.

"Candace?" she says softly, and Candace lifts her head back to her fists.

Ms. Meg smiles at her. "OK. Now who's ready to share?"

I look at my Nike Air Griffeys and pull down my Dodgers hat because I'm not saying crap about my family out loud.

"Robinson?" Ms. Meg chimes. "You haven't shared

with us in a while. Why don't you start?"

My heart beats fast in my chest like I'm stealing home because she never just calls on us like that when we don't have our hands raised. I shake my head no way, but she doesn't move on.

"How about you share something about the day you were born?"

My heart won't stop pounding, but not because of Ms. Meg or the stupid kids in this class. I shake my head no again. "Anything that someone has told you about that day is fine," she says. "Any little detail."

And I'm wishing more than I've ever wished that Ms. Gloria would poke her head in and pull us out for Group Guidance, because even sitting in a small room with Alex Baby Carter would be better than this.

I try not to think about what I know about the day I was born. But with Ms. Meg asking and everyone staring, I can't help it, and no matter how many baseball stats I know I can't remember any right now because I can only imagine my mom and feel that feeling in my gut that I get when I remember that she's dead because I'm alive but I don't even know why because Grandpa is closed up so tight. And that I don't know anything else about my birthday.

"Robinson?"

I bite down hard on my back teeth, but it's hard to

take three deep breaths when I'm doing that.

One of the Brittany/Chelsea girls behind me giggles because I'm just sitting there staring at my Air Griffeys and making huffing sounds that probably make me sound like I'm crazy.

And before I know it my eyes burn and my teeth hurt from biting so hard and I'm trying to think what would Jackie do when Derek turns fast in his seat and says to the Brittany/Chelsea girl, "What's so funny? Nothing. That's what I thought." It's the meanest Derek has ever been, and I'm kind of proud of him, and really glad that I don't have to shove anyone.

Then he tells Ms. Meg to call on someone else already, and she actually listens to him and does.

Derek knows not to put his arm around me or anything like that, so he just shoves my shoe with his shoe and I know what he means. He means everything is going to be OK. But he's wrong.

Kids are still sharing about their moms and dads and cousins when Ms. Gloria pops her head in. I stand up fast and grab my bag before she even says my name.

"See you later," I say to Derek. And I kind of nod my head at him, which means *Thanks*, and he gets it.

We're sitting in that circle around the table again and Ms. Gloria is telling us that we had a rough start yesterday as a group but that's perfectly fine. It takes time and practice. We go over the chart paper of norms again, and she tells us we may meet a few extra times this week before we get in a groove. "So let's check in!"

Candace starts, but it still kind of looks like she wants to have her head on the table.

"I'm a five," she says and passes the talking wand to Ms. Gloria.

Ms. Gloria's a seven. Oscar is a four, which he barely whispers. Alex is a nine, and he says it like a snot because he is one.

I hold the talking wand in my hand and let the sparkles inside fall to the bottom. I'm about to pass because I've done enough talking for one day when before I know it I say, "I'm a three." Then I hand the wand to Ms. Gloria.

"Does anyone want to say more about their number?" Ms. Gloria is holding the wand out, but no one's reaching for it, and before I know it again there's my hand moving toward the talking wand even though I don't want to talk any more about anything. But I grab right on to the wand and squeeze it tight in my fist.

"Because this family tree art project is bull crap," I sputter. "Maybe not everyone wants to share about their family." I've got my Dodgers hat pulled down so far I can only really see the edge of the table and the wand that I'm spinning in my hands, but I look up a little because

I think I hear weird hard breathing or sniffling and I think it's coming from Alex. His face is red and his lips are pushed tight together like he's trying not to burst. "Or maybe not everyone has enough family for a whole dumb tree," I finish.

I pass the wand to Candace, and I'm thinking she's going to say something about why she's only a five, but instead she says, "Robinson?"

Ms. Gloria reaches her hand beneath my brim and motions to me to turn my hat around and look at Candace.

She's wearing a pink sweater with cotton-ball lambs on it that I can't imagine anyone ever agreeing to wear. "I'm sorry you're a three," she tells me. And it's stupid but it makes my eyes do that burning thing and I just focus on the pink lambs on her sweater and think about how ridiculous they are. "I could help you with your project if you want."

I want to say how I don't need anyone's help and I can do it on my own and it's none of her business, but Ms. Gloria makes the wand go all the way around the circle first in case anyone wants to add in. Everyone says "Pass," and by the time I get the wand again I don't really feel like attacking her anymore for sticking her nose in my business. So I just say, "It's OK."

I pass the wand to Alex, who still has his lips pressed

hard together and they're kind of trembling and he looks red and I'm thinking he might have a fever, which means he might have to go home sick and stay there for a few days. I wonder if he knows that I saved his car yesterday. Or that I think his brothers are almost as annoying as he is.

Then the weirdest thing happens. This gigantic jerk bully who makes fun of everyone then sweet-talks teachers starts sobbing. Really sobbing. He's holding the glitter wand so tight his knuckles are turning red and white, and his chest heaves these big breaths and his bruised crooked nose is running and I want to laugh and point and say *Who's tough now?* but all I can do is stare because it's like watching a high-class, fully loaded BMW break down literally right in front of you. Lost brakes, locked steering wheel, wild swerving, and flat tires running on wobbly rims. It's pathetic.

Before anyone knows what to say, the bell rings and Ms. Gloria tells Alex he can stay in for recess if he wants. Even if I feel kind of bad that he's so pathetic, I definitely am not going to miss recess to figure out why he's crying like that, especially a recess he's not there for. So I get up fast and go outside to look for Derek.

Some kids from my class are laying out their book bags for a snow baseball game, and Mr. Danny is circling the yard with his whistle around his neck. Derek is rolling a snowman across the outfield. I wave to him and take out my glove and head for third because that's my base.

"Rob!" Derek sees me and starts running over. The mittens clipped to his jacket bounce as he pumps his skinny arms. He couldn't look any more like a kindergartner if he tried. He's out of breath when he gets to me, but that doesn't stop him from sputtering out, "Ms. Meg told us the family tree is due next Thursday. I'll help you, though."

For some reason knowing the due date for the project makes it worse. Like it's not just going to go away. "I'm not doing it."

I punch my fist into the pocket of my glove and get ready.

"You can't just not do it! What if you don't pass fifth grade?"

"I'm not doing it." I slam my fist in the pocket again.

Everyone is shouting, "Where's Alex?" because he always shoves people out of the way so he can be up first like he's some good lead-off hitter, but he's not, he's just a bully who can hardly even hit the ball. He's probably batting .150.

I bet everyone here would love to know that Alex Carter is crying like a baby in Ms. Gloria's room. And I would love to tell them. But I don't. Maybe it's because of norm number five, that we aren't supposed talk about anything that happens in Group Guidance outside of Group Guidance, and I wrote my name, *Robinson Hart*, on those norms. Or maybe it's just because I want to get this game going already. Recess is the only class that passes too fast.

"He's staying in today!" I holler.

"Yes!" Everyone's pumping their fists, and kids who never played before are lining up to take a turn at bat. Everything's just better when jerks aren't around.

"Can I be backup third base?" Derek asks. Even though I definitely don't need a backup because I never let anything by me, I still sometimes let Derek play backup because it's the only way he'll join in the game.

"Sure."

He slaps my shoulder and steps backward three big steps, close enough that I can still hear him breathing his excited breaths. "I got your back, Robbie," he says. And even though I don't need it, it feels pretty OK knowing he's there.

chapter 12

It's weird seeing Alex after he sobbed in Group Guidance yesterday, but we're sitting in a circle around Ms. Gloria's table for the third day in a row and Alex is acting like nothing ever happened and like he's the king of the world again.

Ms. Gloria asks us to share our check-in number, then comment on how things are going for us in school.

Alex goes first. "Today I'm a ten because my mom's letting me skip school tomorrow," he brags. "So I'll be thinking of all you losers while I'm sleeping in." He's smiling a big annoying smile and nodding his flowy blond head.

"That sounds like a pretty dumb way to spend a day off," I say, because what kind of loser thinks about school when he's not at school?

Ms. Gloria shoots me her no-nonsense look because I talked without the talking wand. And I wish I had the wand because I want to ask why such an amazing king of the world sobs his eyes out, then acts like it never happened. And even if it makes me a bad person, I kind of want him to cry again. I want to watch him break down once for every mean thing he's ever said or done. The room would be full to the ceiling with his salty baby tears.

He doesn't even answer the question Ms. Gloria asked about how things are going for him at school before he passes the wand to Oscar.

"I'm a three," Oscar whispers. I'm expecting him to pass the wand right away like he always does, because he never really says more than three words at a time. But he just sits there with it, not saying anything at all. He rolls the wand between the palms of his hands and stays quiet.

Alex starts to laugh under his breath, and I'm feeling all weird too with Oscar just stalled there. The silence is awkward, so I shift my weight and hope it kind of snaps Oscar out of it.

Then he says in his real quiet voice, "I don't want to do that stupid family tree project either," and passes the wand to Candace.

"Me either," she says. "And I'm a five."

Then I have the wand. "I'm a seven, I guess." I was planning on saying a four, but having Oscar and Candace agree with me that the family tree project is pointless makes me feel three whole points better. I pass the wand off to Ms. Gloria before I remember to ask sissy Alex why he was sobbing yesterday, and now I have to wait until it circles all the way back around.

Ms. Gloria says she's a nine and wants to hear more about this family tree project and passes the talking wand back to Alex.

"It's a project Ms. Meg is making us do," Alex says. "We have to create our family tree. And for the record, I think it's stupid too."

I can't believe that I have any single thing in common with Alex. And even though it makes me feel better to talk crap about the project, it makes me feel kind of worse to be on Alex's team.

"We have to write about the important people in our families and it's such a waste of time," he goes on.

For a second it seems like he's about to sob again like he did yesterday. I can see his chin quiver like the vibration of a hard hit ball off a metal bat, and he's blinking his eyes fast and not looking at anyone. But right before I think he's going to crack, he bites down hard on his teeth and his jaw gets all wide and square with knots and I know that feeling.

"The whole thing stinks" is all he says, then passes the wand to Oscar.

"My family tree is splitting in two, right down the middle," Oscar says, and he says it so quiet that I'm not sure he actually wants us to hear him. I can't believe he spoke so many words in a row, and I wonder if I'm the only one who heard him because he whispered it under his breath and to his shoes and maybe I heard him wrong.

"Seriously? Speak up! We can never hear you!" Alex shouts, and I reach across the table and smack him in the arm because no one said any crap when he was getting all quiet and quivery and sobby.

"She hit me!" Alex screams.

And Ms. Gloria stands up and says sharp as Grandpa's ax, "This is not about you right now." She's looking back and forth between Alex and me. "We are listening to Oscar and what he wants to share with us. Your job is to listen." She's tapping her finger on our signatures at the bottom of the group norms chart.

I hate Alex so much. He's always getting me in trouble when really he's the jerk and I'm the only one doing anything about it.

"Do you want to say more about that, Oscar?" Ms. Gloria asks.

He shakes his head no, because who would want to share anything after bully Alex Brat Carter laughs at you, then calls you out in front of everyone? He quickly hands the talking wand to Candace.

She rolls it between her palms. "Are you sure you don't want to say more?" she asks Oscar. "We're listening. Even Alex." She shoots a fastball of a glare right at Alex that I didn't know good kids like Candace had the capability of shooting. Then she hands the talking wand back to Oscar.

He holds it like he did before and doesn't say anything. Then he takes a deep breath, and I can tell he's getting up the courage to speak. He starts to whisper, but he's not looking up at any of us, his eyes are locked right on the talking wand in his hands.

"My mom probably wouldn't want my dad on my family tree," he says. Then he turns the wand over and lets the glitter fall to the bottom. "And I bet my dad would be pissed if I put my mom on it." He turns the wand over again in his hands. "They hate each other."

The words *pissed* and *hate* seem all wrong coming out of Oscar's small, quiet mouth.

"That's why the project is stupid," he finishes and hands the wand back to Candace.

"That sounds like it really sucks." And now I can't believe that Candace said *sucks*, because that doesn't seem like a Candace word either.

"And you're right," she says. "The family tree thing is hard because sometimes it's hard to think about your family. It's hard to think about my sister right now because I'm pretty sure she hates me." She taps her chipped purple-painted fingernails on the talking wand. "So you're not the only one."

She hands the wand to me, and I can't believe that there's anything wrong or hard about Candace's family and I'm wondering if that's why she puts her head down sometimes.

I'm about to say *pass* and hand the wand back to Alex, but before I know it I'm spilling my guts. And maybe it's because Ms. Gloria was right and that stupid talking wand holds lots of power or maybe it's because whatever happens in Group Guidance stays in Group Guidance or maybe it's because no one here is acting like their normal selves because Alex sobbed and Oscar said *pissed* and Candace said *sucks* so I don't feel so weird anymore.

"I don't have a mom or dad or sister or even a dog, so how does Ms. Meg expect me to make a family tree?" I was going to say that the only branch I have is my grandpa and his memory's getting more and more tired and he snaps into someone kind of scary at night, and I don't even know if someday he won't know my name anymore or why he even named me Robinson. But I take a deep breath and think about Alex's mom raising her eyebrows like adults do and thinking Grandpa isn't fit to raise me. And if Ms. Gloria finds out about Grandpa's memory she'd have to tell Principal Wheeler and then someone might come separate me from my only branch.

The bell starts to ring anyway, which means it's recess and I can go play third base, but I almost kind of wish we had time for the talking wand to go around one extra time. I want to hear more about Candace's sister and maybe Oscar would say something else about his splitting-in-two tree.

I grab my book bag and head for the door when I hear Ms. Gloria's voice. "Robinson? Can I talk to you for a second?"

Alex laughs out loud and I tell him to shut up—at least I don't cry like a baby.

After everyone leaves Ms. Gloria says, "Robinson, I thought you could help me out with something."

She stands right next to me, looking out the window at everyone running outside to recess. Alex is jogging to home base, nudging kids out of the way so he can be first at bat.

"It seems like everyone in this group is having a hard time with the family tree project. What do you think we can do about that?" she asks.

I'm watching Derek, who is watching the door, waiting for me to come outside so he can be backup third base and cheer me on as I scoop up Alex's weak grounders and throw him out at first.

"You could tell Ms. Meg we don't have to do it."

Derek gives up waiting and sits down on the sidelines to watch the game.

"Something realistic, Robbie. Let's come up with something that could help," she says. "What would help you?"

Derek keeps looking toward the door and I wish I could just bang on the window and tell him I'll be there in a second and not to let Alex mess with him because I can't punch anyone today or else the school might find out how tired my grandpa's memory is and then who knows what will happen.

I want to tell Ms. Gloria that nothing can help me, including her, so can I just go play third base now? But because we're standing side by side and looking out and she's not making me spin my Dodgers hat around backward, it feels OK. Then she hands me the talking wand and I think about how I want to find out everything Grandpa knows about my mom before it's gone from his brain.

"It would help if my grandpa would tell me about my mom and what happened. It feels weird putting someone

I don't know anything about on my family tree."

"Have you tried talking to him?" she asks.

"Yeah. More when I was little, but he kept saying, 'Not now,' until I knew he never wanted to talk about her." I can't tell her that I know it stresses him out and makes him sad and makes him worse. That's why he doesn't even have a picture of her. "Sometimes I still try to ask about her, but it doesn't matter."

"We could brainstorm some ways you could try talking to him again," she offers.

I nod my head OK, but really I'm watching Mr. Danny toss extra pop flies to the outfielders for practice.

Ms. Gloria's saying that maybe I could use the family tree project to start the conversation with Grandpa. I could say it's for school and think of some questions ahead of time.

I keep my eyes on Derek the whole time she's talking because it helps me not cry while I'm thinking of Grandpa and how if I ask him about my mom I'll make him shake his head and feel sad, and that I'll make his memory worse.

I nod again and say OK but now I want to play third base.

"Have fun at recess," Ms. Gloria says. I hand her the talking wand and head for the door.

Then I think of something to tell Ms. Gloria before

I leave. "Maybe we could work on the project in Group Guidance instead of in Ms. Meg's room. That might help."

She nods and smiles. "I think that's a great idea, Robbie."

Then I'm out the door to pull Derek off the sidelines so he can back me up at third base.

chapter 13

When I get to the garage after school, Harold's not there again.

"His baby was born this morning!" Grandpa says. "Little girl."

He sounds happy when he tells me, but when he thinks I'm not looking he squeezes his temples and rubs his fingers across his grooved forehead. Maybe he's worried about running the garage without Harold for a few weeks, or maybe he's thinking about my mom and when she was born. Or when I was born. I hope it's just that he's nervous about running the garage, because I can help with that. I know cars.

Or maybe I do hope he's remembering my mom, even if it hurts and makes him rub his forehead, because then maybe he'll change his mind and decide it's not so hard to tell me something about her, like what her name was, and I can put it on my family tree.

"I brought the truck so we can drive over to the hospital and visit them before we go home," he tells me.

"Fine," I say, "but I'm not holding any baby."

"Deal." Grandpa chuckles and nods his head. "Up for an oil change?"

I toss my book bag and my baseball glove onto the wobbly stool and follow Grandpa to the 2013 Toyota Camry that's already parked over the lifts and ready to be raised up. I pop the hood and open the oil tank so the airflow will help drain the oil from the bottom of the car, then close the hood.

Grandpa waits until I push the button that lifts the car above our heads, put on my work gloves, and set up the funnel and drip pan before he heads back to the next bay, where he's replacing brake pads on a red Honda.

I crank the wrench to open the fuel pan under the car, and the old oil starts draining out fast. Changing oil might be my favorite because I like the idea of letting all the bad pour out and getting a fresh, smooth start right out of the unopened bottle.

While the old oil rushes out into the drip pan, I watch Grandpa working on the Honda. He's sliding out the old brake pads and putting antisqueal gel on the new ones, and he seems to be good today and following the right steps and not looking like a deer we caught in the headlights.

When the old oil stops dripping, I get the new filter ready by smearing some clean oil around the gasket ring with my finger, then I install it. I close up the oil pan and lower the car back down. Then I pop the hood, pour the new, clean oil in, close it up, and I'm done. And it feels good.

The man pays Grandpa in cash and drives out his clean-oil, fresh-start Toyota Camry.

"A-plus work, Robbie," Grandpa says. "Now come pump the brakes for me on this Honda."

I climb in and have to slump way down to reach the pedals because I hate adjusting someone else's driver's seat. I pump the brakes with my right foot like Grandpa taught me, and I know the bad brake fluid is bleeding out from under the car and we'll get to fill it up with brand-new, fresh-start brake fluid and the car will run good as new.

"What do you say?" Grandpa asks. "Go check on Harold?"

Even though I want to see Harold because a day at the garage without him feels a little weird, I don't really want to go to any hospital or see any baby. I'd rather do another oil change or headlight replacement.

But I take off my work gloves anyway. "Yeah," I say. "We better go check on him."

The hospital smells too clean, and I feel like I'm messing it up just by walking in.

Grandpa talks to the nurses at the desk and we sit in the waiting room until Harold comes to get us. For some reason I'm feeling nervous to see Harold and Paul's new baby because maybe she won't like me or I'll make her cry and won't be able to get her to stop and she'll spit up on my Nike Air Griffeys.

"Robbie! Charlie!" Harold's hurrying down the hall and his brown hair is sticking up all over his head like it usually does and he's smiling really big. I stick my fist out for a fist bump, but he pulls me in for a hug, and I'm not really a hugging kind of person but it's OK because it's Harold and he knows that, so he makes it quick. "Sorry," he says, tapping the brim of my Dodgers hat. "I've just missed you and I'm so happy you're here."

Grandpa starts standing up slow, pressing down hard on his knees. "Let's go see this body," he says. But he means *baby*. And I'm glad Harold's too busy being excited to notice Grandpa's jumbled words.

Harold pats Grandpa's arm. "OK, boss. Follow me."

Harold walks with his arm around me and asks how school was and how things at the garage went today.

I tell him about changing the oil of the 2013 Toyota Camry and that Alex Carter is still a jerk but I didn't hit him today. He laughs and pats my shoulder and says, "Well now, that's an improvement."

Then we stop at this big window and inside I can see little tiny plastic cribs with the teeniest babies in them. They're so small they don't even look real, like they could all just be dolls. There's one nurse who's wearing all blue and she's leaning over one of the babies, writing something down on a clipboard.

Then I see Paul sitting next to a plastic crib and holding one of the tiny babies. He has his long brown hair pulled back in a ponytail, and the baby is wrapped in a pink blanket and wearing a little pink hat. "Want to go see her?" Harold asks.

I want to say no because the babies are way smaller than I thought, but before I know it Harold is slapping an identification sticker on me and squirting hand sanitizer in my palms and saying that he can't wait for his daughter to meet me. Grandpa gets his sticker and sanitizer too, and we follow Harold in.

Paul stands up slowly and whispers, "Robinson, Charlie. So glad you guys are here." Paul and Harold hug each other with one arm so they don't crush the baby.

"Meet our little May," Harold says, pulling the pink

blanket back a little.

May is sleeping, and her face is kind of red and squishy and blotchy.

"You want to hold her?" Paul asks.

I shake my head no, but he says, "Oh, come on. Sit down." And before I know it I'm sitting in the chair next to her plastic crib and her hot little body is pressed into mine. I make my arms into a strong, stiff cradle and I don't even breathe or anything because I don't want her to start crying. I jiggle my knee by accident and she kind of wakes up and I can feel her little body squirm in the blanket, but she doesn't start crying because I kind of rock her back and forth.

"You're a natural, Robbie," Harold says.

And it feels pretty OK being a natural. So OK that I loosen up my arms a little bit and rock her kind of slow and she stays sleeping. And I'm feeling calm as cruise control.

I ask Grandpa if he wants to hold her and Harold says, "Of course he does!" He lifts the baby out of my arms and I stand up and let Grandpa have my seat.

May makes Grandpa look even older because she's so fresh and new and Grandpa's face is all worn and creased like an old-timer's baseball glove. He's looking down at May and whispering, "Hello, May. Hello." And I've never heard Grandpa sounding so soft. "It's a big world out here," he whispers. "Your daddies are going to protect you." When he looks up his eyes are all red and watery.

"It's OK, Grandpa," I say, and I pat his shoulder.

Then the baby starts crying and Harold says, "Uh-oh. Better give her back to the natural." And before I know it I'm holding her again and she's cooing and dribbling and looking up right at me.

"Good job, Robbie," Paul whispers.

And when I'm looking at her, I can't help thinking about how this little tiny May already has so many branches on her tree. She has Harold and Paul and two sets of grandparents and aunts and uncles on both sides who are all on their way to see her before she's even two days old.

Harold walks us to the lobby of the hospital, and I reach out for a fist bump.

"Good job with the name," I tell him. And I'm thinking how when she's big enough I'll teach her all about Willie Mays of the San Francisco Giants and his twelve Gold Glove awards and how he's in the Hall of Fame. And how maybe I'll even call her Willie.

chapter 14

In the hospital parking lot, Grandpa and I hop in the truck and wave to Harold, who's still watching us from under the entrance awning.

Grandpa starts the truck, and I pull the seat belt across my chest. Harold keeps on waving and smiling, so I wave back one more time. Finally he turns and heads back through the automatic front doors of the hospital.

Then the engine of the truck revs so loud it kind of startles me and then revs again and again, louder.

"Grandpa!" I shout, and I didn't mean to yell it like that, but the revving kind of scared me. "It's in park!"

"I know!" And I don't think he meant to shout either, because now he's shaking his head like he's trying to get all the parts in his brain realigned right. Then he pulls the shift down to reverse and backs out of the parking spot slowly. I'm looking to make sure Harold isn't watching, but he's gone.

When we get to the first stop sign, I say kind of softly and to my shoes, "Left."

"Don't you think I know that?" He's frustrated with me for trying to help, so the rest of the way home I just reach over and flick on the directional for him so the green arrow blinks left or right on the dashboard pointing us home. He used to let me be in charge of the directional when I was little, before I knew how to do all the parts of driving. He doesn't argue about me reaching over, just nods and says it's fine.

Grandpa parks the truck in our driveway and pats my knee three times like he does sometimes, and I know that means that he loves me and everything's going to be OK. And with him calm like this, I'm thinking about what Ms. Gloria said and that maybe this is a good time to try asking him again.

"Grandpa?" My stomach is all full of bases-loaded nerves. "After we collect the sap, do you think I can ask you a couple of questions?" The grooves in his forehead dig deeper. "It's for school," I tell him.

He nods. "Of course."

I unbuckle my seat belt. "I'll go get your ax."

"Two hands," he says. "And grab my flannel."

I run fast to the house to change into my boots and get Grandpa's red flannel shirt that he'll button up over his navy blue jumpsuit from the garage. But the shirt isn't hanging on the black hook inside the door where it always is. And it isn't in the dirty clothes hamper in the closet, and it's not draped over the bench where Grandpa sits to pull on his boots in the morning.

I've never seen his flannel shirt anywhere else, so I don't even know where to look, but I run up the stairs and check his bedroom. It's not hanging on the hooks where he hangs his towels, and it's not in any of his drawers.

I run back downstairs and slide on my socks into the kitchen. Out the window, Grandpa's standing by the sugar maples in the yard, lifting the hoods on the metal buckets to check how much sap we have, which makes me feel relieved because he's not circling in the woods back and forth across the Appalachian Trail.

I'm looking for that stupid flannel shirt in crazy places now, and fast, because I don't like spending too much time away from Grandpa when it's almost night-time. It just makes me feel better when I'm right there at his right hand.

I open the top cupboards where we keep the boxes of cereal and mac and cheese, and the drawers where we keep the silverware. I even open the refrigerator and the microwave. I don't know why anyone would put a dirty outdoor flannel shirt in a kitchen, but sometimes Grandpa's wires get crossed when he's changing his clothes and putting things away.

I keep checking for Grandpa out the window as I open the bottom cupboards where we stack the pots and pans, and that's when I see the red of Grandpa's flannel poking out from between the skillets and pasta pots. And I get these blasts of two feelings at the same time. I'm so mad at Grandpa's brain for making him put his outdoor flannel in the kitchen cupboards when he knows it's supposed to hang on the black hook by the door. But I'm sad too. I'm so sad at Grandpa's brain because I don't know how to diagnose his malfunction, and I don't even know if he knows that his check engine light's on.

I pull on my boots and run to the garage to get our work gloves and carry Grandpa's ax, sharp side down, with two hands, to the chopping block in the backyard.

"Here you go, Grandpa." I hold out his shirt.

I watch his dark fingers push the buttons through the buttonholes, and even though I want to shake him by the shoulders and ask him why his brain thought it was OK to fold his shirt and put it in the cupboard with the pots and pans I don't say anything.

"Thanks, Robbie."

"I got your back, Grandpa," I say, and follow him to the sugar maples.

He pours the sap from the metal buckets while I hold the funnel and cheesecloth over the big plastic holding jugs.

"That's ten more gallons just from today," Grandpa says.

"Yes!" I cheer. That means we have enough gallons collected to make a fire in our pit and boil our sap into syrup, which is the best part.

Grandpa hangs the bucket back under the tap on the tree, walks over to the chopping block, and picks up his ax. I put a piece of wood up there for him and position it just right so it's not wobbly, then I back up three big steps. "We'll need lots of chopped wood for the fire," he tells me, then lifts the ax high above his head and brings it down on the wood. It splits easily, and two pieces fall to the ground. I pick them up, toss them on the pile under the eaves, and set up another piece for Grandpa to chop.

There are little pieces of splintered wood and tree bark stuck to Grandpa's thick red flannel shirt, and I try to make a little reminder to myself to watch Grandpa when we go inside so the shirt ends up on the black hook where it's supposed to be.

And even though I want to give his memory a rest,

I'm also scared that if I wait any longer to ask him questions he might forget all the answers. Then I'll never know. And I won't have a family tree.

Grandpa swings the ax high up over his head again and drives it through the piece of wood, and it's another easy split right down the middle. When I'm setting up the next piece of wood on the chopping block, I take a deep breath. "Can I ask one of those questions now? For school?"

"Sure."

I take another deep breath and say it right to the hard thick bark on the piece of wood I'm adjusting on the chopping block because I don't want to see if Grandpa shakes his head.

"What was my mom's name?"

It feels like a whole minute before he says anything, and I just keep pretending to adjust the piece of wood even though it's sitting sturdy on the chopping block and is ready to be split.

Finally he answers. "Edna Rose Miller." He says it slow, and I can't help but look up and see that he's shaking his head and massaging his temples with his big fingers. "Edna Rose Miller," he whispers again.

And I can't believe he actually told me, that he said her name out loud, and now I know it and get to know it forever.

Edna Rose Miller. I say it a few times in my head and I want it to be perfect, but it sounds all wrong. It's girly and flowery and she didn't even have our last name. My mom's name was supposed to be Sam or Jo. Her last name was supposed to be Hart.

"Why doesn't she have our name?" I ask.

Grandpa shakes his head and raises the ax up high and brings it down hard on the piece of wood on the chopping block. But it's a tough piece, not a smooth split. It's got a knot curled hard at its core, so Grandpa pulls the ax up high over his head again and again and again, but the sharp edge just gets caught up in the knot each time.

"Dammit!" Grandpa shouts, and he slams the ax into the ground. "That's enough, Robbie. It's getting dark."

He starts his side-to-side walk back to the house. I hear the door close and then it's quiet. And I want to yell and punch something hard, so I try counting to ten or taking three deep breaths, but I don't care about that crap. I want to know why Grandpa won't tell me anything else. Why he has to get like this.

My face feels hot, and I try not to think of the stupid family trees that everyone in my class is busy making with lots of branches sticking out all over, but before I know it I have Grandpa's ax in my hands and I'm bringing it up high over my head like I've watched him do a million times, and I let it fall, swinging hard down into our old stump chopping block.

I want to just leave it there, cutting deep into the tough, thick bark around the stump, but it's my job to put the ax away in the shed, so I grab the handle and pull hard, wiggling it up and down until I can free it from the chopping block. It leaves a big gash in the protective bark.

I carry the ax sharp side down, with two hands, back to the shed, then head inside.

I pull off my boots and check the black hook for Grandpa's red flannel shirt. It's not there, and it makes me so mad that I can feel the hot rise up in my face.

"Grandpa!" I call out. Then I run up the stairs, saying a Hall of Famer's name on each step. *Ty Cobb. Lou Gehrig. Roberto Clemente. Jackie Robinson.*

He's sitting in his room on the edge of his bed, still wearing his navy blue jumpsuit from the garage with his red flannel wood-chipped shirt buttoned up over it. His black suitcase is at his feet.

"Grandpa?"

"I'm ready when you are," he says and pats the suitcase at his feet. "Ready for the big day." His dark eyes are wide and glassy and confused, and his thick fingers are tapping out something on his knee. "Ready for this baby to come."

"Grandpa, what are you talking about?"

He's scaring me, and I don't ever get scared by anything, but there's something really wrong and I don't know what it is or how to fix it and I can't ask Grandpa for help. My heart is beating fast.

"Grandpa? It's me. Robbie. Robinson Hart." I lay my hand on top of his to make it still.

He puts his arm around my waist and pulls me close, up onto his lap, where I haven't sat for so many years I can't even remember. With my legs draped over his and my head tucked under his chin, I kind of feel like a baby and it feels OK. And I wouldn't even care too much if he rocked me back and forth a little like I rocked May in the hospital.

"I know that," he says. "I know you're Robbie. I'm not a hundred years old."

He holds me for a second or two more before he puts me down and stands up slow. Then he pretends to walk around like a humpbacked, toothless one-hundred-year-old with a cane and we both get to laughing. "You think I'm a hundred years old?" he asks in a trembling old-man voice.

I laugh because it makes him laugh, and I love Grandpa's laugh because it comes all the way up straight from his belly and makes tears spill from the corners of his eyes. But I'm still scared. Scared that he packed a suitcase and said he was ready to go. Scared that he didn't know who I was. And I'm wondering where he thought he was going. What was the big day he was remembering? What baby was coming?

And I wonder if he'll try to take that suitcase and wander back in time to when Edna Rose Miller was alive and there was some big day to look forward to.

"Come on, Grandpa," I say. "You didn't even take off your flannel. Let's go hang it up and eat some dinner."

He starts walking out of the bedroom and down the stairs and I shove the suitcase into his closet so he won't see it when he comes back up. Maybe he'll forget he even packed it. That he wanted to go somewhere else at all.

chapter 15

The next morning before school I'm sitting on the kitchen stool playing with the rubber bands for my hair as Grandpa brushes out all the knots from sleeping. He tries to hold my hair tight in his hand as he brushes so it doesn't tug at my scalp, but there's always one hair that pulls and makes my eyes water.

He divides my hair down the center and braids the left side first, breaking it into three separate sections and crossing them over and over one another until he asks for a rubber band. I hand one back to him and he wraps it around the bottom of the braid.

"One done," he says. Then I feel him separate the right side into three parts.

I'm trying not to think about last night, but I can't

help it. I keep seeing Grandpa's blank face and his packed suitcase and wondering where he thought he was going and if he thought I was Edna. And if that means I look like her.

And I still want to know why her name wasn't Hart because Grandpa always told me she never got married and that I never had a father. So wouldn't that make her a Hart? And even though I know it'll make me feel like crap, I still want to know what happened when I was born. How she died.

I can feel that one hair that tugs at my scalp every time Grandpa tightens up the braid.

And I don't know if it's because Grandpa's standing behind me and I won't be able to see if he shakes his head or if his eyes get glassy and faraway, or if it's because I know that his memory is doing OK because it's morning but it could get worse fast and then it'll be too late and I'll never get to know anything else about my mom. But before I know it I'm asking him again.

"Grandpa, that thing for school," I start. "I have to know some family stuff. We're making a project."

He keeps crossing my hair over and over, and scoops up the runaway curls at my neck and tucks them into the braid.

"What do you need to know?" he asks.

I take a big breath because I'm scared again. Scared

that I'll send him into a bad place where he forgets who I am and where he is.

"Why was my mom's name Edna Rose Miller, and not Hart?"

That one little hair pulls hard at my scalp. "That was your grandma's last name," he says. "Miller."

"My grandma?" I ask. Grandpa never talks about her, just like he never talks about my mom. "Who was she?"

He clears his throat. "Edna's mom. Your grandma Lucy. Lucy Miller." He says her name all soft and slow and I kind of feel like maybe she was the love of his life, but there was no way I was going to say *love* out loud.

"So then why—"

"That's enough questions, Robbie," he says and asks for the rubber band. I hand it back to him and he wraps it tight around the bottom of the right braid.

"But for my project I—"

"Go get your book bag. Time for school."

When I turn around, Grandpa's eyes are red and watery. And I don't want to make him shake his head or wander off or pack up his suitcase so he can travel back to before I was born, but I do want to cut away at Grandpa's hard, thick bark because it feels really scratchy and crappy to keep rubbing up against it.

"Fine," I snap and grab my book bag and a banana

from the counter and start toward the front door, but Grandpa's voice stops me.

"Your mom was Edna Rose Miller, not Hart, because your grandma and I never got married. We never even lived together. Your grandma Lucy's parents named your mom Edna. Insisted she not have my name. Insisted she be a Miller."

His voice is shaky, and I can't tell if he's going to get mad or sad, but I hate both of those feelings on Grandpa. "They didn't approve of me, of Lucy and me, and they definitely didn't approve of us having a baby."

I turn around. "Why?" But as soon as I ask it, I know. Because of Grandpa's skin. Because he didn't fit right.

And now I'm mad at my grandma Lucy, which feels messed up because she died way too young, before I was born, and because I think she was the love of my grandpa's life, and I only just learned her name. But still, she should have married my grandpa and let him raise Edna as a Hart.

"Why didn't she just tell her parents that they're not the boss of her and that they're stupid and wrong?" I ask.

Grandpa smiled. "Not everyone's as tough as you."

"OK, Grandpa," I say. "And thanks." There are a hundred more questions I want to ask, but I think that's enough for today. Grandpa's memory needs to rest.

The braids feel good and tight like they always do at the beginning of the day. Everything's always better at the beginning of the day. Before school. Before I see Alex Carter. Before Grandpa's memory gets tired and he starts mixing up his words and his places and his people.

I pull on my Dodgers hat and jump over the three steps of the porch to the gravel driveway. When I turn back to wave good-bye to Grandpa, he's standing out on the porch watching me walk.

"Robbie," he calls. "Your mom—"

"Edna Rose Miller?"

"She went by Eddie." He smiles big, and all sorts of wrinkles I've never seen on Grandpa's face before ripple out from his smile.

And I smile big too, because she didn't have some big-pink-bow name that doesn't fit.

I nod back at Grandpa like I know what he means. And I think I do. That I'm just like my mom. My mom, Eddie.

chapter 16

"The family tree project is due next Thursday," Ms. Meg
reminds us. "That's one week from today! And remember that tomorrow is a teacher planning day, so you don't
have school. Lucky you! A day off to work on the project!"
She has to yell the last part because whenever we work
on projects everyone gets kind of excited and loud. Not
me.

The Chelsea/Brittany girls at the table behind us
really did bring in papier-mâché, and they're laying
newspapers out across their table and dipping strips
into this white stuff their moms brought into school in
Tupperware.

And now I'm wondering where Ms. Gloria is because
I told her we should work on this stupid thing in Group

Guidance so we didn't have to be around everyone being all annoying with their big tree ideas.

"Come on, Rob," Derek says. "You have to turn something in. I'll help you."

"I'll help too," Candace adds. She brought in all these pictures of her parents and her aunt Jane and her cousins, and she's laying them out on a big piece of poster board that takes up half our table. "We can do it together."

I open my notebook.

Derek opens his notebook too and starts sketching. "I'm going to make mine like a board game, I think."

"What do you mean?" I ask, even though I don't really care.

"Each square could be a person in my family, and if you land on a square you get to read about who that person is. Or something like that."

It's actually a pretty cool idea, though I'd never say that because nothing about these family trees is cool. Even if I do the project, it won't be creative like Derek's. Or have pictures like Candace's.

But at least my tree will have my mom on it. I've been saying her name in my head all morning and imagining what she looked like. Like Grandpa. Like me. Eddie Rose Miller. Eddie.

I wasn't going to tell anyone about learning her

name because it feels like my own important secret. But before I know it I'm blurting it out to Derek. "I found out what my mom's name was, so I can put her on my tree if I want."

Derek drops his pencil. "What? When did you—? What?"

He's so excited that he's kind of getting loud, so I tell him to shut up and act normal because I don't want the whole class staring at us.

"What is it?" he asks. "What's her name?" He's leaning in and trying to whisper, but he's still so excited that it isn't really a whisper. Candace leans in too.

"Edna Rose Miller," I say. "But she went by Eddie."

"Nice!" Derek exclaims and goes for a high five. "You have to put her on your tree!" Now people are starting to give us funny stares and Ms. Meg gives us that look.

"That's great, Robbie," Candace says. Then she looks right in my eyes, right under my Dodgers hat. "What exactly happened to her?" she asks. "I mean, if you don't want to talk about it, that's OK."

Triples hit, single-season record: Chief Wilson, 36. Dave Orr, 31. If this were last week I would have pushed Candace out of her chair already, but I'm remembering everything Ms. Gloria says about getting mad and taking responsibility for my actions. And I'm thinking about making sure Grandpa never comes back here.

"It's OK, Robbie," Derek says. "Candace is just being nice, remember?"

I unclench my fists and pick up my pen.

"Sorry," Candace says, and she puts her head down on the table. I don't even feel bad for her because who goes around asking about people's moms and how they died? And I'm mad that I don't have an answer. I don't know exactly how my mom died, so even if I wanted to talk about it, I couldn't.

"Why don't you write down your mom's name on your list?" Derek taps his finger on my list of important family members, right beneath Grandpa. "Because no matter what, she was important. If it weren't for her, you wouldn't be here."

And I'm thinking that if *I* weren't here, my mom probably would be.

But I do what Derek says, and just writing it out makes me feel a little better.

Important People in My Family:
Grandpa
Edna Rose Miller

Then I start to draw one of those family trees you see in textbooks sometimes, or on the first page of really complicated books with too many characters. I start with Grandpa and make the tree from there until I have everyone Grandpa told me about and I'm starting to feel like maybe I could do this project.

MEAN OLD MAN ———————— MEAN OLD LADY
(GREAT-GRANDPA)   (GREAT-GRANDMA)

CHARLIE HART ———— LUCY MILLER
(GRANDPA)   (GRANDMA)

EDNA ROSE MILLER (EDDIE) —— ?
(MOM)

ROBINSON HART
(ME)

I don't really want to include my grandma Lucy's mean parents, the ones who thought Grandpa wasn't good enough for their daughter, but I do anyway because it makes it look like I have more family, so if Ms. Meg bends over my work she doesn't have any reason to linger around and try to help me.

Derek leans over and says, "Look at all those people!" and he puts his hand up for another high five when Ms. Gloria pokes her head in.

"Robbie, Candace, Oscar?" she says. "Bring your

projects." She winks at me because this was my idea, that we work on our family trees together.

I nod to Derek and close my notebook. "Oh," I whisper. "This weekend we're boiling. Saturday morning is Maple Day. Tell your mom."

"Yes!" Derek says and pumps his fist. "We'll be there!" And I already can't wait for the weekend.

Candace lifts up her head from the table and grabs her book bag. I guess now I'm starting to feel a little bad that she feels bad because Derek was right. She was just trying to be nice. So when we're in the hall I run a step to catch up and walk next to her and say, "It's OK."

She looks up from the floor and smiles. "Thanks, Robbie." Then she pats my shoulder, and I'm not usually a touching-type person unless it's Grandpa or Harold or Paul or sometimes Derek, but it feels OK, so I don't say anything.

We start with a check-in, but Ms. Gloria says we'll get to use the rest of our time to work on our projects.

Alex's chair is empty, and I can't believe his mom actually let him stay home from school today, especially since we have tomorrow off anyway. I guess she's way cooler than she seems, because I don't know anyone else's mom who would do that.

"I'm a three," Candace says, which is her all-time

low. "Stuff's just hard right now."

Then she passes the talking wand to me. I turn it back and forth in my hands, but then I decide to do what Candace always does because I think she might want to say more but just needs a little help to do it. "Are you sure you don't want to say anything else?" I reach the wand back out to her in case she wants to take it again.

And maybe it's because I asked her nice, or maybe it's because Alex is absent, so there's no one to laugh and break all the group norms and make everyone feel crappy, but Candace reaches back for the talking wand and says, "OK."

She pulls a little on the bottom of her shirt and shifts in her chair. It's kind of hard to see her face from underneath the brim of my hat, and I actually do want to hear what she says, so I turn it around backward. Ms. Gloria nods at me and smiles, and that feels pretty OK too.

Then Candace taps the wand on her knee and says, "My sister and I used to be really close. Best-friends kind of close."

She takes a deep breath and I can tell she's trying not to cry, and I hope she doesn't because I suck at being around crying people. It makes me feel awkward and like I'll do something wrong. Like holding a baby. But I guess I did OK at that with May. So I take a deep breath too and just keep listening.

"She started high school this year and got all these new friends who don't want to hang out with me because I'm just some fifth grader. They'd rather wear makeup and message their friends on their phones and make fun of me for being chubby."

Then she does it. She starts crying, and it's not awkward at all, just like it wasn't awkward to hold May. It's OK, and I actually kind of feel like I could cry right with her about Grandpa and my mom and how Grandpa packed up his bags and he didn't even know why. But I blink my eyes really fast and look away from Candace and think about baseball, and then I don't have to cry anymore.

"She's just so mean now. And she and my mom are always screaming at each other. I miss the old her." Then she passes the wand back to me and says, "Thanks, Robbie."

"That sounds like it really sucks," I say. "Sorry."

Ms. Gloria looks at me and smiles and I know what she means. She means *good job, Robbie* because even though I said *sucks* I helped Candace share and I followed all the norms.

"I'm a seven," I say. "I found out my mom's name, and it's Eddie." I want to say more about Grandpa and all the questions I have left to ask him before it's too late, before his memory wears out and all that information gets locked up tight in his brain. But I think I know what happens to an eleven-year-old when her only branch snaps, so I don't say anymore.

And all of a sudden I'm feeling more like a five or a six than a seven.

I pass the talking wand to Oscar.

Oscar's a six because he and his mom just finished unpacking boxes from their move. "Finally," he says. He's still talking to the ground, but he's loud enough to hear, and Alex isn't there to say something mean. He tells us he misses his dad a lot, but every time they hang out it kind of stinks because his dad talks crap about his mom. "And my mom says all this bad stuff about my dad too. Like I'm supposed to pick a team or something," he says.

He hands the wand back to Ms. Gloria, and she says that she's a seven today because she's sad to hear about some of the hard things going on in our lives but so happy that we are talking through them together.

She also tells us she's looking forward to tomorrow, when all the teachers have a big planning day and the students don't come to school. "We'll be preparing for our big family open house next week."

Oscar laughs a little under his breath and says, "We're looking forward to it too. No school!"

Ms. Gloria smiles. "I bet." She says she's looking

forward to meeting all our families next week. And I'm thinking she's already met Grandpa. Too many times. But I'm not telling Grandpa about any family open house after school anyway.

"Robinson had a great idea yesterday that we could work on our family trees together here in Group Guidance," Ms. Gloria announces.

"Yes!" Candace says.

Oscar nods his head.

"OK, then," Ms. Gloria says. "I'll let you guys work. Let me know if you need anything." She goes to her desk in the corner of the room and takes out her own notebook and a pen.

Candace lays out her poster board on the table in front of us. "How do you think I should arrange these?" she asks as she spreads out a whole bunch of pictures of her family members.

"Which one is your sister?" I ask.

She picks out three pictures. "This one is us at our aunt's house after our first day of swim lessons," she tells me, pointing at the first one. "This is us in our matching Christmas pajamas three years ago. And this one is the most recent. It's the first day of school. Fifth grade for me, ninth for her. My mom always makes us take first-day pictures."

In each picture they have their arms around each

other and are smiling big.

Then she slides over another picture. "This is her ninth-grade class picture."

It makes me feel bad to see the last picture because I can see how much she's changed, which I know makes Candace sad. In the last picture her hair is dyed white blond with two purple streaks down the sides, and she's wearing black makeup around her eyes and bright pink on her lips.

"My mom says she's just adjusting to high school. But they yell at each other all the time. My dad rolls his eyes and says, 'Teenagers,' and my mom rolls her eyes at him and tells him he should be doing more as a father. I hate it all so much."

"What's her name?"

"Tessa."

"Maybe you should put the pictures of Tessa and you at the middle of your project," I suggest.

Then Oscar adds in, "And her ninth-grade class picture could be at the top. You know, like you're all supporting her or something. Like holding her up. Even if she's kind of being different and mean. Like you'll be there for her and love her anyway."

That's definitely the most I've ever heard Oscar talk. And though I'm not going to say it out loud, I like his idea even better than mine.

"I like that," Candace says. "Maybe I could make all my family members into, like, some kind of net at the bottom or something, like we'll be there when she decides to stop being so mean. You know, like those safety nets at the circus or something."

Oscar and I nod and Candace starts arranging the pictures of Tessa on her poster board. "Thanks, guys."

As I watch her sorting through her family I wish that Grandpa had pictures of Eddie. I always wondered why he didn't at least keep one. Even if he put it somewhere secret where he didn't have to see it every day and get sad by remembering.

Oscar's sketching two trees on a blank page in a cool-looking black leather notebook. In the middle of the two trees he starts drawing a picture of himself, and it's really good. Each time he swipes his pencil across the page, the drawing looks more and more like him. He sketches himself with his arms stretched out between the two trees.

Then he catches me staring. "One tree is my mom's side and the other is my dad's," he explains.

I'm thinking this kid is some kind of genius. "Is everything you do always this deep?" I ask.

He laughs, and I guess that means yes.

All this time Ms. Gloria's working on her own family tree project. She's cutting something out of blue construction paper.

"You have to do this project too?" I ask her.

She laughs. "I guess I don't have to." She presses a glue stick into the construction paper. "But it's good to reflect on family every once in a while."

Everyone has some kind of creative idea, even Ms. Gloria, and I don't. All I have are boring lines and the names of some people I don't even know.

For the rest of the period I help Candace smear the glue stick across her poster board and press down the pictures of her and her sister.

When the bell rings we all start to pack up our projects and Ms. Gloria says to have a great long weekend and she'll see us Monday. And I'm thinking how I'll get to spend all day tomorrow in the garage helping Grandpa, then on Saturday we'll boil sap, which is about the most perfect weekend I can think of.

"Hey, Robinson," Ms. Gloria says, and I turn around before I push open the door. "So it went OK with your grandpa?"

I nod. "But I've got more questions."

She smiles and gives me a thumbs-up. That's when I see the beginning of her project, blue birds cut out of construction paper, flying in a V across her white poster board. But there's one bird that's not in the V, one who's flying off in a different direction alone.

I didn't know that a teacher's family could be not perfect. I never really thought about the fact that Ms. Gloria had a family. And I wonder if that was Ms. Gloria flying off by herself and where she was going.

chapter 17

The fire is burning hot in our backyard pit on Saturday morning by the time I hear Derek and his mom pull into our driveway in their Subaru Outback. I peer around the house and see Derek open the passenger door and jump out before his mom even puts the car in park.

"Maple Day!" he screams and runs out to the yard with his purple mitten up the whole way, ready for a high five.

His mom follows behind him, walking carefully through the snow in her big boots. She looks just like the adult version of Derek—short, twig skinny, all bony elbows and knees, and off balance.

"Welcome!" Grandpa calls and walks over to help Derek's mom through the melting snow.

Yesterday in the garage Grandpa and I did two car inspections, three oil changes, and put new tires on a Toyota Prius. All without Harold. And Grandpa talked with customers and didn't get his words crossed either.

"Glad you could make it," he tells Derek's mom.

"Are you kidding? There's no way we'd miss an invitation to boil sap," she says. "Derek talks about this all year."

Today is going to be another good day just like yesterday.

The flames from the fire pit are burning high up over the brick walls that are sunk into the ground. I know that high flames mean it's time for another couple pieces of dry, split wood from our pile.

"Come on." I pull Derek toward the shed. "Let's get your gloves." Derek and his mom have boiled with us for so many years that we keep a pair of gloves for both of them in the shed.

Derek's mom pulls on her work gloves and sits down on the stump chopping block. She helps sometimes, but mostly she likes to watch and take pictures of Derek and me.

"More wood," I order, and Derek and I race to the woodpile. I hold my arms out palms up while he stacks two pieces on my forearms to carry back to the fire.

Derek's always too scared to throw another piece of

wood on the fire, so that's my job every time. Grandpa pokes at the burning wood in the pit and says, "OK, Robbie." That's my cue that I can throw the next piece on and step back fast because the sparks fly up and you don't want them to catch your clothes.

Grandpa's bringing over the metal bars that stretch across the fire and the big lobster pot we'll use to boil. His brain is hardwired for boiling, so he's remembering all the steps, and his memory doesn't seem tired at all, which is good because there's no reason for Derek's mom to raise her eyebrows.

Grandpa puts the lobster pot on the metal bars and the fire starts to heat up the bottom. Then he lets Derek pour the sap from our gallon jugs into the pot until it's three-quarters of the way full.

"Now we wait," Derek says.

Grandpa nods. "Until the staff boils down to half."

And I know he means *sap*. I look quick at Derek and his mom to see if they noticed, and I don't think they did, but I can't tell.

"Then I get to add more sap. Right, Mr. Hart?" Derek asks.

Grandpa nods again and stirs the sap with the big slotted spoon we brought out from the kitchen.

Derek wants to make a snowman while the sap's boiling, but the whole time we're rolling the snow across the yard I'm watching Grandpa as he sits next to Derek's mom on the stump chopping block. I wonder what they're talking about or if they're talking at all and if Grandpa's words are staying straight, so I keep pushing the snow toward them to see if I can spy in.

"Beautiful day." I can hear Derek's mom's voice. "Perfect for boiling, isn't it?" she asks. "Derek always starts getting excited when it's cold at night and warms up during the day. Nothing he loves more than Maple Day." Grandpa nods.

"That's right," I cut in. "Grandpa taught me to recognize perfect sap-running weather when I was little." I stand up from the big snowball we're pushing around for the base of our snowman. "And I taught Derek."

Grandpa slides his work gloves off his hands, lays them on the ground by the stump, and says, "I bet we'll get a few more . . ." Then he looks like he looked the night he wandered off, except this time it's his sentence that wanders off and he can't follow it.

". . . A few more boiling days before the end of the season," I finish for him.

Derek's mom smiles. "Well, that's great! Your syrup is the best in all of Vermont, Charlie." And that's true. And that's saying something.

Derek points to the corner of the yard. "Let's set up our snowman over there."

We push our big snowball across the yard, collecting more and more snow as we roll, and it gets big fast, so by the time we get it over to the corner of the yard it's up past my knees. But it's also far from the stump chopping block, where Grandpa's forgetting the ends of his sentences, and I can't make a snowman and spy in on him at the same time.

Derek's asking me about how deep into the woods the hiker's shelter on the Appalachian Trail is from here and saying maybe he'll go with us one day this summer. I want to tell him it's only a mile, though he'd still never make it, but I'm trying to listen to Grandpa from across the yard.

Then I hear Derek's mom squeal. "Oooooo!"

When I look over, the pot is bubbling over and making hissing sounds. Grandpa stands up quick and Derek and I run over fast. I can tell by the look on Grandpa's face that he forgets this step, he forgets what to do if it boils over.

Even Derek's mom remembers. "Did you bring out the vegetable oil?" and she's running to the kitchen in her big boots, all slow and off balance while Grandpa is frozen to his spot.

"Lift it off," I tell him. "Lift off the pot, Grandpa."

And before I know it he's reaching for the big metal handles on the pot except his gloves are still in the snow next to the stump and I try to shout, "Wait!" in time but I don't because Grandpa's yells are filling the cold air and the pot is overturned and spilling sap into the snow.

Derek is screaming now too.

And Grandpa's shaking his hands and tears are streaming down his face and getting all caught up in his deep grooves.

"Oh my God, Mr. Hart! Mom! Mom!" Derek yells.

She hasn't even gotten to the front door yet and now she's running back and yelling. "What happened?"

I hold Grandpa's elbow and tell him to sit in the snow and he kneels down slow and then sits crisscross applesauce like we learned in pre-K. I make a snowball and tell him to hold it. And I keep saying I'm sorry, I'm so sorry, because if I hadn't told him to lift the pot, then his hands wouldn't be screaming red and he wouldn't have to cry in front of Derek and Derek's mom and if I had remembered the vegetable oil in the first place I would have added a few drops in the foam and it would have simmered down like Grandpa taught me when I was a little kid and if I hadn't been so far away making a stupid snowman in the corner of the yard, then none of this would have happened.

Derek's mom tries to look at Grandpa's hands, but he pulls them away.

"It's nothing," he mumbles. "Just a stupid mistake."

His brain is supposed to be hardwired for this. Hardwired for boiling sap into maple syrup, hardwired for all the steps and details.

I hand him another snowball and he holds it between his hands. I can tell they're stinging bad, because he squeezes his eyes closed tight as the snowball melts.

"Charlie," Derek's mom insists, "let me see." And she reaches out again for his hands. She uncurls his fingers and looks at his palms.

"I'm really fine. It's nothing." He wipes his cheeks with the sleeve of his red flannel shirt.

"It looks like a first-degree burn," she says. "Let's go inside and treat this before it gets worse."

Derek is kind of crying and he's sniffling and wiping the snot off his nose with his work gloves. That's what happens when Derek gets scared. He starts crying and doesn't know what to do. That's why I play third base and he stands behind me.

"I saved some of the sap." He sniffles. The pot is right side up again in the snow, and the fire is still burning hot flames from the brick pit.

"Good job, Derek," I say because I don't want to ruin his day too. That makes him smile, which makes things feel a little more OK. But not really.

We're following his mom and Grandpa inside when I remember that we're not supposed to leave the fire blazing if we're not outside to watch it. I don't want to put it out because it'll take too long to start it all over again and that means that Maple Day is ruined for good. But I don't want to stay outside with it while Grandpa's inside with his stinging hands and Derek's mom's asking him questions. So I take a shovel of sand from the bucket in the shed and carry it out to the yard and dump it on the flames until they die out.

When I get inside Derek's mom is holding a cold cloth on Grandpa's hands. Then she rubs some lotion on his palms and tells him he might want to take some Advil for the swelling. Derek's dad is a doctor. I wonder if that's how she knows all this stuff. Or maybe it's just that she's a mom, and moms know stuff.

"Thank you," Grandpa says. "And Derek, don't you worry. Melted day will . . ."

And I know he means *maple*, and his face looks lost again.

"Maple Day will happen again soon. Maybe next weekend." I look at Derek and his mom. "We'll collect more sap to boil by then anyway."

"Wouldn't miss it!" Derek says. "I'm sorry about your hands, Mr. Hart."

I walk them to the door, and Derek's mom says she'll call to check on us tomorrow. "And please call me for anything." Then she's taking a long look at Grandpa. "Let me write my number down just in case," she says, and I know she's worried because she's raising her eyebrows and wrinkling up her forehead and her eyes look really sad. "Make sure he keeps those hands moisturized. Call if you see any blisters that are bigger than your pinkie fingernail."

Derek's mom pats my shoulder, and before I know it my eyes are getting all burny and I have to blink really fast and look up at the ceiling so I don't cry like some baby.

"You're taking good care of him, Robbie."

I shake my head like that's not true because it's not. "He takes care of me."

chapter 18

On Monday morning I'm trying to braid my own hair before school so I don't make Grandpa's hands worse, but no matter how many times I start over I can't keep all the pieces tied in tight and my curls end up popping out and spilling down to my shoulders. And there is no way I'm wearing my hair down like that to school. I try to pull it back in just a ponytail, but I hate the way the loose ends feel brushing on my neck and I don't want to wear it any different because then everyone will make a big deal about it and it's just stupid hair.

"Need some help?" Grandpa's poking his head in my bedroom.

"But your hands—"

"They're good as new." He opens and closes his

fingers to prove it.

But I know they're not good as new because I spied on them last night when he was sleeping. One hand was flung to the side over his bed and the other was across his chest. I used my hiking headlamp to examine each palm, turning them over softly in my hands so he didn't wake up, and making sure they didn't have any blisters bigger than my pinky fingernail like Derek's mom said. They were red and puffy and looked as hot as the flames from the fire pit.

"Here, turn around," Grandpa says, and he grabs the comb from my dresser and starts dividing my hair in two even parts.

"Maybe I'll just cut off all my hair," I tell him, imagining how good a buzz cut would feel. "I don't know if I'd look stupid, though."

Grandpa snorts a little laugh and bends over my shoulder and kisses my cheek. Normally I say *ewww* when he does stuff like that, but it feels pretty OK this morning, so I just stay quiet.

"I know for a fact," Grandpa says, "you'd look great."

"You can't know for a fact."

He's braiding the left side, pulling each section tight over and over, but I can tell his hands are fumbling more than usual, which means my curls might start popping out before the end of the day.

"Eddie always wore her hair short," he says. I can't believe Grandpa said her name like it was so easy all of a sudden.

"How short?" I ask.

"Boy short. Quarter inch off her head, if that."

And I'm picturing my mom walking down the street and everyone's moving out of her way because she's that tough. And she's giving people fist bumps and nodding with a quick jut of her chin to say *what's up?*

Grandpa asks for the rubber band. I hand it to him and he wraps it around the bottom of my first braid.

"Grandpa?" I try. "What happened to my mom? I mean, I know she—but what exactly—"

"Enough of that, Robbie," he cuts in. "Time for school." His voice is hard, but I don't give a crap because she's my mom and I should get to know how she died. I should get to see pictures and hear all about her. I don't have the guts to tell Grandpa that all of this is bull crap and he has to start telling me stuff before he can't remember anything anymore, so I just huff loud and sit there.

He hurries through my second braid and ties the rubber band. It's not tight like it's supposed to be. It's rushed and loose, and I can feel it unraveling hair by hair before I even grab my book bag.

•••

At school Ms. Meg reminds us that our projects are due Thursday. "And what's even more exciting," she announces, "is that your teachers have planned a fun open house for your families and you'll be presenting your family tree projects as part of it!"

She starts passing out neon blue fliers. One lands in front of me on my table.

YOU'RE INVITED!
**Please join us for an open house on Thursday, March 24,
in Ms. Meg's classroom.
Student presentations begin at 3:30 p.m.**

I crumple the blue piece of paper into a tight ball and flick it off my table. No way am I presenting my family tree project in front of anyone. Derek dives onto the floor and picks up the crumpled flier fast before Ms. Meg can get on my case.

"Put this in your book bags right now so you don't lose it," Ms. Meg shouts over everybody else's excitement. "And don't forget to tell your families!"

Not going to happen.

Out of the corner of my eye I see another crumpled blue paper fly. It came from Alex's table, and he's leaning back in his seat with his arms crossed over his chest. He's wearing a hat today too, which he never does, probably because he's so proud of his flowy, feathery hair, and the brim is pulled down low over his face like mine.

Usually an open house would be another chance for him to show off his perfect life and make fun of other people's projects under his breath. But he just sits there looking down at his shoes. And I remember how he shook and sobbed in Ms. Gloria's room. I guess even bullies might have crap going on.

Everyone else is working on their projects, and all of them are creative and good. Eric is making a tall 3-D tree out of popsicle sticks and Amy brought in an actual potted plant and is hanging little drawings and names off the leaves. The Chelsea/Brittany girls have papier-mâché trees taller than baseball bats planted in the back of the room, and now they're wearing matching pink smocks and covering the floor with newspaper to paint the trees green.

I don't have anything else but what I scribbled in my notebook last week. Just names of people I know nothing about. And I can feel my hair poking out from the right braid, which Grandpa rushed through, and I wish I could tighten it up or chop it off.

I don't even hear Ms. Gloria creak open the classroom door because everyone is so excited about their projects that they can't even talk like normal people. Everything is a squeal or a scream.

Ms. Gloria catches my eye and motions toward the door like she's asking if I want to get out of here. I grab my stuff. "See you later," I say to Derek.

"Meet you on third base," he says.

I follow Alex, Oscar, and Candace down the hall to Ms. Gloria's room, where at the very least it'll be quieter.

Ms. Gloria says we're going to do a quick check-in, then she'll give us time to work on our projects together again. Alex has the talking wand, and I'm waiting for him to tell us all about his day off from school last week and how great his four-day weekend was, and how he's so much cooler than we are. But instead he yells, "I'm an effing zero!"

My jaw actually drops because I'm pretty sure Ms. Gloria knows what *effing* means.

Then he passes the wand to Oscar, but Oscar just stays quiet for at least a whole minute because we're all still watching Alex.

The brim of Alex's hat is pulled down far over his face and his shoulders are shaking and he's making these loud huffing sounds. Candace stands up and stretches all the way across the table and pats his shoulder. She can barely reach him, and the edge of the table is digging into her belly, but she keeps patting his shoulder and says, "It's OK."

At first I'm kind of mad because Candace is supposed

to be our friend, and not nice to a bully like Alex, but then Alex pulls his knees up to his chest and cries loud with his whole body heaving hard. It's like watching that fancy BMW lose control again and drive wild into a brick wall, all its parts coming loose and fluid leaking all over the pavement.

"It's OK," Candace keeps repeating. "You can talk to us."

Alex sniffs and says between choking sobs, "You think I want to talk to you?" He shakes his head and mumbles. "I don't want to talk to some dumb, fat girl."

Candace pulls her hand from his shoulder and I'm trying to count to ten, but I don't make it past three because Candace already has her sister and her sister's friends calling her chubby and she's just being nice to Alex, which she doesn't even have to do.

"You jerk!" I shout. "You're crying like a baby and you still can't even be nice? What the *eff* is wrong with you?" I figure if he can say *eff* I can say it too.

Ms. Gloria stands and claps her hands one time really loud and we all look up. Her windshield-washer-blue eyes are no-nonsense, and I'm sure I'm about to get it because I'm always the one who gets in trouble. But instead she says to Alex, "We can see that you're hurting, Alex, and we are all sorry for that and want to help, but that doesn't mean that you can lash out at others. That's not right."

"Whatever," he sniffs.

"Not whatever," she demands. "Turn your hat around." Alex does it slowly and his face is a mess, red, with tears and snot running everywhere.

"You're not obligated to tell us what sadness you have in your life right now," Ms. Gloria tells him. "That's your business to share if you want. But you do owe Candace an apology for being mean to her."

"Sorry," Alex mumbles under his breath.

"A real one," Ms. Gloria says. "When it's real and you actually feel sorry, that's when you should apologize. We are here to listen whenever you are ready."

Ms. Gloria nods to Oscar, who is still holding the talking wand and I'm wondering if we're just going to go on like Alex isn't sniffling and blubbering. How can a kid whose mom gives him a new snowboarding jacket every year, and a whole day off school for no reason, be crying so hard?

Oscar starts to say that he's a seven because now he at least has an idea for his project and it doesn't feel so bad to work on it, when Alex interrupts. He's not even holding the talking wand, but no one says anything because he's crying so hard we can hardly understand him.

"I'm sorry!" he yells. "I'm really sorry! I mean it!"

Oscar hands Alex the talking wand, and all that power locked up inside with the purple and silver glitter falling from top to bottom must have made him feel safe to share, because he starts blubbering everything.

"My dad—cancer—moved his bed—living room downstairs—" He's gasping and sputtering between every few words and grabbing his stomach and doubling over and crying so much it sounds like he can hardly breathe and his back is shaking like crazy.

Candace gets up and walks around the table to stand next to Alex's chair. She's rubbing her hand across his back now and I'm not even mad at her for being nice to a bully because I want anyone to do anything that will make him stop crying like that.

He's still sobbing hard, and his words come choking out. "Thursday I had to stay home from school—alone with him—Mom had school conference for my brothers and—can't be alone." He lays his head on the table and just keeps crying big, big cries.

And then I do something I never thought was possible. I feel bad for him. I feel so bad for Alex Carter. I imagine him sitting with his sick dad all alone. *Cancer* is a scary word that I never had to think about for too long before, but Alex is sobbing so hard and no one can get him to stop. He probably thinks about it every minute.

"They say three months." Alex trembles.

That's probably why there were so many pills in his mom's car. They were for his dad.

"Thank you for sharing with us," Ms. Gloria says. "That was brave." Then she reaches over and touches his shoulder, and Candace is still rubbing his back. Oscar reaches over too and touches his other shoulder. And before I know it, I'm reaching out over the table and pressing my hand firm but nice on Alex's shoulder too. And we all just stay there quiet like that until Alex's shoulders aren't bouncing so hard up and down from crying anymore.

chapter 19

The whole walk to the garage after school I'm thinking about Alex and wondering if he's going home to sit with his dad and what they talk about and why some people get cancer and others don't and why some people can't remember and others can.

"Robbie!" Harold's walking out of the garage and wiping his hands on a towel, waving at me. "How was school? You staying away from trouble?"

I nod yes, and it's true. I haven't gotten in trouble since I slammed Alex to the lunchroom floor. And even thinking about that now makes me feel kind of bad after seeing him cry so hard and thinking about his dad who has to have a bed downstairs in the living room because he's too weak to walk upstairs anymore.

Harold gives me a fist bump and puts his arm around my shoulder. "How's May?" I ask. "I didn't think you'd be back for a while."

"She's great," he says. "Sleeping and pooping like a champ, so I figured I could come in and help out here while Paul holds down the poop fort at home today."

"Ew, Harold."

Harold was supposed to take a whole month off to take care of May, and it hasn't even been a week since she was born. It makes me nervous that he's here. I'm Grandpa's right hand, so he should know that I've got everything under control.

"There's a Jeep Grand Cherokee whose engine won't turn over. I could use some help," he says.

I nod OK.

The Jeep is parked in the first bay, and Grandpa is vacuuming out the backseat of a Toyota Avalon in the bay next to that.

"There she is," Grandpa says when he sees me, and turns off the vacuum.

"Hi, Grandpa."

"How was school?"

I want to tell him that it would be better if I knew more about my mom and could finish this family tree project already, but I just say, "Fine."

"She's going to help me with this Jeep," Harold tells him.

Grandpa smiles and nods and starts the vacuum again.

It doesn't take a rocket scientist to figure out that the Jeep Grand Cherokee's connecting cables are corroded. I hold out my hand to Harold and say, "Scalpel." That's another one of our things, like the fist bumps. He puts a wire brush in my palm and helps me disconnect the cables from the battery. I have to lean in far to reach the battery, but I remember when I used to have to kneel on the bumper to reach. I'm big enough now that I don't have to do that anymore. While I'm cleaning the end of the cable with the brush, Harold leans in with me and whispers. I can hardly hear him over Grandpa's vacuum.

"Hey, how's your grandpa been feeling?"

"Fine," I say, and keep on scrubbing with the wire brush so when we connect it back to the battery the engine will turn over good as new.

"How'd that happen to his hands?"

"It was an accident."

Harold takes hold of the cables and helps me connect them back to the battery. Then he starts to loosen the other side from the starter just to make sure they aren't corroded there too.

I lean in farther and he leans in with me and right there under the hood he says, "Robbie, I know he's having a hard time." He pats my work glove with his work glove, and I grip the wire brush tight. I don't know if it's because it feels kind of safe under the hood of a 2011 Jeep Grand Cherokee or the hum of Grandpa's vacuum makes him feel farther away, or if it's because Harold's voice is calm and real like Ms. Gloria's is, but before I know it I'm telling him everything.

I'm telling him about Grandpa's flannel shirt folded up with the pots, and about him wandering past our sugar maples. I'm telling him about his suitcase packed up like he might follow an old idea drifting around his head right out the door at any minute, and about the aloe plant I carried home from Dean and Walt's country store to squeeze and rub into his palms at night.

Harold pats my work glove with his again and I'm trying to connect the cables back to the starter, but there are tears blurring up my eyes and I can't. "Here," he says, and takes the cables. "I got it. Let me help." He connects them.

I want to tell him that I don't need help. That I can connect cables back to a starter easy and that Grandpa and I are just fine on our own.

Even though the cables are connected and it's time to try the engine, Harold doesn't close the hood of the Jeep.

We stay there bent over the engine and battery, the oil, and all the tubes and sparks that make everything work right, and Harold tells me that Derek's mom called him and sounded worried after our failed boiling day.

At first I'm mad that she went sticking her nose in our business, but after telling everything to Harold I feel a little lighter somehow.

Grandpa turns off the vacuum and calls, "How's that engine running now?" We stand up fast and Harold slams down the hood of the car.

"About to check it, Charlie," he says and hands me the keys.

When I try the key, the engine turns over quick and easy. Good as new. And I wish there were some wire brush to clean out Grandpa's corroded cables and reconnect them to his starter so he could ride out good as new too.

"A-plus, Robbie," Grandpa says and pats my shoulder with his bandaged hand.

Before we leave, Harold slips a piece of paper into the fold of my baseball glove. "If you need anything, Robbie," he says. "Anything." His hair is wild and sticking up, and I think I can even see a few gray ones poking out in the front. "I'm here. Looking out for you."

His brown eyes are glassy and tired, and I wonder if May ever lets him sleep and I know already I won't call him. Harold's got his family to take care of. And I have mine.

On the walk home I'm wishing my hair wasn't so loose and touching my neck, and thinking that no more adults than Harold can find out about Grandpa's memory.

I take the keys from Grandpa's hand and slide the house key in the front door.

"Hang your flannel here, Grandpa," I tell him when we get inside and point to the black hook by the door.

"I know that," he gruffs. He unbuttons his flannel slowly, then takes off his boots.

"Tuna melts?" he asks. I nod yes and even though I'm pretending to get out my homework, I'm really watching him. Watching him walk to the kitchen and plug in the toaster oven, take out two English muffins and mayonnaise. Watching him get a fork from the drawer and a bowl to mix the tuna in.

Then I'm watching him look at the can of tuna fish. He picks at the can's edge with his thumbnail. Then he tries to pry it off with the fork. Then he slams it hard against the counter. "Dammit!" he yells.

"Grandpa!" I rush to take the can from him.

"Goddammit!" he yells again. "I don't need any help."

My heart's beating fast because it's scary when Grandpa's mad and he does need help but I don't want to make him feel like crap by showing him how to open the tuna. He was the one who taught *me* how to crank the can opener around a can of tuna fish when I was little. It would feel weird and wrong to teach him how to use it now.

I open the drawer and take out the can opener. "It's OK, Grandpa," I say and hold out my other hand. "I'll do it. I remember how you taught me. Just watch and make sure I do all the steps right."

He nods, but I can tell he's still mad because he's huffing big breaths through his nose. I click the opener onto the edge and twist it around the can until the top peels off.

"Good," he says. Then I empty the tuna fish into the bowl with a spoonful of mayonnaise.

Grandpa stirs it up while I toast the English muffins.

Before bed Grandpa unwraps the bandages from his hands and I snap another piece from the aloe plant and squeeze it on his palms.

And later that night when he's sleeping I sneak in again to make sure he hasn't packed up his suitcase to wander off, and to check on his hands. I pull back his wool blanket and as quiet and soft as I can I roll his big hand to face me. I rest my pinky finger soft in his big palm and there aren't any blisters bigger than my nail.

He smells like wood and wool and aloe and his hands look better than they did yesterday. I pull the blanket back up and tiptoe back to my bed, then listen to his deep breaths as I fall asleep.

chapter 20

The next day in Ms. Meg's class Derek takes out his board game family tree. It looks really good already, and it's not even due for two more days. His mom helped him paint a square piece of cardboard purple, and all the spaces around the edge where the game pieces go they painted in white. He's bent over our table writing on the game cards.

"When you land on a square that says *Take Card*, you pick a card and read about a family member. Then you get to add one of these plastic people to your side." He hands me a tiny plastic figurine. "The person who has the most family members by the end wins."

I guess I'm a huge loser, then.

"That's so cool!" Candace gushes.

Candace's project is full of pictures and is almost done too. She has two brown markers out to color the trunk of her tree.

I look down at the drawing I have in my notebook.

MEAN OLD MAN ——————— MEAN OLD LADY
(GREAT-GRANDPA)   (GREAT-GRANDMA)

CHARLIE HART ———— LUCY MILLER
·(GRANDPA)   (GRANDMA)

EDNA ROSE MILLER (EDDIE) —— ?
(MOM)

ROBINSON HART
(ME)

I grab one of Candace's brown markers, clutch it tight in my fist, and press a fat X over my whole stupid family tree. I roll the marker back to Candace, and she and Derek are staring at me with huge eyes.

"What?" I say.

"Do you want me to help you start over?" Derek asks.

I lean back in my chair and bury my hands in the pocket of my sweatshirt. "That's impossible," I say. "I don't even know these people. I don't have anyone to put on a family tree. Besides Grandpa."

Derek moves his foot over next to mine under the table and nudges my Nike Air Griffeys with the toe of his Converse.

"You know me," he says. "You could put me on there."

Then the door creaks open and Ms. Gloria's poking her head in. "I'm here for my crew." She smiles at Ms. Meg and waves us out.

The weird thing is, I'm almost excited to talk to Alex. Maybe it's because his life sucks too and maybe we could say no way to this stupid project together and it wouldn't feel so bad. Or maybe it's because it was a little scary when he sobbed yesterday and I've been hoping that his dad doesn't die.

When we get to Ms. Gloria's room we all sit down around the little table and Alex isn't crying or anything but he looks like he could at any second.

"How's your dad?" I ask.

"The same," he answers. "He's not going to get better, so the same isn't the worst, I guess."

I don't know what to say so I just say, "Sorry," and I do that thing that Derek does when I feel like crap. I slide my Nike Air Griffey toward his foot under the table and just leave it there, the sides of our shoes barely touching. Alex doesn't kick me in the shin or anything, so I figure it makes him feel pretty OK too.

"There's this counselor that comes to our house to talk to my mom and my brothers and me. He's OK," Alex says. "He told us it might be a good idea to write down the things we want to say to my dad and questions we want to ask him before—" His voice catches and his eyes fill up. "Before it's too late, I guess." He looks down.

"That sounds really hard," Candace says.

Oscar leans forward and says in his whisper kind of voice, "Sorry."

I realize that the talking wand is just lying in the middle of the table, and I think it really might be full of magic like Ms. Gloria said it was, because we're all just talking now and everything is going fine. Alex isn't being mean and no one is yelling or flicking bits of paper in anyone else's hair.

And I usually don't believe in magic, but if it does exist I wouldn't be surprised if Ms. Gloria caught some and sprinkled it in with the purple glitter in the wand because instead of wanting to shove or slug Alex Carter I can actually kind of understand how he feels, even if just a little bit, because I want to ask my Grandpa some things before he forgets the answers. But it's too late already. Every time I get to the topic he closes up tight.

"I'm proud of you all for opening up, and for your kindness to each other," Ms. Gloria says. "Kindness is the only thing that can make some of our hurt go away."

Then Alex turns to Candace. "Sorry I said you were fat before. You're not. I was just mad, I guess."

Then he's looking at me. "I won't call you Robin anymore."

I want to ask him, *and how about what you did to Derek?* but I just stay shut because I don't want to wreck his nice streak. It's quiet for a while, but it doesn't feel awkward. It feels pretty OK, actually.

Then Ms. Gloria ruins it. "Projects are due Thursday," she says. "That's two days! I can't wait for your presentations. So let's get to work."

Candace and Oscar take out their projects quickly and get right to work on the finishing touches. Alex and I just sit there with our arms crossed and our hats pulled around in front of our faces and at the exact same time say, "I'm not doing it."

It makes us giggle a little. Then we start cracking up and I try to stop, but I can't. Alex laughs so hard he falls out of his chair and even Oscar starts cracking up too, and he laughs ten times louder than he talks, which makes me laugh even harder, and before I know it we're all on the floor laughing so hard that we're crying too.

At first Ms. Gloria has her no-nonsense voice on, trying to get us off the floor and back to work, but even she breaks and starts laughing and her laughs are these low, deep hoots that rise up from her belly and take over her whole body. She laughs and laughs with us until tears stream from her windshield-washer-blue eyes down her cheeks. We laugh and laugh until we can't laugh anymore.

"Maybe laughter can help us through the hurt too," Ms. Gloria wheezes. "Kindness and laughter." She's wiping her eyes with the back of her hand.

We're all nodding our heads and clutching our middles. My stomach burns and even my cheeks hurt from smiling so wide.

"And I don't mean laughing *at* other people," Ms. Gloria says, and she directs it right to Alex. "But laughing *with* others."

Alex nods like he gets it, and I think he does. And I think I do too. Sometimes people feel so bad they want to make others feel worse. And sometimes people can be so angry at something inside that it spurts out everywhere, like a high-pressure radiator leak.

"Ms. Gloria, are you going to show us your family tree?" Candace asks.

She looks over toward her desk. "I can if you want," she says, and reaches over for it. "I'm not quite done yet either."

It's turning out pretty cool. She glued all the birds on the poster board into a flying V across the sky and wrote names on the wings in black Sharpie marker.

Gloria leads the flock. There's still that one smaller bird who's flying away from the V, off into the white of the poster board.

"Who's that?" Oscar asks and points to the little bird flying off.

Ms. Gloria runs her finger over the outline of the little bird. "That's my son, Devon."

Ms. Gloria explains to us how she was the oldest of her siblings and always felt like she was helping to take care of them and lead them on a good path. "That's why I made my family tree as a flying V. That's me out front," she says and points. "Leading the way." She shows each of her siblings, the birds following behind her, and her other two children.

"Devon passed away when he was eight." Her chin trembles when she tells us. "But I like to think of him flying high and making his own way."

"I believe he is too," Candace says. Ms. Gloria pats Candace on the back and smiles.

"In my next life, I'm coming back as a bird," Ms. Gloria tells us. "That way I can sing to all the people who were great and kind, and poop on all the ones who weren't."

And maybe it's because everything was feeling too sad and heavy or maybe it's because our teacher said *poop*. But before we know it we're all doubled over and bursting out laughing again.

"You better watch out!" Oscar blurts and points at Alex. "Someday when you're an old man hobbling down the street, Ms. Gloria might poop on you if you don't start being nice to everyone!"

And that gets us laughing even harder because Oscar is supposed to be the quiet one who whispers his responses and never says anything if he doesn't have to, and now we're picturing Ms. Gloria flying over Alex's head and white poop splattering on his perfect blond flowy hair.

Ms. Gloria lets out big wheezes to catch her breath and says, "OK, OK, you crazy crew. Ms. Meg will kill me if you don't have your projects ready for Thursday." She points to Candace's and Oscar's projects. "Let's get to work now."

Candace and Oscar start right in, but they're still giggling under their breath.

"I don't have anything," Alex says.

"Me neither."

I show him the Xed out family tree sketched in my notebook. "I don't even know these people, except for my grandpa."

Alex leans in to look, and I can tell he wants to ask me a million things. Like why my grandpa's black and I don't look it. And how my mom died and if I have a dad.

But he doesn't ask, which is good because I don't know most of the answers anyway and having these people on my project makes my whole family tree feel like a lie.

"I just don't want to think about family right now," Alex says, and pushes his notebook away from him across the table. Then his face gets sad and his voice gets shaky again. "But my dad always feels proud of me when I do my schoolwork."

I'm trying not to but I can't help picturing his dad and all the pills and the downstairs bed.

"We just have to do it, then," I tell him. And I push his notebook back across the table.

Alex looks up at me. "OK." Then he reaches out his hand and says, "It's a pact. We'll make our projects. Even if they stink."

"They're going to be so crappy," I laugh. And that makes him giggle a little again too.

I reach out and we shake hands, like it's the end of a long game that went into extra innings and we finally just called the game off because it got too dark.

"Thursday," I say.

"Thursday," he repeats.

Even though it's bad, I'll go home and copy my big lie family tree onto a piece of colored paper and be done with it. I didn't say it was going to be good. Just done.

Then the bell's ringing and it's time for recess and all

I want is third base and Derek backing me up.

Alex slaps me on the back. "Come on, I'll let you bat first."

And I'm feeling the best I can until I hear my name being called over the loudspeaker. "Robinson Hart, please report to the office. Robinson Hart to the office, please."

chapter 21

Ms. Gloria says she'll walk me to Principal Wheeler's. I bet because she knows if I go by myself I'd skip the office and run outside to recess anyway. And she's right. I would. Because Mr. Danny's probably unloading the bats and baseballs from the gym bags right now and I'm supposed to bat first.

We're walking side by side down the hallway and I'm thinking this is bull crap that I have to go to the office during recess and I didn't even do anything bad.

When I get close enough to look through the big glass window of the office I see Grandpa sitting there with Harold and I take off running. "What the—"

I burst through the door and I look right at Grandpa and yell, "I didn't do anything! I swear!"

Harold stands up fast and puts his arms around my shoulders and says, "I know you didn't, Robbie."

And now I'm wishing I didn't say one stupid thing to Harold under the hood of that 2011 Jeep Grand Cherokee because I'm afraid he told some other adult and now we could be in real trouble. He's supposed to be on my team.

There's a woman there I've never seen, wearing fancy black pants and a jacket and carrying a briefcase. I look at Ms. Gloria to give me an answer.

Then Principal Wheeler walks out of her office and says, "Hi, Robinson. Thank you for joining us." She's acting nice. Too nice. And it's making me more nervous because I don't want any meeting or anyone's help and I don't know who this fancy-black-pants woman is and why she has to be here.

"Why did you call my grandpa?" I ask Principal Wheeler. "Why is Harold here? I didn't do anything! They have to go back to work."

I shake out from under Harold's arms and put my hand on Grandpa's shoulder. "You can go," I tell him. "Nothing is wrong." And I'm thinking maybe if he leaves before anyone asks him a question, then we'll be OK and no one will think he can't take care of me anymore. Because he can.

Grandpa's telling me to calm down, but I can't, and I

don't even want to try.

"Hi, Robinson," the fancy lady says. "My name is Grace and I'm a counselor at the Department for Children and Families in Vermont." She reaches out to shake my hand.

"I don't care who you are!" I yell because the Department for Children and Families sounds serious and scary, and I want to get us out of here fast before she says anything else. "I have to walk my grandpa back to the garage now, where he belongs because he can fix everyone in this town's cars."

But that Grace lady just keeps on. "I'm here because I wanted to meet you and to talk—"

"No one asked you to come!" I shout.

I grab my grandpa's bandaged hand from his lap, but Harold squeezes my shoulder and says, "Actually, Robinson, I did. I asked Grace to come here."

It feels like a fastball in the gut because Harold really did quit my team and before I know it we're all shuffling into Principal Wheeler's private office. Grace, Ms. Gloria, Harold, Grandpa, and me.

We're sitting in a circle, but it doesn't feel like the circle in Group Guidance, and there's no talking wand. If there were, I'd take it first and tell everyone to *eff* off, and then I'd never pass it on because I don't want to hear what anyone else has to say. But grown-ups never let kids have the talking wand when they've made up their minds.

"Robbie," Harold says. "I called Grace because I care about you so much, and I care about your grandpa. He's my best friend." Harold's eyes are getting all leaky and his voice is catching. He brushes his hand through his sticking-up brown hair. "I want to help you and your grandpa make a plan."

"We don't need a plan!"

Then Grandpa sits up in his chair and clears his throat into his fist. "Robbie. My memory's not so good. And it's not getting better. You dessert—"

And I know he means *deserve* but everyone staring at him is making him nervous and stressed. I look up to see if Principal Wheeler or Ms. Gloria or that lady Grace noticed, and I'm pretty sure they did because their eyes look sad, and we don't need anyone feeling bad for us because we're fine.

"You dessert—" Grandpa tries again.

And I know he wants to say *I deserve more.*

"No, Grandpa," I interrupt. "That's not true. You're fine." It's not fair that everyone's making him feel lousy. This isn't his fault. I'm the one who made his memory so tired all these years, but I'm good at helping him now.

"I spent the morning with your grandpa," Grace says. "And he told me all about you."

"I don't give a crap what you talked about," I tell her. "My grandpa and I are fine. I know what people like you do. You take kids away from the only *effing* family they have!"

"Robinson!" Principal Wheeler's eyes are wide. "Watch your language, please. We are all here because we care about you and your grandpa Charlie."

I know that's the biggest load of bull crap yet because if they really cared they wouldn't want some counselor around whose job it is to take me away. They'd know that I'm the only one who can find him when he wanders and make him feel OK when he can't open a can of tuna fish. They'd know that I'm really good at finding his flannel and the ends of his sentences.

"I know you're feeling upset, Robinson. This isn't easy," Grace starts again. "But I'd like you to try to listen to what your grandpa and Harold are thinking. You might find that the plan sounds OK."

Before I know it I'm standing up and my hands are tightening into fists because I'm not listening to anyone's plan.

"Robinson," Grace says. "I'm not here to take you away from your grandpa."

I bite down hard on my back teeth. Ms. Gloria catches my eye and I'm counting down from ten and taking a deep breath for each number.

"Your grandpa told me you are a special kid," Grace says. "He told me how good you are at fixing cars and tapping maple trees. He says you are his biggest helper for a lot of things."

"I'm his right hand," I spout through clenched teeth. "Harold's his left."

Grace smiles when I say that. Then she keeps telling me that she's not here to take me away from my grandpa, but I know she is. That's their big plan. That's what people like her do. They want to take me away because they don't think he's a good grandpa and they don't think I can take good enough care of him. But I can. My heart's beating loud in my ears and I just want to get out.

"Maybe we should talk about this another time," Grace offers. "I could come visit you and your grandpa when you're feeling a little better."

"How about never?"

Then Grandpa says, "No need to be rude to this nice lady, Robbie."

Harold nods and pushes himself up from his chair. "Maybe another time is best," he adds. "I can be there anytime."

"I could come by the house tomorrow morning," Grace says. "I'll bring doughnuts and we can talk before you go to school?"

I'm about to say no way, not even the

crispiest-on-the-outside-softest-on-the-inside doughnuts could make me want to ever see this woman again, but Harold jumps in fast and says, "That sounds great. I'll be there."

Grandpa nods and pushes down hard on his thighs to get up from his chair.

"Can I go home with my grandpa now?" I ask Principal Wheeler. I'm thinking there's no way I can go back to class. Not even recess. I don't trust anyone around Grandpa without me there.

I can tell Principal Wheeler is about to say no and that I have to spend the rest of the day in school. So I stare at her hard and say, "I don't feel good. I can't go back to class." I fake a nasty cough and everyone kind of laughs and rolls their eyes and nods.

Ms. Gloria turns to Grandpa. "Mr. Hart, you should be very proud of Robinson's progress. She's been managing her anger and empathizing with others. I know this is tough on her, but I'm confident she'll do a great job listening tomorrow morning." She's looking right at me when she says that last part.

"Thank you," he says. "I know she'll lips . . ." He looks up toward the ceiling as if his words got caught up in his brain somewhere, but he squints his eyes, shakes his head, and gives up.

Ms. Gloria takes his hand in hers and smiles. "Thank

you for coming, Mr. Hart."

Then I hold his hand and he walks side to side, side to side, to the office door.

I know he meant to say *listen*. Not *lips*. *Listen*. He meant to say that I'll listen to him and listen to Harold and Grace, and I wonder what they did to make him so brainwashed. Grandpa can't really think that someone from the Department for Children and Families is going to help us. He just needs to go back to the garage with me. His wires are all crossed because he gets confused in the afternoon, but in the morning he'll be clear and good as new and there's no way he'll want some lady to take me away.

"Let's go to the garage, Grandpa," I say. "I'll help you with the cars."

But as we walk away from the school, my stomach feels all tied up in knots because I know I can't wait around for anyone else's plan.

On the way to the garage Harold keeps trying to explain why he called that lady and finally I blurt, "I don't want to talk about this right now!" which is something that Ms. Gloria taught me to say when I'm annoyed and don't want to listen, and I'm surprised how well it works because Harold just pats my shoulder and doesn't say another thing the whole walk.

I don't want him patting my shoulder, though. Not today. So I shrug away and start walking a little faster.

Grandpa's quiet too, and even though I don't want to talk about anything, the silence is making me feel antsy, so I'm glad when we get to the garage because I can pull on my gloves and get to work.

She Roll is parked outside the garage, and Paul is leaning on the truck with May in a backward-book-bag-looking thing on his chest. He's holding a white bag from Dean and Walt's. I can smell the hamburgers from here because they're that good.

"I thought there might be some hungry workers needing lunch," he calls, holding up the bag. And the fact that he's here makes me feel suspicious. Like he might be in on this plan too.

Grandpa reaches out and touches May's head softly with his big hands. "Still a tiny thing," he says.

"You'd be surprised how fierce she is. She's little but fierce." Paul smiles and May yawns and dribbles a big string of spit on his shoulder.

I go to touch May's head too, like Grandpa did, because I kind of feel like I have to because she didn't do anything wrong. But before I can get to her tiny curls she reaches out her little hand and grabs my finger way harder than I thought a baby could grab and she squeezes tight.

"I told you. She's fierce," Paul says.

May is clutching hard and it's making me laugh a little because I don't actually know how to get my finger out of her grip.

"Looks like you're stuck with her," Harold says.

Then Paul kisses her little fist and starts peeling her fingers off mine one by one. She cries a little when I get free but then pushes her face back into Paul's chest.

He hands the hamburger bag over to me. I take one and pass it to Grandpa and I'm still wondering if Paul is in on the Department for Children and Families bull crap plan too. So I don't ask him how she's rolling and point to the back of his falling-apart old Chevrolet like I always do.

I just eat my lunch in four big bites and say, "Thanks for the burger." Then I ask Grandpa what I can work on even though I kind of wish I could see if May would grasp her fist around my finger again because it felt pretty OK. But I'm mad at Harold and maybe even Paul too.

"Honda Civic needs new brake pads." Grandpa points to the first bay.

Harold pulls on his gloves too. "Robbie and I can tackle that together."

"I can do it by myself," I snap, even though I've only changed brake pads one other time. I know I can remember all the steps if I go slow.

And I don't want Harold's help.

Harold holds his hands up like *don't shoot*, gives Paul and May a kiss good-bye, and starts toward the next bay, where he has to take the winter tires off a Subaru Forester. "I'll be right here if you need—"

"I got it."

Paul starts putting May in her car seat and toots the horn on the way out. "Good to see you, Robbie! Let's hope she rolls all the way home!" he calls out the open window.

I give him a weak smile and start loosening the lug nuts on the front tires of the Civic. And because I'm not asking for help I get a jack. I have to hoist up the car and I can't do that without Harold helping me position the wheels over the lifts. But I'm good with a jack, so before I know it I've got the front wheels up off the ground all by myself and I'm squatting down and removing the lug nuts and pulling the wheels off nice and easy like they're supposed to go.

I spray the caliper bolts with WD-40 and I remember Grandpa telling me about checking the pressure on calipers. If the car is cool and at rest, they should move back and forth easy, but if they're under pressure they'll fly off when you remove the bolts. So I'm careful to stand to the side and check behind me before I fit the socket over the bolts.

I can't get them to move at first try, so I spray more WD-40 and give them another hard crank. I can feel the heat rise up in me, all the way from my belly through my clamped tight teeth and into my cheeks. I'm putting all my weight in and they won't budge and if I can't get these calipers off I can't replace the worn-out brake pads with new ones that stop on a dime. And before I know it I'm punching the stupid things. Punching them hard, and my knuckles are burning through my work gloves and my legs are cramping from squatting because I had to use a jack instead of the lifts but I don't care because bolts are supposed to loosen and they're stuck and stubborn and stupid and I can't get them free.

Then I feel a glove on my shoulder. Harold is squatting behind me like an umpire behind the catcher and trying to pull me away from the wheel.

"I almost got it!" I scream. "Leave me alone!"

"Robbie," he whispers. "Let's take a breath for a minute." He puts his arm around my waist and pulls me back. We both kind of topple on the smooth cement of the garage floor, but I fall mostly on him. My fist is throbbing, and there are tears on my cheeks that I don't even know how they got there.

I can tell Harold wants to laugh because he's biting his lip and smiling and because we're all sprawled out on the floor like a couple of idiots, but I'm not in the mood for laughing. Not with him. Not today. So I roll off him and stand up fast.

"Try this." He holds out a red-and-yellow can. "It's better than the WD-40. I swear by it."

I grab it and give it three hard shakes before squatting back down at the wheel and spraying it on the caliper bolts and giving them a good hard crank with the socket. My knuckles burn when I tighten my fist. The bolts still aren't moving. I'm biting down hard on my back teeth and holding my breath and I want to punch the stupid things again. Then Harold's glove reaches over my shoulder and pushes down on my sore knuckles.

"One. Two. Three," he counts and we give it a good strong turn together and finally, they come free.

We don't say anything after that, and I do the rest by myself, but I know Harold is watching from the next bay.

And the whole time I'm putting on the new brake pads and checking the brake fluid, I'm thinking about the Department for Children and Families and how I'm not waiting around for Grace to come with doughnuts and take me away from Grandpa.

No way.

chapter 22

I need my hair braided up tight before I go to bed, and I try to do it myself, but every time I do my hair falls all loose and out of the braid. It has to be tight for what I'm going to do.

I tap lightly on Grandpa's bedroom door with my hair down long over my shoulders "Grandpa?" I ask. "Will you braid my hair?"

I'm waiting for him to ask why I need it done now so late at night and not before school in the morning like I always do, but he just waves me in and tells me to stand in front of the mirror.

My heart's beating fast and I don't know if it's because at any moment I'm expecting Grandpa to see right through me, right into my whole plan, or if it's because he doesn't even notice anything out of the ordinary.

He combs my hair with his fingers and parts it down the middle, then gathers the right side, separating it into three pieces.

"Tight, Grandpa."

He smiles at me in the mirror and crosses the groups of hair over each other and pulls them tight to my scalp. Tears burn behind my eyes, but it also feels good to have it pulled tight and intertwined like nothing could get between the strands to loosen it up and make it fall apart.

I hand him a rubber band and he wraps it around the bottom of the first braid. Then he braids the left side, crossing the hair over and over and pulling it tight to my scalp.

"Thanks," I say. And before I close his bedroom door I stick my head back in and say, "Hey, Grandpa. Everything's going to be OK."

I want to say what I always say, that I'll see him in the morning, first thing. But I don't want to lie to Grandpa.

I'm waiting for him to remind me about Grace and Harold coming over with doughnuts before school, but he just nods and smiles. "Sleep well, Robbie." And I wonder if he remembers.

"You too, Grandpa."

Wearing my outdoor clothes in bed feels weird. My jeans keep twisting around all wrong and I can't get comfortable. It's dark and the wind is whooshing past my window. I'm going over the plan in my head and looking at my hiking pack leaned against the far wall. It already has my sleeping bag in it so it kind of stands up on its own. I repeat the plan again and again, step by step, in my head to keep me awake until I hear Grandpa's snores through the wall.

When the alarm on my watch beeps four thirty a.m. I blink my eyes fast and let them adjust to the dark. That was part of the plan so I don't fumble around and wake up Grandpa. Then I push off my blanket, hoist the pack over my right shoulder, and tiptoe through the hall and downstairs. I lean my pack against the front door and tiptoe to the kitchen.

The cupboards squeak even when I open them slowly to feel for the loaf of bread. A slant of light shoots across the floor from the refrigerator as I reach in for the cheese slices. I make a sandwich and wrap it tight in plastic wrap like Grandpa taught me so the cheese doesn't slide around and off the bread. Then I turn on the water just enough that it's barely leaking out of the faucet to fill my water bottle as quietly as I can.

I grab the first-aid kit from the hall closet because Grandpa says you never go into the woods without it and stuff it in the pack on top of my sleeping bag. When I hoist the pack up this time, it feels way heavier than I thought it would. But I can carry it.

I adjust my headlamp around my head and pull on my boots, and just when I'm about to turn the doorknob I hear Grandpa cough and shift on his old mattress upstairs. Then I imagine him waking up and not knowing where he is or where I am and maybe packing his suitcase again and wandering off. And I won't be here to follow him and find him and bring him back home.

But I can't be here when Grace shows up to tell me her plan and take me away. And she'll be here soon. If I just disappear for the morning, disappear from Grace and the Department for Children and Families, I can come back and get Grandpa and then we can make our own plan.

Grandpa needs me with him. I'm his right hand.

The light on my watch glows 4:58. Two hours until Grace will be pounding on our door with doughnuts. I have to go.

I turn the knob quietly, but I just can't push the door

open and run. I try again to get the guts, but I can't. I can't leave Grandpa here with no one listening for his breathing and snores through the wall.

I need a new plan.

When I inch the pack off my shoulders, it hits the floor with a thud. "Crap!" I whisper and slap my hand over my mouth as I tiptoe back to the kitchen.

This time I make a sandwich with an extra slice of cheese and slather it with mayonnaise and mustard the way Grandpa likes. The other water bottles are out in the shed, so I fill Grandpa's soup thermos with water, even though it's heavy and will probably kill my shoulders in the pack. But we'll need it. And I can carry it. I grab the blanket off the back of the couch and stuff that in too.

Tiptoeing back up the stairs makes me nervous. I don't want to startle Grandpa because it's still dark and early and his wires will be all crossed and confused.

I knock softly on his bedroom door but he keeps on snoring. I knock a little louder and walk in. He snorts and rolls over. "What? What? Who is it?"

"It's me, Grandpa. It's Robbie."

"What?" He sits up on the edge of his bed and shakes his head, but he doesn't shake anything into place because he's calling me Eddie and wondering if I'm going to come to Vermont. "Eddie, Eddie," he pleads.

"Come stay with me in Vermont until the baby's born."

"Grandpa, it's Robinson." I take his hand and help him stand up. I want to remind him that my mom died so he'll snap out of it and stop calling me Eddie and go back to being normal. But I don't want to make him sad, so I just forget about it. "It's time to go," I say. "Come with me."

I pass him his clothes and he slouches into his shirt and pulls his pants up over his hips. "I'll teach you how to sugar," he says, "if you come."

"I know how to sugar, Grandpa. You taught me. Remember?"

He rubs the grooves on his forehead and pats me on the shoulder. "Eddie. I'm so glad you came. I can't wait to be a grandpa."

Then I realize he's talking about me. And for as many times as I've asked him to tell me what happened to my mom, it feels weird and wrong and a little scary having him talk about her now, when his memory is so tired.

He holds me tight and whispers in my ear, "I wanted to be there when you were growing up, Eddie." Then he squeezes me tighter in the hug and says, "But you're here now and I'm going to be the best damn grandpa in the world." Then he rubs my belly over my sweatshirt and jacket.

"You are," I tell him. "You are the best grandpa in the world." He nods his head and loosens his hug.

"Ready?" I ask and grab a pair of thick socks from his drawer. I put his hand on my shoulder to lead him downstairs to the front door.

"Ready," he says. His voice is gruff and sounds stale, like he hasn't cleared the morning out of it yet.

That's how his memory is too. It's clear by the time the sun comes up for breakfast and he's braiding my hair before school, but it clouds up again when it gets dark and it's time to make dinner and go to bed.

But we can't wait for the sun to rise and his memory to clear. We have to get out of here now. Then we'll be OK and Grandpa can help me think about what we'll do next.

"You're going to need your flannel and a jacket too, Grandpa."

I take his flannel from the hook, but when I turn back around he has one bare foot in his boot and he's trying to pull his sock over the muddy toe.

"Socks first, Grandpa," I remind him. "Socks, then boots." It makes me mad and sad again at the same time that he doesn't know that. How can he forget the simplest things? All the things he taught me when I was a little kid. He's just staring back at me like he doesn't understand, so I reach over and start unlacing his boot. "Socks first."

"Stop it," he huffs. "Stop it, dammit. I can do it."

His eyes are those deer-caught-in-the-headlights eyes, and I just want him to snap out of it and go back to being the grandpa who makes sense, because he scares me when he's like this. But we have to get out of here before Grace from the Department for Children and Families comes to take me away.

chapter 23

The snow crunches beneath our boots and our breath hangs heavy in the air.

"We're going for our little hike, Grandpa," I say. "You remember our favorite route? Up to the hiker shelter on the Appalachian Trail?"

The pack is digging into my shoulders already, and we haven't even made it out of the yard and into the woods.

"You came on the train?" he asks. He's crunching along behind me, side to side, side to side. "Let me take your bag, Eddie. You've come a long way."

"It's OK, Grandpa," I say. "I can carry it." I keep trudging a couple of steps ahead of him so he can follow my footsteps. "Let's find the trail, Grandpa. Then we'll follow it to the shelter."

Our headlamps are bouncing light across the dark morning ground.

"You're going to love it here," he says. "It's the best place to raise a little girl."

He still doesn't understand that I'm me. I'm Robinson.

It scares me that he thinks I'm my pregnant mom, but I also want to know the ending. What happened after my mom came to Vermont to live with my grandpa? What happened when she had me? What went wrong?

"What happens?" I call back to him. "What happens when I'm born? What happens to Eddie?"

He stops and takes a deep breath and squints into the dark morning like he's looking for the answer. "I don't know," he says.

It's like an icicle in the gut because I think he really might not know. Maybe he stuffed it so deep that he actually forgot, and I'll just never find out. I'll never know what happened to my mom.

"I'm so glad you're here, Eddie," he says and starts walking again.

It feels like I'm hiking through the woods with a stranger, except I've lived with him my whole life.

I keep saying over and over in my head that I'm Robinson and he's my grandpa, Charlie, and we're escaping the Department for Children and Families and Grace and Harold and everyone else who thinks they know what's best for us. No one knows my grandpa like I do, and he can't live without his right hand.

I'm weaving through the sugar maples and trudging uphill, shining my headlamp on the snow, looking in the melting snow for the snowshoe tracks of the people who walk this stretch of the Appalachian Trail in the winter.

"Stop!" Grandpa yells and it echoes off the sky.

I whip around fast. "Shhhh!" I whisper. Even though I know Grace probably isn't even awake yet, I imagine her following our footsteps and tracking us down.

"Stop, stop, stop! Don't leave me!" he calls. And I don't know if he's talking to me or to Eddie or someone else his memory stirred up.

"Come on, Grandpa," I whisper. "It's OK. I'm not leaving you."

"Come back!" he shouts and he starts to cry and yell and I'm more scared than I've ever been because I want him to stop yelling and crying, but we can't go back. "Come back!" he sputters. I don't know why he's crying, if he just wants to go home or if he still thinks I'm Eddie and he's begging her to return, which is impossible because she's dead.

He falls to his knees. "Come back! Please! I'm sorry!"

"It's OK, Grandpa," I say. "I'm here. I'm not going

anywhere without you. Let's walk together." I reach out my hand and wait for him to catch up. Then we walk side by side, hand in hand, together up the hill until we reach the Appalachian Trail where Grandpa and I have hiked so many times. He's limping pretty badly on the right side and he keeps mumbling under his breath to please come back, please come back.

"We're close," I tell him and we continue on together up the trail, our things weighing heavy on my shoulders, but I know I can carry them all the way until the end.

We get to the sign that reads *.1 mile to shelter* and an arrow points down the trail.

"Almost there, Grandpa. Then we'll rest." *And the sun will rise up*, I'm thinking, *and you'll be good as new.*

There's no one in the shelter this time of year. All the hikers go through with their big beards and their big packs in the summer, so it's just Grandpa and me now.

"Here we are," I say and drop the pack on the wood floor of the shelter. In the summer, it's a good thing that the shelter has only three sides. This is where Grandpa and I stop to eat our lunch on warm afternoon hikes when school's out and where we dangle our feet from the edge of the shelter and take off our hiking boots and wiggle our toes. Plus, all the hikers who are going a long way with big packs smell like moose crap and I wouldn't want to be shut in anywhere with them. Today, though, I wish that there was a fourth wall, a front to the shelter so the wind wouldn't find its way inside to us.

I unpack my sleeping bag and the blanket from the couch. "Here, Grandpa, take this." I hand him my sleeping bag because it's warmer. "We'll just have a little breakfast and rest for a while. Then we'll go back home." I look at my watch. 7:04. If we can just wait until eight, then the coast will be clear until Grandpa and I can make a better plan.

Grandpa unties his boots and pulls his right foot into his lap. A big blister bubbles from the back of his heel, probably because he didn't tie his boots tight enough and it's hard walking in snow. I should have told him to lace them tighter, but I feel good that I at least remembered the first-aid kit because I can cut Grandpa a piece of Moleskin and wrap his heel with a Band-Aid and medical tape.

"That'll help," I say. He pulls his sock back on over his sore, wrapped blister.

Then he zips himself feet first into the sleeping bag and I wrap the blanket around my shoulders and huddle in close to him. The hair on his chin is rough and scratchy but feels good pressed up on my cheek.

We eat cheese sandwiches and drink water from the water bottle, and I'm thinking any minute now the sun will come up and Grandpa's memory will snap back to normal. But he's rubbing his head and mumbling.

"It's OK, Grandpa," I keep saying. "We'll go home soon."

Then he looks right at me, but I can tell it's not me he sees. "Eddie? Eddie. You can't leave us, Eddie," he says. Then he pushes the sleeping bag off his legs and stands up so fast that he wobbles on his socked feet. In one hand he grabs my pack and cradles it in the crook of his arm like it's a baby. With his other hand he grabs my arm hard. "Come on," he says. "I have to get you to the hospital. Wake up." And before I know it he's pushing me out of the shelter and into the woods.

"Grandpa, your boots!" He's sinking far into the snow in just his socks, and he's zipping the pack into his jacket like he's trying to keep a baby warm and pulling me along.

"We don't have time! We should have gone yesterday. Eddie, I'm sorry. I'm sorry." And he's crying again and pulling me deeper into the woods until I can't see the shelter anymore and we're not on the trail and I don't know if we're getting closer to home or farther.

Now I'm more scared than ever because I think we're lost and Grandpa's memory has never been so bad. He's not just misplacing his flannel or keys; he's misplacing his whole self, and I don't want to lose him. I want him to look right at me and say, *Robinson*. I want him to say he's cold and he needs his boots and that we should go home and what are we doing up here anyway? I want him to put his arm around me and say, *Everything is going to be OK, Robinson. Everything is going to be OK.*

But he's not. He's running wild like a spooked animal and pulling me hard through the woods.

"Hospital," he's panting. "Stay with me. I've got the baby."

I look at Grandpa cradling the pack as he runs, and he's looking down inside his jacket to check. And I know he sees me in there. He sees little baby me. And I wonder what happened to Eddie, what happened to my mom? Why was it too late? But I don't even care anymore. I'd rather have Grandpa back to normal than learn what happened. I want him to stop. He's hurting my arm and he's shaking and scared and his eyes look like he's in so much pain remembering.

We're walking in circles and we're walking fast and I'm crying now too and yelling, "Grandpa! Grandpa!" And I want it to be all over, so I pull back hard on my arm and we both topple into the snow and he clutches hard around the pack in his jacket, protecting it from the fall. And I yell, "It's me. It's Robinson! Eddie's dead!"

I unzip his jacket and pull out the pack and shake it in front of his face. "I'm grown-up, Grandpa. I'm grown-up and I'm fine and I'm right here."

He's crying big cries and I'm hugging him hard and there are cold tears on my cheeks that feel like they'll be frozen there forever. He's shaking from the cold and I know I did a bad job of taking care of Grandpa. I don't even know where we are anymore, and his socks are soaking wet from the snow.

"We have to go home," I say.

I pull him up from the snow and we walk hand in hand, following our footprints backward. Grandpa walks ahead through the thin cold branches, and they whip back fast to lash me on the face. Each cold branch on my cheek feels like a punishment for taking him out here. For making his memory worse.

I finally see the roof of the shelter and I point. "Over there, Grandpa," I say. We duck beneath branches and make our way back to where we started. I help him sit on the edge, and he pulls his boots over his wet socks. I roll up the sleeping bag and blanket and stuff them back in the pack and hoist it over my shoulders. Somehow it feels heavier than when we started.

The sun is beginning to shine down through the branches of the maple trees, and if we wait for one more hour we'll probably be safe from Grace and the

Department for Children and Families, but Grandpa is shaking from the feet up and I don't want him to be scared and wild anymore, so I say, "Let's go," and we follow the Appalachian Trail back down toward our house.

chapter 24

I squeeze Grandpa's hand hard as we step out of the woods and into our backyard. She Roll is parked in the driveway, and I can hear Harold banging on our front door and hollering, "Robbie? Charlie?"

We keep walking slowly, side to side, side to side, across the yard until we can see Harold and Paul on our front steps. Then Grandpa raises his hand above his head. "Here!" he calls. "We're here!"

He squeezes my hand back and says, "I'm sorry."

I'm squeezing as hard as my cold fingers can and even though I'm telling Grandpa that it'll be OK, I don't know that it will be.

Harold rushes toward us and takes Grandpa's arm. "Where were you? Are you OK?"

"Fine, fine," Grandpa mutters.

"Just out for a walk," I say.

Harold looks at me with eyes full of worry, but he doesn't ask any more questions.

"There you are," Paul says, patting my shoulder. He has May in that backward-book-bag carrier thing, and she's fast asleep on his chest. Together we help Grandpa up the front steps and inside.

Grandpa's shoulders are still shaking a little, like a chill got into his bones and he's trying to shoo it off.

Harold puts a kettle of water on to boil while I get Grandpa's boots off and unwrap the bandage over his blister.

"Does it hurt?" I ask.

He looks up and I don't know if he sees Eddie or me, but I can see him searching for his words.

"No," he says. Then he pats my shoulder. "No, Robbie."

And my eyes get all watery because I got my grandpa back.

Harold's pouring a kettle of boiling water into a basin in front of the couch, so I walk Grandpa over, help him sit down, and lift his feet into the hot water.

Harold sits down in our chair near him and rocks May as she gurgles awake. "How's that feel, Charlie? Temperature OK?"

"I'm fine, I'm fine," Grandpa grumbles. "I don't need all this fussing over. I'm not a hundred years old, you know." He shrugs off the blanket I put around his shoulders.

He's sounding more like the real Grandpa already.

Then I hear a car pull into the driveway and I know who it is and I'm not going to the door to welcome her in even though that's how Grandpa raised me. To be polite.

I take the kettle from Harold and go to the kitchen to fill it up and boil some more.

Harold greets Grace at the door and she says hi to my grandpa and Paul and goo-goo-gah-gahs over May. I can hear her unzip her jacket, and I'm thinking, *Keep it on because you're not staying long.*

Then before I know it she's in the kitchen standing next to me. "Your grandpa told me you are one remarkable girl," she says. "Now I really see what he's talking about." I turn on the faucet full blast because I want to drown her out.

Yeah, pretty remarkable, I'm thinking. *I woke him up in the middle of the night when I know his memory is most tired, I got him all confused and turned around, and I almost froze him to death out in the woods.*

The water starts overflowing from the kettle, so I turn off the faucet and put the kettle on the stove. The gas clicks as I start the burner and the flame jumps up.

"He means a lot to you," Grace says. "And I know you'd do anything for him. In fact, it seems like you have been doing quite a lot for him for a while."

I think about all the times I've put his flannel by the door so he wouldn't have to find it in the cupboard and get mad at himself, or how I sometimes turn the blinker on in the truck before the turns come up so he knows which way to go. I think about finding the ends of his sentences.

"You mean a lot to him too, you know," Grace says. "He loves you so much."

I stay facing the stove so I don't have to look at her. And I'm starting to think about Grandpa trying to get my mom to the hospital and how he held that bundle, me, so close to his heart in his jacket. And I'm thinking about all the lines on my stupid family tree that don't mean anything. Except Grandpa.

And before I know it I'm saying, "He's my only family," except I say it more to the kettle than to Grace.

"I know," she says, and puts her hand on my shoulder. The steam from the kettle is starting to whistle through the spout and it feels good on my face. "Why don't you bring that hot water to your grandpa," she says. "I bet he wants you to sit by him."

That's the truth. I'll sit right at his right hand.

I take the kettle into the living room and pour it into

the basin at Grandpa's feet. Then I sit down on the couch next to him and let him put his arm around me and I lean into that rough sandpaper on his chin.

Grace is opening a bag of piping hot fresh doughnuts. I take one and break it in half—one part for me, one for Grandpa.

Harold's sitting across from us with May in his lap, feeding her a bottle, and Paul is next to him and both their eyes look a little watery.

"Can you help me with a problem, Rob?" Harold asks. And it feels like we're back in the garage and he needs me to check under the hood of a sedan to make sure he's done everything right and didn't miss anything.

"Second opinion?" I ask.

He nods his head. Then he starts telling me that Grace and a nurse spent some time yesterday morning with Grandpa and there's something in his brain called Alzheimer's and that's what's making his memory so tired.

"It will get better if I act better," I tell them.

Grace says no, that's not how it works. That this has nothing to do with me. "It happens to some people when they get older. It's nobody's fault."

Just hearing that makes me feel like I dropped a heavy pack off my shoulders, and I take a big bite of the doughnut and it's as good as it smells.

"How can we fix it?" I ask Harold.

Grandpa sighs heavy, and I can feel his breath on my face. It smells like donuts and coffee.

"It's not going to get better," Harold says. "That's the hard part."

He reaches over and pats my knee, but I'm shaking my head and sitting up and looking right at Grandpa. "That's not true," I say. But Grandpa's eyes are getting watery like Harold's and I know that Grace is getting ready to take me away to a place for kids who have no family at all.

"We can't fix it, Robbie. No one can fix it," Harold says. "But we have a plan, and we need your second opinion." He puts down May's bottle and rocks her in his arms.

The whole room looks like it's underwater.

"You and your grandpa are doing great here together right now," he says. "But there are some times when he needs a little more help, like at night, when he's more forgetful. We were thinking of having a really nice nurse come to help you guys in the evenings with dinner and getting ready for bed."

I want to say no way, that I can make dinner and help Grandpa just fine. But I remember Ms. Gloria and think about Harold's plan for a full count to ten. And each count I feel more OK.

"And you'll keep an eye on him at the garage?" I ask. "Just in case?"

"Of course."

My eyes are burning, but I'm still listening.

"Then when Charlie's memory gets too bad and it's too hard for him to be here at home, he told us he wants to go live somewhere that will help him full-time," Harold says.

"What? Grandpa, where?"

Grandpa squeezes my shoulder and says. "Just a place for old guys like me up the road," he says. "It's nice there and you can visible . . ." He shakes his head. "Visible me."

And I know he means I can visit him. "Every day?" I ask.

Grandpa nods his head yes.

"What's it called?" I ask.

Grandpa opens his mouth but shakes his head and looks up to the ceiling like he's searching for the name up there.

"Mountain View," Grace says. "It's only a ten-minute drive from here."

"But what about me? When he goes to . . . where will I . . . ? I can't go with him?"

"Robbie." Something catches in Harold's voice and he wipes his eyes with his shirtsleeve over sleeping May's little face, and Paul reaches out and grabs his hand. They hold hands tight, fingers all interlaced like the braids Grandpa makes.

"Robbie," Harold says, and he waits until I'm looking right at him before he starts talking again, but his eyes look all watery and I'm shaking even though I'm not cold. "Paul and I were hoping you'd come live with us when your grandpa decides to go to Mountain View."

"We love you so much," Paul says. "And we already think of you as family."

I'm shivering hard and the tears trapped in my eyes are running now. I can feel them dropping off my chin.

"And we'll be visiting your grandpa every day anyway," Harold says. "And May would be lucky to have you as a big sister."

My voice is shaking, but before I know it I'm saying yes. Yes to visiting Grandpa every day and yes to living with Harold and Paul and being May's big sister and yes to continuing working on cars in the garage and teaching Harold how to boil sap so we can bring some syrup to Grandpa in case they only have the fake stuff at Mountain View.

"Whenever you two are ready," Harold says to Grandpa and me. "We're here."

Grace is nodding, and even her eyes are a little

watery and I'm starting to think she isn't half as bad as I thought before.

Harold holds out his fist to me and I bump it with mine. "Deal," I say.

Grandpa's kissing my face and telling me that we'll never really be apart and that there's no chance he'll ever forget me, even if it seems like it sometimes.

"You live here in me," he says and taps his thumb at his heart. "Not here," he says, pointing at his head. Then he brings his hand back down and rests it on his chest. "And I'll never lose this."

I lean back into his sandpaper chin and Harold comes across and sits next to us and Paul does too and May's reaching out for my finger and I let her, and before I know it I'm smushed between them and it feels pretty OK. Really OK.

chapter 25

It's easy to talk Grandpa and Harold and Paul into letting me take the day off from school. They're all feeling pretty mushy, so mushy that I bet they'd buy me my own Toyota Tacoma if I asked them nice.

"As long as you do your homework," Harold says. And he's doing that practice dad thing again, which isn't so annoying anymore because I know he's just practicing for me.

I walk Grace and Harold and Paul out to their cars, and Grace tells me that a nurse will come by at five thirty every night, starting tonight. "Her name is Katie and she's the best."

She tells me how Katie will help Grandpa transition from afternoon to evening and into bed at night, and how she'll make sure he has clean clothes, and help with dinner. I tell her that's fine, but really I'm thinking that I'm still going to squeeze the cheese into the mac no matter what because that's my job. And that Grandpa can still braid my hair in the morning.

Harold gives me a hug good-bye while Paul puts May in her car seat and says to call if I need anything.

Back in the house I help Grandpa empty the water from the basin at his feet. It's not hot anymore, but that's fine because we're not shaking like we were before.

"My memory might be rusty," he says, "but that doesn't mean I forgot about that homework you have to do. You're not getting any free day out of me."

I remember the pact I made with Alex. That even though it stinks and we don't want to do it we are going to finish this stupid family tree project so we can pass the fifth grade. And so he can make his dad proud. And it's due tomorrow.

"Will you help me?" I ask.

Grandpa nods so I go to my book bag and take out my notebook and a pen and drop it on the kitchen table. He walks over slow and pulls out a chair to sit.

My stomach is growling. That cheese sandwich we had in the shelter already feels like days ago. Even the doughnut from Grace feels like yesterday. "I'm going to make some oatmeal," I tell Grandpa.

"Make it two," he says.

I stir in the oats and turn down the heat so it doesn't boil over, then I grab two bowls and spoons from the cabinet.

"Don't forget the syrup."

I smile at him because we both know that no one worth knowing can eat oatmeal without maple syrup. But when I go to pour it over the oats in our bowls, the slowest, skinniest stream dribbles out.

"Guess we'll have to boil soon, then," Grandpa says. "A refrigerator without syrup is no good at all."

And I don't know if he remembers when Derek and his mom came over, and if he remembers about his hands and spilling half the sap.

"How about this weekend?" he asks.

"Perfect." I'm already thinking that I'll go out today after I finish this stupid project to collect sap from the buckets and get ready.

I let the last drops fall from the maple syrup jug and bring the bowls of oatmeal over to the kitchen table, where Grandpa is sitting with my unfinished family tree draft.

And that's when I get the idea for my project.

chapter 26

I'm sticking my work gloves into the cracks of the sugar
maple tree and pulling off pieces of bark and snapping
twigs from the branches and collecting it all in an extra
sap bucket.

"I don't have any poster board or anything to put it
on," I say.

Grandpa starts walking to the shed and waves me
along. "Let's see if we can't find something in here."

Our shed is a mess. Grandpa's workbench is covered
with tools and old car parts and bottles of oil. Spare
tires are stacked in the corner, and my baseball bats are
sticking up out of them.

Grandpa's digging through an old metal shelf and
I'm thinking there's no way he's going to find anything

in this place when he holds up an old green Vermont license plate like the ones on our truck. "How about this?"

I'm thinking he must have forgotten what he was looking for, because how can I use a license plate as poster board for my family tree? But then he says, "We'll need some Gorilla Glue too," and starts digging through his toolbox. "Aha! Here it is."

We bring everything back inside and lay it all out on the kitchen table. "Let's make that tree," Grandpa says.

So I turn the license plate the tall way and start laying the bark out on it for the trunk and then add the twigs for the branches. They stick out off the sides of the license plate.

It doesn't look like a perfect sugar maple or anything, but it's way better than the stupid lines in my notebook. Grandpa's turning over the bark, squeezing Gorilla Glue, then I press the bark hard into the license plate and Grandpa presses his hands down on mine to make the glue stick. "This should strike . . ." he says, but he shakes his head and presses harder down on my hands.

And it does. It does stick just fine. So we glue each piece and all the twigs pressing hand over hand over hand over hand until there's a miniature sugar maple glued on the old Vermont license plate. And even though this project is stupid and I don't like artsy things that much at all, it looks pretty OK since I like cars and maple trees.

"Look at that, Robbie!" Grandpa admires, pointing at the project.

But I know it's not done. I still have the hard part left to do. I still have to put on the names.

I push my notebook toward him and say, "This is what I have so far."

Grandpa looks at my draft and runs his finger over Eddie's name. And then over Lucy's name. Then he laughs at "mean old lady" and "mean old man."

"They *were* kind of mean," he chuckles. "But Lucy. Lucy was a gem. Just not so strong as Eddie and you." But then he gets all quiet again just when I was thinking he was going to tell me more. But he closes up tight instead, and I can tell he's not going to say any more than that.

"Forget it," I say. "I don't want to put any of them on my tree because I don't know a thing about them." Heat rises up to my face. "I can't just hand in a stupid piece of bark." I push my notebook clear off the kitchen table.

"Robbie," he says.

And even though I feel bad that I trudged him through the stupid snow this morning, I'm mad he won't actually help me with my family tree. So I say forget it,

I'm going outside to collect the sap from the buckets and I don't need his help.

"Robbie—" he says.

"Forget it, Grandpa!" I yell. "Forget it. Just keep everything inside and to yourself until you don't remember anything anymore." And what I'm thinking is that Grandpa needs Group Guidance with Ms. Gloria to teach him how to tap deep through his hard bark and open up.

The door slams behind me and the cold air feels good. I take my time emptying the buckets and packing the snow back up around the plastic collection jugs, but I can't stay out very long because I rushed out mad without my jacket and I'm starting to shiver again like this morning.

When I go back inside, Grandpa's coming down the stairs. "Sit," he says and points to the kitchen table.

"I'm not doing the proj—"

"I said sit."

I slump hard in the chair, but I grab my Dodgers hat out of my book bag and pull it down over my face.

Grandpa sits down too and before I know it he's sliding a picture across the table. I can't see anything past the brim of my hat, just this picture of a woman with a boy-short haircut, skin the color of sugar maple bark, and a big pregnant belly. In the picture my grandpa's got his arm around her and he's smiling big. He looks a lot younger and like he's not confused about anything at all. Like he knows exactly where his flannel is and where the bathroom is when he gets up in the middle of the night to use it.

Then Grandpa taps his finger on the woman. "That's your mom," he tells me. "That's Eddie."

"Where were you keeping this? Why didn't you ever show—"

"It's here now."

I don't want to be mad at Grandpa, but I am. He had a picture this whole time and who knows if he has any more and who knows all the things about my mom he's keeping from me?

And I think of Ms. Gloria telling me to use the family tree project to help me talk to Grandpa. It hasn't worked that well so far, but it has to work today. It has to work today because I can't wait anymore and I don't know when Grandpa will go live with the old people at Mountain View, and because my family tree is due tomorrow.

"I need to know more for this project," I say. He nods. "When we were in the woods this morning, you kept calling me Eddie," I remind him. "You said you had to get to the hospital."

I look up at him from under the brim of my hat.

"I did?" he asks. "I don't remember—I'm sorry."

"Don't be sorry, Grandpa. It was the most you ever

told me about her." I look down at the picture on the table and turn my hat around backward so he can look right at me. "What happened?" I ask. "Tell me before you forget."

Grandpa takes a deep breath and slides the picture back in front of him. "I don't think I'll ever forget. She lives here too," he says and taps his chest. "Right next to you."

I pat his hand and say that it's OK, he can tell me. He holds the picture between his thumb and forefinger and it shakes a little as he looks.

"She came to Vermont to give birth and raise you here," he starts. "Her mom, Lucy, had passed away from a heart attack. Eddie wanted you to have a relationship with me, a relationship that she didn't really get since Lucy and I never lived together after she found out she was pregnant with your mom."

He puts the picture down and traces her belly with his finger. "I loved her so much," he says. "I made her healthy food for the baby and built her a crib out in the shed from real Vermont wood."

I pictured Grandpa sanding the wood in the shed and hammering the pieces together tight.

He's still looking down at the picture. "It was a hard labor, but she was the happiest in her whole life when you were born. She hadn't named you yet when we brought you home. We called you 'little fighter' because . . ."

Grandpa is losing his words, but I don't know the end to this sentence, so he needs to finish it.

"Why'd you call me 'little fighter'?" I ask.

He nods and taps his finger on the table. "Little fighter . . . because you were small," he continues, "and strong and you balled your fists up tight and made your voice heard all through the night right from the beginning."

I try to picture my mom walking around our house with me in her arms as I cried out at the top of my lungs, and even imagining it makes me feel good.

"Your second and third day home from the hospital she ran a fever. Sweated through her sheets. The doctors had said it might take a few weeks for your mom to feel strong again, so I didn't worry. I thought if the fever didn't go down after another night I'd take her in to get checked the next morning."

Then this morning in the woods all makes sense. Grandpa shoving the pack deep in his coat like it was a little fighter baby he was trying to keep warm, and pulling me through the woods telling Eddie to hold on, not to leave him. He was reliving that moment, trying to get my mom back to the hospital in time.

"The next day she was way worse, wasn't she, Grandpa?" I pat his hand and take the picture from him.

"It was too late," he says. "An infection had dug too deep. And I didn't even . . ."

Grandpa puts his head in his hands and his shoulders are shaking and I know how he feels. Like it's his fault.

"It's no one's fault," I tell him, and for the first time I believe that. It's not my fault my mom died, and it's not his either. It's just plain old unfair bad luck, like Alex's dad and Ms. Gloria's son. Grandpa grabs my hand and squeezes it hard.

"What happened after she died?" I asked.

Grandpa's looking up at the ceiling like he's remembering. "We buried her in a field of sunflowers in New Hampshire. Next to her mom. Next to Lucy."

"I was there?"

Grandpa nods. "I held you the whole time. You balled your fists and cried. Then I brought you home and gave you the strongest fighter name I knew."

"Robinson Hart," I say.

"Robinson Hart."

I'm thinking about the big question mark I have on my family tree. "Did she ever talk about my dad?"

"Your dad?" Grandpa repeats. "Eddie never once talked about your dad, and I just let her be on that." Then he kind of smiles a little while he's remembering. "Eddie wanted a child more than anything." He smiles a little more and I can picture my mom with her big smile and sticking-up boy-cut hair. "You were all Eddie's," he says.

I laugh with him a little because it feels good to laugh. "Now I'm all yours," I say, and he taps his big finger on his heart.

"All mine."

Then I pick up my notebook from the floor and slide over the maple tree license plate. "I think I'm ready to finish the project."

chapter 27

"Your project is so cool!" Derek shouts as if I'm not sitting right next to him, and I don't try to shut him up or anything even though other kids are starting to look over.

I shrug my shoulders like it's no big deal, but I'm kind of happy he's looking at it so close.

"You put me on there?" he says as soon as he sees his name dangling from one of the maple branches. Then he full-on hugs me even though he knows I don't do hugs or anything like that. I don't hug him back, but I don't shove him off either.

He's touching the bark of the sugar maple and running his fingers in the grooves of the Vermont license plate. "It's perfect," he says.

Then he slides his project over to me. His board game idea came out cool too, with a stack of cards in the middle just like a real board game. "Pick the top card," he tells me.

I turn over the top card and there's a picture of him and me holding a big jug of syrup from boiling last year. He's lifting up the jug to his mouth, pretending to chug it, and I'm rolling my eyes. Under the picture it says *Robinson Hart. Best friend I'll ever have.*

I nudge his shoe with my shoe under the table and say thanks. "That reminds me," I tell him. "We're going to try boiling again this weekend. Tell your mom."

"Maple Day! Wouldn't miss it." He nudges my shoe back with his.

Ms. Meg is telling everyone to take out their projects. She says we're going to spend the next couple of periods practicing presenting before our families come this afternoon for the open house. I'm thinking that I don't need to practice because Grandpa will be working at the garage. And I already know he likes my project. And I don't really care what any other parents think.

Candace sits down at the table with us. "Let me see!" She slides my project over to her. And before I know it Alex is huddling around and Oscar is too.

"It looks so cool!" Oscar says. He touches all the names that dangle down from twine off the twigs.

Oscar's is really good too. The sketch of himself between the two trees looks just like him. One tree is for his mom's side of the family and the other is for his dad's. I remember everything he was saying in Group Guidance and I know why he made his project like that. He feels like he's in the middle of his parents splitting up.

Candace finished hers too. I tell her I like how all the happy pictures of Tessa and her are right in the middle of her tree.

Oscar says, "I bet you'll have lots more happy pictures with her too. It'll all work out."

Candace nods and smiles and says she knows.

I turn to Alex. "We had a pact," I remind him.

He unzips his book bag and pulls out a piece of folded white notebook paper. It's small and sketched in black ink. "It's not that good, but I don't care," he says. "At least it's done."

It's a simple drawing of a tree, but you can see the roots digging down below the ground. That's where he labeled his dad.

"It's really good," I tell him and I reach out like Harold does to me sometimes and give him a fist bump.

"I made my Grandpa the trunk of my tree," I say. "But he's kind of like my roots too, I guess."

And it feels pretty OK having everyone look at my family tree project because it's not so bad.

Even Ms. Gloria and Mr. Danny come to the class-room to see our projects and Ms. Gloria puts her arm around my shoulders when she looks at the names dangling from the sugar maple twigs and sees hers. Her windshield-washer-blue eyes get all teary and she says she's really proud of me.

I tell her something that Grandpa told me last night, which is how I figured out how to finish my project. He said that you should hold close the people who push you to be the best version of yourself. "That's what family does," Grandpa said. "They push you to be your best and love you no matter what."

That sounds like Ms. Gloria to me, and everyone else I put on there, except maybe May because she's just a baby. But I guess it's my job to help her be her best version and love her no matter what. And that makes her family too.

Before I know it Ms. Meg and Ms. Gloria are handing out after-school snacks and lining us all up to use the bathroom because parents are starting to come.

Our job is to say "Welcome to our classroom" to all the parents who show up, but I just look down at my Nike Air Griffeys and let Candace talk to the adults.

All the parents are sitting down at our tables and it looks funny to see them in our classroom. Then Candace pokes me and points. "My sister came!" she whispers. "I put the invitation on her bed last night, but I didn't think she'd actually be here." Her sister is sitting in the front row with a purple streak dyed through her hair, and she smiles big when Candace spots her. Then I see her mouth, *Good luck.*

I give Candace a secret thumbs-up.

Ms. Meg is in the front of the room welcoming the parents and telling them how hard we worked on these projects.

"Now it's time to hear a short explanation from the students about the choices they made on their family trees," Ms. Meg announces.

Brittany is the first to go. Then Chelsea. They pretty much have the same papier-mâché tree project, and they talk about how fun it was to paint it once it hardened. Then Ronald goes. He talks about how his brother is really important to him, so he put him at the top of his project. Then Derek presents his board game and his mom cheers from the front row. Alex shares next, and he's looking right at me the whole time he's talking about his tree drawing. He points to the roots that dig deep below the soil. His mom and brothers aren't here, and I don't want to think of what they're doing, so I just look right back at him because I think it's making us both feel OK.

"Robinson?" Ms. Meg says. "Your turn."

My stomach feels like two outs bottom of the ninth, but I stand up and walk to the front of my room and all of a sudden I'm thinking that maybe my license plate tree is stupid and I don't have anything to say about it.

"This is mine," I say and hold it up. I catch Ms. Gloria's eye, which is enough to remind me to turn my hat around backward.

Then before I know it the classroom door is creaking open and my grandpa pokes his head in. "Found it," he says and Ms. Gloria waves him in and helps him to a seat. Behind him are Harold and Paul, and May is wrapped up and sleeping in Harold's arms. Katie, Grandpa's nurse, is here even though it's way earlier than five thirty, and that's when she's supposed to start helping us. I've only known her one day, but she doesn't seem half-bad because she doesn't have to be here and she is and she didn't make my grandpa feel stupid when she was helping him last night, even with the simple things, and she let me squeeze the cheese into the mac. She smiles big and pats my grandpa's arm. Harold gives me an air fist bump over sleeping May.

I point to the trunk of my tree and say, "My Grandpa is my trunk. He's the one who takes care of me." Then I point to Eddie's branch. "My mom was just like me. A fighter with a boy name." Then I point to the other branches. "These people aren't actually related to me, but they're still family. Ms. Gloria. Derek. Harold and Paul and May." I don't really have anything else to say, but it feels like everyone else talked way longer about their projects. Everyone's watching me, expecting more, and it makes me feel weird. I'm looking at Grandpa's nurse Katie and thinking that maybe I should have put her on the tree because she isn't so bad and she's going to be around for a while and she came all the way to school to see my project.

Then I decide I could always add people as I go.

I look at Harold again and I remember how I want to represent my family well, so I try to think about something else I can say.

"I guess family is something you get like I got my Grandpa, but it's also something you make." And I'm looking at Derek, who's nodding his head and giving me a thumbs-up, and then at Grandpa, whose eyes are all misty and proud. Then Grandpa stands up and claps and everyone else claps too and it feels just like sliding into home.

chapter 28

"Maple Day!" Derek's yelling out the window of their Subaru Outback before they even pull into our driveway Saturday morning. "Maple Daaaaaaaaaay!"

The fire's burning hot already, and I'm showing Harold how we put the metal bars over the brick fire pit and fill the lobster pot with sap. I'm telling him how we wait for it to boil down before we can filter it into our empty maple syrup jugs we have stacked high in the shed. I can tell he's paying attention too, because he's nodding at each step.

"While we're waiting for it to boil down, is anyone hungry?" Harold asks. "I can take a quick trip to Dean and Walt's and bring back some burgers."

"Wait! I know!" I say, and I run big strides back to

the house and track slush and mud right through the living room and kitchen to the refrigerator because I'm so excited to show Harold how we boil eggs on Maple Day.

"Can we?" I ask Grandpa when I get back outside, showing him the half-dozen egg carton I took from the refrigerator.

He nods, and Derek and I each drop three eggs carefully in the boiling sap. "Seven minutes," I say.

"Brilliant," Harold says. Then he's asking me questions about Grade A Golden versus Amber and Dark, and I'm explaining about the time of year and how we'll probably get Grade A Dark syrup this time because it's late enough in the season that the snow is starting to melt and it'll really feel like spring soon.

Then I don't even know why, but I start thinking about Alex and whether his dad will be alive when the snow melts and it's the saddest thought, so I try to wipe it out of my head but I can't.

Grandpa uses the ladle to scoop the eggs out of the sap and drops them in the snow to cool the shells before he peels them.

The eggs are perfect. I love when they come out not too hard-boiled so the yolks are still a little soft and they have the slightest maple taste and they're still warm from the pot.

"Heaven," Harold sputters, his mouth full of egg.

I'm glad Harold is learning about how to stoke the fire and boil the sap down and filter the syrup and seal it into jugs. I'm a good teacher and I know it better than anybody because Grandpa taught me.

When the syrup is ready I take the first ladle of it and pour it on the clean snow near the sugar maple trees where there are new buds popping up through the snow. Derek goes headfirst right into it. "Yum!" he exclaims, but his mouth is so full of snow and sugar that you can hardly understand him.

I scoop mine into a loose snowball and eat it out of my hands. The cold snow stings my teeth, but the maple is sweet and perfect and makes the sting go away.

Harold and Grandpa and Derek's mom scoop some up too. And before we know it we're laughing and pouring out more maple for sugar on snow. And I remember when we were all laughing with Ms. Gloria in Group Guidance and how good it felt and I'm thinking that maybe when we boil next year I'll invite Candace and Oscar and maybe even Alex. Little May will be walking and she'll have her first sugar on snow and Grandpa will be here to see the new buds popping up through the snow by the maple trees.

Grandpa puts his hand on my shoulder. "Time to pull out the taps, I'd say." He points to the metal taps we hammered into the trees at the beginning of the season.

"I got it."

As I'm pulling and wiggling the taps out of the trunks, I'm thinking about what Grandpa always says. Everything, even a tree, has sweetness at its core. And I'm thinking maybe that is true, even if it's under a layer of tough bark and all mixed up with splinters and knots.

acknowledgments

Thank you first to my mom and dad. You got me a card to the Shelburne Library before I could even read, and then understood when I wanted to own all the books I loved anyway. I learned, in your laps, that books are comfort and adventure, and would have a forever-place in my life.

And to my big brother, Tyler—you told me that Robinson was worthy and she needed to be sent out in the world. All my life I've been looking up to you and listening very carefully to what you say, and I'm so thankful you said this.

I'm very lucky to be surrounded by great readers who took the time to live in Robbie's world with me as I was creating it. Jess Rothenberg, Jennifer Ochoa, Stephanie

Douglas, Gina Salerno, and Janine Stellacci, thank you for reading, listening, and encouraging.

I'm forever grateful for the Vermont College of Fine Arts community and the magic that exists up on that hill in Montpelier. In particular, thank you to my advisors, Alan Cumyn, Tim Wynne-Jones, Coe Booth, and Shelley Tanaka. I still hear your wise voices in my head while I'm writing.

Thank you to all the students and faculty of MS 324 in New York City. It was in that building, those classrooms, with you, that I realized I must write.

And thank you to the teachers I have had along the way for encouraging creativity and kindness. You may notice bits of yourselves in Robinson's story.

I have the most incredible support and excitement from my agent, Stephen Barbara; editor, Erica Sussman; and the many people at HarperCollins who had a hand in *Just Like Jackie*. Thank you again and again for your vision, your collaboration, and your guidance. You are my dream team.

And to my husband, Kamahnie, and son, Miles— you inspire and motivate me every day. I am most proud that I'm on your tree.